f

WITHDRAWN

BRING MY SONS FROM FAR

A NOVEL OF THE ISRAELI WAR

BRING MY SONS FROM FAR

BY RALPH LYNN LOWENSTEIN

THE WORLD PUBLISHING COMPANY
CLEVELAND AND NEW YORK

Published by The World Publishing Company
2231 West 110th Street, Cleveland, Ohio 44102

Published simultaneously in Canada by
Nelson, Foster & Scott Ltd.

Library of Congress Catalog Card Number: 66-18461

For my mother,
RACHEL BERMAN LOWENSTEIN

The author served in the 79th Armored Regiment,
Army for the Defense of Israel, during Israel's War
of Independence. None of the characters in this book
is intended to resemble any person who was a member of that stalwart regiment. The battles described
in this novel are often fictitious, as are the incidents
around which this story was built.

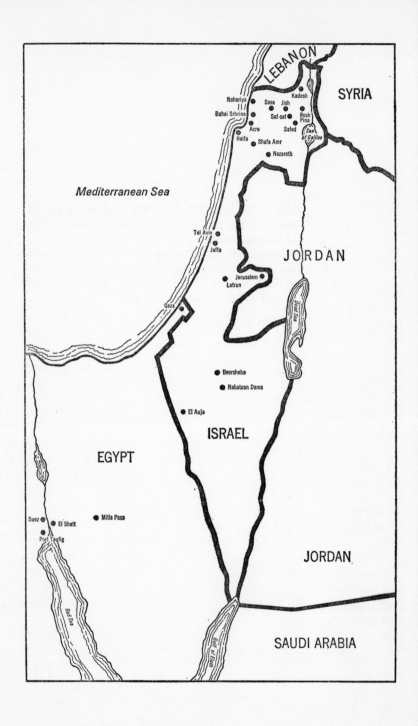

Chapter One

HE WAS A YOUNG MAN—A BOY, REALLY—AND THE new pink sheen of the khaki trousers and the open-necked khaki shirt made him look less a man and more a boy. It was late afternoon, but still warm, and he felt an uncomfortable pinch on his heel and instep as he shifted his weight from one stiff Israeli army boot to the other.

Evan Copperman had been issued the boots at an induction camp near Tel Aviv three days before. He had also been issued two shirts, slightly small, and a pair of trousers, slightly large. The trousers were now held up by his own brown leather belt, and hidden beneath the pants and boots were his own red and white striped socks.

This was his uniform as he stood on the porch of the headquarters building in the north of Israel. He and six other recruits had been deposited here by an army bus only a few minutes before. One by one they were being called into the headquarters building to be assigned to companies and platoons. Evan was the only one who now remained, waiting his turn. He was tall and slender, with a face already deeply tanned by the summer sun of 1948, though it was not yet July. An ordinary chin with a trace of a cleft, a straight nose with a hint of a swell at the bridge, positive but not prominent cheekbones, deeply set eyes, a slightly sloping brow, and hair only a little darker than the skin—it was not an unusual face.

It was, however, an unusually transparent face, its mobile features relentlessly signaling every mood like some powerful transmitter. And when the features were at rest, the face appeared deeply pensive, sadder than it actually was.

Evan's face appeared pensive now as he checked the landmarks around this army post as if to locate himself, as if to pinpoint the one tiny spot on earth that he now occupied. His eyes searched to the left for the needle-like minarets of Acre, the Arab city they had passed a few miles down the road. But the minarets were lost in the haze, too thin or too far away to be seen. On the horizon directly ahead of him he could see a narrow strip of blue, the Mediterranean Sea. It was unbelievable to him even now that within the past week he had crossed that sea on a rusty Displaced Persons ship, that he had been smuggled ashore past the eyes of United Nations observers into this new Jewish state, and that he was now in the uniform, such as it was, of an Israeli soldier. Could it have been only eight days ago that he was still in France? Could it have been only one month ago that he was still in the United States?

A half-century before, his grandfather had stolen away from Russia to escape being impressed into the Czarist army. And now, in June, 1948, that man's grandson—20 years old and without military experience—had left the security of the New World, had come one-third the way around the globe, to join an army. Evan's grandfather, were he still alive, would never have comprehended why he had done it. And Evan's parents—he could not begin to imagine their reactions when they opened the letter that told them their son, their only child, was on his way to Israel, not working and traveling in France.

When he thought about the deceit that he had practiced on his parents, Evan felt a flush of guilt. But it was tempered by the satisfaction that he had had the courage to come this far. And now he was here. He was in the Israeli army, this Jewish army, and he was one with them—no longer an alien among natives, no longer an undissolved particle in a solution.

The Israeli army was six weeks old. It had fought the invading Arab armies for the first month of its existence and now it rested and regrouped during a month-long truce imposed by the United Nations. In two weeks the truce would be at an end, and this Jewish army would be fighting again for the right of Jews to live in their own land. And Evan would be fighting with them.

[2]

A lieutenant appeared at the door of the headquarters office, called Evan's name, then disappeared back inside. When Evan entered the office the lieutenant was sitting at a desk looking over a record sheet. The officer glanced up at him, then turned back to the paper.

"An American." It wasn't a question; it was more a note of disapproval. "We received our first American yesterday. You're now the second. I see there's no specialty listed for you here. Do you have one?"

"I'm familiar with small arms." It was a lie, but Evan had told it so many times in the past three weeks that it was beginning to have the ring of truth, even to him.

"Can you drive?"

"I've driven a car for six years."

"We don't have cars in this regiment. We have American jeeps. We have Israeli armored cars, which are like tanks with wheels. And we have American halftracks, which we use to carry our infantry troops. We will need drivers for new halftracks which we expect to be delivered here soon. But if you have not had experience driving a truck, I do not believe you will be able to drive a halftrack." The lieutenant picked up a pen in his long, bony fingers and turned over the record sheet. "I'll put you in one of the infantry squads."

Evan quickly calculated which would make him look more foolish, attempting to drive a halftrack or trying to take apart and put back together a rifle. "I believe I could drive a halftrack. If you need halftrack drivers, I'd like to try."

The officer, a thin-faced young man with very white skin and very black hair, looked at him suspiciously and held his pen poised in mid-air. "You can try driving tomorrow. We will see how you do." He spoke English smoothly, but with that odd mixture of German and French accent that marked him as a sabra, a native Palestinian. "You can eat tonight at the armored car mess. The halftrack company went up to the lines a week ago to give the infantry troops of another battalion a rest. They will be back tomorrow." He rose from his seat. "Come with me."

Evan followed the lieutenant to one of the nearest brick barracks. Apparently this post had been a British army facility, hastily occupied by the Jews when the British military withdrew from the Pal-

[3]

estine Mandate less than two months before. The interior of the barracks consisted of one large room with a cement floor. Wooden beds—each no more than two low saw horses straddled by wooden planks—were lined up at intervals along each side of the room. A straw-filled mattress cover was folded in half at the top of each bed, exposing the long wooden planks that served for springs.

"This is where the halftrack drivers sleep—when they're in camp. Use any bed tonight. Did you bring any mess gear with you?"

"No."

The Israeli officer glanced at his watch. "The quartermaster hut is closed now. Look up on one of the shelves and see if someone left a mess tin."

Evan reached up to a shelf that jutted out over the head of the first bed next to the door. He pulled down the two halves of an American mess kit. A knife, fork, and spoon rattled inside. The mess kit was filthy. Particles of food were caked along the sides of the aluminum halves. The tines of the fork were clogged. Evan wrinkled his nose.

"That belongs to Nahshon," the lieutenant said. "Get another one."

Evan replaced the mess gear and pulled down the tins from another shelf. These were clean.

"The armored car mess hall is over in that direction. Nahshon is the corporal in charge of the drivers' platoon. When he comes back, he'll see that you get everything you need." The lieutenant turned and left Evan alone in the barracks.

At the mess hall, Evan ate with the Israeli recruits who had traveled with him on the bus. Though he could speak Hebrew, he said very little, preferring to listen to the strange new tones of the Biblical language he had studied for so many years. The Israeli boys spoke in the clipped Sephardic accent and frequently used slang and modern words that Evan could not understand. After eating, they went together to a small one-room building that served as the camp canteen. They bought carbonated grapefruit drinks and sat at a table and talked. Later, the other soldiers returned to the infantry barracks to which they had been assigned and Evan walked alone in the night to the empty drivers' barracks.

He unfolded one of the straw mattresses, pulled off his black boots, sat on the edge of the bed for a few minutes rubbing his sore feet, then lay down and stared at the ridges and troughs of the underside of the galvanized roof. A chill drifted into the barracks and Evan curled up on the mattress, wishing that he had a blanket. It irked him that the lieutenant had put him in a barracks by himself, forcing him to sleep in his clothes without even a blanket for warmth. Evan expected more than that from another Jew. But they were all Jews here, and simply being Jewish did not assure one of any special sympathy. A disadvantage of a Jewish state, he thought.

In the small Virginia city it was different. They needed each other, they reached out for each other, they huddled together for warmth against the cold that surrounded them. There were the times at daybreak when he and his father had driven through the empty streets to a house of a mourner so there could be a *minyan*, the quorum of ten Jewish males thirteen years old or over needed before the *kaddish* prayer for the dead could be recited. And then there were the endless months when they had gathered at the synagogue before breakfast and after supper each weekday so there would be a *minyan* and the mourner could say the *kaddish* for his parent for the full eleven months. And how many times on Saturday morning had he waited, he and the other young boys and the old men and Rabbi Lichtberg, and there was no *minyan* because it was Saturday and the men had to work in their stores. Sometimes on Saturday morning there would be only six of them waiting there. But it was more disappointing on the Sabbaths when there were only nine, because they were so close, but still one short of the *minyan*, and the *Torah* could not be taken from the ark, the Scriptures could not be read, the *kaddish* could not be chanted.

And sometimes when they waited and finally realized they would not have a *minyan* that Sabbath, Evan would walk to the door of the synagogue and stand there at the boundary in his skullcap and prayer shawl. He would look at the street where the Sabbath stopped, where the trucks drove by. All those people out there did not know or care that it was the Jewish Sabbath. They were Christians and it was a Christian world, and in the doorway Evan felt very much alone and apart. It was as though the streets and the trees and even the air were Christian and he could not say that they were partly his. His parents, he suspected, did not feel this awful isolation, nor did the other Jews in the community. They were Americans—Southerners—in thoughts, in accents, in desires. Why,

[5]

then, had this malaise struck only him? How could he play baseball, camp out with the Scouts, win high school honors, attend the state university, mix freely with the Christians among whom he had been born, and still feel like a stranger? Or did his parents and the other Jews in the community feel like strangers, too, and only pretend that they didn't? If they did not feel like strangers, why were they so concerned about the reputation of the Jews in the community, why did they feel so responsive to each other, so responsible for each other? Whatever it was that they felt, it was intensified in Evan, magnified to the point that he felt a great compassion and kinship for all the Jews.

Rabbi Lichtberg recognized this quality in Evan very early and nurtured it with love as though it were some rare plant that was not supposed to grow in southern soil. The other boys abandoned their Hebrew classes at 13, virtually on the day of their *bar mitzvahs*, the religious ceremony accepting them into Jewish manhood. They were happy to be finished with the torture of the after-school classes. But Evan stayed on, learning to translate with speed the books of the Old Testament from Hebrew to English, sharing Rabbi Lichtberg's vast knowledge of the Jewish people. And by the time Evan was ready to leave home for the University of Virginia, he could carry on a sophisticated conversation with the rabbi in Biblical Hebrew. And the literature of the Jews had made him a veteran of the Jewish experience. Their enemies throughout the millennia were his enemies. He bore the scars of all their wounds. And when, during this past year of college, his third at the university, the United Nations had voted to partition Palestine into a Jewish state and an Arab state, Evan had felt the triumph of a Jewish victory. And when the Arab armies invaded the new Jewish state from every direction but the sea on the day of its birth—May 14, 1948—Evan had felt the pain of a Jewish tragedy. As he sat in his classrooms at the university, listening to the last lectures before final examinations, his mind wandered to those battlefields, and he wanted to shout to the Jews in Israel that if they needed one more man he would be there—they must wait.

Evan awakened the next morning into the bright strangeness of the Israeli barracks. Someone had placed a rough army blanket over him during the night. He lay under the warmth of the blanket and looked around the deserted room. One of the other straw mattresses was unfolded and a balled-up blanket lay on the empty bed. Next to the blanket was a dusty Sten gun and a gritty-looking ammunition magazine full of cartridges.

Evan pulled on his boots, tucked his shirt into his trousers and walked over to the mess hall. The cook reached into a pot and pulled out a hard-boiled egg. He put it in Evan's mess tin and with the same wet hand tossed a piece of yellow cheese on top of it. Evan held out his cup to be filled with tea, then walked toward the table where his friends of the night before were eating. Before he could get there, an olive-skinned soldier sitting at a table by himself motioned for Evan to come over. The man resembled an Arab more than a Jew. He was hunched over an aluminum mess tin half filled with egg shells. Some of the shells overflowed and scattered onto the table. His mouth was full of bread and he was gulping tea from a large aluminum cup. A black handlebar mustache gave the cup wings as he drank. He motioned for Evan to sit down.

"*Shalom.*" Evan set his mess tins and cup down at the place opposite the man.

The soldier nodded, then took another huge bite from a slice of rye bread, chewed it with his mouth open, and examined Evan with small brown eyes. "I am Nahshon," he said in English. "Eliyahu—the lieutenant—told me that you are an American. Do you speak Hebrew?"

"I have a Biblical vocabulary and the wrong accent. But I'm trying to pick up the new words as quickly as possible."

"You have driven before?"

"Yes."

"What?"

"Cars—for six years."

"Have you ever driven trucks?"

"I drove a pickup truck once. But not a large truck, no."

"There's a difference between a car and a halftrack," Nahshon said. "A car weighs about one ton and has four gears. A halftrack weighs eight tons and has ten gears."

"I think I can drive one if you'll just show me where the gears are."

Nahshon grunted and nodded his head cynically. "First you need other equipment. Why didn't you get blankets last night?"

"The lieutenant said the quartermaster hut was closed."

Nahshon's eyes narrowed. "Eliyahu is a bastard. A brave bastard, but still a bastard. Fortunately, he is only a lieutenant. If Gingi, our company commander, had been here, he would have kicked down the door of the quartermaster hut and taken blankets for you." He cut a chunk of rye bread off a loaf lying on the table. Picking it up, he grabbed his plate and walked over to the garbage can. He used the piece of rye bread as a scouring pad to scrape bits of hardboiled egg and shells out of the plate, then tossed the piece of rye bread into the garbage can. "After I shave, we'll get you a Sten gun and blankets at the quartermaster." He left the mess hall and walked past the other men who were cleaning their mess tins with sand and water.

The small quartermaster hut was a hodgepodge of blankets, bullets, weapons, and items of clothing. As Nahshon stood by with the protective yet aloof attitude of a rich aunt buying her impoverished niece a good practical outfit for the new school year, the quartermaster clerk issued Evan a Sten gun, a British helmet, a pair of blue coveralls, a canteen, a box of bullets, two blankets, two deep rectangular metal dishes and eating utensils that comprised the British mess gear, an enamel cup, and a clean palliasse cover that could be filled with straw to make a mattress. Except for the bullets, every item had been used before, initiated already into the life and perhaps the hazards of a soldier.

"There's no straw in camp now," the quartermaster said. "We will have some in a few days."

Nahshon grunted sourly, then turned to Evan. "The halftrack company will come back from the truce line today, so leave everything but your weapon in the barracks. Bring your Sten gun with you to the halftrack."

The nearer Evan got to the halftrack the larger it looked. Thick plate steel surrounded the sides of the cab and bed. The steel also made a sharp rectangular box around the motor, with the nose of the hood covered by slatted steel plates. A large winch, encircled by part of the steel bumper, jutted out ahead of the hood. The cab of the vehicle looked much like that of a regular truck, except there were steel flaps that could be swung up in battle to cover the side windows. Another steel flap which could drop down to cover the front window was now propped open and rested parallel to the hood like a monstrous sun visor. Hard rubber tracks ran more than half the length of the heavy vehicle and large puncture-proof tires sat under the steel front fenders.

Nahshon opened a door and climbed into the driver's seat. He turned a switch, pushed a button, and sat back as the motor caught quickly, making a loud clattering noise as it idled. He showed Evan the movements of the gears, yelling above the motor noise. He pointed out the three additional levers forward and to the side of the gear shift lever. One was for five additional sub-low gears that could give the halftrack even more power than the lowest gear in the normal shift. A second lever switched on the front wheel drive, and the other lever was the clutch for the winch on front of the halftrack. Nahshon released the brake and the halftrack rumbled slowly forward. As soon as the halftrack was barely moving, he put it into the next gear.

"This first gear," he yelled, "is just used to take the halftrack from a standing position to motion." He stopped at the regimental police hut near the gate and showed the man on guard there a trip ticket. The regimental policeman raised the striped pole that blocked the entrance to the camp and waved the halftrack past. As Nahshon swung the vehicle skillfully through the four forward speeds, the halftrack moved quickly to a cruising speed of about 30 miles an hour on the asphalt road. He turned off the highway to a narrower black-top road and then turned off again to a dirt road. Nahshon stopped the halftrack and climbed out of the seat, motioning for Evan to drive. Except that all the pedals were metal, the feel of the driver's seat was much like that of a car to Evan. The steel hood sloped flat and gently down in front of him. A large roll of barbed wire propped on top of the winch peeked over the front of the hood.

Evan shoved the gear shift lever into first and let out the clutch gently until the gears began to mesh, then pushed the accelerator down farther and let the gears take a deep bite into each other. He shifted up through the gears until the halftrack was moving smoothly on the dirt road. Nahshon was standing next to Evan's seat, hold-

[9]

ing on to the machine gun track. His large nose was a prow that cut the wind for the weather-lined face. His chest and head rose above the steel rim of the halftrack like a mast.

"Slow down ahead," Nahshon said. "There's a detour around a section of road that's mined."

Evan shoved his foot on the brake pedal. The heavy halftrack slowed only a tiny bit.

Nahshon looked down at Evan's feet, then shot a glance at the American's face. "Shift down to third!" he shouted.

Evan took his foot off the brake pedal and threw in the clutch with his left foot. He rammed the gear shift lever from fourth gear to third. There was a loud, rasping noise of grinding metal. The gear wouldn't go into third.

"No! No!" Nahshon looked excited.

Evan, panicky now and unable to decide whether he should shove down on the brake or force the gear into third even at the risk of stripping it, held in the clutch. With the clutch in, the halftrack was now free-wheeling and moving ahead slightly faster. They were rapidly approaching the mined area, which was marked by large white cans that blocked the road. Evan had the same feeling of desperation that he experienced once before when a horse he was riding broke into a run and refused to respond to the reins no matter how tightly he pulled on them.

"The brake!" Nahshon was pointing at the floorboard, looking quickly from Evan's feet to the barrier ahead and back to Evan's feet.

Evan jammed his right foot on the brake pedal again, and, bracing his back against the back rest of the seat, pushed down on the pedal as hard as he could. Again the halftrack began to slow a little. Evan applied more pressure and it slowed slightly more, but he could see he could never stop the halftrack before it got to the white cans.

Nahshon dropped down on his side, placed one foot against the instrument panel of the halftrack and slowly began to pull on the emergency brake lever. As the brake caught, the halftrack made a thumping skid on the dirt road, throwing Evan forward against the steering wheel. Nahshon released the handbrake an eighth of an inch, then pulled it back slowly again. Again the halftrack skidded as the hard-rubber tracks locked.

[10]

Evan, still flat against the steering wheel, felt the wheel turn a few degrees.

"Turn it back!" Nahshon shouted angrily. Evan shifted his weight on the wheel and stared ahead at a large oil drum that was now only a few feet from the bumper. There was a loud hollow thump and a split-second later the halftrack came to a halt. Evan fell back from the steering wheel to the driver's seat and looked next to him at the mustachioed face now only a few inches from his own.

Nahshon lay there and gave him an unbelieving stare for a few seconds. Then he pushed himself to his feet. "You bloody idiot! You almost killed us!" he shouted, his face contorted in anger. "Don't you know how to stop a bloody truck?"

"The brake wouldn't work," Evan said.

"The brake works the way it's supposed to. You can't stop eight tons of halftrack with a foot brake. Even if you could, you'd burn a new brake lining out in one morning. You have to use the gears."

"It wouldn't go into a lower gear."

"You're bloody well right it wouldn't." Nahshon shook his head in disgust. "Did you think you were shifting gears on a motor-cycle or a jeep? These gears are large, and when you shift down you have to double clutch and rev the motor so the gears will mesh at the same rate of speed. God knows the damage you did to the brake lining on that try, and you came close to stripping the third gear."

"I'm sorry."

Nahshon ignored the apology and craned his neck to look back at the long skid mark the halftrack had left in the dirt road.

"I still think I can drive this thing. I'd just forgotten about double-clutching." Evan had made no move to leave the driver's seat. He was hoping that Nahshon would tell him to back the half-track up to the detour and try driving again.

"I'll take the wheel," Nahshon said.

Evan gathered in his humiliation and dejection and climbed over into the seat on the other side of the halftrack. Nahshon started the stalled halftrack, threw it into reverse, and backed slowly to the detour. He now turned the wheel sharply, let the gear remain in first as the halftrack nosed down the steep incline that led off the road, and followed the detour around the mined portion of the road. When they were back on the road again, Nahshon increased the speed until they were churning up a cloud of dust in their wake. Then suddenly he shoved the clutch to the floor, slipped the gear lever from fourth to neutral, let out the clutch, gunned the motor, jammed the clutch to the floor again, slapped the lever into third, and let out the clutch. The gears meshed and the heavy vehicle slowed with a jolt. He repeated the same process, swiftly and deftly, from third to second, and then from second to first until the half-track was barely moving along the road. Only then did he apply the brake and stop. He pulled on the emergency brake and cut the motor.

"That is how you stop eight tons of steel," he said. "With the gears, not with the brake." He reached in his breast pocket and pulled out a box of cigarettes, removed one, and rolled it between his hands until the loosened tobacco was dribbling out of both ends. Then he wet one end of the paper with his lips, placed it in his mouth, and lighted the cigarette. "These halftracks are the only decent armored weapons we have. We can't afford to lose one of them on a mined road during a truce. We can't strip gears or burn out brake linings, because we have no spare parts, no work-shops—nothing."

Evan sat there silently, angry at himself for the fool he had made of himself, angry at Nahshon for the lecture.

"Do you know where these halftracks came from?" Nahshon asked.

Evan shook his head.

"Italy. You Americans used them as personnel carriers and then left them there when the war was over. There are hundreds of them there rusting away in junk metal yards. We got our hands on a few dozen, but we couldn't bring them in until May 15, and then the Arabs were already on top of us. But the halftracks gave us an armored regiment—no tanks, no armored cars—just two dozen halftracks with German light machine guns mounted on the rims. This armored regiment was formed in one day from truck drivers like me, from boys in other infantry units, and from D.P.'s who had just gotten off the boats. And the next day they sent us to attack the Arab Legion at Latrun in the Jerusalem corridor."

Nahshon puffed on the cigarette as it dangled from his lips. The end of the ash fell on his shirt. "Do you know what happened? The bastards wiped us out. They sat there behind the walls of the Latrun police station and with bastard British anti-tank guns and with bastard British officers directing their fire, they picked us off one by one. In two days they eliminated the only armored regiment in the Israeli army. Most of our halftracks and half of our men went up in smoke at Latrun." He pulled the butt of the cigarette out of his mouth and flicked it into the road. "Now we're starting all over again. Some Israeli agent at this minute is paying some bastard Italian junk yard dealer ten times what these halftracks are worth. He's paying him in hopes that he can then find some bastard ship owner and pay him ten times the usual freight to bring the halftracks into Haifa and unload them at night so the bastard U.N. observers won't see that we're violating the truce by bringing them in. And in hopes that we get the halftracks, we are trying to find drivers."

"I'm not exactly the answer to your prayers, am I?"

Nahshon looked at Evan and shook his head. "I have been told that there are Jews in America who are admirals and generals, and that Jewish scientists built the atomic bomb. Is that true?"

"Yes."

"The Americans sent us a colonel. One. His name was Marcus. He fought with us at Latrun. He was a good man. He was killed one night by one of his own sentries because the sentry challenged him in Hebrew and Marcus could not understand the language. It is good that you know Hebrew." He started the motor, shifted into gear, and headed down the road.

Evan realized that Nahshon was bitter that Americans with military skill were not flooding into Israel to help their fellow Jews. The dark-skinned corporal could not understand why only a handful—perhaps less than a hundred so far—had come from the largest Jewish community in the world, from a nation that had over five million Jews. The failure of Americans to come in greater numbers was something he did not completely understand himself. All it took was a boat ticket to France. He had proved that. And yet it took more. It took a combination of factors. It took a love for the Jewish people. It took enough will to break away from the possessive, protecting love of your parents. It took enough courage to risk losing your American citizenship and your life.

And, Evan now thought for the first time, it took one more thing —a deep-seated and abiding hatred for bullies. But perhaps you

[13]

couldn't love Jews without hating bullies—God, there had been so many of them in Jewish history. Evan had had few encounters with the physical bullies. There was the time in the fourth grade when one of his Christian classmates had picked on a smaller Jewish boy. Evan, despite his fear of the bigger boy, had stepped between the two and dared the bully to pick on someone nearer his own size, and the bully had backed down. But there were other bullies that you could rarely fight, the anti-semitic bullies who made slurring comments about Jews, usually when they thought there were no Jews around. The name Copperman kept him from having much experience with that type. The Jews without Jewish names picked up the insults from that quarter. And then there were the intellectual bullies who were just bullies, and Judaism had nothing to do with it. Like the authoritarian professors—there were only a few—at the university who demanded that you accept their scholastic prejudices as truth. Evan had argued with them in class, usually to be told later by his friends that he was a damned fool because it would lower his grade. But it took a certain amount of courage to risk getting a lower grade, too. So one had to be a fighter of bullies to be here, too, because the Arabs were bullies, and they would fight only as long as they thought the Israelis were weaker than they.

The halftrack was approaching the narrow streets of an Arab village, and Nahshon shifted down into a lower gear to slow the armored vehicle. The main street of the little village was barely wide enough to admit the halftrack. Iron grill work guarded every window of the buildings, but the doors now hung open carelessly. Magazines, photographs, trash spilled out of some doorways into the dirty street. Nahshon stopped the halftrack in the street next to one of the larger mud-brick houses.

"The whole village is deserted," he told Evan. "Get used to it. You'll see many like it. The villagers left before the fighting could even begin. They put everything they could on the backs of their donkeys and fled to the east. Their leaders told them we would shoot them and mutilate their bodies. They were also told they could come back in a few days, as soon as the Arab armies had flung us into the sea." Nahshon grinned. "It didn't work out that way." He opened the door of the halftrack. "This was the house of the *Mukhtar*, the village leader. Gingi, our company commander, is using it for Plugah Gimel's headquarters. Come inside and meet him."

Evan followed Nahshon into the house, through several bare rooms, and into the back room. A muscular man in his early thirties was standing in front of a mirror shaving with a safety razor. An old enamel pan filled with water sat on a small table in front of him. There was lather on his neck and face up to the close-cropped hair of his blond sideburns. He was bare to his waist and over the short khaki pants he wore a thick canvas belt which held a canvas holster. His black army boots were dusty, but the long khaki stockings were tight and folded neatly below his knees. The thick muscles in his calves caused knotty bulges in his stockings.

In the corner of the room, a girl in khaki shirt and long khaki trousers sat before a radio set that was partially covered by a greenish canvas case. A pair of earphones was an oversized hairband for her dark brown hair, which was pulled into a loose bun at the back of her head. Nahshon raised a devilish eyebrow in greeting to her. The company commander opened his mouth to tighten the skin for the stroke of the razor and observed the two soldiers in his mirror.

"*Shalom,* Nahshon. What do you have with you?" he said cheerfully, not turning from the mirror.

"An American *yeled,*" Nahshon answered unhappily. Evan felt himself growing red and glanced at the girl—*yeled* was the Hebrew word for "little boy."

Gingi peered at Evan in the mirror and gave him a warm smile. "If he came to Plugah Gimel all the way from America, he's a man, Nahshon. How are you called?"

"Evan Copperman, sir."

The girl at the radio set smiled. Gingi waved his razor in the air. "We don't use 'sirs' in this army. Ask Nahshon. You call me Gingi. I'll call you Evan. How did an American get a fine Hebrew name like Evan?"

"By accident. My parents thought it was a fine Anglo-Saxon name," Evan said. The girl laughed. "They named me for a grandfather called Ezekiel, but they wanted to give me an American name I could live with, so they chose Evan. They had no idea that it means stone in Hebrew."

"Then we have something in common. My parents named me

[15]

Zechariah, and my friends couldn't live with it, not even in Israel. So they called me Gingi." He bent down near the enamel pan and sloshed water on his face. The lids were closed over the green eyes as he aimed a finger at his head. "It's the hair. You Americans would say 'blondy.' Gingi is the word here." The captain reached for a towel and wiped his face. "Where are you from in America?"

"Virginia."

"Oh, where the cigarettes come from. Did you grow tobacco there?"

"No, I lived in a city."

"Too bad. You could have taught us how to grow it here and then we wouldn't have to send all the way to Virginia." He put on his shirt, reached into a pocket for a box of cigarettes, and offered one to Evan. Evan shook his head. Nahshon, uninvited, reached over and took one, then lighted Gingi's cigarette and his own.

"Well, how is he?" Gingi asked Nahshon.

"I think he would be better off in one of the infantry platoons."

"Why?" Gingi looked surprised. "Can't he drive?"

"He's very good at starting," Nahshon said, "but bloody miserable at stopping."

Gingi grinned and looked intently at Evan. "You have just described the perfect quality for an Israeli soldier, Nahshon. If we get more halftracks, we'll have to have drivers ready. Take as much time as you need during the next few days to teach him to drive. If you aren't successful, tell Eliyahu to transfer him to one of the infantry platoons."

Chapter Two

NAHSHON DROVE THE HALFTRACK AWAY FROM THE *Mukhtar's* house, out of the village and down the road about a half a mile until he came to a grove of olive trees. There were eight other halftracks parked in the grove, their drivers lounging in the shade of one of the trees. Nahshon introduced Evan to the other drivers as the 'Yeled,' the 'Kid.' Four of the drivers had spread a blanket under the olive tree and were playing a game of rummy. Nahshon ejected one of them from the game and moved in to take his place.

At mid-morning, trucks loaded with infantry troops from the armored unit's sister battalion drove into the olive grove. The men were coming back to the truce line after a week's rest back at their base. Each man wore a different combination of khaki clothes. Some had on long trousers, others short pants. Some had sweaters tied around their waists. Some had sleeves rolled up, others had them down, and some had short-sleeved blouses. There was a variety of weapons and helmets—Sten guns, German rifles, a few British Enfield rifles with the wooden stocks that came right up to the muzzles, several German light machine guns, helmets from at least three different armies, Palestinian knit stocking caps, and even a few kibbutz hats, which looked like sailor hats with the brims pulled down. The men hopped down from the trucks, formed into squads, then straggled off toward the nearby hills.

About twenty minutes later, the infantry squads that belonged to the armored regiment began arriving from the hills. For motleyness, they were near duplicates of the squads that had just relieved them, except that their uniforms were a little dirtier and some of the men had the stubble of several days' growth of whiskers on their red and brown sunburned faces. With a few exceptions, they were very young, many about the age of Evan, some younger. By comparison, the halftrack drivers seemed to be a much older group. The soldiers began throwing their gear into the back of the halftracks and climbing in after it.

"Hey, Rebel!" one of the new arrivals called to Evan. Bernie Schwartz had left the induction camp one day ahead of Evan. He now wore a British helmet, the weight of which seemed to push the stocky little American closer to the ground. He wiggled his eyebrows. "Don't tell me they sent you to this same regiment."

"Yes. They're going to try to teach me to drive one of those."

"Good. Maybe you'll drive the one I ride in and take it easy over the chuckholes. I've got a sore ass from sitting on rocks for the past two days. How do you like these jerks? I report in to the camp, they give me a rifle, some slugs, two blankets, and a helmet, put me in a jeep, and an hour later I'm on that friggin hill digging a foxhole."

"You wanted action. You're getting action."

"Yeah. I'm getting a lot of rocks jammed up my butt."

"Schwartz!" a man hollered from one of the halftracks. Then the man yelled again in Hebrew, "Hurry up, come along quickly!"

"I can't understand anything these creeps say," Bernie complained.

"He said to hurry up, they're waiting for you."

Bernie made a dirty gesture with his finger toward the man in the halftrack. "Take it easy, meathead," he yelled. "I'm coming." He turned to Evan. "One day when we have lots of time, explain to me how a Heeb from Virginia can understand this language while a bum like me from New York can only say hello and goodbye, which is the same word. I'll see you back in camp. Don't get no traffic tickets."

Bernie and nine other Americans had been with Evan in the D.P. camp in Marseilles. All but Evan had been sent to the D.P. camp directly from America, since they had skills that the Israeli army needed quickly. Evan had met Bernie for the first time one afternoon when they walked next to each other down to the beach near the D.P. camp.

"That Tamar is really nice, uh, Rebel?" Bernie had declared, his eyes focused on the legs of the Israeli girl, one of the camp directors, walking a few dozen feet in front of them. He punched Evan with his elbow. "Think I could get next to her if I tried? Or do you figger these Israelis have a closed shop?"

"Why don't you try Gerry?" Evan suggested. Gerry was one of the two nurses in the American group.

"You ever been in New York?"

"A few times."

"Then maybe you know enough about the place to know that to a broad like Gerry I'm from the wrong side of the tracks. She's a snob from Central Park West and I'm just a lousy kike from the East Side."

Evan was sorry Bernie had used the word "kike." It was a word that always made him bristle, even when a Jew used it. "Anyway, Gerry is a few years older than you."

"When it comes to what makes me a man and what makes her

[18]

a woman, a few years mocks friggin nix." Bernie was trying to say "macht nichts" with the "friggin" thrown between, but he couldn't make the German guttural sound. "Them rich bitches get hot pants and squirm for it the same as girls in my neighborhood. If I was marriage bait she'd be crawling all over me."

"This your first time away from New York?" Evan tried to change the subject.

"Think they'd of sent me over here if it was? I joined the army too late to do any fighting in the war. I was on occupation duty in Germany two years and got discharged as a sergeant this spring. I know my weapons. How about you?"

"I went to a military school in Virginia," Evan lied.

"Them friggin Germans." Bernie shook his head slowly. "I hate them bastards. They hated me, too, but didn't have guts enough to do anything about it. I'd get a fraulein up in a hotel room, and she'd strip down, and I'd strip down, and I'd stand there in front of her, and I'd say—" Bernie gritted his teeth, his neck muscles tightening. "—I'd say, 'Look at me, you Dutch bitch. See, I'm a Jew, I'm a Jew. What the hell are you going to do about it?'"

"What would they say?"

"They'd say, 'Come on, baby, I love you.' They didn't give a frig if I was a Jew or a Arab or a man from Mars. As long as I had the *gelt*, that's all they cared about. They're all a bunch of whores." Like a punch drunk fighter coming out of a daze, Bernie looked around as though surprised to find Evan beside him. "Look, Rebel, the truth now, you come from a rich family in Dixie, don't you?"

"No, not really." Evan, still mentally in the German hotel room with the naked Bernie confronting the naked German prostitute, was unprepared for this bridgeless sweep to a new topic.

"You can't figger a guy like me, Rebel, can you? The truth now. I'm just a guy who wants to do some shoving. People have been shoving me since I was a kid—my old man till he started pushing up daisies, my old lady till I joined the army. Now the Arabs are trying to shove me around. By God, we'll do some friggin shoving back, uh, Rebel?" He punched Evan with his elbow again. "And when I come back to the East Side after this fighting is over and walk down Delancey Street in my Israeli uniform, them old Jews'll come out weeping and shake my hand. 'You're a good boy, you're a good boy,'

[19]

they'll say. And the girls. Brudder, I'll have to fight 'em off." Bernie had laughed then, his short muscular body rippling in anticipation of the homecoming.

Evan thought he had been able to "figure" him, because in Bernie there was some of them all, and the openness of his emotions revealed what many of them were hiding. Under the layer of reasons that they all gave for going to Israel—and there was truth to the reasons, too—there was the hard flint of revenge, the urge to shove back, finally, and at last.

They could all catalogue the incidents for which they were now, belatedly, seeking their own kind of revenge. There was the time, for example, when he was a child and his father was walking with him from their store to the car. They passed two house painters who were standing in the foyer of a pool hall, and one of the painters pointed to Evan's father and said to the other painter: "No, you're wrong about that. Copperman don't have no Jew nose." "Sure he does. Look at it. That's a Jew nose if ever I seen one." "No, you're wrong." "The hell I am." And the two men had laughed at Evan and his father. Evan's father had continued walking, pretending he hadn't heard them, but he had. But what did Evan expect him to do, walk up and begin brawling with two house painters? No. Yes!

The fights, the snubs, the insults; why did he always remember those? There were so many more good things to remember about growing up in the Virginia town: the Christians who were good, who if they disparaged the Jews at least kept it within the privacy of their own homes, who were "Christian" in their contact with Jews. Why didn't he remember those things? What kind of warped person had he become that the memories of the few humiliations, the conflicts, stayed like living, breathing things, while the unrecalled kindnesses decomposed?

The poor Arabs. How did they have a chance to win? To the Jews they had become a reincarnation of the Romans, the Inquisitors, the Crusaders, the Cossacks, the Poles, the Germans, and every enemy, real and imagined, that had ever hurt an Israeli soldier in his own lifetime.

The last of the infantry troops had now arrived back from the hill, and they were climbing over the sides or through the rear doors of the halftracks that were not yet filled. Only three men walked up to Nahshon's halftrack, the command vehicle. One, a small, skinny young man with a red star of David on a white background painted on his helmet, opened the back door and shoved a large canvas satchel into the vehicle, then climbed in after it. He was followed by two soldiers carrying light machine guns and metal boxes full of ammunition. The first was an older man, a stocking cap teetering on the back of his almost bald head.

It was the second machine gunner, however, who captured Evan's attention and held it. The man was solid black, and Evan's surprise to find a Negro here was followed by the realization that there was something about the tall black soldier that made him different than any other Negro he had ever seen. His hair was longer, a mass of glistening raven ringlets, and his nose and lips were quite thin. Still, his skin was black, and Evan stared at him, transfixed. The Negro was setting his machine gun into a mount on the rim of the half-track and tightening it into place.

Nahshon threw his cards down on the blanket and stood up. "*Chaverim,*"—Comrades, "let's go." He motioned to Evan. "Yeled, come with me."

They climbed into the halftrack and the corporal turned in his seat and called to the three men in the back of the vehicle. "*Chaverim,* this is the Yeled, an American. Yeled, the little one back there is Mordecai, our medic. The ancient one is Itzik, a machine gunner and kibbutznik. And the other machine gunner is Radhai Hayehudi-Ha'acharon, our colonial troop, a gift from Haile Selassie. We pick up now a radio operator and a captain and the command halftrack is ready to go home." Nahshon started the motor and threw the halftrack into gear. The tall aerial near the driver's seat swayed wildly as the corporal jerked the vehicle around and headed out of the olive grove. The other halftracks swung in behind him. Some of the soldiers in them were seated precariously on the steel rims of the tracked vehicles, swaying too, like fleshy aerials above the hard, unyielding bodies of the powerful brown armored carriers.

Nahshon led the convoy back to the village. He stopped at the *Mukhtar's* house and the other vehicles stopped behind him. "Yeled," Nahshon ordered, "go in and help Shulamit with the radio."

When Evan walked into the back room, Gingi was rolling up a bundle of maps and sticking them into a map case. The girl was wrapping up the earphone wires.

"I'll carry this," Evan said, getting a hold on the set.

"No, it's too heavy. Let me take this end," the girl said.

They carried it to the halftrack and lifted it up to the men inside, who placed it on its mount just behind the driver's seat. Gingi followed them out of the house with the map case and his own and Shulamit's knapsacks. Evan sat next to Shulamit on the raised metal cabinets that ran along each side of the interior of the halftrack, leaving a well for the feet in the center. Gingi gave a signal with his hand for the convoy to get underway.

"Are you the only girl in this regiment?" Evan asked, trying to yell above the noise of the halftrack motor.

She motioned toward her ear. He slid closer to her and repeated the question, louder.

"No," she said. "The only one in Plugah Gimel—this company. Sorry. I do not understand English so well. Speak Hebrew." The motor of the halftrack was not so loud now.

"My accent is very bad and I don't know the new words," Evan said in Hebrew.

"You won't learn them unless you speak Hebrew all the time," she said in Hebrew. Evan noticed that her eyes were tan, almost the exact same shade as her skin, which had been sunburned to a light reddish-brown. Her elliptical face, firm arms, and slender fingers hinted that an equally attractive body was hidden within the baggy khaki shirt and loose-fitting long trousers.

Evan spoke in Hebrew again. "All right. I will speak to you in Hebrew. You speak to me in English."

"No." She held up one of her long fingers in the manner of a teacher admonishing a student. "This is Israel. Hebrew is our language. We both speak Hebrew or we do not speak at all."

"All right," Evan grinned. "Do you sleep with us?"

She looked at him curiously for a minute, then laughed. "You mean in the barracks?"

"Yes."

She shook her head, a glint of amusement in her eyes. "I sleep with the nurse (she made the motion of giving herself an injection) and two regimental secretaries (she picked up an imaginary pencil and began scribbling on her hand)."

Evan nodded that he understood.

"Are you very disappointed?" she asked, feigning a comforting tone.

"Yes," Evan said. He grinned broadly, then glanced over at the other three soldiers in the back of the halftrack to see if they were listening to the conversation. Itzik was sitting upright, his eyes closed, his head posting with the vibration of the halftrack. Mordecai, the medic, had one foot on the bench that ran the length of the halftrack. He was looking over the edge of the vehicle at the rocky fields that were slipping away behind them. Radhai, the Ethiopian, was watching them. Evan turned again toward Shulamit and spoke to her in Hebrew. Using the ancient language in the back of a rumbling halftrack made him feel like a Biblical character awakening suddenly to find himself in the middle of the Twentieth Century. Nahshon down-shifted to slow the vehicle and negotiated it through the detours that skirted the mined sections of the road. The last detour was the one that Evan had missed. The can he had hit was lying on its side, a deep dent in its white hide.

When they arrived back at the barracks, Nahshon stopped first at the long building that housed the regimental and company headquarters and the girls' quarters. Gingi climbed out through the front door. Shulamit grabbed her knapsack, opened the back door of the halftrack, and climbed down to the ground.

"*Shalom,*" she said to Evan. "Remember. Only Hebrew."

Chapter Three

THE HALFTRACK COMPANY DID NOT ARRIVE BACK IN the camp until noon, so it was later than usual when the men came into the mess hall for the mid-day meal. Evan was standing near the end of the mess line when Nahshon walked in quickly, followed by two other drivers. He held his mess tins high in his right hand. "Drivers first!" he called. Then he and the two other drivers squeezed into the front of the line. Evan noticed that no one grumbled about the intrusion.

"Why do drivers go to the front of the line?" he asked Itzik, who was standing behind him.

"They don't," Itzik answered. "Just Nahshon, and anyone who is with him. He takes special privileges—but he also takes special responsibilities, so everyone lets him get by with it."

The meal was a gristly lamb stew and a salad, which the cooks dashed into the mess gear, and a thick sweet concoction of fruit, which they poured into the cup. There were a few loaves of unsliced rye bread on each table and in the center of each table two large tin cans. One contained jam, the other sharp-smelling herring. Large, yellow-podded bees hovered around the cans like whirring, stalkless daisies. Sometimes they would light on the spots of fruit drink that had been spilled on the wooden tables. The fruit concoction served as both the drink and the dessert. First a soldier drank off the juice, then speared the bloated dried fruit on the bottom of the cup and ate it.

When Evan returned to the barracks, most of the men were lying on their beds, resting during the mid-day heat. Nahshon and three others had continued their card game, using Nahshon's bed as a table. Evan put his mess gear on the shelf, flattened the empty palliasse on the wooden planks of his bed, and then folded his two blankets on top of the palliasse cover to put some sort of cushion between himself and the boards. He lay down on his back, and the planks gave slightly with the weight of his body, but when he turned the wooden slats jabbed into his hipbones and shoulder.

There were dozens of lethargic flies around his bed. When Evan hit at them, they would give an indolent hop a short distance into the air and then light on the same spot again. One of the drivers had managed to get a mosquito net from some place and was comfortably sleeping under it. Evan rolled down his sleeves, hid his face under the pages of an open magazine, and put his hands in his pockets. Now every part of his flesh was protected from the flies and he could rest. But instead of resting, he told himself, he should be writing a letter to his parents telling them that he was now assigned to a permanent army unit and he was well.

He had written them twice, once just before the D.P. ship left from Marseilles, telling them that he had joined the Israeli army, and again the day the ship docked in Haifa, informing them that he had arrived in Israel safely and giving them the address of the American-Canadian Club in Tel Aviv, which would forward his mail to his permanent camp. In Marseilles, he had also written Rabbi

Lichtberg and asked him to comfort his parents in whatever way he could. Rabbi Lichtberg would understand why he had come to Israel. His parents would not. His first letter to them, he knew, would not only be a shock, it would be a knife. He loved them, and it pained him that he had to make a decision that would hurt them. They had given him everything material they had to give—and even more than simply material things. They instilled in him a sense of justice, which probably accounted for his desire of many years to become an attorney.

Nor had they neglected to give him the example of the Jewish traditions, even in the small southern city. His mother always purchased kosher meat (from the meat market that kept a separate cutting block and slicing tools for the Jews, yet also sold ham and other non-kosher meats). She kept two sets of dishes, silverware, and pots and pans. One set was for meals with meat products and the other set was for meals with milk products. But she served bread made with both milk and lard at both kinds of meals. It was the only bread available in the city. And although they ate only kosher meat in their home, they had no qualms about eating out at restaurants where non-kosher meat was served. Evan himself had often laughed at the gross inconsistencies, but he always accepted them with no more feelings of guilt than his parents. The Coppermans preserved in Judaism what they conveniently could. They made adjustments for the things they conveniently could not. Most of the Jewish families in the town found it convenient to observe far less than the Coppermans. His parents enrolled him in Hebrew school in the same year he started public school, and they were immensely pleased that he chose to stay on after his *bar mitzvah* and study further with Rabbi Lichtberg. They did not see it as a contradiction to encourage their son to attend synagogue services on Saturday morning, yet expect him to come and help them in the clothing store on Saturday afternoon.

The store had been founded at the turn of the century by Evan's grandfather, who had lived with the Coppermans until his death. He once told Evan that the first time he had opened his store on Saturday he had hidden in a back room for shame and let a clerk wait on customers. In business, his grandfather had learned to make the American adjustments to his religion. In the home and synagogue, he could never quite grasp the changes. He would arise early and say the morning prayers by himself in his room, wearing the phylacteries—the two tiny Scripture cases with long leather straps—on his forehead and left arm next to his heart. He complained to his daughter-in-law, Evan's mother, one evening before supper: "The Jewish home in America! Do you smell sweet and sour cabbage? No! You smell model airplane dope." And the sermons of Rabbi Lichtberg on Friday evenings and on the holidays were to him nothing more than an emulation of the Christian services, an unwarranted interruption of his prayers. Walking home from services one evening on Yom Kippur, the Day of Atonement, he described for Evan the services in the little synagogue in the Russian village that had been his home. "It was nice then," he said. "We had a simple faith. There was a God who would punish sin. No theologians, no appeal to reason from the pulpit. A man could stand on his feet all night and all day on Yom Kippur and then sit down to read the Law after sunset. He could deal with God. And God could deal with him."

There were times when Evan knew that he himself was living with one foot in the ruins of the little Russian ghetto and the other on the emancipated ground of the southern city. Almost all his friends in high school were Christians and he was accepted in his own crowd without reservations. Yet his parents did not want him to date Christian girls—it might lead eventually to marriage. Because he did not want to hurt his parents, and because there were no Jewish girls his age, he took out no one. He simply envied the dating habits of his classmates from a distance. Just as he envied from a distance Christmas and Easter and church on Sunday morning and all the things that set him apart from his friends. Evan often wondered if, after he went to the university and became a lawyer, he would come back to this town, or another like it, and know that he, like his parents, could give his children everything but the one thing he could never purchase—a sense of belonging in a total way to the community in which they lived.

This spring, when he had told his parents that he wanted to take part in a National Students Association program in which American students would work on French farms during the summer, they agreed, reluctantly, to let him go. They feared he would not be safe in France by himself. When he came home from the university at the end of May to pack his clothes and tell them goodbye, he knew it was possible that he would now go farther than France. But how could he tell them? First, they might prevent him from going. Second, he would hurt them needlessly if he told them and then the Israelis would not accept him.

From the first, it seemed doubtful that the Israelis would. When Evan had walked into the newly-opened Israeli Embassy in Paris, carpenters and plasterers were still working on partitions and walls, transforming what had been a private residence into a modest office building. A secretary sitting at a desk before a steep winding staircase seemed to be on guard, ready to man the heights of the staircase, if necessary, to beat back the outsider and keep him from gaining the second story offices.

When Evan told her that he wanted to see someone who could take his application for the Israeli army, she regarded him for a moment suspiciously, then picked up a pencil, wrote an address on a white pad, tore off the small piece of paper and handed it to him.

"Thank you," he had said. The woman had not replied. Evan turned and left the embassy. It was his first encounter with either the State of Israel or an individual Israeli.

The man who reluctantly allowed Evan to enter the room over the second-rate movie house was even less cordial. The room was bare except for a desk and chair. Tacked onto the dirty yellow wallpaper were several fresh posters, each with the word "Haganah" emblazoned across it, and each showing a tough, heroic man in the act of battle. The men on the posters seemed to be growling. One was dressed in a sweater and stocking cap in addition to khaki clothing and boots. He was throwing a hand grenade. The man in the room was shorter and stockier than the heroes on the posters.

"Why do you want to join the Israeli army?" he asked Evan impatiently.

"I'm a Zionist."

"Are you Jewish?"

"Of course." Evan tried to give a belligerent tone to his voice to match the hostility of his interrogator.

"Prove it."

Evan reached into his sport coat pocket and pulled out his green U.S. passport. "You can see here that I have a Jewish name."

The man opened the passport to the identification page, looked at the passport photo and then looked back up at Evan, searching for dissimilarities between the young man in the passport photo and this hazel-eyed, brown-haired youth before him.

"Evan Andrew Copperman. Copperman. Copperman could be anything. Perhaps even British."

"Would speaking Hebrew satisfy you?"

"Let me hear the *aleph-bet*."

"*Aleph, base, vase, gimmel, daled—*" Evan could say the Hebrew alphabet as easily as he could spell his name. Twelve years of Hebrew in which he had learned to translate rapidly and accurately not only the Bible, but the Aramaic commentaries as well, and now this man was asking him what he had learned on the first day when he was six years old.

"That's enough," the man interrupted. "We need only men who have had experience with weapons. Were you in the American army?"

"No. But I was in a military group for four years in high school. I'm familiar with the M-1 and other small arms." Evan avoided explaining that the military group was nothing more than a fancy drill company which high school youths had entered to avoid taking physical education. Their weapons were dummy rifles.

"According to this passport, you are only twenty years old." He gave Evan a hard, appraising look. "We would need proof that you have your parents' permission."

"How could I go about doing that? A letter would take too long, and I couldn't put a message like that in a cable." The belligerency in Evan's voice now was real. His parents would never give their permission.

The man seemed undecided. "I do not know. We have had no case like this before."

"Look," Evan said. "My parents have always been Zionists. I'm doing what I think they would want me to do."

"I do not give you a definite yes," the man said, "but if you are willing you can begin taking the necessary physical examinations. I will let you know later if you have been accepted."

Those were the first two, the cold, wooden-faced secretary at the Israeli Embassy, and the harassed, impatient man at the secret room over the movie house near the Arc de Triomphe. They were like Eliyahu. By the strange inside-out attitude that they affected, they made you think *they* were doing *you* a favor to allow you to

[28]

join the surrounded Jews in Palestine. If your desire was strong enough, they would try to help you—perhaps. There had been a spark of warmth from the woman doctor, but possibly Evan imagined even that because of her resemblance to his mother.

Dr. Mathilde Arbenson's name was on a mimeographed sheet the man had given him. The sheet listed a number of doctors, their addresses, and the part of the body that each would examine. It also gave another address he was to report to in two days, after all the physical examinations had been completed. Dr. Arbenson was a chest specialist and her office was in a tree-lined residential section of Paris. A thin, gray-haired woman, she was sitting in a straight chair in the empty waiting room reading a medical journal when Evan entered. Dr. Arbenson held the medical journal in one hand and took the papers from Evan with the other. She ushered him into the examination room in a relaxed, but businesslike manner, and then looked at the mimeographed sheets.

"Are you English or American?"

"American."

"Take off your shirt, please." She placed the plugs of a stethoscope in her ears. "You are quite young. How old?"

"Twenty." The doctor tapped Evan's chest and then placed the stethoscope to his back and chest. Afterwards, she positioned the youth in front of the fluoroscope and told him to breathe in and out deeply.

"You have the chest of an athlete," she said, observing the expanding and contracting skeleton in the screen.

"I was on the track team at college."

"How did you get to France?"

"I came over on a student ship. I was supposed to work on a French farm this summer."

"Do your parents know of what you are about to do?"

"No. But they wouldn't mind." He was sure Dr. Arbenson knew he was not telling the truth. Those large brown eyes that reminded him so much of his mother seemed to be peering into his thoughts, just as they had examined the skeleton and shadows in the fluoroscope. And while her face reflected nothing, in the brown eyes there was warmth and sympathy. "I believe I understand," she said. She looked down at the mimeographed form and began writing.

Somewhere, at the ephemeral headquarters in Paris, his name

had been approved, or at least allowed to slip by, and he had found himself on the train to Marseilles. He had lived in the D.P. camp and taken the new name, "Zerach Itzkovitch," along with D.P. papers that might enable him to fool the U.N. observers who would be awaiting the ship in Haifa. Only bona fide displaced persons were permitted by the U.N. to come into the country during the truce that followed the first month of official war between Israel and the surrounding Arab nations.

The truce was elapsing and the U.N. worked with benevolent ineptness to seek out ways of delaying the hour when the bell would ring for the second round. But the combatants on both sides knew they would clash and kill again, and they laid plans for attack and defense. Arab troops were crossing freely into Palestine from Lebanon, Syria, Trans-Jordan, and Egypt. United Nations observers, however, awaited every ship that arrived in Haifa from the D.P. camps of Italy and France to make certain that the Jews, at least, obeyed the rules of the truce, even if the Arabs didn't. Evan and Bernie were aboard one of the ships, and as it came closer to the coast of Israel Evan became more concerned about the U.N. observers than about his parents.

In the late afternoon, Nahshon took Evan for a practice drive on the road to Nahariya, and after supper he took him out again for a night driving session—without lights.

"We don't use our lights when we travel at night," he explained. "The Arabs can hear us, but they can't see us. They usually estimate that we have three times as many vehicles as we really do. It's an advantage to have a frightened enemy."

In the darkness, Evan learned to watch the light sand at the edge of the asphalt road for direction. Other vehicles that approached the darkened halftrack cut off their lights to keep from blinding the driver. Two small cars failed to douse their lights, and, for frightening seconds after they passed, Evan was driving blind. His pupils had contracted in the glare of the lights and they could not expand rapidly enough to allow him to see in the dark.

The next day, regular training resumed for all units of the armored regiment. The truce was almost in its last week, and the Israelis were uncertain about whether it would be prolonged. The

Arabs had already declared that they would not agree to a continuation of the month-long halt in fighting.

Nahshon told Evan to fill up his canteen and bring along his Sten gun. "Today we try cross-country driving." There was a half-concealed look of mischief in the corporal's bloodshot eyes. "Come, the medic waits."

Mordecai, his medic's satchel beside him, was already in the halftrack. He grinned and waved the palm of his hand in greeting when Evan climbed over the side and sat next to him. Nahshon drove up to the company headquarters, got a trip ticket filled out, then poked his head in the office next door, where Shulamit was talking to the regimental secretary.

"Shulamit, come. I need a radio operator."

"Where are you going?"

"To the east. The Yeled has to have cross-country experience."

"And who said I was to go?" she demanded, putting her hands on her hips.

"I did. What higher authority is there?" He twirled the tip of his handlebar mustache and winked at the regimental secretary. "Besides," he said plaintively, "suppose the Yeled wrecks the halftrack when we're off the road. Suppose we're attacked by Arabs. Would you leave old Nahshon and those two children out there helpless?"

"You know how to operate the radio. Use it if you get into trouble."

"Ah, my dear, but that's not my job."

"Oh, you Moroccan bully," she said in exasperation. "I have one day free after being in that smelly Arab village for five days, and you have to come and take it away. I was going to wash everything I own today."

Nahshon rubbed his big nose with a finger and glanced from her sandals up the full trouser legs to the baggy khaki blouse. "Everything you have on passes inspection, my pretty one. Get your canteen and hop aboard. You can wash your things tomorrow."

Shulamit disappeared into a room at the end of the long building and a few minutes later came out with a canteen and a rolled up pair of earphones. Evan opened the back door of the halftrack and held out a hand to help her climb aboard.

He asked Mordecai in Hebrew, "Do you speak English?"

"Only Yiddish, Hungarian, and Hebrew," Mordecai replied.

"That's all right," Evan said, "I have to speak Hebrew to her because she's so—" He turned to Shulamit and began making the motion of saluting. "What is that?" he asked.

Shulamit, who had been pouting over her interrupted plans, suddenly laughed. "Patriotic."

"Yes, Mordecai, she is very patriotic."

"Good," Mordecai said. "Then we will all speak Hebrew together."

As they drove toward the main gate of the camp, they passed another halftrack loaded with infantry troops. Standing out in stark contrast to the lighter-skinned Jews was Radhai.

"I have to look a second time everytime I see someone so dark among us," Evan commented to Shulamit.

"He's a Falasha, an Ethiopian Jew," she said.

"I didn't know any Jews lived there. They have strange names in that country. If I understood Nahshon correctly, he called him Radhai Hayehudi-Ha'acharon."

"You understood him correctly. Radhai The-Last-Jew. It's a name Wingate gave him."

"You mean the General Wingate of Burma?"

"Yes. But he was first in Palestine with the British army. He formed special squads of Jewish youths to protect the settlements from Arab marauders, although most of the other British officers opposed his doing it. Then he fought in Ethiopia during the war, and then in Burma. He sent Radhai here when he was in Ethiopia."

"Was Wingate a Jew?"

"No," she said. "But he was a Zionist. If he were alive and with us now, this war would have already been won, and we would have all of Palestine, not just a small part of it."

She spoke so rapidly that Evan had missed a few of the words. He touched her hand. "Slowly, slowly."

"Sorry."

Nahshon headed out the same road that they had taken the day before, then turned north on another dirt road. Evan and Shulamit talked to each other above the roar of the motor, and Mordecai, sitting across from them, asked an occasional question, but mostly listened.

"Shulamit is a beautiful name," Evan said. "It was taken from 'The Song of Songs,' wasn't it?"

[32]

"Do you know the Bible?"

"If I could translate the difficult verses in Isaiah, my rabbi let me read the poetry of 'The Song of Songs' for dessert. 'Return, return, O Shulamit; return, return, that we may look upon thee.'"

She laughed. "Please. Don't quote any more. You will embarrass Mordecai."

"Will I embarrass you?"

"You will find that I do not embarrass easily."

"Have you been out upon the world so long?"

She smiled, but did not answer.

"Were you in the Hebrew University?" he asked.

"No. I finished high school in Jerusalem a year ago. I was going to begin in the university last fall, but 1947 was not a vintage year for starting a university education in Palestine. So I decided to postpone it. It's just as well."

"What did you do before the war started?"

"Which war? The war that started last November, when the U.N. passed the partition plan, or the war that started this May, when the Arabs invaded?" She paused for a second. "Last summer, I volunteered to work with the Irgun's secret radio station, and—"

"You were a terrorist?" he asked incredulously, using the English word 'terrorist.'

Shulamit stiffened and gave him a withering look. "'Terrorist' is a word the British called us, not the Jews." She turned away from him.

"I'm sorry," Evan said, surprised that the word had had such an upsetting effect on her. "It's just a word the American newspapers use when they mention the Irgun Zvai Leumi or the Stern Gang."

"'Stern Gang' is another British term. For a Jew to use it is an insult to the memories of the soldiers who fell in battle against the British and Arabs."

Evan was silent. He really didn't give a damn about either the Irgun Zvai Leumi or the Stern Gang, but he was sorry he had offended her by calling them what everybody he had ever heard always called them. He wondered what he could say to move the conversation back toward a more pleasant direction.

But Shulamit, as though realizing the childishness of her burst of anger, relaxed and smiled wryly at Evan. "You thought a member of the Irgun would be some kind of madman, a fanatic?"

[33]

"No," he lied. He had thought members of the Irgun were fanatics, but not madmen.

"Then why are you surprised that I was a member?"

"Well," he hesitated. "Well, you are very quiet."

She nodded. "That's why I'm still alive. That's why most of the Irgun members are still alive. They are all very quiet."

He listened, slipping through the Sephardic accent and tackling the speeding words one by one.

"Many of my friends in school joined Haganah, the 'proper' defense organization of the Palestinian Jews," she continued. "I joined the Irgun, the 'improper' organization, your so-called terrorists. My friends in Haganah believed what they were doing was best for the Palestinian Jews. I believed what I was doing was best."

"Then you aren't angry with them."

"Why should I be? They love Israel as much as I. So do their leaders. But their leaders are wrong. They were wrong then. They are wrong now. Haganah thought it would get a Jewish state through politics. So they played politics and kissed the British and the British stayed. The Irgun kicked the British and the British mothers got tired of seeing their sons killed in Palestine and the British left."

She reached for a strand of brown hair that had blown down into her face and pushed the end of it back into the bun at the back of her head. "Now Ben-Gurion thinks he can call to the politicians of the world and get the Arab nations to leave Palestine. He will learn that the Irgun was right. The Arabs will understand only force."

"What would you do, break the truce?"

"Yes, of course. The Arabs will break it when they are ready. Why should they have surprise on their side?"

"But world opinion will be against us if we break it."

"Something else Ben-Gurion hasn't learned yet, but the Arabs already know. World opinion has no meaning. It's a streetwalker whose memory lasts only as long as the money or the thrill of a customer, then turns to a new customer with a new thrill and a new handful of money. World opinion has already forgotten the German slaughter of the Jews and the Arab invasion of Palestine. How long will it remember that the Jews broke a truce?"

The halftrack slowed and pulled to a stop in the middle of the dirt road. "Yeled," Nahshon called. "Drive now."

[34]

Evan slipped into the driver's seat, shifted into first and released the hand brake. As soon as the halftrack was moving, Nahshon pointed to the left, indicating for Evan to turn off the road and drive down the slope of a hill that led toward a maize field. Nahshon ordered him to stop on the slope of the hill so he could show him how to move another gear that activated the front wheel drive. When Evan started the vehicle again it pulled firmly with its front wheels as well as with its hard-rubber tracks.

Like a dull and aimless reaper, it cut a swath through the maize field, flattening the stalks in its path but allowing them to pop back up at drunken angles in its wake. It seemed a senseless destruction of the grain, whether or not any Arabs would be around to harvest it. There had been a dozen barren fields that they could have as easily ridden over. Near the end of the field Evan turned up onto the road again and looked back at the path of crippled stalks. Perhaps many of them would grow back tall again.

They followed the main dirt road for another few miles. Then Nahshon directed Evan to turn up a smaller dirt road that rose at a slight angle for a few hundred yards, then climbed steeply to a little Arab village at the top of the hill. At the base of the hill Nahshon reached over and shoved forward a lever which shifted the gear box into sub-low gears for more power. The heavy vehicle inched slowly up the steep hill. Mordecai and Shulamit had to clutch the side of the halftrack to keep from sliding down to the back door, and Nahshon, standing beside the driver's seat, braced his legs and leaned forward slightly.

The first Arab houses were near the top of the hill. As the halftrack approached them, Evan could see several people walking in the narrow road. He felt on the floor for his Sten gun, but Nahshon waved a hand at him.

"Don't worry, Yeled. This is a Druse village."

Evan gave him a questioning look.

"Drusim," the corporal said. "They are Arabs, but not Moslems. They are friendly to the state of Israel. Some of them even serve in the army."

This was the first Arab village with real inhabitants Evan had seen. A young girl walked by carrying an armful of faggots. A long white linen shawl covered her hair and flowed down behind her back. Her black gown was wrinkled and smudged with dust. She wore no shoes. Yet her face was smooth and lovely—a small chin, straight prominent nose, and large dark eyes. She reminded Evan of an illustration of Ruth he had seen once in a children's book of Bible stories.

Then he remembered the other Arab village he had seen, the deserted one. The life there had probably once been much like the life here. These people were tintypes of the ancient Jews. They lived now and looked now much as the Jews had lived and looked long ago. But now they were deserting their villages in the path of these Jewish warriors, these modern Jews whose ancestors had been exiled from the land, who had spent 2,000 years in the wilderness of other lands, changing their way of living, changing their way of dressing, even changing the way they once looked, but always carefully nurturing their children and their children's children for the time of the return, for the time when the white skins and the brown skins and the yellow skins of a thousand features and a hundred languages would sweep back into the land like a whirlwind and blend into a nation again and take the land from those who now looked as they once had looked, who now lived as they once had lived.

The girl who looked like Ruth disappeared. The halftrack was approaching the shops at the top of the hill in the center of the village. The youngsters in the village ran up to the shops to see the instrument of war, then clung to the walls of the mud-brick buildings, keeping their distance, but staring curiously. The halftrack was a monstrous intruder in this village street. The soldiers inside were intruders, too, and Evan, at least, perceived it with great discomfort.

Nahshon told him to cut the motor, then jumped down to the dirt street and motioned for Evan to come with him. Evan followed the Israeli corporal to one of the shops, which was more of a market that opened full onto the street. Soiled vegetables and fruit were set out on a paper on the ground. A thousand flies crawled over the items or buzzed around them. The owner of the shop was thin and bewhiskered, but the black twin cord band that held on his white headdress was set at a jaunty angle on his head. He wore wool pinstripe trousers that were dusty and creaseless. At the far interior of the shop, a woman—probably his wife—sat with a small baby on her lap. The child was sleeping, but a cluster of flies crawled around sores at the corners of the child's eyes. The mother made no attempt to brush them away.

Nahshon haggled in Arabic with the shopkeeper, who was insistent about not accepting a price he thought too low. First the corporal bought a small watermelon, which he handed to Evan to carry. Then he bought two bread cakes, a hunk of goat's cheese, four pomegranates, tobacco, and tobacco paper. The shopkeeper half bowed when he gave Nahshon the change. They exchanged farewells in Arabic, and Nahshon and Evan carried the supplies back to the halftrack, handing them up to Mordecai and Shulamit.

"We go now, Yeled," the corporal ordered.

Evan started the motor and reached over to pull back the lever that would take the halftrack out of the sub-low gears. Nahshon grabbed his hand. "The hill to the village is as steep going down, my boy, as it is coming up. You'll need the sub-low gears to brake you until you get to the bottom."

The halftrack moved back down the hill as slowly as it had come up. With the vehicle in sub-low gear, Evan actually had to push lightly on the accelerator at times to keep it moving at a steady rate of speed. They turned back into the main road and in a few miles turned again into a narrow asphalt road that seemed to wind higher into the round, rocky hills of the Galilee. The hills were brown and bare of growth. They apparently produced rocks, however, in great abundance, for the surface of each hill was thickly speckled with pebbles, rocks and boulders of all sizes. The hills were low and mound-like, but they somehow seemed very close to the cloudless blue sky.

Every now and then an Arab village clustered at the protective peak of a hill. Large rocks had been gathered to make fences around plots of ground on the lower slopes, but many rocks still remained in the fields, as though no matter how many were gleaned each cut of the plow pulled more to the surface.

As the halftrack moved slowly around a hairpin turn in the road, Evan glanced ahead and saw lying beneath the hot distant haze a long broad plain checkered with patches of green and yellow.

He tapped Nahshon on the leg and pointed toward the plain.

"The Emek," Nahshon shouted. "We won't go there today. Too far."

[37]

At the next bend, the corporal shouted for Evan to stop. Evan down-shifted and brought the halftrack to a smooth halt.

"Set the front wheel drive gear and turn off the road down to that small grove of olive trees," Nahshon said.

Evan headed off the asphalt road and tried to guide the halftrack so the big rocks would go between the wheels and the tracks. Sometimes when he would swerve the front wheels to miss a boulder, a back track would hit another large rock and the vehicle would tip up to one side at an angle and then come crashing back to the ground again. Evan drove into the shade of one of the largest olive trees and stopped the halftrack.

Nahshon reached under the driver's seat and pulled out a rusty bayonet. He cut each of the two small loaves of bread in half and then divided the hunk of cheese into quarters. The blade of the bayonet left heavy rust stains on the sides of the first quarter of cheese, and lighter ones on the last pieces he cut. He flung the bayonet back onto the dirty floor of the halftrack and looked up at the three young faces that had been watching the operation. "Well, help me carry this stuff. We came here to eat, didn't we?"

He picked up the watermelon and two of the pomegranates. Mordecai, Evan, and Shulamit took the rest of the food, grabbed the straps of the canteens and followed Nahshon out the back door. They sat on the ground in the shade of the olive tree, ate the cheese and bread, and washed it down with water from the canteens. The bread cake had a very thick crust, but was white and grainy on the inside. The soft cheese had a pungent, fermented smell. But Evan was hungry and both the cheese and the bread tasted good.

"How's this for a holiday in the hills of Galilee?" Nahshon said, one side of his mouth bulging with bread and cheese. He winked at Shulamit. "A lovely girl alone with three handsome men, two young and one ancient. Now aren't you glad you came?"

"No. I wish I had stayed back at camp and washed my clothes," Shulamit answered curtly. She had set her bread and cheese on her lap, and was rolling the bottom of her trouser legs up above her ankles so they wouldn't hang in the dirt while she was sitting on the ground. Her ankles were thin and brown, as well-shaped as the clean small feet that filled the leather sandals.

"You would rather wash clothes than be here?" Nahshon combed his fingers through his long, dark hair. He turned to Mordecai. "This is the sensitivity of a sabra." He leaned against the rough bark of the olive tree and stared at Shulamit's feet. "Would you believe, my child, that old Nahshon was once a sandalmaker?"

"There's nothing I wouldn't believe about you, Nahshon, except that you ever considered the feelings of anyone else."

Nahshon laughed. He polished off the rest of his cheese and sucked the end of his finger. Then he walked back to the halftrack, opened the door next to the driver's seat and reached for the bayonet.

"Not to use on you, you ungrateful sabra," he said pleasantly, "but for this fine melon that that bloody Druse probably sold us green."

He cut open the melon. It was pink, but very seedy. Nahshon hacked off four slices and stuck the bayonet tip into the remaining portion. He gave Mordecai one slice, Evan a slice, and then bowed low as he offered Shulamit a slice. She took it and began to nibble at it. Nahshon stuck his face deep into the fourth slice, surfacing only to spew the seeds in a high arc to the ground.

"There were two sabras who ran our D.P. camp in Marseilles," Evan told Shulamit. "Their names were Tamar and Yochanan. Do you know them?"

"What were their last names?"

"I don't know."

"Unless they were in my high school in Jerusalem, I probably wouldn't know them anyway. I'm a different kind of sabra."

"Every sabra in Israel is different," Nahshon said. "But they have one thing in common. They are all ungrateful to Nahshon."

"Poor man," Shulamit said. "I would gladly pay you the ten mills for my share of this feast, but you forced me to come so quickly that I left all of my money in camp."

"And I haven't gotten my pay from the army yet," Evan said, joining in the joke, but thinking at the same time of the six dollars a month that an Israeli private received.

"I've already spent mine from last month," Mordecai added.

Nahshon nodded and puffed his mustachioed lip out skeptically. "It's all right, children. I'm rich."

"How would you like a tour of the Emek now?" Shulamit asked. "We can probably see most of it from the top of the hill over there."

Mordecai and Evan got to their feet. "Come on, Nahshon," Evan called. Nahshon shook his head and pulled out the package of Arab tobacco he had bought. He took a piece of cigarette paper and cupped it with his finger.

"Leave the old man here to watch the halftrack," Shulamit said, dusting off the seat of her trousers. "He probably couldn't make the climb, anyway."

"Do we need our Sten guns?" Evan asked.

"No, but I'll bring one along," Shulamit answered. She reached into the halftrack and pulled out Evan's Sten gun and its magazine clip. She snapped the clip expertly into the empty slot on the weapon and slung the strap of the small submachine gun over her shoulder.

Nahshon was leaning back against the tree, the misshapen cigarette dangling through the bush of the mustache. He was not more than thirty years old, Evan knew, yet in contrast to the three young people who had eaten with him Nahshon seemed much older. And for some reason he himself persisted in contributing to the fiction that he was ancient.

Shulamit and the two young men walked from the olive grove to the gradually rising slope of the hill. They walked side by side with Shulamit in the center. Mordecai and Shulamit were about the same height, Evan a head taller. The large rocks and steepness of the climb made it difficult for them to keep even with each other as they went up the hill. They climbed for a full ten minutes before they neared the summit—it had looked like a shorter, easier climb from the olive grove.

Near the summit, some of the rocks they stepped on were so loose that they gave way and rumbled down the hill, making a sharp click, like the sound of billiard balls, when they hit other rocks. Evan and Mordecai gave an extra kick to make the last few steps to the top, and a covey of little rocks avalanched down the hill behind them. They turned at the summit and reached their hands down for Shulamit, a few steps behind them. She grabbed their hands and they pulled her to the top with them. When they let go of her, she limped on one foot.

"Ouch. There's a sharp rock caught in my sandal. Just a minute." She pulled the Sten gun off her shoulder and draped the sling over Mordecai's, then sat down and began unfastening the sandal strap.

"Look!" Mordecai whispered. Thirty feet ahead of them the top of the hill fell off into its opposite slope. Appearing above this slope now was a white headdress, followed by two more headdresses, and the sound of churning rocks. Then there were three dark faces, peering down at the ground on which they were trying to get a foothold. Their khaki shirts rose up from the slope. They were carrying rifles. The Arab who was slightly ahead of the others glanced up for a second and saw the three youths facing them. He was stunned. His two companions saw him stop and they looked up, too. The two groups stared at each other almost hypnotically for what seemed a very long time, but for what was really less than a second.

"Arabs!" Shulamit shouted. She grabbed a rock with each hand, scrambled to her knees, and let the first rock fly. It hit one of the Arabs on the hip. "The Sten gun!" she cried to Mordecai. "The Sten gun!" She threw the second rock at the surprised Arabs and advanced toward them, picking up other rocks. Her unfastened sandal had fallen off her foot as soon as she had stood up. Evan scooped up rocks and hurled them, also, while he walked in a crouch beside Shulamit toward the Arabs. The Arabs picked up stones and threw them back at the Jews, but they were inching backwards, back down the hill. The three Arabs were half sliding down the hill now, but they were still facing the Jewish youths and making an attempt to throw rocks at them with their right hands while they braced themselves against the hill with their left hands. A large rock hit Shulamit on the shoulder, but she and Evan were letting go with a fusillade of rocks from the top of the hill now, and the Arabs were at a disadvantage because they were sliding.

One of the Arabs turned to run and the other two turned also and began running down the steep slope of the hill. Evan reached down for a smooth, round rock the size of his fist. He wound up like a baseball pitcher and hurled it at the fleeing trio with all his might. It hit one of the men in the small of the back. The Arab let out a shout of pain, tripped, and fell headlong down the hill, scattering rocks in front of him. The strap of his rifle broke and the weapon fell off to the ground at his side. Still sliding forward on his stomach, he clawed himself to his knees, then to his feet, and ran faster to catch up with the other two.

"The Sten gun! The Sten gun!" Shulamit shouted again at Mordecai. She looked back. Mordecai was still standing where they had been when they first saw the Arabs. The Sten gun was still slung over his shoulder. She raced back to him, jerked away the submachine gun, then raced back to the rim of the hill. She pulled back the cocking lever and aimed the weapon—then looked up from the sight and lowered the short barrel of the submachine gun. The three Arabs were at the bottom of the hill, still running crazily. Their figures were very small and getting smaller.

"It would be a waste of bullets. They're too far away now," she said.

Evan looked at her. Her face was flushed a deep brownish red and tiny drops of perspiration had broken out along the high bridge of her nose and under her eyes. She was panting for breath. So was Evan. Mordecai was walking toward them with Shulamit's sandal.

"I'll get the rifle," Evan said. He clambered down the hill to pick up the rifle the Arab had dropped. When he returned, Shulamit was sitting on the ground again, fastening the strap of the sandal.

"How's your shoulder?" Evan asked. He touched her shirt near the place where he had seen the rock hit. She winced slightly. She unbuttoned her shirt down to the top of her white brassiere and pulled the collar back over her left shoulder. There was a harsh red spot where the rock had hit. She felt the bones around the area.

"Nothing feels broken," she said. She examined the rifle Evan held in his hand. It was in excellent shape, its stock scratched only slightly by the fall to the ground. "It's an Enfield, a good catch."

"Why didn't you use the Sten gun?" Evan asked, turning to Mordecai.

Shulamit interrupted. "For the same reason the Arabs didn't use their rifles. Everybody was too surprised to reach for anything but a rock."

"If you hadn't run toward them," Evan told Shulamit, "and forced them down that hill backwards, all three of us would have been killed."

"An Irgun rule. When in danger, attack. A surprised enemy is already half beaten."

"Force," said Evan mockingly, holding the Enfield rifle high above his head like the arm and rifle on the insignia of the Irgun Zvai Leumi. "The only thing the Arab understands."

"Correct," she said smiling, the pink lips parting to show white, even teeth.

"Now are we ready to see the Emek," Evan asked, "or shall we dig trenches first?"

In the distance they could see the Valley of Jezreel, laid out for

[42]

them as if they were viewing it from an airplane. Below them was the green and brown patchwork quilt of cultivated fields, and far off to the east was the towering grayness of Mt. Gilboa.

But Shulamit was already turning away from it, walking to the slope of the hill that led down to the olive grove. "The Emek can wait," she said. "I think we should go back. Those Arabs may have friends near here."

"But this is Israeli territory," Mordecai said.

"Controlled by Israel, yes," she answered. "But there are few Jewish settlements in this area, and Arab infiltrators can move freely as long as they don't travel the roads." They walked back down the hill, following the slope at an angle so the descent would not be so steep.

Nahshon was asleep under the tree. He awoke when he heard the sound of their approaching footsteps. "Back so soon?" he said sleepily. Then he saw the rifle. "Where did that come from?"

Shulamit picked up the canteens lying near the trunk of the tree and climbed up into the halftrack. "We took it away from three Arabs who were going to use it on an old Jew they heard was asleep next to a halftrack."

"Another thing that the sabras have in common," Nahshon said, climbing into the halftrack. "They all have a very sharp sense of humor. Yeled, continue driving."

Evan settled into the driver's seat, smugly delighted that Nahshon was not sure whether the younger soldiers had really taken the rifle away from a frightened Arab or whether they had simply found it on the ground someplace, where it had been lost in the night. The American felt the intoxicating exuberance of victory. He had had his first taste of battle, the inimitable trauma of fright accompanied by recklessness, followed by extreme relief. It didn't matter that he had been led into battle by a girl or that the weapons of war were the most primitive in the history of man. What mattered was that he had fought and that he had won and that he was safe.

While Evan drove back toward the base, Nahshon stood beside him at the front of the halftrack, his feet spread apart, his hands gripping the steel rim, his dark mustache and black hair playing in the wind. It was a hot, desolate, unfiltered breeze, and from the Druse village atop the hill they were now circling came the smell of over-ripened fruit, mud bricks and embers.

[43]

Nahshon pointed toward the village and said to Evan, "Would you believe that old Nahshon once lived in a village like that in the Atlas Mountains of Morocco?"

"Was it a Jewish village?"

"No. Berber. We were the only Jewish family there."

"There were towns like that near us in Virginia. Only one or two Jewish families in the entire place. On the high holidays they would come in to pray with us in our synagogue. Then we wouldn't see them again until the next year."

"So, there are such Jews in America, too." He shook his head with surprise. "The more one sees of the world, the more it looks the same. I have always been told that the Jews in America live in the big cities like New York and Chicago."

"Most do. But there are Jews in almost all the small cities and towns, also. There were less than a hundred Jewish families in our city. Sometimes Jewish friends from one of the big cities would come to visit us, and I could see them thinking, 'How can Judaism survive in a town this small?' But I was no different. On the high holidays I would stare at the strangers in our synagogue who had come in from the little towns in which they were the only Jewish families, and I would think, 'How can a family stay Jewish when they are so alone out there?' "

"Someday, Yeled, I will tell you." Nahshon breathed in the familiar odor of embers and thought about the distant village in the mountains of Morocco. Asabadin was much smaller than the Druse village they were now passing. Asabadin had only two streets, and only a few of the mud-brick homes and shops held valuables worth being protected by bars. The shop of Yoseph Ben-Mizrachi, the silversmith, had bars. Squeezed between two other shops, it had a tiny interior. A small, felt-covered table held a few items of woven silver jewelry in the daytime. Next to the single barred window was the workbench, its top scarred and nicked by the tools and silver of more than five generations of Ben-Mizrachis, its half a dozen remnant-filled drawers worn loose by more than a hundred years' daily friction.

An old straw-woven chair sat next to the doorway—for a customer, may God be merciful. The room behind the shop was no larger than the shop itself, and the dirt courtyard in back of the two-room building was only about the size of the two rooms combined. The room behind the shop was lighted by only one window, as was the shop.

There were two beds, a wooden table with benches, and a hearth. The parents slept in one bed, the grandmother slept in the other, and the three children slept on mats on the floor. Shimeon was two years older than Nahshon; Sura was one year younger. They had slept in chronological order on the mats from the time of Nahshon's earliest recollections—Sura nearest the hearth, Nahshon next, and Shimeon farthest from the hearth, but nearest to his parents' bed.

In the courtyard were a goat and a few chickens. Outside the village was a small graveyard, populated only by Ben-Mizrachis. The Ben-Mizrachis were the only Jewish family in Asabadin. For at least five generations, and perhaps more, they had been the only Jewish family there. Each generation had been silversmiths. No one knew how the first Ben-Mizrachi had found the little farming village. There had been Jews in Morocco since before the Babylonian exile, but Yoseph Ben-Mizrachi could only be sure of five generations. There were only four tombstones in the cemetery that marked the graves of adult male Ben-Mizrachis. Possibly there was another generation or two whose tombstones had been carted away, or which were never erected.

There was an unwritten agreement in Asabadin that there would never be but one Jewish family in the village. Each generation of Jews and Moslems knew of the agreement, which made necessary a tradition that the eldest son inherit the silversmith shop and that the other brothers and sisters be sent off to Demnate, the nearest city with a Jewish ghetto. There was a tale told that Yoseph's grandfather had had a twin brother with whom he was inseparable. But the silversmith shop was to be Yoseph's grandfather's because he was minutes older. The younger twin had been sent away to Demnate, but when their father died Yoseph's grandfather sent to Demnate for his brother and the brother's wife and children. Just behind the courtyard, the two men dug a pit, made mud bricks, and built a one-room house. The younger twin, his wife, and children moved into it.

The first Friday after the house was completed, the Moslem villagers came out of the mosque, and instead of separating their ways to go home they stayed in a band, picking up large rocks as they walked. They strode silently into the silversmith shop, walked through the room behind the shop, through the courtyard, and back to the new mud-brick house. As the younger twin's wife and children ran out in panic, the villagers began to hack away at the walls of the new house with their rocks. They broke down the walls, then picked up the clods of bricks and dashed them against the parched ground. The younger twin and his family went back to Demnate. There was still a portion of the destroyed walls at the end of the courtyard.

There was a small advantage to the agreement, however. When Yoseph was a young man, another Jewish silversmith had tried to open up a shop in Asabadin. On the first Friday morning the new Jew was in Asabadin, the villagers brought baskets full of dung and threw it into his shop, until the dung reached over the top of his workbench. On Sunday morning, after the Sabbath, the man left Asabadin.

If there was this one advantage to being the only Jewish family in the small village, there were a far larger number of disadvantages. There was the loneliness of prayers, of holidays in which the family could share its joy in Israel only with each other. Nahshon would always remember especially the Passover evening when he had been a child. Following the *seder* dinner which celebrated the exodus of the Jews from Egypt, Nahshon's father, Yoseph, had placed some *matzot*, unleavened bread, in a sack, flung it over his back, and, in the custom of the Moroccan Jews, gone out into the street to tell others about his deliverance from Egypt. For according to the *Haggadah*, which is read on the first night of Passover, "Not only our forefathers did the Holy One, blessed be He, redeem, but also ourselves did He redeem with them." So Nahshon's father had gone out into the street with his sack of *matzot* and approached the first citizen of Asabadin who passed by.

"Stop a minute, Hasim, my friend. Let me tell you of the wonderful miracle that just happened to me."

The Moslem paused impatiently. "All right. But hurry, Yoseph. That shrew of a wife of mine will scrape the wax from my eardrums for being so late from the field."

"I have just come from the land of Egypt," Yoseph declared. "Oh, there were great miracles there. The Lord our God, may His Name ever be blessed, forced the Pharaoh to release me from bondage."

"May Allah rescue me in the same way," the Moslem said. He had heard of the strange customs of the Jews on some of their holidays. The story was told in the coffee house that on one night of the year, after an orgy of feasting and drinking wine, they were seized by the spirits of their ancestors. They became so obsessed that the ghosts of the past took over their bodies for the one night and lived again and walked the earth as human beings. The Moslem was becoming slightly frightened. This was no longer Yoseph, the mild-mannered Jewish silversmith. This was a ghost four thousand years old, the possessor of Yoseph's body for a night.

"And He sent plagues of blood and frogs and locusts and boils down upon the Egyptians," Yoseph was saying. "But Pharaoh would not let me and my people go. Do you know what He did then, Hasim, my friend?"

Hasim's feet were nailed to the ground. His body was rigid. He shook his head.

"Then our angry God sent down His Angel of Death, and the Angel of Death slaughtered in their sleep the first-born of every Egyptian family, even the eldest son of Pharaoh himself."

Hasim nodded dumbly. He glanced out of the corner of his eyes to see if he could find succor. The street was deserted.

"And Pharaoh let us go. We left the land of Egypt so fast we did not have time to let our bread rise, so we baked the unleavened cakes in the sun. Here, I still have some left." Yoseph reached into his sack and pulled out a piece of the irregular round and warped *matzot*. He gave it to the Moslem, who held it limply in his hand.

"And we left and arrived at the Red Sea. But the Pharaoh had sent his armies to kill us, to the last man. But the merciful God, blessed be His Name forever, parted the waters of the sea, and I myself walked across that sea on dry land."

"Yes, yes," said Hasim, beginning to back slowly away from Yoseph—or the spirit that inhabited the body of Yoseph. "Allah is great. He can stop the sun in the sky or lift the sand from the desert. Who can doubt that He could part the waters of the sea."

"But wait, my friend. I am not yet finished."

The Moslem stopped, reluctantly.

"I was one of the last to cross the Red Sea. And when I came to the other side and looked behind me, lo and behold, the warriors of the Pharaoh were coming through the opening in the Red Sea, also."

Hasim looked up at the stars. Praise be to Allah. Would this nightmare never end?

"They were fully armed and galloping on their huge horses. We were at their mercy. We had neither horses nor knowledge of battle. But God closed the waters of the sea. A lance, the nostrils of a snorting horse appeared for a second above the foam of the bubbling turmoil. Then all was silent. And so I am safe, here with you tonight, my friend Hasim."

"May you live a thousand years, Yoseph. And then another thousand. Allah is great." Hasim began to inch away nervously.

"It was a great miracle," Yoseph said quietly.

"Good night, my friend," Hasim said hopefully. "That shrew of a wife of mine, may Allah tie her tongue in a knot."

"Good night, my friend Hasim." Yoseph turned to go back into his shop, where his wife and children were in the midst of clearing away the table from the Passover meal.

The Moslem walked quickly down the street. Allah was indeed merciful. He had delivered him from the ancient ghost. But the methods of Allah were mysterious, too. He had taken the Jews out of Egypt to the land on the other side of the Nile, but then had turned around and brought them back to Egypt and to Morocco, which was on this side of the Nile. And the very ghosts of the people He had originally rescued He now forced once a year to inhabit the bodies of their descendants, who were now exiles from the Land of Israel. The moment of fright had now left Hasim. He could be amused by the incident in front of the Jewish silversmith's shop. He would tell it tomorrow in the coffee house. But would his wife believe it tonight?

The hours that Yoseph worked in the shop were long, but at night by the yellow light of the lantern in the summer and the glow of the shrinking flames of the hearth in the cold months he taught his two sons to read the sacred Scriptures. For was it not written, "And you shall teach them to your children"? The two boys were first taught to read the holy words, and when they could read the Hebrew quickly, without hesitation, Yoseph taught them the meaning of the words. They read the laws and the stories, and Yoseph explained gently that the Holy Land of their ancestors was much like this mountain land of the Berbers that they now lived in. Only there were more trees in the Holy Land and perhaps the nights were a bit cooler during the summer months.

Nahshon remembered that he would often pretend that Asabadin was really a village in ancient Israel, and that the Moslems who came to the shop and passed by in the street were really Jews. It was a boyish dream, but it had a grain of truth, because there were Arabs in the Holy Land, he knew, and they lived much as the Berbers of Asabadin. And even now, so many years later, when he went into an Arab village in this Land of Israel, he wondered if it had a Jewish family, a Ben-Mizrachi struggling to keep a miracle alive. The Druse girl with the faggots might have been Sura. If only she were Sura—Jew or Druse or Moslem. He squeezed the steel rim of the halftrack as if to crush the metal, and he felt the same tight grip on the inside of his throat and heart as the image of his sister, naked and disgraced, flashed before him again and again, identical as the stalks of maize whisking by the fender of the halftrack.

Chapter Four

EVAN AWOKE TO HIS FIRST SABBATH MORNING IN Israel in complete darkness. He had pulled the blanket over his head during the night to ward off the mosquitoes. The Israeli nights, he had discovered, were filled with the close whines of mosquitoes and the distant wails of jackals. He poked his head out into daylight. Nahshon was still asleep. So were some of the other drivers. He noticed that a number of the drivers' beds had not been slept in at all during the night.

Evan stepped into his blue coveralls, put on his socks and boots, pulled his mess equipment from the shelf, and walked sleepily toward the mess hall. He met Bernie on the way and the two of them went in together and ate the Sabbath fare of rye bread, jam, cheese, margarine, and cold tea. The cooks were recruited from the religious Jews, and they wouldn't prepare hot meals on the Sabbath.

After breakfast, Evan returned to the barracks and brought his Sten gun out to the porch for a thorough cleaning. The bullet magazine was covered with grit from the halftrack trip of the day before, but he couldn't figure out how to take it apart. He called to Mordecai, who was walking past the barracks on his way to the mess hall.

The little medic came over to him and squinted his blue eyes at the object in Evan's hand. Then he shook his head. "I'm sorry, but I know nothing about guns." He smiled apologetically and walked off toward the mess hall.

Bert, the only Christian in the halftrack company, was standing in the doorway of the barracks stretching. He had put on his khaki uniform, but hadn't buttoned the shirt or tucked it into his trousers.

"More than a hundred men in this company," the British driver said, "and you have to pick the only one who can't tell you how to take the spring out of a Sten gun magazine." He stepped out onto the porch, took the magazine out of Evan's hand, and slid a piece of metal at the bottom of the slot. He pulled out the long spring and examined it.

"I forgot that Mordecai doesn't carry a gun," Evan said.

"Not just that. The little booger's a conscientious objector."

"A what?"

"Oh hell, you know. Doesn't believe in war and all that." Bert tossed the magazine back to Evan and handed him the spring. "Rather sandy. You can clean it, but it won't do you too much good. Just get sandy again." He combed his blond hair back with his fingers and yawned.

Evan examined the Sten gun magazine and remembered the day before when Mordecai had stood on the hill with the gun hanging from his shoulder while he and Shulamit were heaving rocks at the Arabs. A conscientious objector! If the Arabs had had the presence to use their rifles, he and Shulamit—and Mordecai, too—would have been dead, because Mordecai wouldn't have used the Sten gun, even if all their lives had depended on it. Evan shivered at the thought.

He wondered what made a man refuse to fight, even for his own life. Cowardice, perhaps. A medic went in at the tail end of the assault and didn't have to poke his head above a rock to shoot a rifle. It was the Mordecais, Evan decided, who had filed into the gas chambers without a sign of protest to die a gutless death and make the extermination of the Jews easy for the Germans. They were animals led quietly to the slaughter. They had died like animals just as they had been conditioned to live like animals.

In the D.P. camp in Marseilles, fights had broken out almost everytime the D.P.'s had lined up for a meal, with people shoving and pushing to be at the head of the line, as though the food would not hold out. And when the meal was finished, many of the D.P.'s would take pieces of bread back to their beds and hide them between the blankets, like a dog burying a bone, keeping the bread even after it became hard and moldy, for fear that there would be no next meal. Evan had felt compassion for those Jews then and a special burning hatred for the Germans, not for the millions they had killed, but for what they had reduced the living to. But despite his attempts to fight it, Evan had also felt distaste for this product of the Germans. He had felt contempt for the husband and wife on the *Pan York* who had told him that they were sorry they were going to Israel instead of to the United States, where life would have been easier for them. And he had felt raw anger for the young D.P. who had lounged to the side and not lifted a hand to help when Evan was hosing out the wooden latrines built on the deck of the ship, but had cursed Evan with the vilest Yiddish words when Evan had accidentally touched him with the crap-smeared hose.

But as much as he had come to dislike some of the D.P.'s in the Marseilles camp and on the *Pan York*, he had told himself that they would be rehabilitated in the land of Israel. He had expected an immediate, miraculous transformation, and Mordecai had now given the lie to this. The little D.P. was in his own country now, and he could have wiped away the shame of the death camps by fighting proudly as a Jew. Instead, he preferred to remain the victim, and he had almost made Evan and Shulamit victims, too.

Evan followed Bert back into the barracks. "I can't understand why they would put a pacifist like Mordecai in a combat unit. He could have been a cook or a clerk or something where he couldn't endanger other people's lives."

Bert looked at the American curiously. "Mordecai saves lives. He doesn't endanger them."

Evan told him about the rock-throwing incident with the Arabs the afternoon before. What had been the most exciting experience of his life now sounded ludicrous in the retelling. The listener had to laugh—as Bert was now laughing—at either the Arabs or the Jewish youths or the entire incident. Evan made up his mind not to tell the story again.

"Well, at least you learned something," Bert chuckled. "Mordecai is the wrong person to let hold a gun." He sat down on his bed. "I don't think Mordecai enjoys being in this company any more than you like having him. He asked to come here as a medic because his twin brother is in one of the infantry platoons—in fact, he's in the squad that rides in my halftrack."

"I take it, then, that he's not a conscientious objector like Mordecai."

"I rather wish he was. Barely eighteen years old, and he's a bloody butcher. He'll shoot anything that walks, crawls, or burrows. Once, when we were mopping up a village we had just captured in the Jerusalem corridor near Latrun, Aaron shot two dogs and then put a bullet into the belly of an old man standing in a doorway. The old boy must have been at least ninety. I shouted at him, 'My God, man, what have you done?' He merely shrugged his shoulders."

"Did the man die?"

"What do you think? Gingi gave Aaron a tongue-lashing and warned him if anything like that happened again he would shoot him on the spot, but I don't think it made much of an impression."

"He sounds like a savage. But I would rather have had him with us yesterday than Mordecai."

"Yes, I suppose you would, wouldn't you?"

Evan sat down on the foot of Bert's bed and wiped the grit from the magazine spring. "Don't take this the wrong way," he said, "but how did an Englishman like you get into the Israeli army?"

"First of all, I'm not English. I'm a Scot. I was in the British army here. When they left, I stayed behind."

"Did many British soldiers stay?"

"Only a few. It meant deserting. The ones who stayed mostly had Jewish wives or Jewish girl friends. I had neither."

"Then why did you stay?"

"It's rather hard to explain. Why did you come here all the way from America? Because you are a Zionist?"

"That's what I told them in France. I suppose I really am a Zionist, although I never belonged to a Zionist organization—there weren't any in my hometown. I've always believed that there should be a Jewish state, that there ought to be at least one place in the world where Jews could live as a majority on their own terms."

"And that's the reason you came all this distance to join an army? You don't think you were interested in being a hero, just a tiny bit?"

"A hero, no. A Jewish hero—probably. I wouldn't have turned a finger if the Kurds were fighting the Hindus for Palestine. But if the Jews were fighting for their lives in Tanganyika, I think I would want to be there. I came here because everything in my experience has bound me to the Jewish people. I know my reasons for coming aren't the same as everybody else's. But whatever our reasons, I think there is some general destiny that is bringing us all together again, after all these centuries, to fight next to each other. Without our quite being certain why, we were drawn to this place at this time. Are you familiar with the Old Testament, Bert?"

"I suppose I learned about as much in church as the next fellow. But I'm no Bible scholar."

"Well, there's a passage in Isaiah that prophesied exactly what is happening to all of us now. It goes, 'I will bring thy seed from the east, and gather thee from the west; I will say to the north: "Give up," and to the south: "Keep not back." Bring My sons from far, and My daughters from the ends of the earth.'"

Bert smiled. "That sort of leaves me out of the picture, doesn't it?"

"No, I'm not sure that it does. After all, you *are* in the picture." Evan grinned broadly. "But don't expect the history books to say, 'The Jews and one Scot defeated seven invading Arab armies.' And come to think of it, you still haven't told me why that one Scot decided to remain here."

"Well, you came here because you love Jews. I stayed here because I found I'd grown to love this land. Others besides Jews can love this land, too, you know."

"But in Israel you're going to be different from your neighbors."

"We're all different from our neighbors, no matter where we are, aren't we? I've got more in common with the average Israeli than I have with ninety per cent of the people who live on my street in Glasgow."

Bert helped Evan clean and reassemble the magazine, then showed him how to oil the few moving parts of the Israeli-made Sten gun. When they were finished, Evan leaned the weapon against the wall behind his bed, reached into his duffel bag, and pulled out a handful of dirty socks and a brown cake of laundry soap.

The laundry building held eight sinks, with a rough stone counter on each side sloping down to drain into the sink. The building was empty except for Shulamit, who, dressed in the same baggy khaki uniform of the day before, had several articles of clothing already washed and wrung into thick khaki coils and was at work on another pair of long khaki trousers. The trousers were stretched out wet on the stone counter and she was scrubbing them with a brush. Her hair was bound in a blue kerchief knotted at the nape of her neck.

Evan tossed his dirty socks and the cake of laundry soap down on the counter facing her. She looked up and smiled at him. "*Shabat shalom*"—Good Sabbath. "You see I'm doing today what I told Nahshon I wanted to do yesterday," she said in Hebrew. They had spoken no English to each other since shortly after their first meeting in the Arab village.

"Good," Evan said. "I thought I'd be the only one violating the Sabbath." He turned on the faucet to wet his socks.

"Violating," she said. "What is violating? The Sabbath was made for man to enjoy. If you would rather wash socks on the Sabbath than do something else, why shouldn't you?"

"I'm afraid the Orthodox Jews don't think that way."

"I know what the Orthodox Jews think," she said, picking up the cuffs of the trousers to scrub them with the brush. "Are the Jews in America so religious?"

"From what I've heard and seen so far, I think American Jews are more religious than the Jews in Israel—as a group."

"Oh? But I have heard that the American Jews work on the Sabbath."

"Well, most do work on the Sabbath. But they go to synagogue on Friday night, and belong to congregations and see that their children have some kind of religious education."

Shulamit looked puzzled. "These same people that go to synagogue on Friday night, do they work on the Sabbath?"

"Yes."

"Strange. You'll find that most of the Jews in Israel don't go to synagogue on Friday night, but no one works—in a business, I mean —no one works on the Sabbath. Does that make us less religious than you Americans?"

"It's not the right comparison," Evan explained. "Most American Jews have to work on Saturday, because the Sabbath in America isn't until Sunday."

"The first day of the week?"

"Yes, that's the Christian Sabbath."

[54]

"Then why don't the Jews close their stores on the Jewish Sabbath and let the Christians close their stores on the Christian Sabbath?"

"It just wouldn't be practical."

"I understand," Shulamit said, a wrinkle appearing in her high forehead. "You mean there are so few Jewish shops that no one would trade in them on the Christian Sabbath."

Evan wondered how the conversation had ever evolved to this position. "That would be true in some places. But in a number of cities there are as many stores owned by Jews as by Christians. The point is, though, that the United States is a Christian country and the Jews really have to observe the Christian Sabbath."

She looked at him as though she had not really understood him completely.

"Let me explain it another way. The United States isn't really a Christian country. I mean there's no state church, and the Constitution calls for complete freedom of religion. The Jews don't really have to observe the Christian Sabbath—that is, they don't have to worship on Sunday. In fact, some Jews—a few—do close their stores on Saturday and open on Sunday in some places where it isn't against the law. I mean there are state laws, not national laws, in some places that say you can't open on Sunday." Evan had almost forgotten what he had started to say, and he could see that he had explained it so poorly that Shulamit had no idea what he was talking about. "What I'm trying to say is that the Jews are a small minority in the United States, and the Christians are a very large majority. Therefore, the Jews find it financially convenient to stay open on Saturday, when the Christians are working, and to close on Sunday, when the Christians are resting."

"When do the Jews rest?"

"On Sunday, too."

"So Sunday is really the American Jews' Sabbath."

"I suppose it is in actual fact. But theoretically the Sabbath is still Saturday, just like yours."

"Then I don't think American Jews are as religious as Israelis. And most of us aren't very religious at all. It just seems to me that American Jews make a mockery of the Sabbath."

"You're right. Most of them do." Evan smiled in genuine amusement. One had only to explain how most American Jews observed their "Sabbath" to realize that it was a Sabbath in name only, whereas

[55]

Israeli Jews who did not observe the Sabbath still had a Sabbath in fact.

Shulamit had rinsed the trousers and squeezed them to get some of the water out. She handed the legs to Evan. They both twisted until they had wrung the last drops from the coil of cloth.

"I'm going back to my room and hang these out now," she said. "Are you going anywhere this afternoon?"

"Where is there to go?"

"How would you like to go with me to see the Bahai shrine?"

"Can we get a pass?" Evan asked.

"We don't need a pass. It's right behind the fence of the camp here."

"Good. I'll go with you."

"There's a place to swim there. I'll borrow a bathing suit for you."

"I have a bathing suit," Evan said. "It's in the barracks."

Shulamit gave a short laugh. "Who can understand a *chocolatnik?* You come all this way to help us fight the Arabs, and you bring your bathing suit with you."

"What's a *chocolatnik?*"

"It's our name for Americans. They're always eating chocolate bars. Meet me at my room after you've finished the noon meal." She left with her bundle of laundry.

Evan washed his socks, then took them back to the barracks and hung them on a line stretched between two posts beside the building. Hanging out the wash on Saturday. There were Jews in Virginia who would do that, too. But they would never hang it out on Sunday for fear of offending their Christian neighbors. In that trivial little reality, Evan thought, was all the poignancy of the position of the Jew in America. How different for a Shulamit, who had grown up in a city where the Jews were the majority. She had no conception what it was like to be part of a minority, nor could she comprehend the serious adjustments a member of a minority had to make to live without friction in a world that was not his own. Evan remembered his own feelings when he had first left his old world and come into this new world of the Shulamits. He and the other Americans had been packed into the hold of the little tugboat and taken to a dock in Haifa harbor that was hidden from the view of U.N. observers. Within minutes they were unloaded from the tug and were being driven in a bus through the semi-deserted streets of the Arab section that surrounded the harbor. Then the bus began the steep ascent of Mt. Carmel and quickly it was in the Jewish section of Haifa.

The stores were open and there were people on the sidewalks. They might have been people in France, or England, or the United States. But Evan knew they were all Jews and they were going into Jewish buildings on Jewish streets. Down below, in the purple bay, he picked out the *Pan York*, nursing at the dock. Such as it was, it was a Jewish ship and a Jewish dock, and up above them were a Jewish mountain and Jewish air. It was a good feeling, for the first time in his life, to be part of the majority.

They had arrived on a Sunday, and now this air had been his for almost a full week. Evan looked up at his American socks dripping on the line. The warm morning air would dry them quickly.

After the noon meal Evan put on his khaki trousers and open-necked shirt. He rolled his bathing suit inside a towel and walked up to the headquarters building where the four girls in the armored regiment had their room. Shulamit was waiting for him on the porch. At a distance, he thought it was one of the other girls, but as he came nearer he recognized the reddish-bronze skin and the thin high bridge of the aquiline nose. She wore a khaki skirt—it was the first time he had ever seen her when she wasn't wearing trousers— and a white sleeveless Russian peasant blouse, with the top few buttons of the neck flap unbuttoned. The blouse was tucked tightly into her skirt, showing the outlines of a full, shapely bosom that her baggy khaki skirt had always managed to hide. She still wore her leather sandals, but she had woven her dark brown hair into two tight braids and pinned them up in circlets around her head. She had a bathing suit and towel under her arm.

Shulamit led Evan to the back of the headquarters building and then to the high barbed wire fence that surrounded the army base. They followed the fence for about fifty yards until they came to an opening in the barbed wire fence that was large enough to drive a jeep through.

"How can such a large hole be here and the officers not know about it?" Evan asked.

"They know about it," she answered. "We have two gates to this camp—the official one that the regimental police guard, and the un-official one that the regimental police ignore. We have a civilian army and no one wants to make a soldier a prisoner. So if anyone wants to leave at night or on the Sabbath, unofficially, he can use this hole. Come on." Shulamit stepped through the hole, turned, and reached her hand out to Evan. He caught the long-fingered right hand and stepped through the hole, also. He held on to her hand, gently, and she made no attempt to lift it away.

A grove of fir and eucalyptus trees was on the other side of the barbed wire fence. Flowering bushes of several varieties were sprinkled between the trees. A red-roofed house lay in the center of the grove. A heavy, olive-complexioned man with a bald head was kneeling near the door, digging in a flower bed.

Shulamit let go of Evan's hand and spoke to the man in Hebrew. "May we see the house?"

The man rose. He was quite large. "Come with me." At the door, the man removed his slippers from his stocking feet. Shulamit bent down and unbuckled her sandals, then stepped out of them. Her feet were bare. She motioned for Evan to take his shoes off. He sat down on the stoop, unlaced his black army boots and pulled them off. He looked down toward the bottom of his trousers, where the khaki stopped abruptly to become civilian red and white, and wiggled his toes self-consciously.

The large man explained to them that the rooms in the house had been maintained as a shrine to the memory of Prince Hussein Ali, the Bahaullah, who founded the Bahai religion almost a hundred years before. Bahaullah—the splendor of God—was a Persian, as were the present caretakers of the shrine. The man showed Evan and Shulamit into the bedroom, where the covers were turned down and the Bahaullah's slippers were next to the bed, just as they had been when the religious leader died fifty years before. Evan found himself listening inattentively to the guide. The relics of the dead religious leader paled in comparison to the lovely, living girl that was now at Evan's side. He was anxious to be alone with her, away from the ascetic, musty-smelling rooms.

He was glad to leave the house and get out into the sunshine again. He laced up his boots while Shulamit put on her sandals. They walked down the broad dirt road that led away from the house through the grove of pine trees. Following the sounds of shouting children, they went along a path that cut off from the road and came to a large rectangular pool that was surrounded by firs and eucalyptuses. About two dozen children were standing near the edge of the pool, squealing happily to each other. They ranged in age from about six to ten, and dangled wet bathing suits from their hands. The boys had on dark blue shorts and faded blue shirts. The girls wore dark blue bloomer shorts with elastic trimmed legs, and blouses like those of the boys. All wore sandals and the turned down khaki sailor caps typical of the Israeli farmer. Still wet dark and blonde hair fell below the inverted cup of the caps on most of the girls' heads. A short, stocky woman, also deeply sunburned and dressed like the girls, except she wore no cap, gave an order for the children to form two lines. Then, with the woman walking beside them, they marched noisily down the road.

"Children from a kibbutz near here," Shulamit said. "Very pretty, aren't they?"

"Yes," Evan said, still hearing the sounds of the departing children and thinking about what an unrealistic presence they were in this armed nation surrounded by enemies. And yet in the setting of this huge garden they were as natural as the flowers and the scent of firs. The war was not only remote from this spot, it was non-existent. "Maybe we should have asked the man at the shrine if we could swim here, too," he said.

"He doesn't mind. This isn't really a swimming pool. They have it here to beautify this area. Then the water is used for irrigation."

Colored tiles lined the edge of the pool. Trees and flowering shrubs grew just beyond the water's edge. Dead leaves bobbed on the top of the water, which had not yet digested all the turbulence of the children. The images of the trees on the other side of the pool reflected and rippled and broke on the blue mirror. There was a heavy silence now, and in the magical beauty Evan could imagine that the garden and the pool revealed themselves only in the sunshine of a Sabbath, disappearing for the rest of the week.

"Let's put our bathing suits on," Shulamit said. She walked over to one of the large eucalyptus trees away from the path and stepped behind it. "My dressing room," she shouted.

Evan could see the brown wrists and slender hands folding a wisp of the skirt that appeared from behind the tree and then placing it neatly on the ground. He went over to the side of another tree and quickly undressed and stepped into his bathing suit.

He was folding his clothes into a neat pile when Shulamit stepped

[59]

out from behind the tree and walked over to him. Her uniform—even the khaki skirt she had just removed—had made her seem much shorter than she now looked in the navy-blue bathing suit. Her legs were not thin, but they were tapered gracefully from the slim ankles to the full, firm thighs. Evan took a short breath. The surroundings already had the shapes and colors of make-believe, and now Shulamit was an apparition, a houri in this Arabian garden. She sat on the tiles at the edge of the pool and dipped her feet into the water. "Umm, it's warm," she said, and then, as if reading his thoughts, "It's hard to believe at this moment that this is a country at war and we're soldiers."

Evan sat down beside her. "You like being a soldier, don't you?"

She looked at him, surprised by the question, and thought about an answer for a minute. "I think it would be better if no one were a soldier. But as long as soldiers are necessary, yes, I'm glad women are given a chance to fight, too."

"I suppose women are needed in the army. But it seems strange to see them in a combat unit."

"Americans think a woman is inferior to a man. So do the Arabs. Israelis don't."

"It's not that. Americans just believe a woman has one duty and the man another."

"Here our duty is the same," she said. "It's better that way. I would hate to tell my children that I sat at home and knitted sweaters while their father was being shot at by Arabs."

"There's a difference, though," Evan said, "I have a feeling that there's nothing you sabras enjoy like the thrill of danger—that you almost welcome a good fight."

"That's not true," she said. "We want peace, but not the kind of peace that's offered to us like a gift of charity. Since the first Jewish settlers came here, we've had to fight for every inch of land. It was never given to us on a silver platter."

"And you're proud that you had to fight for it, aren't you?"

"Proud, yes, but not glad, because many lives were lost. But now the land will have so much more meaning to us and our children." She splashed a brown leaf that floated near her toes. "I knew a South African during the fighting in Jerusalem. He was a member of the Irgun Zvai Leumi organization in South Africa and he came with others from South Africa to help us fight. I asked him once why he came all the way from South Africa and he said, 'Because things aren't good for Jews in South Africa. They may get worse and some-day I may have to come to Palestine to live. And when I do, I don't want any bloody sabra to tell me that everything is peaceful in Palestine now but I should have been here when the fighting was going on.' Is that why you came here?"

"No, I'm afraid not. I had different reasons. I never worried about what a sabra would say ten years from now. And the Jews in America don't have to worry about being jailed or driven out of the land."

"As long as they observe the Christian Sabbath."

"I didn't do a very good job of explaining that this morning. The Christians have nothing to do with the way Jews observe Sabbath. The Jews do it by their own choice. There are Christians who are Seventh Day Adventists and don't do a particle of work on the Sab-bath, our Sabbath, and they've never been persecuted."

"Are you planning to go back to America when the fighting is over?" She lay down on her back and closed her eyes.

He looked down at her cleft chin, at the closed pink lips, and at the broad arched eyebrows over the closed eyelids. "Getting here was so big a problem for me, Shulamit, that I haven't had a chance to think about the problem of leaving yet."

"Wait until you've been here longer." She uncovered the tan eyes and smiled at him. "You'll find you've become attached to Israel with a bond no one can break."

"I already feel very close to Israel. But I think I would have felt pretty much the same way if I had never come here. Can you understand that?"

"About Jews who have never seen Israel loving her? Yes. That's what brought the pioneers here. But they didn't like the lands they were in."

"Well, I think that's how most American Jews are different. They're happy where they are, but they have an affection for this land, too."

"Perhaps," she said. "But they have to like one country more than the other. If they love Israel more, they should come here to live."

"How do you measure love? Does a mother love one child more than she loves another? I think a person could have enough love for two countries if each were somehow a meaningful part of him."

Shulamit sat up and straightened the shoulder straps of her swim suit. "A mother doesn't have to choose between her children, but a

[61]

person has to choose the country he loves most and live there, no matter how difficult it might be, no matter how many family ties he must break. That's why we have Israel—because people chose to love Israel here, not from a distance."

"But Israel is also here," Evan answered, "because millions of Jews also chose to love her from a distance. They sent the money that bought the land, and they're sending the money that's buying the weapons we're fighting with. Israel owes them a debt, too."

"We owe them nothing! What do they know about this land? It's nothing but an orphanage to them, a place where their fatherless relatives now live and where still more of their orphan relatives may have to come to live. How many have made a real sacrifice for the land? The money is a salve for their consciences. It soothes their guilt that they haven't sacrificed more, and that their orphan relatives live so meanly while they live so well."

"At least you admit that they have consciences."

"Yes, for their orphan relatives. Not for the land. Suppose it was the Jews in the Arab lands who were massacred by an Arab Hitler, and there was nothing but dark-skinned Jews in Israel. Would the American Jews care as much or give as much?"

"I don't know," Evan said. "Perhaps they wouldn't."

Shulamit nodded. "There's a difference between compassion for orphan relatives and love for the land of Israel. The people who give us money are repaid. Their consciences repay them. The only debt we owe is to those like you who chose to come to Israel and help us to hold the land with their bodies."

"You owe me nothing, either. I always thought it was my fight as much as yours, otherwise I wouldn't be here."

"Good," she said, pulling herself toward the edge of the pool. "Then we start even. And you can see for yourself why you should stay with us." She slid into the water slowly, taking special care not to get her hair wet.

Evan waited until she had swum to the center of the pool. Then he made a flat dive into the pool and coasted underwater until he saw her legs. He grabbed one of the slender ankles and pulled her under, then popped to the surface. Her head bubbled out of the water next to him. She opened her eyes and, holding onto Evan's shoulder with one hand, felt her soaking braids with the other.

"You . . . You . . . *chocolatnik!*" she pouted, pretending to be
angry, and splashed water in his face. Evan splashed her back. They
swam around the pool several times, not talking. Then Evan climbed
out of the water and helped Shulamit up to the edge. She wrapped
her towel around her hair and lay down next to Evan, so close that
her shoulder and arm lightly touched his. Evan felt the warmth of
her flesh. It was a delicious sensation. He wondered if their arms,
side by side and touching now, had been attracted to each other in
the same way he had been attracted to this people and this land—
if there were some force drawing him to this Israeli girl and forming
a bond between them that neither would be able to break.

Chapter Five

EVAN AND SHULAMIT COULD HEAR THE SHOUTS OF
sergeants and the noise of motors even before
they stepped back through the hedge of the Bahai shrine. They ran
to the hole in the barbed wire fence and jumped through, then
trotted to the headquarters building. Several jeeps and halftracks
were parked at odd angles in front of the building. Eliyahu was
walking hurriedly from the regimental office to the company headquarters next door.

He saw Shulamit and stopped at the doorway. "Where have you
been?" he asked angrily. "Gingi's been trying to find you for an hour."
He noticed the towel and the bathing suit rolled up inside it in her
hand. Then his eyes moved from her towel to the towel in Evan's
hand and finally came to rest on Evan's face. He shook his head bitterly and stalked into the company office.

Shulamit followed him, Evan tagging along behind. Gingi was
standing behind his desk, his hands spread apart on top of a map
to keep the edges from curling in. He might have been a rabbi,
Evan thought, preparing to read the Scroll of Esther on Purim. But
there was the large canvas holster strapped to his waist.

[63]

"When do we leave?" Shulamit asked.

Gingi studied a spot on the map for a few seconds, then looked up. "At four o'clock. Go get ready now. You, too, Evan."

Shulamit turned and ran toward her room. Evan sprinted to the barracks. The drivers inside were cleaning their weapons and packing their personal gear.

"We've been looking for you," Nahshon said. "We thought perhaps you had already deserted. Where were you?"

"Swimming," Evan said sheepishly.

Nahshon grunted. "Three drivers still aren't here."

"Where are they?"

"In Haifa—in bed with their wives, probably. But they'll be here by the time we leave. If not, you'll have to drive one of the half-tracks."

"How will they ever know to come back in time?"

"Kol Yisrael, the radio station, is making an announcement every ten minutes for all members of this unit to report back to camp. They'll hear about it, if they ever get out of bed."

"Well, it seems that the truce is over," Evan observed.

"No. We still have six days left. The Arabs are probably just trying to improve their positions before the fighting really begins."

Nahshon drove the halftrack to the quartermaster hut. Evan helped him heave a small footlocker into the vehicle and then a gunnysack that felt like it was loaded with lead. The gunnysack was full of loose hand grenades, two for each man on the halftrack, and the footlocker was filled with several cans of cheese, several of meat, a few large cans of orange juice, hard crackers, and a lot of loose hazel nuts, enough food to last several days if the halftrack was cut off from the regular mess supply.

Gingi gathered all the men in his company at an area of open ground near the barracks. The men arranged themselves in a large circle, the ones nearest the center sitting, those behind them kneeling, and the last ring standing. The blond, muscular captain held a small branch in his hand and began using it to draw a road in the dirt. Then he drew the concentric lines denoting a hill on each side of the road, and skipped over a foot of ground and drew other hills adjacent to the road.

"*Chaverim,*" he said curtly. It clipped off the talking among the men. "Most of you are familiar with this territory. It's the same area

[64]

we guarded earlier this week while the infantry battalion had a rest. Here's the village where I had our headquarters. Here's the olive grove and here are the two hills that command the road on our side of the wadi. This morning our boys observed three companies of Fawzi El Kaukji's Arab Liberation Army moving toward this point on their side of the truce line. We believe they are going to try something, perhaps this afternoon, perhaps tomorrow—perhaps not at all. It will be our job to reinforce the troops already on these hills. Remember, our first job, in case the Arabs attack, is to hold these hills. After we have done that, our plan is to counter-attack across the truce line, moving seven kilometers down this road to Deir Funduq, the Arab village at this crossroad. All of Kaukji's troops in this area are supplied by Deir Funduq. Our sappers will blow up all the food and ammunition they can find. Then we'll return."

Gingi paused and looked around at the men. "Now this is important. If the Arabs attack this afternoon, we must be back to at least the olive grove by dawn. The Israeli government will not report there has been a truce violation until our counterattack is well underway. That means that the U.N. boys should get there to make an investigation shortly after dawn. We'll have no one over the truce line at dawn. Understood? Good." He tossed the branch down on the ground and walked away.

Evan had already changed into his coveralls and checked his Sten gun before the briefing. Now he filled his canteen and went back to the barracks to get his sweater, blanket, and helmet. It was almost four in the afternoon and the men were beginning to climb aboard their halftracks. All the missing drivers had either heard or been told about the announcement on the radio and had arrived back at camp a half an hour before. Evan was relieved that he wouldn't be driving a halftrack into his first real battle. He had pulsations of fear in his stomach and chest. The day before, when they had thrown rocks at the three Arabs, he hadn't had a chance to be afraid. Now he had an opportunity to think about going into combat and it frightened him. He had sometimes thought of dying, and had felt the cold chills that accompanied such speculation—how the world could exist without him, whether the world was only a figment of his imagination, what the world would be like a hundred years or a thousand years after his death, what it felt like to be dead, the fear that there was no afterlife. He had always turned such thoughts from his mind and tried to think of more pleasant things, reminding himself that, barring an accident, he still had many years to live and that he could think the chilling thoughts later. But now there was no turning away from his thoughts. A war did away with the actuarial statistics. He tried to force himself to think of something else, but his fear was a gyroscope that returned him, each time he veered away, to doubts on immortality.

Evan climbed into the halftrack and sat there by himself, quietly, thinking of his home and family and wondering how he could have been fool enough to put his head on the block for any cause. "It's a dream," he told himself, "a long dream. The swimming pool at the Bahai shrine was the sweet part of the dream and this is the nightmare portion. In a minute I'll wake up and I'll find myself in a hot sweat in the bed in the Paris hotel, or in the bunk of the student ship, or in my room at college." He pinched himself hard, until he could feel the sharp pain. He winced. He was awake and he was in the halftrack.

Mordecai, Itzik, and Radhai climbed into the halftrack with their equipment, Itzik and Radhai mounting their machine guns on the rim of the halftrack. Then Shulamit, who had changed to her trousers, climbed aboard with her helmet, blanket, Sten gun, and earphones. She dumped her equipment next to Evan, plugged in the earphones, and turned the radio on. She listened for a minute, then moved the earphones forward to her temples. She looked at Evan and smiled. "*Shalom, chocolatnik.*"

"Eliyahu was slightly angry," Evan said.

"Eliyahu is always angry. It consumes him," she said. "He hates many things and he loves only two things, his country and himself—but his country first."

"Do you know him well?"

"We are together often in our duties. We have gone on several dates together."

"He's so unlike Gingi."

"You would like to put people into little slots, wouldn't you?" she said, not unkindly. "There is no mold that a man must fit. Eliyahu is a very good fighter."

Evan felt a pang of jealousy, though he knew he did not possess this girl. In fact, he had an uneasy feeling that it was she who was beginning to possess him. He had convinced himself that there was a certain bloom in her face that she had brought back from the afternoon water and sun. Yet she would not remain like a blossom at home while her lover went out to war. She would go with him, and she would possess her lover in the field as well as in the garden.

There were five companies in the armored regiment: two armored car companies, one halftrack company carrying infantry troops, one heavy machine gun company also equipped with halftracks, and one mortar company which traveled in jeeps. But only the halftrack company and one armored car company were being sent to the truce line that afternoon. Ten halftracks were now strung out in single file. There were to be eight armored cars in the column, and four were now moving past the halftracks, through the gate and into the road that led to Acre and Haifa. The torso and head of a man with earphones clamped to his head poked out of each turret like a jack-in-the-box whose lid had just been tripped and was now waiting to be pushed back down again.

Although the halftracks were American-made, surplus of World War II, the armored cars were pure Israeli. They were really short trucks with armor plate welded around them. Each one mounted a light machine gun through an opening in the right forward side and a heavy machine gun in the turret at the top of the vehicle. The great weight of the steel plate was supported inadequately by the chassis springs, giving the armored car a very high center of gravity, and the truck motor was not powerful enough for the weight it had to pull. In the hilly Galilee, the Israeli vehicle did a competent job as long as it could stay on the roads, but, unlike the halftrack, was unmaneuverable and unreliable off the road.

Nahshon released the handbrake and let the halftrack jolt forward as the last of the four armored cars passed him. Gingi signaled with his hand and one by one the other vehicles in the column moved forward, also.

The column of vehicles, led by a jeep carrying the regimental commander and brought up at the rear by a gargantuan wrecking truck and a small armor-plated ambulance with the red star of David painted on it, rolled noisily down the highway for a few miles, then turned east toward the danger spot on the truce line. The column moved through the deserted, silent Arab village, past the house of the *Mukhtar*, and down to the same olive grove where they had picked up the troops several days before. Everyone but the drivers and Shulamit dismounted from the halftracks at the olive grove. Evan, his Sten gun slung over his shoulder, walked with Radhai and Itzik toward the nearest platoon formation. They stepped into ranks at the tail end of the platoon. Evan found himself standing next to Bernie.

Bernie had a German light machine gun balanced on his left shoulder. Two metal boxes filled with ammunition were on the ground next to his feet. He wiggled his eyebrows at Evan. "How about giving me a hand with these ammunition cans?" Evan picked up the heavy little boxes. Eliyahu gave a command for the platoon to face right and begin marching toward the hill next to the olive grove. Bernie faked a monster look on his face, distorted the fingers of his one free hand into claws, and walked stiffly toward the hill. "Lead me to them Arab bastards," he said gruffly. "Lead me to 'em." Then he laughed out loud.

When they arrived at the top of the hill, Eliyahu assigned all the men to defense positions. He told Bernie and Evan to set up a machine gun position halfway down the forward slope of the hill. Below them to the right was the dirt road that led back past the olive grove and up to the deserted Arab village. On the other side of the road was a higher hill, also held by the Israelis. The road continued east for about three hundred yards across a rocky valley and then needled through two larger hills held by Kaukji's Arab Liberation Army. It was this road that Gingi intended his forces to use if they had to counterattack into Arab territory. At both sides of the valley, the road was blocked by huge boulders—one wall erected by the Arabs, the other by the Jews.

Evan and Bernie began building a semi-circular rock wall around the machine gun. "Every army's the same," Bernie said. "The new men always get the shitty end of the stick. This position is exposed from every direction but hell."

"We at least seem to have height here. They have to come up to us."

"If we're lucky enough to have them come that way. But suppose they take that hill first." Bernie pointed toward the Israeli-held hill across the road. "Then they can spit down on top of us."

"You know something? I've never fired this Sten gun."

"It don't surprise me. This is a Jewish army. They don't believe in wasting bullets on targets." Bernie reached over and grabbed Evan's Sten gun. "Let me tell you something about this pea shooter. Don't bother aiming it. The barrel's shorter than the barrel on most two-bit pistols. That means you ain't gonna have no accuracy beyond twenty-five yards. The best way to shoot this thing is to hold the butt at your hip like this and spray your fire. That way, maybe one bullet will hit something."

"Twenty-five yards," Evan said. "My God. I thought I had a real submachine gun."

"What you got, buddy, is a flit gun. We used to call them grease guns. They're okay for close-range, house-to-house fighting. But out here—" He handed the Sten gun back to Evan and looked across the wadi toward the Arab-held hills. "I wonder if them Arab bastards over there got any broads with 'em to keep 'em warm at night."

"Crap, Bernie. Is that all you can think about, Arab bed warmers?"

"What'sa matter? You a queer or something? You want me to sit here and figure out some strategy that'll win the war in two days? I was just wondering what they do at night for fun."

"They toss coins to see who'll have the first chance at castrating you."

"See this?" Bernie asked, holding up a finger. "Sit down on it and rotate."

Evan laughed and shook his head.

"Well, admit it. This is a helluva way for a red-blooded American boy to spend a Saturday afternoon," Bernie said. "You know what I'd be doing at home now? I'd have a broad at the beach. And by this time of the afternoon I'd already be feeling her up a little bit, getting her all warmed up for Saturday night. Jesus H., I must have rocks in my head. To think that I could be doing that—and I'm sitting here playing nursemaid to a machine gun with a German swastika stamped on its barrel." He showed Evan the Nazi die-mark. "Those kraut whores would get their kicks if they could see me now, wouldn't they? I should'a stayed in Marseilles with that little French piece."

Evan remembered the afternoon in Marseilles when he and Bernie had watched the teen-age French girl walk down the cement steps to the beach. She was short and blonde, and her uplifted breasts shoved against the tight-fitting blouse as though straining to be free. A little boy held on to her hand. The two of them walked to the edge of the beach and disappeared behind a large boulder. In a few minutes they reappeared, the little boy in a pair of undershorts and the girl in the skimpiest bikini Evan had ever seen. The top was red and only half-covered her full-burst breasts. The bottom appeared to be made of two tiny triangles of white cloth, and the triangle in front started well below her naval cleft and the swell of her stomach.

She ran into the surf with the little boy. Then she ran back up onto the beach, her blonde hair plastered to her head and dripping from the fringes around her neck. The triangle of white cloth, cemented by water to her skin, had become almost transparent. She turned to run into the water again, and it looked as though a nude nymph, a narrow string of red across the top of her back, was frolicking in the foam. Bernie got up from the towel on which he and Evan were sitting, walked across the narrow beach, and strode deliberately through the surf to the girl and the little boy. Then there were three heads bobbing in the sea, and when they came out onto the beach later the little boy was holding one of Bernie's hands and the girl was holding the other. Evan's thoughts shifted to Shulamit, then back to the French girl, until the scenes merged, and the French girl in her skimpy bikini and Shulamit in her bathing suit were standing next to each other on a hot beach out there in front of him. Yes, he definitely preferred Shulamit—Shulamit in a Bahai garden on a Sabbath afternoon that now seemed light years ago.

The sound of a double thump echoing through the hills shattered the images racing through Evan's mind. It was a sound similar to that of a shoe being dropped to the floor, the heel hitting first and the louder slap of the sole immediately after.

"That's a mortar!" Bernie shouted. "Get low!"

Within seconds they heard the whining of a mortar hurtling toward earth. But it wasn't coming toward their hill. It was to the right. A mortar shell was landing on the Israeli hill on the other side of the road. There was a blast at the top of the hill. Then there was another blast on the top of the hill, and three more.

Evan cocked his Sten gun and Bernie examined the machine gun to see that the safety was off and it was ready for firing. They could still see no Arabs advancing toward their hill, but far off to the right, on the far side of the Israeli hill next to them, they could see groups of small figures with white headdresses dashing across a point where the valley narrowed, and they could see little puffs of smoke hit near the figures. The Arabs had waited until just before sunset to attack. The afternoon was beginning to fade into dusk.

"They're trying to outflank us," Bernie said. "I told you. If they take that hill they'll be looking right down on the top of our heads."

More mortar shells were landing now on the top of the hill. Evan and Bernie could see the Arabs running across the last stretch of the valley and beginning a crouching climb up the hill, but mostly they were on the side of the hill hidden from the view of the two Americans.

"Bernie," Evan shouted. "Turn the machine gun around and aim it near the top of the hill across the road. Maybe we can help those guys over there."

Bernie shifted the machine gun around. It had been facing down the slope of the hill toward the Israeli roadblock at the near end of the valley. Now the weapon was aimed slightly below the Israeli position at the top of the opposite hill. The mortar shells were still landing on the hill, and there was the irregular crack, rising in pace now, of rifle fire. The quick barrage of mortar bursts and attack of the Arab soldiers had apparently caught the Israeli defenders on the hill by surprise. At first they rallied, but now they seemed to be withdrawing from their positions in the face of the heavy attack.

When the withdrawal of the men from the opposite hill began, Bernie aimed his machine gun at the positions they had just vacated, hoping to slow the advancing Arabs at that point and give the retreating Israelis a chance to get out safely. The heads of the first Arabs came into view over the rise of the hill, and Bernie and Evan opened fire. Bernie handled the German weapon with skill, sending short, rapid bursts in the direction of the Arabs. Evan's Sten gun had a slower rate of fire. He was surprised that there was little kick as it fired. The heads on the opposite hill quickly disappeared as the Arabs flattened their bodies against the ground.

"You're wasting ammunition, Evan. You couldn't get those Sten gun bullets as far as that hill if you batted each one when it comes out of the muzzle." Bernie pulled out his handkerchief and used it as a glove for his left hand as he grabbed the hot barrel of the machine gun. "Get the ammunition boxes. We're going to get the hell out of here. As soon as our guys retreat off the hill and the Arabs find they ain't in a crossfire anymore, we've had it."

Bernie picked up the machine gun and began carrying it up the slope of the hill to the Israeli positions on the crest. As he walked, he managed to fire short bursts from the heavy and unwieldy weapon toward the neighboring ridge now occupied by Arabs. Evan followed with the ammunition cans. Less than a minute after they began climbing the hill, bullets started kicking into the dust near them and whining overhead. They dropped to the ground. But the shots weren't coming from the Arab positions across the road. They were coming from the top of the very hill they were climbing. Some of the men in their own company were firing down at them.

"Christ!" Bernie gasped. "They must think we're Arabs attacking their positions. Can't they see we were shooting at the other hill?" He left the machine gun on the ground at his feet and stood up quickly. He waved his hands back and forth over his head. "Hey, you dumb punks! We're Jews! You're shooting at Jews! Let us up this friggin hill!"

"Get down, Bernie!" Evan shouted. "Get—"

Bernie slumped forward and fell to his knees. His body wavered there for a few seconds, as though trying to balance itself. Then Bernie's eyes closed and the body fell over face forward onto the rocks and pebbles. The bullets were still hitting around them as Evan crawled over to him and turned him over on his back. His face, nose, and forehead had been badly scratched by the fall onto the rocks. Blood was flowing out of two wounds in his neck, one at the left front base of the neck and the other on the back side of his neck, a little lower.

Evan glanced over at the hill across the road. There was still the sound of heavy firing from both ends of it. The Jews hadn't retreated all the way off the other end of the hill yet. He prayed silently that he could pull Bernie back down to the safety of the rock wall before the Israelis withdrew completely from the hill.

He began sliding feet first on his belly down the slope. Then he grabbed Bernie's ankles and pulled Bernie toward him. The wounded American was on his back, his face over to one side, his ear and cheek scraping along the ground everytime Evan gave another pull. Evan wondered if he were pulling a dead man. Bernie's eyes were closed and a thin stream of blood still flowed out of the wounds. It left a line of red on the rocky ground as the body was dragged down the hill. First Bernie's cheek and then his dark hair brushed the wet line and widened it.

Bullets were still vibrating low overhead when they neared the rock wall that they had erected as a shield for the machine gun position. Evan pulled Bernie down below the wall. They needed protection from the Jewish rifles at the crest of the hill, not from an Arab attack up the wide valley. Now the bullets were beginning to come from two directions, from the Jews at the top of the hill and from the Arabs who had just secured the hill across the road. It was beginning to get dark, but it seemed to Evan that the lingering daylight was taking an eternity to quit his and Bernie's spot on the hill. Bernie's chest rose and fell. He was still alive. Evan unbuttoned and removed his own shirt. Then he pulled his undershirt off and began ripping it into large pieces. He wrapped the strips of undershirt tightly around Bernie's neck, covering the wounds. Blood still soaked up through the cloth, but Evan hoped it wasn't coming out as fast. The pressure point. He couldn't remember where the pressure point was to stop blood going up through the neck. He sure as hell couldn't put a tourniquet on Bernie's neck. The shoulder? No. Where was it? He recalled vaguely that when he took the test to get the first aid merit badge in the Boy Scouts someone had asked him that same question, and he hadn't known. But he had passed the test, anyway.

He checked his Sten gun and loaded more cartridges into the magazine to replace those he had fired. The machine gun and ammunition boxes were still on the slope at the spot where Bernie had fallen. Evan wouldn't go back for them. He pulled his handkerchief out of his pocket and poured water from his canteen onto it. He used the wet cloth to wipe the scratches on Bernie's face and dab at the dirt embedded in his right cheek. The cheek had been skinned almost raw when Bernie was dragged down the hill, and dirt had been ground into the open flesh. He wondered if he

[73]

should leave Bernie and try to make a dash for the crest of the hill now that it was dark. A bullet hit one of the rocks in the wall and made a loud clipping noise. Evan slid down closer to the ground.

He was out in space falling and there was no way to tread air like the cartoon characters and reach out and pull himself back. He was always shoving himself out into the air. The last time had been when the *Pan York* arrived at the Haifa dock. There was a happy pandemonium among the D.P.'s who crushed forward to get to the gangplank. But the Americans knew they would have to pass the scrutiny of U.N. observers, so they had hung back, gathering at the rail on the sea side of the ship. A small tugboat tooted twice as it came alongside the *Pan York* and gently bumped the bigger ship. Evan looked down at the little tug bobbing softly in the water. A sailor jumped out of the wheelhouse of the tug and reached down into the hold. He dragged out a large, air-filled rubber mat and pulled it to the side of the tug's deck that lay adjacent to the *Pan York*.

"Hello! You Americans up there!" he called.

Their group leader, Jess, a heavy-set Philadelphian, peered over the rail and looked at the sailor inquisitively. "What do you want, buddy?"

"You men are Americans, yes?"

"Yeah."

"Then drop your baggage over the side and then jump down here."

"Okay." Jess turned to the young men around him. "This is where we make our exit. Bernie, you jump first. If you survive, the rest of us will join you. All right?"

"Mocks friggin nix to me," Bernie said. He dropped his cheap metal suitcase over the side. It hit the pad and the sailor caught it on first bounce. The sailor carried the suitcase over to the hold and dropped it inside. Bernie climbed over the rail, gripped the pole only for a few seconds, and then let go. He fell free for almost twenty feet before his feet hit the pad. He fell to his hands and knees. The sailor grabbed him and led him to the hold of the tug. Bernie looked up at the larger ship and grinned before disappearing into the hold.

"Your turn, Evan." Jess took the canvas suitcase out of his hand and dropped it down to the tug.

Evan climbed over the rail, stood on the edge of the deck for a second, then pushed himself off, out into the air. It was easy. It was just like jumping off the garage roof at home. He was off the roof and into the air. Too early to predict the damage, too late to climb back onto the roof. This was the kind of bravery he was made of.

He had learned this kind of bravery as a small boy. It was fragmented bravery, calculated courage, packed into a thimble of determination and emptied into a void of fear. He had learned it on the roof. He had been dared by two playmates to jump off a garage roof higher than any roof the three had attempted before. When Evan had looked over the side, the ground seemed too far below. He had not had the courage to leap the entire distance to the ground. But he had learned then that he had the power to split himself into a second person, and for an instant to allow that second, crazy person to take command, to push his cowardly body out into space. It was only for an instant and then the second person would dissolve. But Evan Andrew Copperman would be out in space, wishing for some mystic power to pull his body back onto the roof, back from danger. His source of courage had never been the motor—it was the battery, storing the tiny particle of energy that would push him beyond the point of return. He had used it as much in the past few months as he had in his lifetime before that; at the entrance to the Israeli Embassy in Paris, at the doorway to the Haganah office near the Arc de Triomphe, at the steps to the train that would take him to Marseilles, and on the dock near the gangplank that led up to the *Pan York*. It had taken every cell of courage he possessed to put him on the first step of the gangplank, to make the last break with the security he had always known. And after the first step courage was no longer necessary. There was no turning back, not now.

Evan hit the pad hard, and shock waves rippled up from his soles to his knees. His hands helped break the fall. He bounced off the pad and onto the deck, falling on his side. He let himself be led to the darkness of the hold. Bernie was there in the dark waiting for him. And now they were in the dark together again, on the slope of the Israeli hill. Or was it by now an Arab hill? They had been in the Promised Land one week.

Evan nudged Bernie's shoulder. His friend's eyes were still closed. "Bernie. Bernie. Can you hear me?"

Chapter Six

EVAN HEARD THE SOUND OF BOOTS AGAINST ROCKS. He cocked his Sten gun. "Jews or Arabs?" he called in Hebrew.

"Sons of the covenant." It was the prescribed answer.

"All right. Come quickly."

A patrol of four men approached the wall cautiously.

Evan stood up and pointed to Bernie. "You bastards shot him. Now help me get him to an aid station. His machine gun and ammunition boxes should be up above us there."

The soldiers helped Evan carry Bernie up to the top of the hill. Then they carried him to a first aid tent. A young doctor looked at him and shook his head. "Still alive. But he needs surgery and blood quickly. We'll send him back to Haifa at once."

The khaki ambulance had a red star of David in a white circle painted on both sides. There was already another man near death inside. They shoved the stretcher with Bernie in the back, also, and bounced off toward Haifa.

It was midnight before the Israelis could recapture the lost hill and launch the counterattack into Arab territory. All the squads were now back in their halftracks, and the armored column was moving down the road toward the wadi that served as the truce line. The heavy steel windshield and side window covers had been swung into place. Nahshon was leaning forward over the steering wheel to squint through a small square opening in the steel windshield cover. Gingi was standing straight, his chest and helmetless head appearing above the protecting shield of the halftrack. Shulamit was picking up messages on the radio and relaying them to Gingi. Once Gingi stepped back to the radio, put one of Shulamit's earphones to his ear and spoke directly through the microphone to the regimental commander.

There was still the sound of firing from the opposing hills on either side of the wadi, and there was the occasional slap of a mortar being sent on its way. So far, no bullets had come in their direction. It seemed to Evan that it would be a simple matter to shoot a bullet down into the halftrack, and if an Arab did so Evan would get it in the chest. He felt the top of his helmet with his hand to reassure himself that it was below the rim of the half-track and curled down lower on the bench. His legs were sprawled over the gunnysack with the hand grenades inside, and the grenades bounced and bumped against each other as the halftrack rumbled over the dirt road, past the roadblock at the Israeli side of the truce line and into the wadi.

Evan could not get the picture of Bernie's lifeless-looking body out of his mind. His fingers were still stained red from his attempt at dressing Bernie's wounds. Bernie's blood was caked beneath Evan's fingernails.

As the column approached the hills on the other side of the wadi, the sounds of rifle and machine gun fire from the heights intensified. Then there was the answering fire of the four armored cars at the head of the column. Evan could see tracers from the machine guns in the armored cars now rocketing up into the hills. The air was filled with the staccato of bullets and the phosphorescent wake of tracers. Though closer, the voice of Shulamit speaking rapidly into the radio and the roar of halftrack motors virtually blended into the night silence, unimportant background noises next to the sharp, abortive spit of weapons and the hiss of bullets. Both Itzik and Radhai were now beginning to send bursts of machine gun fire into the Arab hills. Evan crawled over and held the cartridge belt so the bullets would feed smoothly into the jaws of Radhai's German light machine gun.

Near the Arab side of the wadi the column came to a halt. "They say they need a squad of men to remove the Arab roadblock," Shulamit called quickly to Gingi.

"Tell them we'll be up there in a minute." Gingi turned and

signaled with his hand to the halftrack behind them. The squad of men in the halftrack jumped over the side to the ground, and Eliyahu, helmetless, led them at a trot to the head of the column, where he directed them in moving the boulders the Arabs had used to block the road. By the time he and the squad returned, the armored cars were moving forward again, still firing at the hills.

The column of vehicles began to move up a slight rise that led between the two hills. The armored cars at the rear of the column were within range of the Arab-held positions now and they opened fire on the hills also. The Arabs, in turn, were firing down at the column with rifles and machine guns. When the bullets were high overhead they made a thin whining sound. The low ones buzzed in bass like overweight bumblebees. Occasionally, a bullet would thud against the thick hide of the halftrack.

Several of the men in the halftrack immediately behind Nah-shon's were silhouetted against the moon-lit sky above the edge of their vehicle. They were sitting on the edge of the rim, as though oblivious of the bullets ripping through the air. One man was leaning over the side of the halftrack and—Evan noted with near disbelief—urinating.

Eliyahu without a helmet, the Palestinians sitting nonchalantly on the rim of the halftrack—they were heaping the highest insult on their enemies. They were the bullfighter turning his back on the bull and strutting away with cape dragging behind him. And if it wasn't contempt for the enemy, it was more; it was contempt for danger itself, as though danger, like fear, was only a state of mind that could be pretended away. It was a steel-tempered form of courage that the Israeli officers had made a rite of war, and which the enlisted men took heart from and imitated.

The column was now arriving at the back slopes of the two Arab-held hills. Gingi jumped over the side of the halftrack and directed six vehicles to pull off the shoulder of the road. The squads in each one dismounted and three squads began climbing up each of the back slopes, Eliyahu leading one group, a sergeant leading the other. Mordecai opened the back door of Nah-shon's halftrack and jumped down with his medic's satchel to join one of the groups.

The other halftracks closed up the gap and the column began

moving again. The firing from the hills receded in the distance
and Evan stood up. In the dim light of the quarter moon he could
see the outline of the hills on either side of the road and the dim
mass of the armored cars ahead, moving beetle-like toward Deir
Funduq, the village they were to attack. Deir Funduq lay on
either side of a slight rise in the road. Two hundred yards before
the convoy neared the first building—low mud-brick and stone
huts that huddled against each other in the night—the first armored
cars opened fire, spraying bullets and tracers into the windows
and streets. There was no answering fire. The villagers might have
been warned or might have heard the terrible motor noise of the
convoy and fled up into the hills. Or they might be crouched in
their homes waiting for the blade of the Jews. The convoy pulled
up to the edge of the village and stopped. Then the two armored
cars at the head of the column moved slowly through the street
that split the town and took up positions on the road at the other
edge of the village.

There were now only about two hours left before dawn. Gingi
checked his watch, then stepped down out of the back door of
the halftrack. "Both machine guns stay in the halftrack. Evan,
come with me."

Evan followed the captain as he gathered the last three squads
of infantry troops, spread them out, drew his revolver out of the
canvas holster on his hip, and led the men into the village. The
soldiers, wearing sweaters in the chill night air and a variety of
helmets, followed the blond hair of the muscular officer as though
it were a standard. Then they fanned out in groups of two's to check
each of the buildings to find the ammunition and stores. Evan
remained by Gingi's side. His finger was on the trigger of his
Sten gun—he expected the white flame of an Arab rifle to come
spewing out of every doorway and window. Gingi, he noticed,
walked down the narrow street as if he himself were the *Mukhtar* of the village, as if he had walked down this street a thousand
times before.

Gingi stopped in front of a building that appeared to be a storehouse rather than a dwelling. "Wait right here, Evan. But be
ready to shoot." The captain lifted his foot and used his boot as
a battering ram against the door of the storehouse. The door flew
open at the first kick and Gingi dashed inside. There was silence,

[79]

then Gingi's voice telling him to come inside. Wooden boxes, probably filled with ammunition and grenades, were stacked against the walls. French and Arabic words were stenciled on the sides of the boxes. "This must be the main storehouse," Gingi said. "Let's get the other boys to help us carry this stuff out."

The soldiers hauled as many crates as they could carry to the halftracks for half an hour. Then Gingi, who was constantly checking his watch and the sky above them, told them to stop and blow up the rest. Exploding ammunition and fires lit up the village as the three squads climbed back into their vehicles.

"Tell the armored cars on the other side of the village to pull back now," Gingi said. Shulamit transmitted the message. In a few minutes the two armored cars had rejoined the main column. All the other vehicles now began to turn around in the narrow road. It was a simple maneuver for the halftracks, which could move off the road and down toward the gully on either side. But the armored cars, which couldn't leave the road without a great deal more danger to the vehicle, inched back and forth like great indecisive turtles until they had turned completely.

The convoy headed back toward the Jewish lines, but this time Nahshon's halftrack was the last in the column of halftracks. The jeep with the regimental commander squeezed past to take up the lead at the other end of the column, but the other vehicles were too large to pass each other on the narrow road. When the convoy arrived back at the point where it had dropped off the six halftracks, it halted once again.

The soldiers were just coming down from the hills. There was no firing now. The only sound was that of feet scuffling the pebbles in their path. One soldier was seated in a chair of hands made by Mordecai and another soldier. His boot was off and a blood-soaked bandage was wrapped around his ankle. They lifted him to the helping hands of the men in one of the halftracks and Mordecai climbed into the halftrack after him.

"Both hills are clean. Only one man wounded in the leg. No one killed," Eliyahu reported laconically to Gingi.

The six halftracks pulled back into the line again and the convoy proceeded down the gradual incline that led toward the opening in the Arab roadblock. An explosion ahead of them ripped a red gash in the night. The convoy stopped, and Gingi looked quickly over to Shulamit, waiting for her to tell him what had happened.

"The first armored car hit a mine going back through the roadblock," she said as soon as the message came through.

"Nineteen vehicles came through that space three hours ago," Gingi said. "It must have hit one spot we all missed before. What about the wrecker?"

"It's already on the way," she said. "The jeep just radioed for it."

"Good. Nahshon, see if you can pull around this line and get us up to the roadblock."

Nahshon put the halftrack into front wheel drive and, steering half in the gully and half on the road, slowly passed the other vehicles until the halftrack came to the roadblock. The damaged armored car had gone almost all the way through the opening in the roadblock when it hit the mine. The explosion had ripped away one rear wheel, flattened the other, and bent the axle. The armored car had been turned by the explosion so it now effectively blocked the road to the Jewish lines. A tall bank jutted up on both sides of the road at the point of the roadblock. Men from the crippled vehicle and stalled convoy were standing near the wreck surveying the damage.

The sound of a rifle firing up on the hill sent all of them crouching for cover. There were a few more cracks from the hill and bullets whizzed high overhead.

Nahshon cursed in Arabic. "The Arabs we chased off the hills are coming back." He looked at his watch. "The sun will be up in half an hour. If that armored car isn't moved in a hurry, we'll be easy targets for them."

The armored cars answered the Arabs with a hail of bullets from their machine guns. But the rifle fire, probably not from more than two or three rifles, still came down at them.

The big wrecker sped across the wadi toward them and stopped on the other side of the roadblock. A skinny, balding soldier jumped down from the running board and looked over the damaged armored car. He crawled back into the cab of the wrecker and, slapping it from one gear to the other, quickly turned the huge vehicle around and backed it up to the armored car. He pulled large wooden blocks from the back of the wrecker and put them behind each of the wrecker's rear wheels.

"Nahshon!" he called across the roadblock. "You lazy Berber. Come give me a hand."

"The halftrack's yours, Yeled," Nahshon said, sliding out the door. The Moroccan crawled through the roadblock and began helping the wrecker driver tug at a cable. They hooked it onto the back corner of the armored car.

Evan slid into the driver's seat of Nahshon's halftrack, put his feet on the clutch and brake pedals, and rested his hand on the gear shift lever. He felt a surge of confidence in himself that he knew he could not have possessed a day before.

Amid the increasing chatter of bullets from the hill, the wrecker driver and Nahshon worked quickly to pull the smashed end of the armored car around and reel it up into the air next to the rear of the wrecker. Finally Alex, the wrecker driver, was ready to pull the armored car completely out of the roadblock while Nahshon sat in the driver's seat of the damaged vehicle, steering the only two wheels now touching the ground.

As soon as the road was cleared, the convoy began to roll again. The first rim of gray light simmered at the crest of the eastern hills and the bullets began coming closer to their targets, but the convoy was speeding across the wadi now and was quickly out of range of the Arab rifles. The column of vehicles, led by the wrecker and the armored car it was pulling, followed the gently rising road between the two Jewish-held hills, then turned off into the olive grove and went as deeply into it as it could before coming to a stop.

The soldiers immediately began breaking off branches from the olive trees and using them to camouflage the armored cars and halftracks. Gingi broke off a large limb and dragged it behind him to the road. Using it like a broom, he erased the tire and track marks that led from the edge of the road into the olive grove.

"This seems completely pointless," Evan complained, draping a branch over the back door of the halftrack. "We're in Jewish territory." He looked up at the tree that spread over them. Tiny green olives, themselves camouflaged among the elliptical leaves, hung from each small limb.

"Silly, but not exactly pointless," Shulamit said. "This is all part of the way the contest is played." There was a trace of dis-

[82]

gust in her voice. "We lodge a complaint that there has been a truce violation before the Arabs do. That gives us several points. It happens to be the truth this time, but even if we attacked first, if we could make the complaint to the U.N. first it would still give us points, because the U.N. believes that the party that complains first is really the party that's been wronged."

"But what rule have we broken by having our own military vehicles in our own territory?"

"None, but it weighs in the point total. If the Arabs attacked us, as we say they did, it is perfectly all right to counter attack and in our zeal accidentally spill over to the Arab side of the truce line to do a little damage. We lose no points for that. But if we send an armored regiment to cross the truce line, strafe the hills, and blow up a village, then we're guilty of aggression that hasn't been properly provoked, and we lose points."

"Asinine," Evan declared. "The Arabs know that we had armored vehicles in their territory last night, and that men from halftracks blew up part of the village."

"Certainly," said Shulamit. "But it was dark, and the Arabs are likely to say anything, just as we are likely to say anything. The U.N. observers are neutral, and can only report what they can see. We spend half of our time letting them see as little or as much as we want them to see, depending on the points at stake." She shoved the last branch into the grate on the side of the halftrack and sat down, wiping her hands on her trousers. "We shouldn't even be here now. We should be back at that Arab village we just blew up. We should hold onto every inch of ground we won last night, instead of crawling back here and hiding like thieves afraid of being found out."

"But you contradict yourself. You just said that this would make us lose points. Maybe even get sanctions slapped on us."

"Points are in a game for children," she said bitterly. "A government must be as brave with the world as its soldiers are with the enemy."

"A government has to consider the consequences of its actions, too."

"The Arabs haven't worried about the consequences," she said. "They've invaded Palestine and occupied more than half the land.

[83]

There are no sanctions against them—not even the threat of sanctions—and no one will make them give back the land, to either the Jews or the Palestinian Arabs. They'll divide it among themselves while we worry about the consequences. What we can take by force we should keep by right. If the Arabs can do it, why can't we?"

"Because we are small and weak," Evan said. "As you said, there are rules and regulations, and the U.N. has different sets of rules according to the size of a country."

"We should have stayed in the village and held it," she maintained. "A threat of sanctions wouldn't hurt us. The sanctions themselves—perhaps. There would be time to get out later if we had to, but not because of fear of what the U.N. might say."

Evan could share her low opinion of the U.N. He remembered how enthusiastic he had been about the U.N. less than a year before, and how disappointed he was in it now. It had passed a resolution providing for the establishment of a Jewish state. Now the state had been established and invaded, and the U.N. had promptly placed the Jewish state in the exact same category as the outside aggressors. Israel was to refrain from bringing in arms or military volunteers while the truce was in effect.

The U.N. was a strange organization that lived in a never-never land of non-partisanship. It could examine facts objectively and order the establishment of two states—one Jewish, one Arab —out of a mandate area entrusted to it. Then it could stand objectively aside and watch a handful of its own members attack the Jewish state in an attempt to destroy it at the same time that they were trying to gobble up the new Arab state. Then the U.N. could step in objectively and mediate between the invaders and the invaded without ever mentioning that one side had been violently breaking the law. It was like imposing an equal sentence on both the rapist and his victim on the grounds that both had been participants in an incident that had disturbed the peace.

Shortly after dawn, in the stillness of the olive grove they could hear the sound of a motor approaching from the direction of the deserted village. A white jeep was speeding down the dirt road, churning a cloud of dust in its wake as it passed the olive grove. Two men in khaki uniforms were sitting in the front seat and a small blue flag rippled from a thin mast on the front fender. The jeep disappeared down the road that led to the wadi.

Shulamit put her earphones on again and began talking to someone in the Jewish positions on the hills.

"Tell them to let us know when the U.N. jeep passes the Arab roadblock," Gingi called.

Half an hour later, the radio operator at the other end reported to Shulamit that the U.N. observers had finished inspecting the Jewish positions and taking the Jewish reports of the Arab attack. The jeep was now moving through the Arab roadblock where the armored car had hit the mine, he said.

"Tell the armored cars to move out," Gingi ordered, beginning to toss the olive branches away from the halftrack. He tapped Evan on the shoulder. "We'll follow them."

After they arrived back at the base, Evan sleepily helped unload the halftrack at the quartermaster hut. He gave the quartermaster back the locker of food and the sack of hand grenades. He also made him a present of the captured Arab ammunition.

The wrecker with the armored car in tow had lagged far behind the convoy. Nahshon's shoulders were stooped with fatigue when he walked into the mess hall. Everyone was already eating so there was no line for him to shove in front of. To compensate for the lost privilege, the dark-skinned corporal demanded two hardboiled eggs instead of the usual one. A rotund cook pretended to be angered by the request and shouted at Nahshon. The Moroccan scowled back from behind his hook nose and returned the insult. They both cursed each other. Then the cook laughed and tossed the extra egg on Nahshon's plate.

The Moroccan sat down next to Evan and hunched over his food. He littered his section of the table with egg shells and began to stuff the food into his mouth.

The exuberance that Evan had felt when he first arrived back at the olive grove had now disappeared, giving way to languid shock. He felt as if the energy had been pumped out of him. He was sitting at the table staring at nothing, thinking of nothing, when something bumped his shoulder. It was a young sabra from one of the infantry platoons. He had walked up to the table and was reaching over Evan's arm to take Evan's knife. He took the knife, cut a thick slice from the rye bread sitting in front of Evan, and then reached over to slash the knife into the margarine in front of Nahshon. He spread the margarine thickly over the slice of bread, then tossed the knife down onto the table.

"*Toda raba*"—Thank you very much, Evan said with heavy sarcasm as the sabra turned to go back to his table.

"*B'vakasha*"—You're welcome, the sabra said matter-of-factly, his back now to Evan.

Evan picked up the knife and examined it. There was a thick smear of margarine all over the blade. He dropped it onto his plate.

"Goddam it! What's wrong with these people? Aren't they ever taught any manners?"

"Look, Yeled," Nahshon said, his jaw bulging with a large bite of bread, "understand one thing now. Don't expect manners from a sabra. They don't mean to be rude. It's just that a sabra doesn't give a damn about you and he doesn't give a damn about me. But most important, he doesn't give a damn about himself. That's the reason we've won most of our battles so far. The sabras just don't give a damn about themselves." He folded a piece of cheese and poked it into his mouth. "If the sabras cared as much about their lives as you care about yours or I care about mine, we'd all be wading in the Mediterranean now. The only bloody thing they care about is this country."

He swallowed the cheese in a gulp, drank the rest of his tea, and wiped the bottom of his mustache with the back of his hand. "I don't know. Maybe they care about their families and friends, too. But themselves—no. Did you see what we had to fight with last night? Imagine a European army going into battle with nothing but light arms. When the Arab armies first attacked in May, the sabras went into action with one rifle and two hand grenades to divide between three boys. And each one had a weapon he could use. These boys were bred for guts. The manners will have to come later."

Evan remembered the boys he had seen sitting nonchalantly on the rim of the halftrack while the bullets whizzed around them. "I suppose you're right. I can't quite comprehend either their cold nerve or their manners. But if I have to choose between good manners and the guts, I'll take the guts."

He went back to the barracks and fell down on his mattressless bed. It was hard, but at least it was horizontal. He reminded himself that when he woke up he would have to see someone and demand straw for his palliasse.

Chapter Seven

THE LETTERS ARRIVED IN THE AFTERNOON. ONE WAS from his mother, the other from his rabbi. Both had been opened by the Israeli censor and re-sealed with heavy sticky-tape. Evan examined the envelope on his mother's letter, delaying the moment when he would have to open it and read what he knew would be the depressing message inside. She had written "Please Forward" twice on the front and once on the back, each time underlining "Please." Next to "Israel" she had put in parentheses "Palestine."

Evan plowed a jagged furrow in the flap with his thumb and pulled out the typewritten letter. It was short, which surprised him, and written in an unnaturally stiff style, as though she had rewritten it several times before mailing it. She told him that his letter revealing his plans to go to Israel had been a terrible shock. She and his father were beside themselves with worry and grief. They still could not believe, she said, that Evan, who had always been most considerate of them in the smallest details, would make a decision of this magnitude without first discussing it fully with them.

"But Dad and I are attempting to forget our own selfish feelings in this matter and consider your decision from a logical point of view," she continued. "Israel does not need brawn or bodies from America—there are enough D.P.'s for that. Israel needs brains, and if you really want to help Israel, you will return to college at once and finish your education. We have called the Israeli embassy in Washington and been assured that you will be released within days if you will only request it. We hope you will put in such a request right away. We know you have acted out of the best of motives, but the motives have been misguided and might result in tragedy for both yourself and Israel."

She concluded: "Cable us and tell us how much money you will need for your return trip. We are expecting you home on the first ship or plane you can take."

Evan read the letter over a second time. He tried to blink back the tears of disappointment. He had known they would tell him they "expected" him to come home at once, though he had hoped for the remote possibility of their telling him to stay if he wanted to, that they were proud of him. But this. This wasn't a letter. It was a note to a naughty child from the firm, experienced, and for-the-time-being tolerant hand of a parent.

He would answer them in kind. He would write them that Israel needed halftrack drivers, not lawyers or physicians or merchants. He would say that he was his own man in a country where he could be a man, that he would stay in Israel as long as Israel needed him, and perhaps forever. And he would make some cutting remark about the depth of their Zionism, which extended to the surface of time and money, but stopped at the loan of their son.

Evan had prepared himself to receive a frantic, tearful letter from his mother. Possibly that was what he wanted to get from her. But in the dispassion of her letter she had abandoned him emotionally, and he was suddenly a trapeze artist swinging gracefully through the air only to look up and discover that his hands were grasping nothing. As much as he was disappointed in his parents at that moment, that much he loved them also, and he could not polarize the two sensations. He held the letter limply in his hand as he sat there on the edge of his bed, and he did not try to trap the few tears that trickled out of his eyes.

"So you finally heard from home, Yeled." It was Nahshon. The Moroccan wore only the baggy undershorts that hit just above his knees and the sleeveless undershirt. The olive brown of his skin contrasted sharply even with the dingy gray of the underwear.

Evan nodded. Nahshon glanced down at the typewritten letter Evan was holding in his hand, then searched the wet hazel eyes. He sat down on the foot of the bunk near the American who now felt very young and very much alone.

"All of us sometimes have to fight a longing for the home of our

[88]

parents," Nahshon said. "But we must do what we think is right before we can go home again. Your parents will be proud of you. You'll see."

"They won't be proud of me," Evan said bitterly. He handed the letter to Nahshon.

The Moroccan gave it back to him without looking at it. "I learned to speak English in the British army, but I was never too good at reading it. You read it to me."

"I don't know if I can read it again," Evan said. He glanced around the barracks uneasily. More than half the beds were still filled with soldiers sleeping off the fatigue of the night's battle. In a voice just above a whisper, he read the letter to Nahshon. He did not look up at the Moroccan until he had finished. Then he examined Nahshon's face for a reaction. Nahshon said nothing for long seconds. His eyes narrowed and he stared out the window, slowly wringing the end of his mustache with his thumb and forefinger.

"You are very lucky, Yeled. Your parents want you. Look around this room. How many men are there here who can even remember the sound of a mother's voice? I think there are only one or two whose mothers are alive."

"But she doesn't have any understanding of what I am, of what I feel, or why I came here," Evan said. "I expected more of her than that."

"Don't blame her, Yeled."

"Do you think she's right?" Evan asked dejectedly.

"No. You belong here. I know you will stay here. But don't cut yourself off from your parents because you have been hurt, and don't write anything that will make their pain greater. That is Nahshon's advice."

"I don't know. I've done what I think is right. And yet I believe that they hate me for doing it."

"Perhaps I can tell you a story that will explain why I give you this advice. Do you remember speaking to me a few days ago of a family that lived in a small town and only came to your synagogue once a year? We were such Jews, but we came into a synagogue only once or twice in a lifetime. The nearest synagogue was four days' journey away in the city of Demnate. It was too far.

My father had been to Demnate only twice, once when his father took him there for his *bar mitzvah* and the second time when he went there to get a wife."

Nahshon leaned back on his elbows and told Evan about his family in Asabadin. His father, Yoseph, made his third trip to Demnate when Nahshon's older brother, Shimeon, was thirteen and ready to take his place before the Torah as a Jewish adult. Yoseph and Shimeon left Asabadin with a large ration of food and a change of clothes slung in sacks over a rented donkey. Ten days later they returned, and Shimeon was full of tales about the huge city of Demnate. There were palaces in the city, he said, and thousands of Jews lived together in the *Mellah,* a walled portion of the city. The *Mellah's* streets were narrow and dirty, but there were a hundred different kinds of shops there, selling foods and goods that the Berbers had never heard of. And he, Shimeon, had changed into his Sabbath clothes and gone to the synagogue with Yoseph. An old bearded man had called his name and he was allowed to walk up to the *bima* and kiss the ancient parchment of the Torah and read his portion of the Law. Nahshon listened to the tales in awe. He wanted to reach out and touch the arm of his brother, who had seen such wonders.

Nahshon waited with anticipation and a certain fear for his turn to be taken to Demnate. Could he be as confident as Shimeon when the bearded one called his name? He studied his portion, and learned to wrap the phylacteries around his arm and head. He memorized whole portions of the daily prayers. Yoseph praised the diligence of his youngest son.

And finally the time came for Nahshon, the son of Yoseph, to take his place as a man among Jews. Yoseph said that this time Sura would go to Demnate, also. Nahshon's mother packed the two children's clothes in a large sack along with Yoseph's, and in another sack she tenderly placed the dried meat and hard *pitta,* the bread they would eat on the long journey to Demnate. Early the next morning, Yoseph brought the small rented donkey to the gate of the shop. He tied on the sacks of clothes and food and the kid skin filled with fresh water. The thirteen-year-old boy and the twelve-year-old girl kissed Shimeon and the old grandmother. Yoseph looked away as the weeping mother kissed her youngest son

[90]

and then kissed and hugged her only daughter as though she would never let loose. Yoseph, his eyes on the ground, gently pulled Sura away from her mother and lifted her onto the donkey, where she sat between the bundles.

They left on their journey, Yoseph and Nahshon walking in front of the donkey and Sura riding. The two children turned and waved to the Ben-Mizrachis in Asabadin until the village was out of sight.

It was a long four days to Demnate. Down out of the mountains and into the foothills and then to the hot, dusty plains. The nights they would spend in a stable in a small village, where the donkey could eat and drink and rest, and the Ben-Mizrachis could sleep in the straw. Nahshon and Sura, already homesick, would huddle together until they fell asleep.

Towards the end of the fourth day, the low gnarled buildings of Demnate came into view. At the outskirts of town, Yoseph lifted Sura down from the donkey. Jews, he explained, were not allowed to ride through the streets of Demnate. They led the donkey through narrow dirt streets until they came to a broad, cobbled road. There were indeed large houses, half hidden by walls and iron grills, that must have been inhabited by princes, if one city could truly have so many princes. There were arched shops, also, and artisans busy inside in the shadows that brought relief from the summer sun.

And then there was the high, narrow gate to the *Mellah*, the ghetto of the Jews. The streets became much narrower, with filth of all kinds running down the center gutter. Here a butcher slaughtered a lamb and let the blood course from its throat to the street; there a fishmonger de-gutted one of his scaly creatures and flung the entrails into the street. The smells of food, waste, dirty bodies, and fermenting latrines mingled into one pot as the smell of the *Mellah*, and the pot was stirred by the raucous noises that came from the small shops and close, crowded buildings.

Whether the *Mellah* was originally built to separate the Jews or simply offer them better protection from their Moslem neighbors was a question that even the sages in the *Mellah* no longer argued. The *Mellah* was the *Mellah*. Separation there was. Protection there was not. But a Jew could have the peace of the present in the

[91]

Mellah. In the past? There were still stories told of several hundred years before when the city of Demnate was attacked by the mountain Berbers. The sheik who had directed the successful attack did not have enough money to pay his troops, so he gave them a free hand to take the spoils of the *Mellah.* The women were violated. The shops were looted. A hundred men of the *Mellah* were killed. The high walls of the *Mellah* had been a trap, not a barrier. And who knew what the future would bring? Was it not a Moroccan proverb that "You may kill seven Jews without punishment"? The pogrom of Demnate was but yesterday, the destruction of the Temple the day before. It was important to live for today.

The thin men in the streets and shops, with their skullcaps perched on their shaven heads, were unlike the Jews Nahshon had imagined. They ignored the Ben-Mizrachis in the street before them. They showed less warmth than the Berbers of Asabadin.

Yoseph stopped before the shop of his second cousin, Moises Ibn-Eli, the sandalmaker. Moises came out to greet them and sent one of his apprentices to take care of the donkey. That night, after supper, the three Ben-Mizrachis slept in a small room with Moises' two apprentices and six children. The dark eyes of several of the children were already half closed by the trachoma that was pollinated by the fog of flies that hovered over the *Mellah.*

The next night, on the Sabbath eve, Yoseph took Nahshon by the hand and led him to the nearby synagogue. Nahshon had imagined it would be a Temple. The synagogue was a little narrow building, close and hot, filled with the babble of a hundred nodding men chanting their prayers as if only each one and God and the synagogue existed.

The next morning, Nahshon and Yoseph arrived at the synagogue early. Nahshon said his prayers and tugged at the fringes of his new prayer shawl, as proud as though it were the multi-colored cloak of Joseph in the Bible. And then one of the old bearded men who huddled around the Torah that had been set on the *bima* in the center of the synagogue called out "Nahshon ben Yoseph," and the thirteen-year-old boy, the son of Yoseph, walked quickly up to the *bima*, bowed and kissed the yellowing parchment on which was written the word of the Law. He said the blessings and then read his portion, hardly seeing the Hebrew words on the scroll, because he knew the portion by heart. Nahshon was now a man, and when he returned from the *bima* his father kissed him on the forehead.

When Yoseph and Nahshon and Sura had awakened the next morning, and the father and son had said their prayers and removed the leather phylacteries from their arms and foreheads, Yoseph took his Sabbath clothes out of the bag of clothing and put them into a separate sack.

He rose, holding the small sack. "My children, your father is a coward. I have waited until the last minute to tell you this. Perhaps it would have been easier if I had told you back in Asabadin." Yoseph paused. His eyes were covered by a thin, wet film. Nahshon reached down and grasped the hand of his sister. "You know," Yoseph continued, "that only one Ben-Mizrachi family can stay in Asabadin, and that this inheritance must go to Shimeon." He looked at his son. "I want you to stay in the city, Nahshon, and make a life for yourself. Moises will keep you here as an apprentice in his shop." He turned to Sura. "My daughter, you are a child now. But in a few years you will be a woman. There are no husbands for you in Asabadin. Here there are many. One will be worthy of you. You will stay here and help the wife of Moises. Nahshon is a man now. I leave him here to watch over you."

Yoseph took his bundles of food and clothes and walked to the arch of Moises' shop. He tied them on the donkey that was being held by an apprentice and stepped back to the two children, who were too stunned to talk or cry. Yoseph placed his hands first on the head of Nahshon as he moved his lips in an inaudible prayer. Then he did the same to Sura. He kissed both children on the forehead, took the halter string of the donkey, and walked toward the *Mellah* gate. He did not look back.

Sura tried to run after her father. Nahshon held her back. She thrust her face into the chest of her brother and wept. Nahshon felt the warm tears soaking through his blouse. He wanted to cry, too. But he was a man now.

He stroked the soft black hair of his sister and whispered, "Quiet. Quiet now. Your brother is here with you. He'll always be with you."

Nahshon got up from Evan's bed and stood there, shaking his head. To tell the story was to relive it. "What I told her was a lie. The *Mellah* made it a lie. The *Mellah* forced me to make it a lie."

He stared into Evan's eyes for long seconds. "So tell me, now. Is a letter from a mother who wants to hold on to you so awful? Is it really a horrible fate for you to have such parents?"

"Your parents—are they still in Asabadin?"

"Yes."

"And Sura—is she still in the *Mellah?*"

"Yes," Nahshon said. "She is still in the *Mellah.*"

The Moroccan went back to his own bed, whipped one of his balled-up blankets to unfold it, and pulled it over him. But he couldn't close his eyes. It was the afternoon sun sending a bright shaft of light through the window next to him. Little particles of dust, sucked in from the darkness, hovered and spiraled in the drafts of the light beam, then faded away into darkness again. The weaning of a child, he thought—it left another scar, another navel, and sometimes it never healed. His scars. Sura's scars. If only there had been no *Mellah,* and no Moises, and no Shaul, the green tea merchant. He thought about what they had done to her, what he himself had done to her, and felt again the ancient guilt.

Through the shaft of light, which gave each thread of dust a living second, Nahshon glanced over at Evan's bunk. The American was still sitting in the same spot, but now he was writing something on a pad of paper.

The day before the truce was scheduled to end, an additional halftrack was ferried into the armored regiment and Evan was assigned to drive it. Excess men from the other infantry squads were formed into a squad for the newly-arrived halftrack. Of the eight men assigned to his halftrack, Evan knew only one, Radhai. He was glad that the tall Ethiopian would be beside him, but he couldn't understand how he had been lucky enough to get him. It was true that Nahshon's halftrack, which didn't carry a squad of men, needed only one machine gunner. But Nahshon had a way of keeping his friends with him despite the desires of headquarters, and Nahshon and the Falasha were close friends.

The other seven men were all very young. Five were Palestinians and two others were D.P.'s who had already been in the country for more than a year. The second machine gunner, who would move out with the squad while Radhai stayed with the halftrack, was a Palestinian named Uzi. A round and flabby youth with aqua eyes and a stubby nose, he had carried a concertina with him when the squad had boarded the halftrack for the first time. "Are you from New York?" he had asked Evan.

"No. Virginia."

"Virgeenia?" Uzi repeated and held his hands up as though he were holding the handles of a plough. "Does your father make tobacco?"

"No."

Uzi rubbed his thumb back and forth across the other four fingers of his hand and raised his blond eyebrows in anticipation of an answer. "Business?"

Evan nodded, smiling.

Uzi grinned and reached out to shake the American's hand.

The truce was to end at 6 a.m. the next day, Friday, July 9. Shortly before dusk the entire armored regiment was engaged in the deliberate final activities of preparing for battle. The regiment was preparing to maintain itself in the field for an indefinite period of time, since the U.N. had not allotted a specific number of days for the fighting, as it had for the truce.

Radhai and the men in the infantry squad helped Evan load aboard the halftrack the locker of food as well as abundant supplies of hand grenades and ammunition. They also strapped to the side of the halftrack two five-gallon cans of water and one five-gallon emergency can of gasoline.

The regiment formed into a convoy inside the camp. A company of armored cars led the line of vehicles, followed by the four halftracks of the heavy machine gun company, then the halftrack infantry, another company of armored cars, several jeeps carrying light mortars, and finally two more armored cars.

Most of the ultra-religious Jews in the regiment were in the heavy machine gun company. Some of them wore *paot,* the long sideburns that hung down in curls before their ears. For the sake of military appearance, however, they would tuck the curls up over their ears, as one would a pencil, and pull their berets down to make the curls inconspicuous. All the meals served in the mess halls were kosher. The cooks used two sets of pots and pans, one for meat dishes and another for milk dishes, and meat products were never served at the same meal with dairy products. But almost all the soldiers in the armored regiment ignored the dietary

[95]

prohibitions against mixing milk and meat as far as their own mess gear was concerned. They would put cheese in their mess tins in the morning and then meat in the same mess tins at noon. But the religious men in the heavy machine gun company each had two cups and an extra knife, fork, and spoon. They would use one cup, one set of eating utensils, and one half of their two-piece mess gear for the milk dishes, and the other set of utensils and mess tin for the meat dishes.

As the regiment prepared to go into battle, even the halftracks of the heavy machine gun company were different from those of Evan's company. Biblical phrases and slogans had been chalked in Hebrew print on the steel sides and doors of the four halftracks: "If I Forget Thee, O Jerusalem," "I Will Lift Up Mine Eyes Unto The Hills," and one, "Ride On In Behalf Of Truth," that sent Evan's hand unconsciously to the breast pocket of his shirt. He felt the edge of the envelope inside the pocket, then pulled the letter from Rabbi Lichtberg out of the envelope and read it over still another time:

Dear Evan:

It is somewhat difficult for me to express the feelings which have moved me from the moment that I read your letter informing me of your momentous decision. Following that I lived with your parents through hours of terrible distress. You can well imagine the effect of the news upon your mother, who had to take it completely unprepared at a moment when she was expecting to get a letter from you telling all about your wonderful first experiences in France.

But your letters bore ample evidence that you had drawn all that into the realm of your deliberations before you took the fateful action.

Let me give you an analysis of the situation as I see it. My first reaction was immense pride that you had mustered enough idealism and Jewish substance to feel that your place was with your people in such a dangerous hour of Jewish history. While my wife was crying and my own throat was choking, I had a deep feeling of satisfaction because in all humility I felt that mine was a share in a great and noble thing which you had done.

I have always tried, and sometimes, I admit, with a lurking

sense of frustration, to imbue all my students with Jewishness in all its implications. Here I saw irrefutable proof that something had taken root and produced wonderful results. That feeling will always be with me. No matter what will happen now or later, I have been proud of you, Evan.

Your parents have asked you to return immediately. They have not asked me explicitly to add my plea to theirs as some of the family have. To them I have said what I would say to your parents also: I cannot ask you to return. Such a decision must be your own, either positive or negative. But in either case it should be preceded by sound and practical reasoning.

You are twenty now and just in the middle of your education. There may be grave repercussions concerning your draft status and other complications in regard to your citizenship. On the other hand you must ask yourself this all important question: Is your contribution to the cause of Israel in your present stage of preparation, skill, and potential usefulness important enough, or important at all, to warrant such a revolutionary turn in your life? Or would it be wiser and ultimately more beneficial to you personally and to the cause of Israel if you could first equip yourself more thoroughly and then place yourself at the disposal of the cause?

That, I believe, is the proper way to look at the whole matter. Now that you are on the spot you must again weigh all these factors carefully. You must listen to the advice of people who are qualified to consider all factors fairly and dispassionately. That much you owe to your parents, to yourself, yes, and also to Israel.

If, after conscientious deliberation and honest soul searching you still feel that your place is in Israel now, then, I believe, I would not feel morally justified to call on you to come back. My blessings and my prayers would be with you, as expressed in the ancient words of the Psalmist: "Ride on in behalf of truth."

I remember many an occasion when, with your great argumentative powers, you tried to prove to me that there was not much sense in learning Hebrew. Now, of course, you are grateful for the good background you have. I am looking forward to receiving a Hebrew letter from you soon with all the latest vernacular.

[97]

Now, Evan, may G-d be with you and guide you in whatever you will do, and may everything turn out for the best.

Affectionately,

Rabbi Ernst Lichtberg

Evan folded the letter and put it back in his breast pocket. His "great argumentative powers"—if only he could use them to convince the rabbi and his parents that there was no decision to make. The decision had already been made at Paris and at the gangplank of the *Pan York*. If it had taken all the courage he possessed to come to Israel, it would surely take more than he possessed to leave when the fight for the land was still in progress. They would be shocked, all of them in Virginia, Evan thought, if they knew that the decision beginning to face him was not whether to go home now, but whether to go home ever.

For many years, Evan had wanted to be an attorney. He wanted to use a lawyer's brain and a lawyer's tongue to help those caught in the powerful undertow of injustice. It was a romantic notion, he knew, to pretend that mortgages, wills, divorces, and petty suits didn't exist, and that only the big challenges were awaiting him. But he knew that the big challenges were there, and they would remain there for the man ascetic enough to ignore the morsels. This would be his quest for immortality. But weren't there challenges in Israel, too? Weren't there underdogs among the Jews? Wouldn't there be the ignorant and the innocent and even the oppressed here? And wasn't this a far more receptive climate for the man who called himself a Jew? Here he could be a lawyer—period. Not a Jewish lawyer. Here there would be only injustice to attack. Not injustice plus the cold thin metal of resentment that it was a Jewish lawyer who was doing the attacking. All of which was a dichotomy whose resolution could very well be postponed, he thought wryly, considering that he was now sitting in the driver's seat of a halftrack on the eve of battle and the most important challenge facing him was staying alive tomorrow.

The plan for the convoy was to follow the highway toward Haifa and then turn to the southeast, where the regiment would help clear the Southern Galilee of the troops of Syria, Lebanon, and Fawzi El Kaukji's Arab Liberation Army. The great walls, round domes, and peaked minarets of Acre passed on the right, a huge black facade,

[98]

a disembodied expressionless face. And then there was unbroken night, and silence. For there was a great eye of silence in the hurricane of noise enveloping the convoy.

Radhai was part of the night as he stood next to Evan, ready to warn the American if he came too close to the halftrack ahead of them or too near the shoulder of the road. In all Evan's readings about the history of the Jews he could not remember seeing one word about the African Jews. He had read of black Jews in Harlem, but they had been former slaves of Jewish plantation owners.

"Radhai, are there many Jews in Ethiopia?"

"There were once many, many thousands. Part of Ethiopia was a Jewish kingdom hundreds of years ago. But now many Falashas have been converted to Christianity or Islam. Others have been slaughtered by the Amharas or the Italians. I don't know how many are left."

"The word Falasha. It doesn't mean the same as Ethiopian?"

Radhai smiled. "Hardly. We called ourselves *Beta-Israel*, the House of Israel. The Amharas—the Christian Ethiopians—called us Falashas, which is the Amharic word for 'emigrants' or 'intruders.' My uncle used to say that Falasha was a fitting word for us, since we were only sojourners in the land, and the time would come when the Messiah would be sent by God to lead us back to the Land of Israel."

"That makes it sound as though you were newcomers to Ethiopia."

"But we were newcomers." Radhai laughed and squatted down next to Evan's seat. "We had only lived there 3,000 years." He checked Evan's face for the signs of disbelief he knew would be there. "You are wondering how that is possible. Our legends tell us that the Queen of Sheba had a son by Solomon. His name was Menilek. When she came back to Ethiopia with Menilek, she brought Hebrew scholars and artisans so her son would receive the same education as the royalty of Jerusalem. They were our ancestors. So for 3,000 years we lived completely apart from the Amharas, waiting for the arrival of the Messiah. He never came."

"But you are here, anyway. Shulamit told me that General Wingate sent you."

"Yes. He had served here in the British army during the 1930's. The British transferred him out of Palestine in 1939 because he had become too friendly with the Jews. He always thought he would return here to lead a Jewish army to independence."

[99]

"Do you ever miss Ethiopia?"

"Why should I?"

"Well, because—"

"Because I'm different? You don't have to be embarrassed. It is an honest question. You have men in America whose skins are black. Do you treat them differently from those whose skins are white?"

"Yes, I'm ashamed to say."

"Do they miss Africa?"

"No. They can't really go back to Africa."

"Neither can I. Everything that I loved there is destroyed. If I went back now I would feel as different from the Ethiopians as if my skin were white." Radhai stood up. "We should be getting close to the truce line now."

The Falasha put his hands on the forward rim of the halftrack and watched the road that was about to pass beneath them. The asphalt was very black, but easy to follow because of the white, sandy shoulders. He thought about his conversation with the American. He had been told by Wingate that almost all of the Jews in Palestine were white-skinned, so he wasn't surprised to find that it was true. But he could not understand at first why the white-skinned Jews had come back to the Holy Land while the Falashas, the real Jews, had not. In the beginning, he had felt that the white-skinned Jews were different. Later he had felt that he was different, known that he was different, a black Jew, proudly sheltered in his preserve, as unique and as interesting as a white rhinoceros. Not that the kibbutzniks of Ein Dvorah had ever treated him as anything but one of themselves. They had received the letter from Wingate and they had welcomed the barefoot Ethiopian, assigned him quarters with the other unmarried men, and made him a part of the communal farming settlement. Radhai became an assistant in the dairy barn. They found a pair of wide and long soft leather boots and made Radhai wear them as a protection against nails and broken glass—and the wrath of the women in charge of the communal dining hall.

But there was no denying that his skin was black and theirs was white. And even when they became deeply sunburned in the summer months, the darkest of them was still white when he stood next to Radhai. He noticed that visitors to the kibbutz often stared at him, and once, when the British came to the kibbutz for a periodic search for arms, one soldier became so absorbed in the sight of the black Jew that he was almost left behind when his comrades departed.

Radhai went with the young men and women of the kibbutz on their Sabbath excursions. They danced together and swam together. But the girls tried too hard to be friendly, as if it were an effort they tried to disguise as effortless. When he went with Avinoam, his red-haired roommate and fellow worker in the dairy barn, to neighboring settlements to sell or trade cattle, more than once the small children had run behind him gleefully, calling *"Cushi, Cushi!"* He knew they did not mean it as an epithet; the word simply meant "African," or at worst, "black man." He was indeed a *Cushi* and the children only called out his difference, while their elders thought it. But saying it was so much sharper than thinking it, and those were the times when, in his humiliation, he had wanted to take the great flying boat back to Cairo, and the smaller plane back to Ethiopia, to search for the Falasha villages that Wingate had said were still there, to search for the people of his own kind and be with them.

Radhai thought about Debra Hakim, the village of his birth. His earliest memory was of the day the Christians from the nearby Amhara village of Kumansa had been visited by a new Coptic priest. In a Sunday sermon, the new priest reminded the Amharas of the deicide of the Falashas, who had killed the Savior, and the villagers had set out in a spontaneous crusade to convert the Falashas to the cross of redemption. The Falashas hid behind the hedge that they had planted around their village as a protective barrier, and when the Christians, running at full stride, swept toward the village in a wide, shrieking line, the Falashas fired their ancient single-shot rifles in a volley that downed some of the attackers. Then they gave their rifles to their wives to reload and ran out beyond the hedge with their swords and shields to fight back the Amharas.

If Radhai tried very hard, he could still remember sitting alone in his parents' hut that day and hearing first the volley of shots from the hedge, then an answering volley from the attackers, and then the clashing of metal against metal and the hoarse shouts of men killing and being killed. The shouts were very much the same. Then, when the Amharas had retreated, the Falashas had pulled their dead and wounded back behind the hedge that protected the village and waited for the second assault. The second wave never came. The first hand-to-hand fight with the Falashas had sobered the Amharas and dashed their religious fervor. The Christians left their dead and their dying in the brown sweep of the plateau, and only half as many men who had set out from Kumansa in the morning returned in the evening.

After the day of the clashing swords, Radhai went to live with his Uncle Ya'qob. His mother and Ya'qob's wife had been killed by the first volley of the Amharas. The bullets had penetrated the hedge and sought them out as they reloaded their husbands' rifles. Radhai's father's left arm was severed at the shoulder, and he died during the night. Both Radhai's father and Ya'qob were priests, and when Radhai was young and growing up in his uncle's hut, Ya'qob would take out his father's white turban and show it to the boy and promise him that someday it would be his.

When Radhai was old enough to fast on the numbered holy days, Ya'qob sent him to the *mesgid*, the synagogue, each day with the other boys his age and older. The *dabteras*, the scribes, taught them how to sing the prayers and how to read and write Geez so they could understand the words in the Book of the Law and translate the stories in the other books of sacred writings that were kept in the *mesgid*. The young boys would sit on the cool earthen floor of the *mesgid* and curl their bare feet under their long tunics. They would memorize the prayers that asked God to make the Land of Zion fertile again and bring his people of *Beta-Israel* back across the wild Takkaze River and the broad sea and the desert into the Land of Zion.

Sometimes when he was singing the prayers that he had learned by rote, Radhai would lose himself in a daydream, and he would imagine that God had sent the Messiah into the mountain fastness that surrounded Lake Tana to bring the Falashas back to the Land of Israel. And when the Amharas saw that the Falashas were marching out, just as the Children of Israel had marched out of Egypt, they got down on their knees and begged the Messiah, the seed of David, to take them, too, so they could dwell in the same land that had been the land of their God, Jesus Christ. And the Messiah, who really didn't look very much different from the Falashas and the Amharas, except for the reddish glow that surrounded his white turban and flowing white toga, had gently but firmly pushed the Amharas aside and shaken his head, and, holding the Amharas back with an outstretched arm, had stood by the side of the road and waved the members of the House of Israel past. Whenever he was caught daydreaming, the *dabteras* would scold him and threaten to tell his uncle, since Radhai was destined to be a priest and needed to learn more than the other boys.

His Uncle Ya'qob, in his wisdom, had once told him that the Falashas had waited patiently for 3,000 years for the return to their ancient land and had not tried to hurry the Messiah. No one, he said, could judge the wisdom of God, who would order the Messiah at the right time, just as he ordered the seasons and the coming and going of man.

Wingate had been his Messiah. Wingate had sent him here. He was part of Wingate's dream for Israel, of Wingate's flair for the spectacular. When Wingate became leader of the Jewish army, it was to be Radhai's task to serve him as the symbol of the phoenix Jew. If Wingate had only come it would have been all right. But first there was word that Wingate had been denied permission to return to Palestine. Then he was sent to Burma, where, as leader of the long-range penetration groups behind Japanese lines, he became one of the great heroes of the war and was promoted to major-general. Then the word came to Ein Dvorah in 1944 that he had been killed in an airplane crash in Burma.

The kibbutzniks of Ein Dvorah wept that day, as did other Jews throughout Palestine. But Radhai could not mourn in public. He went into the barn, took off his boots, and sat in the corner of a stall occupied by a cow ready to calve. Here there was the rich smell of the cows and the barn, and the coolness of the dirt under his toes. In the barn there was solitude and he sat there a long time after the last light faded from the open door. At least he had not been robbed of solitude. He had been robbed of everything else and he could not understand why. He could no longer believe as deeply as Ya'qob had believed. He wanted to fathom God's will and find out where this raging stream was taking him. Why had he been set apart to walk the earth alone, a Cain with a mark on his forehead that distinguished him from other men? If there was a destination, a resting place in life, he asked God to show it to him, and he pleaded in the stall of the barn that at least God would stop throwing signs of false hope in his path.

Radhai became master of the dairy barn. He slept in the barn when each new calf was due and brought it into life with tender hands. And although the people of Ein Dvorah cared little whether an animal was killed ritually or not, Radhai became the self-appointed *schochet*, the religious slaughterer, making sure that each animal returned to darkness as quickly and unknowingly as it had come into the light. In time, he learned that he could love the people of Ein Dvorah without resenting the difference that they all knew existed between them.

In somewhat the same way, he had nurtured a bond of comfort toward the occupants of Nahshon's halftrack—with Gingi because he was a spark of Wingate, with Nahshon because his skin was brown and his heart capacity large, with Mordecai because he dared to not kill, with Itzik because he was gentle and slow to speak, with Shulamit because she treated him no nicer than she treated anyone else. She talked, laughed, argued with him without the over-compensating effort he had learned to detect so well. And when she was in one of her moods, she ignored him without apology, just as she ignored the other men in the halftrack.

He wondered if any of them really felt his absence tonight. This had been Nahshon's doing, this business of transferring him to the American's halftrack. Nahshon had denied it, but had left his tracks and scent. Perhaps he should be flattered that Nahshon cared so much for the safety of this boy that he had sent Radhai to watch over him. But Radhai did not want to play the noble savage to the young American or educate him to the delusion that just beneath the pigment they were very much alike. He had had enough of that in his six years in Palestine.

As the convoy turned off the main road eight miles below Acre, the sounds of battle could be heard plainly over the roar of the motors. Troops on both sides were anticipating the end of the truce and firing random shots at each other. Peace passed into war long before the arrival of the dawn deadline and the sounds of combat were no longer isolated notes. They crashed and ricocheted against each other and merged into the rhythm of a war fought ineptly by nations that had not made war a science. The bullets were first, the snare drum, and then the strings; the mortars were the bass, then the cymbals; the machine guns the pizzicato; the engines the French horns; the boots the steel brush against the face of the drum; the cocking of a rifle the brief castanet that preceded the quick dance and the clap of the heel against the floor. These were the sounds, and the nearness and the distance gave them tone, and the momentum of the battle gave them pace—the reluctant first movement, the angry third movement, the crash of recapitulation, and then nothing. The audience was silent and attentive. They were silent and attentive during the concert and after the concert, and only the musicians worked, following the score, and afterwards feeling relief and satisfaction that the performance was done, and waiting for the applause from a silent audience. Then they counted their fellow musicians to determine whether to play an encore or wait until the next night for another Concert Under The Stars.

Somewhere in the distance, many hills and many miles away, was Nazareth. Nazareth was the goal. Nazareth stood astride the main paved road from Haifa to Tiberias. It was the key that would unlock the Southern Galilee. But there were a dozen villages that guarded the approach to Nazareth. Some were large and some small, but all were heavily fortified now and each one would have to be taken before the Israelis could reach the key.

The armored cars moved in a line to the front of the Jewish positions, and, like a handful of turrets atop an ironclad, began to lay down a heavy fire with their light and heavy machine guns. Men dashed out to clear a roadblock and the armored cars rolled forward through the roadblock toward the living and dying flicks of light coming from the dark buildings in the distance. The light mortars were deployed out from the road, and the halftracks turned off the road and moved out into the fields to surround the village and prepare to let the infantry troops dismount on the village flanks.

There was a large flash followed by a bass crack from the village. It was an artillery piece opening up on the line of armored cars. The artillery missile zoomed woefully high over the armored cars. The mortars adjusted their fire to close in on the spot the flash had come from. The duel between the village and the armored cars continued for an hour as the armored cars crept closer to the buildings, to a point where they could lay down an accurate blistering fire.

Evan's halftrack was out in the field now, alone. The nearest halftrack was more than a hundred yards away. The helmetless Gingi had hopped on the running board and positioned Evan there, then hopped off to run across the field and place another halftrack in position. The artillery piece was still trying to find the range of the armored cars. Bullets from the village were whining down at the halftrack and sometimes thudding against the steel plates. Evan leaned across the steering wheel to grope with his eyes through the slot in the lowered steel windshield. In the halftrack, four of the men in the infantry squad were dozing, their helmets on their heads and their blankets wrapped around their bodies to ward off the penetrating chill of the night. Evan marveled again at their ability to sleep through battle, with all the sounds of war warning them of danger. But they slept. The others who were awake were quiet. And sometimes when they talked they whispered as though there were no sounds of battle, as though there were silence in the field and they would be found out if they talked in normal tones. Radhai crouched next to Evan, his hand on the trigger of his German light machine gun, his eyes and helmet poking above the rim of the halftrack.

"Start the motor," Radhai whispered in Hebrew. "The other halftracks are beginning to move."

Evan looked through the slot on the side door. The nearest halftrack was now in motion, digging its tracks into the dirt of the field and moving toward the village. Evan started the motor and let the clutch out to send the halftrack into its slow first gear, then shifted into second. He saw an opening in a low rock wall and threaded the halftrack through it. Radhai aimed and fired bursts from his machine gun. The noise was deafening, gashing at Evan's eardrums. Two hot shells somersaulted through the air and fell on his lap. He tried to sweep them off without looking down at them. A larger rock wall loomed ahead of the halftrack. They were almost at the edge of the village, and bullets were thudding against the halftrack with frequency now.

"*Chaverim!*" Radhai called back to the other men. "All passengers off. *L'hitraot!*"—until we meet again!

One of the sabras was still not completely awake. A friend was shaking him to jog the sleep out of his head. The men opened the back door of the halftrack and jumped out, one at a time. Then they ran in a crouch to the front of the halftrack and sprawled behind the wall.

"Get your Sten gun," Radhai said. "When they get ready to run for those first houses on the other side of the wall, we'll provide cover with every bullet we can shoot."

[106]

The corporal of the squad, a quiet youth with the face and body of a peasant, was at the center of the squad, three men spread out on either side of him. He got off his knees and hunched his body over to stay behind the protection of the wall. Then, looking from one side to the other along the line of his men, much as a football quarterback before calling signals, he threw a knee over the wall and began running toward the nearest building. The other men were right behind him. Radhai opened up with a long burst from his machine gun and Evan peeked above the rim of the halftrack and tried to spray his Sten gun bullets at the window of the building. Both he and Radhai stopped firing as the squad approached the mud-brick structure. The seven men dropped to the ground below the window and hugged the side of the building. The corporal threw a hand grenade through the window and all the men in the squad flattened themselves against the ground. At the blast, shrapnel and debris exploded out of the window, but the wall held. The corporal stood up and fired his Sten gun into the room. Then two of the men climbed in through the window while the others split up and disappeared around the sides of the building.

By dawn the village was won. There were no civilians in the village. They had departed a week before, taking as many of their belongings as they could with them. There were about fifty Arab soldiers left alive, all members of Kaukji's Arab Liberation Army. They were a scraggly-looking bunch of irregulars wearing an assortment of uniforms, many of them the wrong size. They were loaded aboard a truck and sent back toward Haifa.

In the early morning, troops from an infantry battalion marched past to take up advance positions and occupy the village. The squad from Evan's halftrack returned. They were all alive, although there had been light casualties in the other infantry squads. Evan turned the halftrack around and drove back to the road, then up to the edge of the village where the other halftracks were already parked. Uzi, the squad's machine gunner, had the locker of food open. He poured orange juice into Evan's cup and then handed him some crackers and a hunk of cheese. Evan put the cup of orange juice down on the floor near the clutch and brake pedals, and slipped out the side door of the halftrack with his cheese and crackers. He examined the little nicks in the side and windshield cover of the halftrack. The bullets had sounded as though they might dig all the way through the armor plate, but they had made only the slightest dents in the surface of the steel.

Evan walked up the road to Nahshon's halftrack. The Moroccan had one half of the steel hood folded back and was leaning inside poking at the fuel pump.

"This bloody thing is going to give out on me completely one of these days," the dark-skinned corporal said. "It was sputtering this morning."

"Where's Shulamit?"

Nahshon nodded toward the halftrack. It looked empty to Evan. He climbed up on the running board and looked inside. Shulamit was lying on the bench behind her radio set. Her blanket covered her legs and body. She was asleep, threads of hair, loose from the bun, brushing over her face. Itzik was also asleep in the back of the halftrack. He had taken off his stocking cap, folded it on top of the sack of hand grenades, and used it as a miniature pillow. Except for a fringe of hair, he was bald. His blanket was pulled up under his chin.

Evan released his grip on the side of the halftrack and jumped back down from the running board. "A peaceful scene in there," he said, munching on a cracker. "How did they get to sleep so fast?"

"We arrived before you. The officers are already in the village, making plans for tonight's attack."

"How can they keep their eyes open long enough to look at a map?" Evan yawned. "I'm going to get a few hours' sleep."

Nahshon pulled his head out of the halftrack. "Good—just as soon as you check the oil and water and fill up with petrol. The petrol truck will be here soon."

"Okay. I'll take care of it as soon as I wake up."

"Yeled!" Nahshon shouted, his eyes narrowing down to black and bloodshot slits. "You'll take care of it now. We don't know when we'll have to leave again."

Evan nodded wearily. He pulled away the spring snaps and heaved the heavy steel hood cover of his halftrack open. The oil was all right. The water was low. He unstrapped the heavy five-gallon water can and poured water into the radiator until it overflowed. The gasoline truck was about fifty yards away, and its driver was handing down five-gallon cans of gasoline to an armored car driver.

If he drove the halftrack down to the truck, Evan knew he would disturb the eight men who were already trying to go to sleep in, under, and beside the armor-plated vehicle. Evan opened the door of the halftrack and drank down the warm orange juice. The sun was rising now above the flat roofs of the Arab village. He unbuckled his ammunition belt and pulled off his sweater, throwing both of them on the driver's seat. Then he trudged down to the truck and asked for four five-gallon cans of gasoline and a funnel. He carried two cans back to the halftrack, then returned for the other two. The weight of the cans stretched his arms and jerked at his shoulders as he carried them. He let the last two cans drop next to the hard rubber tracks and gave an exhausted sigh.

"Do you need help?" It was Mordecai. The scrawny little medic was right behind Evan, and the unexpected sound of his voice startled him.

"I think I can manage it by myself." Evan climbed up on the side of the halftrack, unscrewed the cap of the gas tank on the left side, and inserted the funnel in the tank opening.

"Let me help you," Mordecai persisted. He heaved one of the gasoline cans up to Evan. "You've been angry with me since the day we met the Arabs on the hill, haven't you?"

"No," Evan lied. He began pouring the gasoline into the tank.

"I could have fired the Sten gun, you know. I was tempted to fire it. Can you understand why I didn't?"

"To tell the truth, Mordecai, no. I can't begin to understand."

"I would like for you to. It would make me feel better about what happened on the hill if you did." He stuck out his left arm and showed Evan a series of faded, tattooed numbers on his wrist. "The numbers are hard to read. The Germans put them there when Aaron and I were children. Our arms have grown. The skin has stretched. But the numbers on our arms are exactly alike, except the last number on my arm is two and the last one on Aaron's is three."

Evan handed him the empty gasoline can and Mordecai lifted another full one up to him. "Aaron and I don't look very much alike, even though we're twins. But our mother always dressed us exactly alike, even on the day when we were to leave for Auschwitz. That is what saved us."

Mordecai told Evan how his entire family had been loaded aboard the cattle car in Debrecen, Hungary, for the trip to the concentra-

[109]

tion camp. When they arrived at Auschwitz, all the other children, including their brothers and sisters, were put aside into a group that eventually would be sent to the gas chambers and crematoria. But a Jewish orderly at the train depot at Auschwitz noticed that their clothes were alike and asked if they were twins. When he discovered that they were, he placed them to the side with several other sets of twins who had come on the same train. They were sent to F Lager, 15th Barracks, known as the *Zwilling Lager,* the Twins Camp. With them in the *Zwilling Lager* were more than fifty sets of male twins, ranging in age from four years old to seventy, and in another camp more than seventy sets of female twins.

The twins offered interesting possibilities for medical research, so they were skimmed off of each arriving trainload of subhumans by the Germans. Even so late in the war, the Germans had an abiding interest in the freaks of nature. In the same barracks with the twins, the Germans also collected midgets and mongolian idiots. They had been preceded in the barracks by Gypsy twins, all of whom had been destroyed like used up white rats when the experiments on them were over. The twins slept on one side of the barracks and the midgets and mongolian idiots slept on the other. They slept six to a bed, three tiers high—eighteen in each three-tiered bunk.

The Twins Camp had been a temporary reprieve from the gas chambers they all knew existed. The Germans wanted their bodies to be healthy for the medical experiments, so the twins were given additional rations of soup and bread, and they were encouraged to play soccer in a field behind the barracks. The Jewish physicians, mostly from Belgium and Czechoslovakia, often risked their lives to cheat on the experiments. Instead of performing the operations they had been ordered to, they would often simply make incisions and then sew the boys and girls back up again.

Most of the German soldiers were kind. After all, the Germans were human, too. They loved children and these were the only children in Auschwitz they were allowed to spare. Even Dr. Josef Mengele, the Angel of Death, the man who determined which of the inmates were healthy enough to continue working and which were sickly enough for the gas chambers—even Dr. Mengele was fond of the twins. Once, while making an inspection of F Lager, he stopped in front of Mordecai and pointed to the pocket of the boy's shirt.

"The pocket," he said in Yiddish, "what do you have in there?"

Mordecai shivered with fear. There were two snapshots in his pocket, one of his mother and one of his father. All the Hungarians had been told to turn in their belongings, including photographs, when they got off the train months before. But Mordecai had hidden the two pictures and now he always carried them with him. Rarely could he bear to look at them, but there was the comfort that they were always there, near him. He took the snapshots out of his pocket and gave them to Dr. Mengele.

Mengele looked at them, then examined the features of the fourteen-year-old twins. Then he looked back at the pictures again. "I'll keep these a few days and have them enlarged," the Angel of Death said. "Then I'll see that they get back to you." He reacted to the stark terror written on the faces of the two twins in a way that was not unkind. His lips curved upward with curious good humor. "In your Hebrew schools," he asked, "what did they teach you about the gentiles?"

The boys, stricken dumb, made no attempt to answer him. Dr. Mengele stared at them for a long moment and then moved on.

In the months that followed, Dr. Mengele remembered their names, and he would call to them sometimes as his black Porsche moved slowly through the *Zwilling Lager* compound. Often Mordecai would wave back.

Mordecai could not believe that these men were cruel, or that they wanted to bring this heartache to the Jews. He could feel, even through his own sense of despair, that these men performed their macabre tasks unwillingly, only because they were ordered to.

"Unwillingly!" Aaron had looked at him as though he were looking at a stranger. Then he had laughed an empty, hopeless laugh. "Yes, as unwillingly as they shave, or shine their boots. They are gassing us and cooking us over there. Everybody says so. And if you don't believe what everybody says, breathe deeply and smell the roasting flesh of your mother and father, or taste their ashes—they float down here every day from the chimneys. But don't tell me to feel sorry for their murderers. I hate the diseased bastards. They are all as guilty as Hitler—the one who locks the door, the one who

[111]

lights the oven, the one who guards this gate. There are orders, and there are orders."

But Mordecai thought often about these Germans who he knew wanted to be merciful, but whose weakness made them like the blades of a thresher, powerless to alter their course or desist from cutting the grain that came beneath their edge. He decided simply, but resolutely, that he would never be the blade of a thresher, that no force, no matter how powerful, could make him take a bullet or a knife or a pellet of death to another human being.

Not Aaron. Aaron hated. He hated the Hungarians who had spit at the Jews as they were herded into the cattle cars in Debrecen. He despised the Jewish doctors who could be ordered like menials to slice into the flesh of the Jewish children. But most of all he hated the Angel of Death in the black Porsche and the members of his Teutonic race who could fill the bellies of the children and smile at them and call them by name—and in the operating rooms, when the arms they had tattooed lay limp, transfer their blood, peel off their skin for grafts, and transplant their vital organs. He hated with a powerful and awful hatred the Aryan scientists who, in the pursuit of science, in the search for everlasting truth, could order the midgets to fornicate with the normal women and the mongolian idiots to fornicate with each other—and wait breathlessly for the products of the unions.

Aaron was full of longing for his parents and brothers and sisters. He wanted to be in the part of the camp they were in. He wanted to share their hunger and their pain. And if they were to be killed, he wanted to share their deaths in defiance of a pointless life. At fourteen, Aaron had come into Auschwitz with the firm belief that there was a God and a Heaven. At fifteen, he clung only to the hope that there was a devil and a Hell and an afterlife for those he hated.

There were only a few thousand living Jews in Auschwitz when the Russians liberated the camp. Among them were eighteen sets of twins, the youngest eight years old, the oldest thirty-five. As soon as they were freed, Mordecai and Aaron began a search through Auschwitz for their brothers and sisters and parents. From other inmates they learned that all their brothers and sisters had been killed, but that both parents had been shipped away many months before to a slave labor factory. No one knew where. The two twins lived in D.P. camps in Austria and France, always questioning every refugee about their parents. That no one they spoke to knew the names of their parents Mordecai saw as hope that they might still be alive. Aaron saw it as proof that they were dead.

The twins had come to Palestine a few months before the establishment of the State of Israel. They came in a small refugee ship that slipped through the British blockade. Once ashore, Mordecai continued his quest for his parents, writing letters to every Displaced Persons center in Europe. But Aaron buried his parents and began his quest for Germans. Every Arab was a German, every dog was a German, and he lived for the realization of his dream that one day he would have at his mercy a real German.

"And even though I can never take a human life," Mordecai told Evan, "I understand exactly why Aaron feels the way he does. I don't love him any less because of it."

"I think his attitude is more understandable than yours," Evan said. "Revenge is a normal desire."

"Were any of your relatives killed by the Germans?" Mordecai asked him.

"None that I knew existed."

"Do you have relatives in Israel?"

"No."

"Then there is something about you that I cannot understand. Why have you come so far to kill?"

Chapter Eight

THE ARMORED REGIMENT ATTACKED THE NEXT VIL-lage at dusk, overcame it by midnight, and pushed on to take still another village before dawn. Each battle was different, yet somehow the same: the sounds of bullets resonating in the low hills, the tight sensation in the stomach and gut, the exhaustion in the early morning, the deserted stone and rubble buildings of the villages, the ill-clad Arab soldiers looking like they

[113]

wanted to sleep and be reborn again free of the Jews, and the dead Arabs and dead Jews looking like they would awaken soon from their bloody rest. Evan should have been saddened and filled with compassion at the sight of the twisted, inert bodies beside the road, crushed so irrevocably in the first fullness of manhood. But he was too pleased to be alive, too happy that he was not the red-stained sleeping figure next to the road.

On the sixth night, the armored regiment led the attack on the town of Shafa Amr, which lay across the main road to Nazareth. Evan's halftrack was again in a flanking position, with the armored cars attempting to force themselves through the broad road that led into the center of the Arab town.

The infantry squad from Evan's halftrack ran into the town along a narrow dirt street. They were firing straight ahead and checking each house that they came to for Arab soldiers. Evan guided the halftrack into the street and drove just behind them while Radhai gave covering fire with spurts from his machine gun. The jagged sounds of gunfire and exploding grenades surrounded them with a wall of noise as oppressive as the walls of the stone, one-story houses fronting on the narrow street.

The halftrack moved slowly down the street, following the squad of infantry. Evan opened the slot in the windshield cover all the way so he could see better. There was an ample amount of moonlight, but he was finding it difficult to judge the distance from the buildings, which were only a few feet on either side of the halftrack. Ejected shells from Radhai's clattering machine gun were spinning into the air and plunking against his helmet as they came down.

Ahead, a half a block away, he could see another halftrack stopped. Its machine gun was spitting little flames at something farther down the street. As he came closer to the vehicle, Evan could see the aerial that marked it as Nahshon's halftrack. The tip of the aerial, he noticed, was almost as high as the edges of the flat roofs on both sides of the halftrack. As his eyes glanced at the aerial, Evan saw a dark figure crawl on its hands and knees across the roof of the building to the right of Nahshon's halftrack and stop at the edge almost immediately over the hood of the vehicle. Evan was stunned for a few seconds, paralyzed almost in the same way he had been when the Arabs' heads first appeared above the crest of the hill in the rock-throwing incident. He reached out and hit Radhai's left arm hard.

"Over the halftrack!" he shouted.

Radhai looked quickly up to the roof beside Evan's halftrack.

"No!" Evan shouted again in panic. "Over Nahshon's!"

Radhai saw. But it was too late. The Arab was throwing what looked like a rock over the side of the building. It fell into Nahshon's halftrack. Within another second Radhai had opened fire on the figure, which was now standing to run back across the roof, and Itzik, in Nahshon's halftrack, had turned his machine gun hard to the right and aimed up at the edge of the building. The door next to the driver's seat flew open and Nahshon came hurtling out, missing the running board and hitting the ground on his left shoulder. Another figure leaped over the side of the halftrack, hitting the ground on its feet, but then tumbling over on its back and contracting into a tight ball in the dirt.

The running figure on the rooftop fell and disappeared from view, either hit by one of Radhai's bullets or tripped. An explosion in Nahshon's halftrack for a split-second drowned out all the other noises of battle. Flames and smoke geysered out the top of the steel vehicle. Then there was the relative quiet of distant rifles and machine guns again. A machine gun, its muzzle pointing straight up to the sky as the butt hung below the inside rim of the halftrack, stood alone on the front edge of Nahshon's vehicle.

"Great God!" Evan whispered. It had happened so fast. If he had been inside the halftrack, he knew he wouldn't have escaped. He would have sat there stunned while the grenade blew him to bits. He opened his door, grabbed his Sten gun, and scrambled out into the street. Radhai had vaulted over to the hood and was now leaping to the ground.

The infantry squad from Evan's halftrack was already at the two figures sprawled on the ground when Radhai and Evan got there. The figure that had jumped over the edge was Shulamit. She was sitting on the ground, her legs sprawled out in front of her. Nahshon was lying on his back. Two men tried to lift him to his feet. Nahshon gritted his teeth in pain. "Stop! Let me back down." He was down on his back again. He closed his eyes briefly, then opened them. "Now, *chaverim*, pull me up by my right arm. Don't touch the left one." They reached for his right arm and pulled him to a sitting position, then up to his feet. The left arm hung by his side. "Go along," he ordered the men in the infantry squad who had paused. "We're all right now. You're needed up ahead."

Radhai and Evan were kneeling next to Shulamit when Nahshon walked over to them.

"You're sure you aren't hurt?" Evan was asking the Israeli girl. She nodded her head. "Where's Itzik? He got out, didn't he?"

"I yelled for him to jump," Nahshon said.

"Only two people jumped out of the halftrack," Evan said.

Shulamit put her head in her hands. Her hair was completely disheveled and powdered with dirt from the street. "He may be alive," she said. "See if you can help him."

Evan was afraid to look. But while Radhai climbed up on the tracks to peer inside, the American poked his head through the open door. It was difficult to see in the dark. The instrument panel was shattered and twisted. Next to the driver's seat, shoved up against the gears, was the crumpled body in a glazed pool of blood. The helmet, dented by shrapnel, was still on Itzik's head. The entire right side of his body, from the helmet to the frayed clothing and ripped boot, had been badly chewed by the direct burst of shrapnel. Evan looked away. There was a ragged hole in the floor of the halftrack bed. The grenade had apparently been lying at that point when it exploded.

Evan stepped back down to the road. "He's dead." He tried to fight the erupting sensation of nausea, but even more he tried to fight the thoughts in his mind that kept telling him it was better that it had happened to Itzik rather than to Evan Copperman.

"Why didn't he jump over to the hood?" Nahshon said. "I yelled for him to jump."

A life could vanish so swiftly, Evan thought. It could be torn away with such haste that there were those who would sleep tonight and wake up tomorrow morning with the secure feeling that Itzik was still alive. "Did he have a family?" he asked.

"He had a wife and two sons," Shulamit said. "His wife is still on a kibbutz near Hadera. One son was killed in the fighting at Latrun. The other one is in an army unit in the Negev."

"It's over for him now," Nahshon said curtly. "Come. We've got to get this halftrack out of the street."

"Why?" Evan asked. Machine gun and rifle fire and the sound of exploding grenades were now coming from the far end of the town.

"Because I say so," Nahshon declared angrily. "Don't ask so damn many questions and do as I tell you." The Moroccan grabbed the steering wheel of the damaged halftrack and tried to pull himself inside. He winced as his left arm hit the door. He stepped back down from the running board.

"That arm's really hurt," Evan said. "Let me take a look at it."

"No point," the Moroccan said. "I think the collar bone is broken. I hit it bloody hard. See if the halftrack will start."

Evan climbed into the driver's seat. His right hip brushed against the helmet on Itzik's head. He pushed the starter. The motor turned over, but wouldn't catch.

"The damn fuel pump," Nahshon said.

The crazy Moroccan, Evan thought. The whole inside of the halftrack had been destroyed by shrapnel, yet he was blaming motor failure on a bad fuel pump.

"Leave it in neutral," Nahshon called. "Radhai, get in and guide where I tell you to. Yeled will push with his halftrack."

While Evan walked back to his own halftrack, Radhai climbed into the damaged vehicle. The Falasha looked down for a moment at Itzik, then looked up again. With Nahshon directing with his good right hand, Evan pushed the damaged halftrack up about two blocks to a place where the street widened. There was now room for other vehicles to pass the crippled vehicle. Shulamit and Radhai helped Nahshon climb through the back door of Evan's halftrack, then followed him.

"Gingi is probably wondering where the hell we are," the Moroccan said. "He expected us to be right behind him. Come on."

Evan followed the street, which soon led into the main road through town. He drove east and passed two deserted halftracks. There was only the sound of an occasional shot off into the hills when the halftrack arrived at the other edge of town. Most of the vehicles in the armored unit were parked at the edge of the road. Gingi was in the middle of the road, the gunnysack of grenades slung over his shoulder. He saw Nahshon standing in the front of the halftrack next to Radhai and came over to them. Nahshon explained what had happened.

"Then that makes three halftracks we lost that way tonight. Bert and his machine gunner were killed. Ephriam managed to get out of his. They were waiting for us on the roofs. They know the half-tracks have no protection from that direction. Tell all the drivers, Nahshon, that from now on no halftrack will go into a town or village while fighting's in progress. Another night like this and we won't be able to move."

"My halftrack's all right," Nahshon said. "If I can get the fuel pump working we can still use it."

"If you can get your arm working," Evan interrupted. "His collar bone is probably broken."

"Get it taken care of," Gingi said. He climbed up on one of the rubber tracks and lifted the gunnysacks gently into the back of Evan's halftrack. "Lucky for you," he told Nahshon, "that I took these hand grenades with me. Turned out we didn't need them." He looked at Shulamit. "Are you all right?"

"I sprained my ankle a little. Otherwise I'm fine."

"Good. I'm going to see if we can't borrow or steal another radio." Gingi walked back down the road looking for regimental head-quarters.

Nahshon went to the back door, sat down, and slid to the ground. "I'll hitch a ride with an ambulance going back to Haifa. Yeled, take Gingi, Shulamit, and Mordecai in your halftrack until I get back tonight or tomorrow. Tell Alex, the wrecker driver, where my halftrack is and ask him to check the fuel pump. Tell him I'll pick it up here on my return trip."

The armored regiment paused the remainder of that day and evening, and the next night dashed fifteen miles through the hill country for the attack on Saffuriya, the source of Nazareth's water supply. This time the Arabs made a strong stand before the village in the wooded hills that bordered the road. They fired down on the armored column from the heights, and the column had to halt for a number of hours while the infantry troops charged up through the trees on the hillsides and cleared the area of Arab soldiers.

Evan's halftrack was now temporarily the first halftrack in the column since, in addition to the squad of infantry, he now carried Gingi, Mordecai, Shulamit, and a newly-acquired radio. He was relieved of those duties that afternoon in Saffuriya, however, when Nahshon came speeding into the Arab village. Despite the fact that the instrument panel in the halftrack had been shattered, the trouble, Alex discovered, was indeed in the fuel pump, and he had patched it together so Nahshon could continue to drive the vehicle in combat. The doctor at the hospital in Haifa had wanted to put Nahshon's shoulder in a cast, but the Moroccan had talked the doctor into giving him a corset brace for the cracked bone so he could use his arm and drive the halftrack.

"I checked on your American friend, Yeled," Nahshon said. "He is still more dead than alive. He lost a tremendous amount of blood before the doctors could sew him up. The doctor told me he will recover, however. It will be a long time."

Nahshon had arrived back just in time for the assault on Nazareth. But the battle for the main prize proved to be an anti-climax. The city fell too easily. The armored regiment knocked out six of the eight armored vehicles the Arabs sent out to face them, and before dusk controlled all the roads leading into Nazareth. The Israelis then opened a hole in a roadblock to send two jeeps with machine guns blazing through the main street. The last bit of resistance came to an end in the city proper and the armored regiment attacked the police fortress on the outskirts only to find it had been abandoned by Arab troops.

Another truce was scheduled to go into effect in two more days and perhaps afterwards there would be no more battles in the land. Even now they had news that the Egyptians were being hammered back in the northern Negev, the corridor to Jerusalem was being widened, frantic efforts were being made to recapture the Old City of Jerusalem from the Arab Legion, and in the Eastern Galilee frontal attacks by the Iraqis and Syrians had been repulsed.

But the victorious entrance of the armored regiment into Nazareth had a different character than any of the other victories the Israelis had won. Perhaps it was because almost all of the inhabitants of the city were still there and few of the buildings had been damaged. But it was more than that. Although Nazareth was an Arab city, it had a Christian character. Many of the Arabs were Christians. There were monasteries on the hillsides and numerous Christian retreats and churches throughout the city. Even the Israeli soldiers' exuberance at reaching their goal was tempered with the awe that they were the conquerors of such a city.

Radhai stood straight and proud in the front of the halftrack as it rolled slowly in a show of might through the city. But when the armored column pulled to a stop next to a row of deserted shops,

[119]

Radhai shook his head with dissatisfaction. "This is not the way to parade into a conquered city. Gingi or the regimental colonel should have been at the head of the column on a white horse."

"A white horse!" Evan laughed.

"The white horse is a symbol of victory. It's important that we let the people of Nazareth know who the victors are. When we won Addis Ababa from the Italians in 1941, Wingate rode a white horse at the head of the parade that brought Haile Selassie back into the city. He wanted the emperor to ride the horse, to prove to the people that the city was his and that the Italians would never take it again. But the emperor preferred to ride in an open car."

"Did you see the parade, Radhai?"

"I marched in the first row of the 2nd Ethiopian Battalion, right behind Wingate. I was about your age, but I had already been fighting the Italians for four years."

He had been sixteen, he told Evan, when he had come down from the mountains above Lake Tana and joined the forces of Lij Hailu Balao, chieftain of a patriot group fiercely loyal to Haile Selassie. Balao had believed Radhai's story that he was a Christian whose village in the Semien district had been destroyed by the Italians.

Balao had been chief of the Amhara Saint district east of the Blue Nile before the Italian conquest. Now he and his band of fighters roamed the area to the south of Lake Tana, raiding Italian outposts and patrols, never giving up hope that the emperor would one day return and vanquish the invaders.

Balao's patriot group used as its headquarters the small village of Safarboto, not far from Bahrdar Giorgis on the southeastern point of Lake Tana, where it spills into the Blue Nile. Radhai returned there with them. They gave him a spear to use in battle—the only guns they had were those they took from the Italians, and these were often without ammunition—and Radhai used his weapon with a blood lust that sometimes made him ashamed. Whenever he felt the spear thrust into the body of an Italian or one of their colonial troops, he received such a feeling of satisfaction that he often lunged it into the body again and again.

Radhai's body matured into that of a man in his four years with Balao. He laughed and ate and fought with the Amhara warriors, for he had determined that he would live the way he had been told some of the villages of the Falasha monks had lived. Outwardly they were Christians. Inwardly they were of the House of Israel. He learned early that he could be as close to the Amharas as flesh to flesh and still stand apart. For whether he ate with the Amhara warriors or slept with an Amhara woman, he was still alone, fulfilling the needs that would allow him to stay alone as a Falasha.

Sometimes he asked himself why he wanted to remain a Falasha, even secretly, if he was indeed the last of his kind. Then he would remind himself that God had had a reason for preserving him. He would await the will of God. Only when he fought was he one with the Amharas. When they fought in the night, creeping up on Italian sentries or waiting in the daytime to ambush Italian patrols, he was an Amhara and they were Falashas. He could be one with them then.

Early in 1941, Balao received a message that the emperor and Ethiopian troops commanded by British officers had re-invaded Ethiopia the month before and were now fighting the Italians near the Sudanese border. The message said that a British army was also attacking from the south. There was great rejoicing among the patriots. When word of the double invasion spread, hundreds of men who had shown no interest in war for five years joined the forces of Balao. Soon, Balao marched his ragged band of men to Burye, which had just been captured by Ethiopian troops fighting under the British officers.

The Italians had built fortifications on the hills to the east of the small town, and it was in this area that the Balao irregulars rested. The hill on which Radhai and the Amharas made their temporary camp was truly a rotten spoil of war. Barbed wire and communications wire, severed in a hundred places, lay lifeless across the open ditches and mounds of dirt that marked the interlocking trenches. Donkeys and mules, shot several days before in the battle for the area, remained unburied, bloated and stinking. A few stone command huts sat uneasily on the top of the hill and looked down at the filth of humans and animals.

The Balao men had arrived in Burye in the late afternoon. The next morning the corpulent Balao formed his barefoot men in jagged lines to be reviewed by the British colonel who headed the Ethiopian regulars.

While Balao's irregulars stood in the files, gripping their rifles and spears, some of the regular troops in the 2nd Ethiopian Battalion squatted on their ankles nearby watching the show. The battalion had been formed of Ethiopian refugees in the Sudan, and they had been trained by British officers and non-commissioned officers for the invasion. They joked among themselves about the tramp-like attire of the patriots. One of the Ethiopian soldiers kept staring at Radhai. When Balao walked down the line to give his troops a final inspection before the British officer arrived, the soldier stood up and shouted at the chief. "Oh Lij Hailu Balao," he said good-naturedly, "is there such a shortage of men in Ethiopia that you have enlisted Falashas?"

Balao turned and advanced toward the man menacingly. "You son of a jackal," Balao said, "do you dare to stand here and insult my men, who by themselves have turned back the entire army of Ras Hailu?"

Surprise crossed the soldier's face. "I meant no harm," he retreated. "But you do have a Falasha with you." He pointed toward Radhai.

The chieftain turned his head and examined Radhai, as though looking at him for the first time since he had joined the patriot band.

"He lies," Radhai said, lifting his spear and holding it in the position of attack. He stepped out of line and walked toward the soldier.

"I could lie about many things," the soldier said angrily, pulling a gleaming bayonet out of the sheath on his belt, "but not about a Falasha. I lived near a Falasha village for thirty years. I can tell a Falasha as soon as I am near enough to see the shape of his face." The two men were circling each other now, each waiting for the other to make a mistake in his guard that would open the way to death. Balao's men had broken ranks, such as they were, and were shouting for Radhai to kill the soldier. The soldier's comrades were also shouting encouragement, and some of them were drawing their bayonets. Balao stood in the tightening circle with the two combatants, like an unwilling referee. He was afraid that his men and the soldiers would fall upon each other as soon as blood was drawn in the circle, but he didn't know how to break up the fight without losing the respect of his men.

Suddenly there was a fourth man in the circle. He was a white-skinned British officer dressed in a dirty khaki uniform and khaki sweater. A short beard covered most of his face, and he wore a huge pith helmet which almost hid his eyebrows and ears. The man had forced himself through the wall of soldiers and patriots and was shouting "Stop!" in Amharic as loudly as he could. He stepped between Radhai and the Ethiopian soldier. First he turned to the soldier and threw his fist into the soldier's stomach with all his might. The soldier doubled over, then fell on his side in the dust. He looked at the British officer out of the corner of his eye and began pushing his body backward through the dust toward his fellow soldiers. The British officer turned toward Radhai and reached for his spear, putting a hand on the shaft and pulling on it. Radhai tightened his grip and defiantly refused to let go. The officer let loose of the shaft and shouted at Balao, "Is this how you parade your men?"

Balao shook his head. "The parade was ready. But one of your soldiers called this man a Falasha."

The British officer's features shifted immediately from anger to curiosity. He peered at Radhai from under his enormous pith helmet. His eyes were a piercing light blue, and they were set deep, yet close together as they flanked the prominent hawk nose. He reminded Radhai of an exotic jungle bird that somehow had once flown into the Semien mountain country. The white-skinned man with the strange hat was in the center of a host of blacks, almost all of whom were taller than he. Yet the original reason for his breaking into the circle now apparently escaped the man. He continued to examine Radhai, first walking to one side to catch his profile, then walking in front of him to see his full face, as though he were an artist preparing to paint a portrait.

"Yes, yes, by heavens, he is a Falasha," the officer declared.

"Perhaps. Perhaps not," Balao said firmly, recovering his composure of command. "I don't care. He's one of my best soldiers. He fought the Italians for years while these warriors of yours were wallowing in the whorehouses of Khartoum."

"Certainly. He's a good man," the British officer said. "Send him to my quarters to see me as soon as the parade is over." The officer stepped aside and took no further notice of Radhai while Balao yelled at his men and shoved them back into their uneven lines. The regular Ethiopian soldiers drifted away from the area. The British officer walked up and down the lines, checking the unusual attire of the irregulars. Radhai wore an Italian officer's jacket that was three sizes too small for him and a pair of short trousers that had been washed until they were completely bleached and frayed. He wore an empty leather ammunition belt around his waist and, of course, no shoes.

After the British officer departed, Balao made the men stand in their files for fifteen more minutes, during which he shouted at them and warned them that he would hack off their heads with his sword if they ever again disgraced him as he had been disgraced that morning when they left their positions and gathered around to watch the fight between Radhai and the Ethiopian soldier. Then he told Radhai to report to Col. Orde Wingate and dismissed the men.

Radhai did not want to see the officer. First of all, he didn't trust the white-skinned man. Second, he was afraid the officer wanted to whip him for causing the disturbance at the inspection. He decided he would take his spear with him. When he arrived at the stone headquarters building at the top of the hill, he was directed to Colonel Wingate's room.

When Radhai entered the room, Wingate was lying on a cot completely naked. He was scratching his stomach and legs with a thick tree branch. Two other white-skinned men sat on a cot on the other side of the small room, but they were wearing their clothes.

Wingate spoke to Radhai first in a language the Falasha could not understand, then waited a moment. When Radhai gave no answer he said in Amharic, "Ah, then it's true. You Falashas have no knowledge of Hebrew."

Radhai shook his head.

"Sorry. My Amharic is very bad, I know," the British colonel said. "I picked up a bit of it years ago when we caught Ethiopians trying to poach elephants in the Sudan. And several times I visited Coptic churches across the border in Ethiopia. But I haven't had a chance on this mission to do more than brush up on it. Do you speak Arabic?"

Radhai shook his head again at the strange naked man.

"A pity," the colonel continued in Amharic. "I can speak Arabic almost as well as English and better than Hebrew." He hopped up from his cot and circled Radhai again. He spoke in Hebrew now to the two men on the cot. "A perfect Falasha type. This is the first one I've ever seen. He has all the Hamitic characteristics, with just a trace of the Semitic. Notice the light black color of the skin and the regular Caucasian features—straight nose, thin lips, high forehead. Look at the face. It has the Agau influence—according to the books I've read, this lad's Semitic ancestors married into and converted the Agau tribe. Mark that his face isn't as long as the Amharas and his eyes are slightly smaller."

Wingate's face transmitted the excitement of an anthropologist who has made an important find. "Take off your jacket," he ordered in Amharic.

Radhai unbuttoned the small Italian officer's jacket with one hand and held on to his spear with the other. Now he knew he would get the whip. There was no doubt of it. But he debated whether he should take the punishment, or take only as much as he thought he could stand, or run away before the first lash fell.

Wingate examined the dark muscular chest and back. "Yes, it's quite apparent." He was speaking in Hebrew again now. "The bone structure is heavier than that of the Amharas. We have a discovery here. A perfect Falasha." He lay back down on the cot and began scratching himself with the stick again. "All right," he said in Amharic. "You can put your jacket back on."

Radhai was bewildered. Wingate took no note of it.

"What's your name?" the naked colonel asked.

"Radhai."

"What are you doing in these parts? I didn't know there was a Falasha village for hundreds of miles."

"There are no more Falasha villages," Radhai said. "The Italians have destroyed them all."

"No. You have to be wrong. There are several dozen just three or four hundred miles northwest of here." He pulled a rolled-up map from behind his cot and spread it out on the floor. "See, here they are. Our aircraft have passed over them in the last few weeks, and they've reported no destruction."

"They're all destroyed," Radhai insisted. "The Falashas have been killed."

"You're wrong. There are thousands and thousands of Falashas still alive in Ethiopia."

Radhai shook his head. Wingate turned to the other two men and told them in Hebrew what Radhai had said. One of them said something to Wingate in Hebrew and Wingate spoke again to Radhai. "My friend here says that he knows of several families of Falashas living right now in Jerusalem."

Radhai gripped his spear with angry tightness. These men were trying to bait him. First they had tried to frighten him by threatening to whip him and now they were trying to make him admit that he was lying. "Your friend does not tell the truth," he told Wingate. "The people of the House of Israel cannot return to Jerusalem until the Messiah comes and leads us there. And if the Messiah had already come, I would know it, for of all the House of Israel, only I remain." It was a point that they could not refute and Radhai made it triumphantly.

Wingate stared at Radhai for a moment. He had not understood the meaning of some of the words Radhai had spoken, but the message the Falasha was trying to get across was beginning to dawn on him.

"Are you saying that you believe you're the last Jew left alive in the world?"

Radhai nodded.

The naked officer lay back on his cot and began chuckling. He closed his eyes and chuckled more intensely, the white skin on his stomach percolating with each convulsion. He was unable to talk for a few minutes. Then he turned again to the two men on the other cot who did not yet know the reason for his amusement. He could hardly translate for them what Radhai had just said before he fell back into the paroxysm of almost-silent laughter. After another few minutes he regained control of himself, and, with an amused look on his face, pointed to the two grinning men on the cot and said to Radhai, "What would you say if I told you that these two soldiers are Jews, also?"

Radhai looked at the two men curiously and not without some anger that the officer was persisting in the joke. That there were other Jews still alive was perhaps possible. But even a child would not believe that there were Jews who looked like Italians and Englishmen.

"And that they both live in the Land of Israel?" Wingate continued.

Radhai had already lost his secret that day, but not his pride and self-respect. They were making him play the fool. He moved his hand toward the balance point of the shaft, and the heavy iron point fell forward until the spear was horizontal with the floor. He went into a slight crouch and began backing toward the door.

"Wait!" Orde Wingate was an extremely sensitive man. He realized now that the tall muscular Falasha was not sophisticated enough to be treated with humor. He stopped smiling, sat up on the edge of his cot and gave a curt command to the two men on the other cot. They immediately stopped grinning, although for one it was a mighty effort.

"You don't really believe these men could be Jews, do you?"

At the first command, Radhai had stopped retreating. But he was still in the half crouch, his spear poised. "No."

"Radhai, I'm transferring you to the 2nd Ethiopian Battalion. I would like to have you as my personal guard. Is that all right with you?"

Radhai was confused. But he could see the fun-making was over. The British officer had said the words sincerely. Radhai nodded.

"Good." Wingate turned to one of the men on the cot. "Put him on the roster as my batman." The corner of his mouth curled into a half smile. "And I don't give a damn what his last name is. His name on our rolls will be Radhai Hayehudi-Ha'acharon—Radhai The-Last-Jew."

They took away Radhai's spear and replaced it with a Springfield rifle. In place of the Italian officer's jacket, they gave him a turtleneck khaki sweater. He wore new khaki shorts and the olive drab wrap-around leggings from his ankles to his knees. And on top of his rippling black curls they perched a misshapened cotton khaki overseas cap. A long leather belt that held bullets for his rifle was wrapped three times around his waist. Like the other Ethiopian soldiers, Radhai wanted no shoes and wore no shoes.

The Falasha soon discovered that Wingate did not expect him to assume the formal duties of a batman. Wingate had no desire for a personal servant as did some of his subordinate British officers. But he kept Radhai as close to him as he did his Jewish aide, and whenever he had the opportunity he pumped Radhai for information about the Falashas and their customs. Slowly, Radhai's attitude toward the strange man changed. He found that he was not in the position of being a black-skinned Jewish slave to a white-skinned Christian overlord. Rather, Wingate treated the Falasha as a companion, giving him orders only because he was older and wiser, and accepting the services of Radhai because the tall Falasha was his friend.

When Wingate knew that he had won Radhai's confidence, he told the Falasha that the legends of his people contained some inaccuracies—not because his ancestors had intended to deceive, but because of their centuries of isolation. Although almost all of the Jews in ancient Israel had been dispersed by the Babylonians and Romans, he said, there were still millions of Jews in the world. There were even a few who had never left the Holy Land, and their descendants lived there even today. The Jews who left the Holy Land lived among other peoples for thousands of years, and they began to look like those people in whose lands they lived. Many had the white skins and even the blue eyes of the people of the north. Some of these Jews, like their Falasha cousins, were waiting for the Messiah to lead them back to the Holy Land. There were others who never wanted to return. And there were still others who had determined to return at once to the land of their forefathers to seek refuge from their oppressors.

And now, Wingate told him, the Jews were returning to Israel by the thousands. They were building cities and making the desert green with crops, but still their enemies did not relent. And he, Wingate, had promised them that he would lead a Jewish army and help them wrest the land from those who would deny it to them. The time was near for the struggle, Wingate said, and when it came he wanted Radhai to be there to help fight for the land that was his, also.

Radhai's new-found faith in the English officer was such that he believed the story. But Radhai said he could not help wondering how deep these other Jews' devotion to Israel really was, considering that their ancestors had intermarried and become white-skinned and therefore thinned the Jewish blood in their veins.

Wingate smiled. "They would probably wonder the same thing about you, Radhai. They believe the skin of the ancient Jews was white—or at the worst a very, very light brown."

Radhai dismissed this argument. It was well known by even the greatest enemies of the House of Israel that the Falashas rarely mixed with non-Jews and never intermarried with them.

Wingate did not try to disillusion the Falasha. In Palestine he had once told a German-Jewish engineer who was a friend of his that there was anthropological evidence that the Israelites who fled from Egypt had deep brown skins, considerably darker than those of the Canaanites with whom they later intermarried—and Wingate had noted that the man listened to the argument with angry, silent disbelief written on his face. Wingate had discovered that man always created God in his own image, and the fetishes of organized religion, whether they were ancestors, Olympian gods, fertility statues, or messiahs, were no exceptions. The farther north one got, the lighter the pictures of Christ became, and the farther south the darker, until Swedish portraits of the Savior showed him with blond beard and blue eyes, and the Ethiopian murals made him look very much like Haile Selassie.

In the battles leading up to the capture of Debra Markos, Radhai learned why Wingate had already earned a reputation as an outstanding fighting man. One night he and the English officer manned the mortar by themselves, and on another joined a machine gunner whose ammunition carriers had been killed. Everywhere there was Wingate, giving orders as if he had had them memorized for weeks, sending Radhai as a runner to the flanking positions when radio communications broke down, encouraging the Ethiopians to assault the enemy and destroy him.

The Falasha was at Wingate's side at Dambacha when word came that the Italians, thinking Wingate's Gideon Force was one hundred times its size, had evacuated Debra Markos. Radhai hopped in the back of the truck that rushed Wingate to Debra Markos and saw him accept the surrender from an Italian captain in the central fort. While they were in the fort a telephone began ringing and Wingate told an American newspaper correspondent who spoke Italian to answer it and tell the Italians on the other end of the line that Debra Markos had surrendered and that a British division ten thousand strong was marching toward the Blue Nile. As a result of the phone conversation, the Italians abandoned their defenses before the Blue Nile and dashed across the river in retreat, leaving the way open to the recapture of Addis Ababa.

The longer Radhai was with Wingate the more he began to suspect that Wingate was not a Christian at all. The Englishman's abiding love for Israel and his affinity for Jews convinced the Falasha that Wingate was actually a Jew in disguise, operating something like the elusive (at least Radhai had never seen one) Falasha monks who pretended to be Christians but really practiced Judaism in secret.

One night, while they were chasing the retreating Italians to the north, Radhai and Wingate sat around a fire the Falasha had built in front of the command tent. They were in the mountains now and they seemed to be nearer the stars that pierced the cloudless black sky. Wingate stared into the flames and listened to the crackle of the sticks that were being consumed. There were other camp noises in the distance—men shouting and pack camels whining in the unfamiliar mountain air. But as long as there was only Radhai along, Wingate could expect silence at the fireside. The Palestinian Jews, when they were around, rarely stopped talking. The tall Ethiopian Jew hardly ever opened his mouth. Wingate believed Radhai could go weeks without saying a word, but it was a quality which the British officer appreciated. Wingate was a brooder, and often when he brooded he didn't like his thoughts to be interrupted. When he talked, he liked to do most of the talking.

"I read somewhere that a Falasha girl who's found to be unchaste is made to leap into a flaming fire," Wingate said. "Is that true?"

"No. Why would we make the girl leap into the fire and not the boy who is also guilty?" The British officer was asking again about the Falashas. Radhai knew he would have to ask the question that had been on his lips for weeks.

"You are not a Christian, are you?" he asked the British officer. "You are a member of the House of Israel. If it is so, you can tell me now and I swear by my belief in the One God that I will never reveal it to anyone."

Wingate did not answer for a number of seconds that seemed like minutes. When he did answer, he did not look at Radhai, but at the center of the fire. "No, Radhai, I'm sorry to disappoint you, but I'm not a Jew. I believe in the sweet teachings of Jesus, and I believe he was really sent by God to show the world a better way, but the world would not listen. I don't believe that Jesus was God, or that there was a virgin birth, or that his body rose up to heaven, or in the fetishes or myths. But I don't believe a person has to. If anyone called me a Christian I would be very honored." He glanced over at Radhai, who was looking at the ground in disappointment. "And I have never forgotten that Jesus came from the Jews and considered himself a Jew until the moment of his death on the cross. We Christians have tried to make a Christian out of him, but he lived and died a Jew. I envy you Jews, because you were chosen by God to be a light unto the nations. That is your destiny. It's mine to help the Jews become a nation again."

Months later, after Wingate's Gideon Force had defeated and captured an Italian unit twenty times its size and put an end to the fighting in the north, they returned to Addis Ababa, where Wingate learned that he was to report to Cairo for new orders. Radhai rode to the airfield in the back of the truck with Wingate's luggage. At the airport, the British officer gave Radhai one of his hawk-like looks.

"Radhai," he said, "I hope while in Cairo to be given permission to return to Palestine and form a Jewish army. I can't imagine, now, having a Jewish army without a Falasha. When I told the emperor goodbye this morning, I asked only one favor of him—that he release you from the 2nd Ethiopian Battalion and allow you to return to Palestine with my Palestinian volunteers. He gave it. Will you go?"

"Yes."

"I expected you would. I've already written to friends at Ein Dvorah in the Valley of Jezreel. You'll live with them until I can set up some kind of headquarters in Palestine. Then you'll join me again."

Wingate turned to his Jewish aide and told him to make sure Radhai got out of Ethiopia and to Palestine. Then he shook hands warmly with the aide and Radhai, walked to the plane, and disappeared inside. The plane fanned up a huge cloud of dust as it gathered speed for the takeoff. Then it was airborne and became a small dot vanishing toward the land of Egypt.

Radhai had been unable to talk with the Palestinian doctors attached to Wingate's staff in the almost three months he had been with Wingate. They could speak only a few words of Amharic. But now that he was with them much of the time, they began to teach him Hebrew. The language came easy for Radhai, as if somewhere in the recesses of his brain there was a memory pocket that recognized familiar words and phrases.

Within two months Radhai and three of the doctors were on a British cargo plane flying in the direction of Cairo. Far below them the Nile River took strength from its tributaries and twisted and turned with young power through the mountain country, then matured into an ever-broadening stream, and slowed and straightened for the long trip to the sea.

From Cairo the four men were transferred to a large flying boat that was on its way to India. The plane climbed above the Sinai Peninsula, crossed over Beersheba and headed northeast to the Dead Sea. Below were the mountains and hill country of Israel. As Radhai stared spellbound at the earth passing under the struts of the great wings, he had a feeling that, just as in the case of the Hebrew language, there was a familiarity to this land, too. The flying boat circled for a landing near Kalia on the north shore of the Dead Sea, and the doctors pointed out Jerusalem, half hidden in the mountains to the west. As the large airplane glided in to touch the thick waters of the Dead Sea, Radhai said a short prayer in Geez to the merciful God who had blessed him with this vision of the Land of Israel— not the view of a pilgrim, or even of those who were to follow the Messiah from the 3,000-year exile, but the very same view that the Angel Sanbat would see when she came up from Africa and broke through the clouds to prepare the way for the Messiah and the House of Israel that was to follow him.

"I think God loves this land so much because he always sees it from the sky," Radhai told Evan.

Evan smiled. "I had never thought of it quite that way." His mind still held the image of the strange Wingate saying goodbye to the tall Falasha for the last time. "Were you happy at Ein Dvorah, Radhai?"

"Yes, as happy as a person could be in a new and very different world. But I will not be going back there after the war. My friend Avinoam—my fellow worker in the dairy barn—and I are leaders of a group of boys and girls from Ein Dvorah that will form a new kibbutz. We have already picked out a site in the Negev. It will be a new beginning for all of us—if the Israeli army is able to push the Egyptians out of the Negev before this war is over."

The armored regiment broke into smaller units for mopping up operations in the small villages near Nazareth, but found virtually no opposition. A day after the truce went into effect, the regiment left by companies at night to return to its home camp. About ten miles out of Nazareth on the paved highway that led through the Valley of Jezreel, the convoy of vehicles in the halftrack company halted. Nahshon, whose halftrack was at the head of the column, was having trouble with his fuel pump again. When Evan walked up to the stalled halftrack, the Moroccan had the hood folded back. He was kneeling on the fender and hammering on the fuel pump with his rusty bayonet.

"Curses upon the breasts of your mother," he muttered in Arabic to the motor.

"We'll leave the halftrack here and send Alex for it in the morning," Gingi said. He turned to Mordecai and Shulamit. "Come, let's get into another halftrack."

"I can get this beast back myself," Nahshon argued. "All I have to do is feed the fuel directly into the carburetor. Leave the Yeled with me and let Ephraim drive the Yeled's halftrack back."

Gingi shrugged his shoulders. Like all the men in his company, the Israeli captain looked more like one of Fawzi El Kaukji's captured soldiers than a Jewish victor. His sweater and trousers were wrinkled and dirty, his face was sunburned a thick, rusty red, his lips were chapped and swollen from exposure to the sun, and there were dark circles under his eyes. He had received far less sleep than his men. The days had been spent in planning the details of the battles with the other officers of the regiment, and the nights in leading his troops into combat. The blond, curly-haired officer checked his watch. "I'll give you five minutes to see if you can get this thing started. If not, we leave without it."

Nahshon unbuckled the spare five-gallon can of gasoline from its stand near the running board and lifted it onto the hood. He pulled a long rubber hose out of a cabinet in the back of the halftrack, placed one end deep into the gasoline can, and sucked on the other end of the hose until he had drawn gasoline into his mouth. He pinched the end of the hose and spit gasoline onto the ground, then jammed the hose into the carburetor. "Now, make sure the other end stays in the petrol," he told Evan, and ran around to the driver's seat, the brace across his back bulging out through his shirt and sweater. He pushed the starter and the motor caught.

"All right," Gingi yelled over the roar of the motor. "Wait here and tag on at the end of the convoy. Keep up as best as you can. I'll give you Radhai and Uzi so you'll have protection if you need it."

"And Shulamit, too," Nahshon said. "I still have the radio."

The captain glanced at Shulamit, huddled in her blanket like an

Indian squaw. "You don't fool me, Nahshon. You can operate a radio as well as anyone in this brigade. But all right, Shulamit, too."

Ephraim, who had lost his halftrack at Shafa Amr, transferred to Evan's halftrack, as did Gingi and Mordecai. Nahshon was left with Radhai, Uzi, Shulamit, three extra cans of gasoline, and Evan, who was now sitting on the raised steel windshield and holding the rubber tube with one hand and the gasoline can with the other.

Gingi waved to Ephraim to pull away and gave the signal for the rest of the halftracks to follow. When the last vehicle had passed, Nahshon pulled out into the road. Only enough gasoline was coming through the tube to allow the halftrack to go about fifteen miles an hour, and the convoy quickly outdistanced the limping halftrack and disappeared from view after the first few bends in the road. Radhai, Uzi, and Shulamit, their blankets wrapped tightly around them, were soon droned to sleep by the sound of the halftrack motor, leaving the night to Nahshon and Evan.

The halftrack was still in the Emek, the Valley of Jezreel, when the sun pushed up over the hills far behind them to the East and evaporated the shadow that lay over the flat, full land. Sprinklers were already twirling in some of the fields. Far off the road, near a little cluster of trees, buildings, and barns, a lone woman was working, bent down over a row of bushy plants. She had long, sunburned arms and legs and wore the bloomer shorts and short-sleeved blouse of the kibbutznik. A blue bandanna was wrapped around her hair. When she heard the sound of the halftrack motor, she stood up and waved. Evan raised his hand high above his head and waved back.

This was the Emek, a panorama colored with rich strokes of green and sparkling with the suspended crystals of sun-tinted dew. The distance from the road to the buildings and trees and the woman in the field made them miniatures of life, cast without blemish. And Evan, Nahshon, Radhai, Uzi, and Shulamit were the giant Gullivers who had taken Nazareth and made this beautiful Lilliputian valley secure.

Uzi awoke and reached for his concertina. Sitting back against the side of the halftrack, his blanket still lying across his legs and his legs arched across the jagged hole in the floor of the halftrack, the chubby youth played a song about the Emek. He played it slower than it was usually played, but it was beautiful and fitting for the hour of the day, and the motor of the halftrack provided a monotonous, but not unpleasant bass rhythm. After he had played it through once, he played it again, and this time he sang, and the rest of them sang with him. The notes came from the concertina, but the music came from the land. The land was the composer and the lyricist, and even now the voice.

Chapter Nine

EVAN AND SHULAMIT WENT AGAIN TO THE BAHAI garden and one evening they hitchhiked to Nahariya,-where they sipped bottles of soda at a sidewalk cafe and then walked down to the beach to listen to the timeless sounds of the surf and shiver in the drafts that came from both the sea and the nearby mountains of Lebanon. The first days of the Second Truce were vacation days, and they lived them to the full measure of their freedom.

Once Shulamit went with Evan to the hospital in Haifa to visit Bernie. The wounded American, his neck still swathed in bandages, lay thin and listless in his hospital bed. Evan was amused and pleased that Shulamit flirted with Bernie coquettishly as they sat and talked to him. It was as though she realized that this was the best therapy for Bernie. And it had its effect. Before they left, Bernie was laughing and making verbal passes at the Israeli girl.

There had been another letter from Evan's mother, this one in answer to a long letter he had written her describing his reasons for coming to Israel. She wrote:

I could read in your letter an undertone of bitterness toward America that I never knew existed, and I have asked myself if somehow Dad and I are at fault. Were we so busy with the store, so occupied with the material things in our lives that we failed to teach you the values that we always felt but never expressed? Perhaps it is your tragedy, my son, that you are one generation too far removed from Europe.

[135]

Our own parents knew the life of the Jews in Europe, the hardships, the oppressions, the fear of pogroms. Grandpa Copperman, as you know, came here to escape the long army service that under the Russian system would have forced him to abandon not only his family, but his religion as well. Our parents were immigrants—greenhorns—but they loved America and her freedom with a passion that I think you would find a bit strange, despite their disappointment that their children did not follow all the traditional religious rules.

Though immigrants, they passed on this love of America to us. And I'm ashamed that as native-born Americans Dad and I failed to do the same for you. Perhaps we took it for granted that you would feel what we felt. We love America. This is our country. We belong here. There is prejudice here, but there will be prejudice any place where there are people, until we have reached the millennium. What makes America different is that the same laws that protect the majority protect us. We are not in fear of our lives or our property, and we have hopes that our Christian friends will understand us more as we live with them longer.

We would have sent you into the American army without a whimper of regret. All of us owe America something, even our lives, for the freedom she has given us. But to volunteer to serve in the army of a country you have never seen, that is something else. I know there is something noble in you and a feeling of compassion for your fellow Jews that led you to do this thing. But that does not satisfy me. You did not owe them your life—*our* lives. You say it was your decision to make. I say it was *our* decision to make, and you owed it to us to discuss it fully with us before making such a decision. But now you have done it and apparently you refuse to change your mind. I suppose there is nothing we can do but pray that you take care of yourself, protect yourself, and come back to us safely, as soon as you can.

You wrote that my first letter to you seemed cold. Yes, it was. I tried to guard my emotions and appeal to your sense of reason to return. But if you want to know how I feel, I will tell you. Everytime there is news of another battle in Israel, I see you lying dead or wounded, with no one near who loves or cares about you. I lie awake at night and see your bones bleaching on some forgotten desert. I think about you every minute. I feel the utmost contempt

[136]

for the authorities who permitted you to join that army. And if anything happens to you over there I will hate Israel until my dying day. These are hard words from a woman who has worked for Israel and Jewish causes all her life. But what more can you expect from your heartbroken

Mother

The last paragraph of her letter brought tears to Evan's eyes. If only there were some way to alleviate her pain and anguish. And yet somehow this letter from her, which sounded so much like her, had also cleared the air. Everything she said was true. They understood each other now. The difference between their feelings for America, for Israel, for the Jews, was not a difference of fact, but a difference of intensity.

The dance, scheduled one week after they returned from Nazareth, was designed to celebrate the victory of the armored regiment. Buses were to bring girls from brigade headquarters in Acre and from army offices in Haifa. Uzi and his concertina and two other men with harmonicas would provide the music.

Evan and Nahshon walked together toward the dance, which was to be held in the paved area in front of regimental headquarters. Nahshon had spent two hours shaving, combing his hair, and trimming his mustache. Evan was amazed at the transformation. Usually the sloppiest looking soldier in the entire regiment, the Moroccan now looked like a much younger Middle Eastern dandy. His khakis were clean and unwrinkled, the tight skin on his face shone from the close shave, and his neatly-parted hair had a raven glow. The brace bulged through the back of his khaki shirt, but pulled back on his shoulders to give him a stiff, dashing military posture.

"But you won't be able to dance the *hora* with that cracked shoulder," Evan told him.

Nahshon felt for the tip of his mustache and twisted it tighter. "My good luck," he said. "You will learn tonight, Yeled, that Israeli dancing is more physical training than physical contact. You have to wait until you're off the dance floor to find out the difference between little girls and little boys."

"And the little girls let you?" Evan asked teasingly. "Then everything I've read about Palestine in the novels is true."

"Those writers. A curse upon the breasts of their sisters, who are whores," Nahshon swore in Arabic. "I read a book once that had been translated into Hebrew. According to the author, all the unmarried kibbutzniks worked hard in the fields all day, fought off Arab attacks for one half the night, and played the close buttocks game in the trenches the other half." He reached over and swatted a mosquito that had just landed on Evan's sleeve. "The Israeli girls are smart, and, as you Americans say, know when there's a seller's market. I was in one of the convoys to Jerusalem last winter, and I met a girl there who was a clerk for the Haganah. We went for a walk that night and then we came back and sat in my truck. I moved close to her and put my arm around her shoulder. She pointed to her waist and said, 'From here up is for fun. From here down is for marriage.' How's that for free love?"

Uzi and his two fellow musicians were practicing a song together softly. Shulamit was sitting on the porch of the headquarters building listening to them. She had her hair done up in the tight braids wrapped around her head and was wearing her khaki blouse and skirt.

"How are the ankles tonight, my pretty one?" Nahshon asked, sitting down beside her.

"Almost completely healed. I'm ready to leap over the side of another halftrack." She moved her face closer to Nahshon's, pretending to peer at him. "Are you really Nahshon, the ancient Moroccan? Or are you perhaps his handsome young brother?" Nahshon grinned and curried his mustache with his forefinger.

"When he heard there were going to be women here tonight, he became a new man," Evan said.

"My feelings are hurt," Shulamit teased. "I'm always by his side in the halftrack and he's never failed to look like a beggar."

Nahshon put an arm around her and patted her shoulder. "Because, my sweet," he said, "you're like a daughter to me. Some of the women here tonight might be more mature."

Shulamit pretended to take a swing at him, and Nahshon hopped up and trotted away. The Moroccan stopped in the center of the asphalt area and watched a regimental policeman lift the barrier at the main gate and wave in three buses that were filled with girls.

Nahshon directed the buses to a parking area and then stood at the front door of the first bus, solicitously taking the hand of each girl and helping her down the last step to the ground. Almost all the girls were dressed in khaki uniforms similar to the one Shulamit wore, but a few had on civilian dresses. At first the women gathered in little knots, but they were so greatly outnumbered by the men of the armored regiment that soon there seemed to be only one girl in the center of a circle of a dozen men. Uzi and his band began to play a *hora*, the fast-moving, unsophisticated Israeli folk dance in which the boys and girls arrange themselves in a circle and skip clockwise, pausing briefly every few steps to kick in toward the center of the circle.

"Come, let's dance," Shulamit said, standing up.

"I don't think I've caught on to the steps yet," Evan said.

"Don't worry. I'll teach you."

"You go on and dance this one," Evan said. "I'll watch."

"Then I'll wait, too," Shulamit said. "We'll join the next one."

The circle was getting larger now as more couples broke in and picked up the step. Radhai walked over to Evan and Shulamit and held out his hand to the Israeli girl. As he smiled, his white teeth were like perfect ivory insets in the purple lips. The small black eyes were made darker by the clear white eyeballs. The nose and lips were thin and the face had a finely chiseled quality. If he were white, Evan thought, he would be extremely handsome.

Radhai led Shulamit over to the dancing circle. They broke in and clasped the arms of their neighbors to complete the circle again.

Uzi and his companions began a new chorus of the song, and the dancers moved faster now in the revolving circle. The dancers breathlessly sang the words to the *hora,* and the soldiers who crowded around the circle sang also, clapping their hands to the fast beat of the music.

Radhai gripped Shulamit's arm tighter to keep her from being pulled away from him when the circle hesitated for a kick and then whipped forward again. He could feel her hand on his arm answer with a tighter grip, and they looked at each other and laughed as they sang. The *hora* was a happy, though at times frantic dance. It used the body to help express the nationalistic fervor of the song, as though not only the throat and lungs were thrown into the power of the words, but the torso and limbs as well.

As the *hora* reached its peak, with the circle twirling as fast as it could without breaking apart, Radhai felt the sensation of flight,

[139]

similar to when he had flown in the airplane and the turbulence of the air had pitched him up from his seat. There was a smaller turbulence, too, in the chest and in the shoulders, as when one dances and skips and throws the knees up into the air to break the legs and body away from the pull of the earth. And Radhai was still dancing, throwing the strong black legs up into the air and bobbing the head down and up and to the side, feeling the dizziness that was caused by the hypnotic circling of his head and the fasting on the Day of Forgiveness in the Falasha village in Ethiopia.

Radhai was wearing a toga, as were all the other men in the *mesgid,* the synagogue of the Falashas. And as he danced on the afternoon of the Day of Forgiveness, he felt the lightness of the draped cloth, and it matched the lightness in his head and heart. All of the men were dancing now, and they were singing the praises of God in the melodious Agau dialect of Amharic. Another Day of Forgiveness was coming to an end, and the Falashas danced with joy, as the Scriptures said their ancestors had danced at the Temple when the scapegoat had been sent into the wilderness and they had felt the relief of the absolution of sin, the precious moment of the year when their souls were cleansed and pure.

But the vision of that other dance so many years before faded almost as quickly as it appeared, and he could feel the strong hands of Shulamit pulling him back to the *hora.* The long fingers grasped his arms and dug into them as the *hora* circle twirled like a potter's wheel. And suddenly he and Shulamit were in the center of the circle. His arm was around her waist and hers around his. They were laughing as they skipped and kicked with the rhythm of the dance, and everyone was clapping and shouting the meaningless and almost unintelligible words of the song. And as suddenly as they had found themselves out in the center of the circle, the music stopped. The circle disintegrated and Shulamit's ankle gave way. She would have fallen to the ground if she had not reached for Radhai's neck with both hands. Radhai quickly put his hands under her arms to support her and she laid her head breathlessly against his chest. Radhai could feel the warm moisture of her blouse as his hands pressed the cloth against her underarms, and he could smell the sweet wetness of her forehead.

They stood there for a minute, holding on to each other, while they both caught their breaths. Then Shulamit filled her lungs with air and opened her eyes, and the first thing she saw was Evan, standing among the circle of spectators, watching her. She pulled her head away from Radhai's chest and looked up into the black, handsome face, gleaming wetly now under the bright lights.

"Do you want me to carry you to the porch?" he asked.

"Let me test the ankle again. Funny, but it didn't even hurt when we were dancing." She put her weight on the foot gingerly. There was no pain in the ankle and this time it seemed to hold with ease. "I think I'm cured."

"Good."

Uzi and his musicians began a fox trot. Radhai put his right hand around Shulamit's waist and lifted her right arm with his left.

"No. I'd rather not dance this dance," she said. "I need to cool off."

Radhai guided her to the porch, down a little way from where the musicians were playing, and they sat there and watched the couples dancing. The Israelis danced the *hora* for the sake of nationalism and the fox trot for the sake of sex, deriving equally as much pleasure from each. Nahshon, who had abstained from the hearty exercise of the *hora*, was now attached to a blonde and was dancing around the asphalt area with nimble feet.

At the end of the fox trot, Uzi announced that there would be another folk dance, but not a *hora* this time. The men who knew the steps lined up on one side and the women on the other, facing them. Uzi counted down the line and found he was one man short. He walked down the porch and grabbed Radhai's arm. "Ah, here's a kibbutznik," he said and pulled the reluctant Falasha toward the line of men. Everyone shouted encouragement to him, including Shulamit, and he gave a sheepish grin as he took his place at the end of the line.

The music started and the crowd of observers closed in around the two lines until finally there were a number of people standing in front of Shulamit. She heard footsteps on the porch and Evan was beside her.

"You said you were going to have the next dance with me," Shulamit said.

"I know." He sat down next to her. "But you had company. I didn't want to interrupt."

"You were jealous," she said, amused.

"No. Not at all."

[141]

"Then you were angry," she probed. "Because he's a Falasha?"

"No, I wasn't angry," he said firmly. "I like Radhai." There was a glint of disbelief in her eyes. "Look, Shulamit, I don't fear or dislike black men. I'm used to them. There were many in my hometown."

"And they danced with white women." It was a statement, and its sharp edge cut through the disclaimers to the rock core of prejudice that Evan himself had never been able to assay.

Evan gave a short laugh, acknowledging the thrust. "No, they didn't dance with white women. Where I was born and raised," he said seriously, "prejudice wasn't a state of mind. It was a way of life. The difference between me and most of the others who lived where I lived was that I knew our way of life was wrong. But prejudice can become a conditioned reflex. I would lie if I said I weren't still affected by it."

"You were taught to hate a man because his skin was black?"

"No. We were taught to love many of them. But we were also taught that the Negro was a different kind of man, that he was a primitive who had less capacity for learning—that he had his world and we had ours and there wasn't to be any mingling between them. It's much the same as the line drawn between the Jews and the Arabs in Israel.

"But we don't dislike the Arabs because their skin is brown. We dislike them because they would take our homes and throw us into the sea."

"Can you truthfully say there aren't Israelis who consider the Arabs inferior just because they're Arabs?"

Shulamit paused for a minute, then nodded in concession. "There are some Israelis who believe that. But certainly not all."

"Well, there are many Americans who believe that about Negroes."

"But in any case," she said, "Radhai's not a Negro. He's a Hamite mostly."

"There are Southerners in America who ask those who want equality for Negroes, 'How would you like your sister to marry one?' Would Israeli parents have no objection to their daughter marrying a Hamite?"

"Don't ask me about parents," she said. "Their ideas are different from those of the sabras. There are some who wouldn't want their children to marry anything but German Jews, others who prefer Poles, and many who would die if their children married a brown-skinned Yemenite. Still, their children marry whomever they please —Yemenites, Moroccans, Litvaks. And I've heard of no parent committing suicide yet."

"Would your parents object to Radhai?"

"My parents would probably object to you." She smiled enigmatically. "You should have asked if I would object to Radhai." She rubbed the side of her face with the palm of her hand. "I feel that there is no great purity in the blood and genes that made my skin this color. My father has blue eyes and fair skin. He did not come by it from Abraham. So I'll love my children just as much whatever the color of their skin or the shape of their noses and lips. Radhai is extremely handsome. He is mature and he is brave and he is sensitive. But I could never marry him."

She ignored Evan's raised eyebrows.

"First," she continued, "I'm not in love with him. That's quite apparent. Second, he's a gunbearer. I could never be happy for long with a gunbearer."

Evan was puzzled. "I don't understand. What did he do, work on a safari?"

"No, no," she said impatiently. "It has nothing to do with the color of his skin or where he came from. Most immigrants to Israel are gunbearers, and they can live here a lifetime and never get over it. They're used to carrying the rifle for the great white hunter. They carry the rifle around, keep it clean, expose themselves to all the dangers—and when the time comes to shoot the lion between the eyes, they loyally hand the rifle to the white hunter, who gets all the glory."

"No sabra, of course, would ever be a gunbearer."

"Not many," she said. "A sabra would shove the white hunter aside and have a try at the lion himself."

"To prove that he was brave and superior," Evan said.

"Or immune to lions." She smiled. "Wingate was Radhai's white hunter. Now it's Gingi. I don't know who it was on his kibbutz. If only he'd kick Gingi in the pants once or refuse to obey a sergeant's order, I would hug him. But he follows all the regulations. He does everything the master tells him to. He wouldn't even step through the hole in the fence back there."

"Has anyone ever urged him to?"

She looked at him wryly. "Does it take urging?"

"And am I a gunbearer, too?" He asked it lightly, but waited expectantly for an answer.

She stood up, put her hands on both sides of his face, and pretended to look deeply into his eyes. "Perhaps you came to me in time," she said in mock seriousness. "I'll let you know after further examination." She took his hand and pulled him to his feet. "On the Friday after the next one, I'll have a leave for three days. Try to get one, too, and come to Jerusalem with me. I'll show you the city."

They returned to the dance area. The *horas*, which required a reservoir of energy that was only available at the beginning of an evening, were finished. Uzi and his companions played a series of slow dance numbers that Evan had never heard before, songs that apparently were popular in Israel. Evan held the Israeli girl close to him and let her nearness and warmth drug his consciousness to the stares of the other soldiers, the roughness of the dance floor, and the uneven tempo of the music.

After Evan had danced two numbers with Shulamit, Radhai asked her to dance again. Evan stood among the onlookers and watched the Falasha and the sabra girl dance. They danced into the shadows and out again into the bright lights, aware that they were being watched, content that no one watched them without envy.

Chapter Ten

Jerusalem was a city that derived much of its magic from the eyes of the beholder. Evan couldn't be sure how much of what he saw was really there and how much he only imagined was there. In Jerusalem the present absorbed, yet kept the flavor, of the past as smoothly as the quarried rose stones gleaned from some ancient rubble fitted into the modern walls in the New City. And everywhere there was the enveloping presence of those who had walked these hills in the past and left a breath alive in the city.

[144]

He and Shulamit had caught a ride to Jerusalem on the top of a supply truck leaving from Tel Aviv. It was loaded with sacks of flour piled up higher than its sides and tied down with criss-crossing ropes. As the truck labored up the narrow winding Burma Road that by-passed Arab-held Latrun, its top-heavy load would shift precariously on the hairpin curves and Evan and Shulamit would throw their weight to the opposite side, like yachtsmen ballasting a sailboat by leaning over the rail.

The dirt road cut a tortuous path through wadis and sharply-climbing hills, past several deserted Arab villages until it finally turned back into the main paved road to Jerusalem. The paved highway passed through the Judean hills—some completely bare, some partially reforested but still left with bald tops, and others completely covered with pines—then dipped down into the New City of Jerusalem.

And now, as the first long shadows of a new Sabbath began to fall over the Holy City, Evan could feel the sanctity of the place close in around him as he and Shulamit dropped their small military bags over the side of the truck and jumped down after them. They walked down Jaffa Road to the center of the city. Cement roadblocks, barbed wire, and oil drums jutted across many of the intersections. The occasional report of a rifle, then the quick burst of machine gun fire came from the direction of the fortress-like walls of the Old City. Evan and Shulamit walked along the eastern side of the street, staying close to the walls to protect themselves from drifting rifle bullets. The truce, which was in such strict effect in the rest of the country, could never be enforced in Jerusalem, a breached city where there were constant exchanges of small arms fire and sometimes mortar and artillery duels across the no-man's land.

The difference between the other Israeli cities and Jerusalem during the truce, too, was that the young men and women, soldiers of the city, walked along the streets with Sten guns and rifles slung over their shoulders as matter-of-factly as the Sorbonne students Evan had seen carrying their loaves of bread back to their rooms at night.

Evan checked into a small hotel near Ben Yehuda Street. Shulamit went with him up the steep, straight stairway that led to his room, then glanced outside at the gathering dusk.

"I'll have to leave my bag here until tomorrow night," she said. "It's already Sabbath, and I don't want to be stoned by the good citizens of Mea Shearim."

They left the hotel and walked up Ben Yehuda Street, crossed the Street of the Prophets, and entered the narrow alleys of Mea Shearim, the ultra-orthodox section of Jerusalem. It was sundown and the cobblestone lanes were virtually deserted. The men were in the synagogue, the women and children in the homes, already enfolded in the Sabbath.

Shulamit turned into a doorway and led Evan down a dim hall, then opened a door marked "5." The furniture in the room was old and shabby, the walls bare of ornament. But in the center of the room was a table with a bright white tablecloth and five place-settings of silver. Each chair around the table was different; only the chair at the head of the table had arms. There was the smell of freshly-baked bread in the room.

A middle-aged woman in a large green apron came out of the kitchen when she heard the door close. She was small, with fine features, very white skin, and the light brown eyes that she had passed on to her daughter. She wore a lifeless brown *sheitel*, the wig worn by the ultra-orthodox women. She began wiping her hands on her apron as soon as she saw them and ran over and put her arms around Shulamit's neck and kissed her. "*Mein kindele, mein kindele,*" she said tearfully, holding her daughter close to her.

Shulamit turned and pointed to Evan. "This is the American friend I wrote you I was bringing with me," she told her mother in Yiddish. Mrs. Zephron reached out and shook Evan's hand, holding his hand between the two of hers warmly.

"I'm glad we got here in time," Shulamit continued in Yiddish. "I see you were expecting us."

"I have a few more things to do in the kitchen," Mrs. Zephron said apologetically. "Your father and Carmi will be home from the synagogue in a little while. You two go and prepare for the Sabbath."

Shulamit pointed to another door in the room. "The bathroom is between the two bedrooms. You go first. I'll stay here and talk to mother."

"Your mother hasn't learned to speak Hebrew after all of these years in Palestine?" Evan whispered.

"My mother's family has lived in Jerusalem for six generations, my father's for four. Hebrew for them is a sacred language,"—she put sarcastic emphasis on the word 'sacred'—"too holy to be used for anything but the Torah, the prayerbooks, and the commentaries. They wouldn't defile it by using it in everyday conversation."

A half-hour later, the door burst open and a boy about eight years old hurtled through it and ran over to Shulamit shouting breathlessly, "Shula! Shula!" She lifted him and hugged and kissed him, the tightness of her embrace knocking off his black skullcap. His hair had been cut very close to the scalp, except for the sideburns which hung down in half curls on the smooth skin in front of his ears. Shulamit put her brother back down to his feet. "This is Carmi. And Carmi, this is Evan, a real *chocolatnik*." The boy grinned at Evan with an open face that looked much like his mother's, and leaned against his sister's arm.

A minute after the boy entered the room Shulamit's father followed him. Mr. Zephron was a big man and he looked even larger in the black *caftan*, the long coat that hung down to his knees. He wore a magnificent *shtreimel*, a fur-trimmed hat that bushed out over his face like cantilevered fox tails. A full dark beard, shocked through with long lightning streaks of gray, framed the thin, high bridged nose and intense deep-set blue eyes. He looked at Shulamit, then quickly turned his eyes away and nodded to Evan. Still wearing his *caftan* and fur-trimmed *shtreimel*, he pulled his chair away from the head of the table and stood there while the others came and stood by their places. Carmi brought Evan a skullcap. Then Mr. Zephron poured the wine and sang the *Kiddish*, the Sabbath blessing over the wine. He got up from his chair and disappeared into the bathroom for a half-minute, then returned, rubbing his hands together. He said the blessing over the bread as he cut the loaf and passed a piece around to each person at the table.

Mrs. Zephron and Shulamit brought in the bowls of food, which consisted primarily of heavily breaded ground meat patties and mashed potatoes.

"Mother says to please forgive the meal," Shulamit whispered to Evan in Hebrew. "The Sabbath dinner is always special in this house, but these days there's very little food available."

Mr. Zephron glared at Shulamit. She pretended not to notice him. At the end of the meal, Mrs. Zephron brought a glass of water and an empty bowl. Shulamit's father poured water over his fingers into the bowl and passed the water to Carmi, who did the same thing. Evan took the glass and poured it over his fingers, also. Mr. Zephron reached behind him to a bookcase and pulled out four books. He gave everyone at the table one but Shulamit. Carmi showed Evan the place and the American joined in the chanting of grace after the meal. Shulamit sat at her place quietly while the other members of the family and Evan sang several *zmee'rot,* songs of the Sabbath, from their books. Evan kept one eye on Carmi's finger, a good indicator of when Mr. Zephron was going to skip a verse or repeat a line. The boy, for his part, was obviously glorying in sitting next to an American.

Later, when Evan and Shulamit were in the darkened alley walking toward Jaffa Road, Evan said, "I felt a little foolish at the table. The only language I can talk to your father in is Hebrew, and he won't speak it."

"Don't let it bother you. If you knew all the languages in the world you couldn't speak to him. He lives in a completely different world, a thousand light years away from us."

"It's an interesting world, though," Evan said. "I've always envied the Chasidim. The happy love they have for God and religion is something I wish I had."

"Be glad that you don't." She caught his hand. "Their kind of religion imposes a world that cannot change. I haven't been back here in six months, but I feel as though I only left yesterday."

"Your father greeted us like he had just seen us an hour before."

"My father tries not to notice me any more than he has to, and I'm afraid my friends get the same treatment," Shulamit explained, saying it as though she didn't care. "When I broke away from the grip of this ghetto three years ago, I stopped existing as far as my father was concerned."

"Three years ago? I thought you said you were here six months ago."

"Only for a visit. I left Mea Shearim in 1945 and went to live with my uncle, my father's brother, in a newer section of the city. There was a time when I thought I would always live in Mea Shearim. Then I began to read the picture magazines and see the way the other Jewish children in Palestine lived. A few times I would walk along this street out of Mea Shearim and watch the

[148]

other young girls and boys, and I became jealous. I wanted to be like them, to dress like them, to go to school with them, to have their freedom. That was the beginning. The end was when I left. My uncle understood. He had done the same thing a generation before." She gripped his hand harder. "Can you imagine me living in Mea Shearim and waiting dutifully for my father to arrange a marriage for me with a *yeshiva bachur,* a Talmudic student I had never seen?"

"No. But your father's such a large, powerful man. He doesn't look like the type to put up with a rebellion."

"My father's weak. He's an addict. Not to drugs. But to the Scriptures and commentaries, and commentaries on commentaries. There was a Chasidic way of life that died and was embalmed a hundred years ago. Each generation since then has embalmed itself with it. If anything tries to disturb the dead or the pattern of the trance, my father simply wipes it away from reality. I don't think he recognizes the Arabs or the war or the fact that his fish shop hasn't had any fish to sell since last November."

"But in a sense that's what we're fighting for, isn't it? So the Jews who want to live this way and dress this way can do so without fear of ridicule or laws that make them conform."

"A very democratic thought. But do you know what my father would do if he were Ben-Gurion and all his friends from Mea Shearim held the powers of government? He would pass laws that would set down what you could eat, what kind of clothes you and your children could wear, and how many times a day you would have to pray. He would make you conform in every way in his power, and Israel would end up as a copy of Mea Shearim."

"That's fiction. I'm talking about the fact of his own freedom."

"And I'm talking about the fact of mine—and Carmi's. If I could only show Carmi that there is another world out there and all he has to do to break away from this mausoleum when he's older is to challenge the authority of his father, just as I did!"

"You make it sound as though Mea Shearim is a place of the living dead."

"No. I didn't mean that. Very few of the people here are as completely embalmed as my father. You'd be surprised, though, how many of them won't look up from their prayers to see whether God is still around."

"Do you believe in God, Shulamit?"

She waited a minute before answering. "Yes. But possibly not the same one my father believes in. He knows exactly the personality of his God. I don't. But I believe in God because I love Israel and I believe in her destiny. If there isn't a God, why did every force and every circumstance fall into place at the exact right moment to give us our land? The exodus of the refugees from Europe, the wealth of the Jewish community in America, the weakening of the British Empire, and all the other miracles. It was like tossing a mirror into the air a hundred times and having it land on its edge unbroken each time."

"That's a pretty materialistic reason for believing in God,"

"I'm a materialist," she said. "I love what I can see and admire and hold onto. I can't adore from a distance."

They were out of Mea Shearim and at Jaffa Road now, closer to the Old City walls and nearer the sounds of the rifle fire. They ran across the intersection and paused at a darkened window that displayed woven silver jewelry. There were no lights in the street, but the three-quarter moon overhead illuminated the tiny silver daggers and camels in the window.

"Sunday," he said, "I'm going to buy you that little pin that looks like an Arab dagger. No Irgunist should be without one."

"Can I thank you now?" She put her hands on his shoulders, stood on her tiptoes, and closed her eyes as she kissed him softly. Then he circled her body with his arms and pressed her close to him, and she kissed him hard and deep.

Evan slept blissfully, luxuriously—the first time he had felt the comfortable smoothness of sheets next to his skin since leaving Paris two months before. The next morning he ate at a soldiers' dining hall and attended the Sabbath services at Jeshurun Synagogue.

The congregation in the large synagogue was made up of soldiers and older, clean-shaven men in suits. They covered themselves with their large prayer shawls and read their Sabbath prayers with dignity and decorum, the voice of the cantor echoing in arcs from the domed roof of the great synagogue. But it was too much like the services Evan had seen all his life. He was a little sorry that he hadn't gone with Mr. Zephron and Carmi to their Chasidic synagogue in Mea Shearim. Evan envisioned the Chasidic Jews swaying back and forth with the rhythm of the prayers, losing themselves in each prayer until, in the crowded room of a hundred voices saying a hundred different words, the prayer became an earnest, heartfelt supplication from one tiny man to the Great God in heaven, and there were no other worshipers, no roof, no distance between the tiny man and God, and God turned an ear to the Chasidic plea.

It was possible that Evan needed the Chasidic synagogue to help him absorb the real flavor of Jerusalem, for these were difficult times to catch the mood of the city. Although Jerusalem had seen a hundred sieges in its history, it was essentially a city of peace, and the spell of the city was broken by the incessant snap of sniper fire and the occasional blast of a vengeful mortar.

Shulamit was waiting for him when the services ended. They walked toward Mt. Zion along King George V Avenue until they got to Julian's Way. Then Shulamit turned into a path that led sharply downhill through a stretch of rubble that had once been homes. He followed her through trenches and paths that brought them to Dormition Church on Mt. Zion, just outside the walls of the Arab-held Old City. They went through a labyrinth of rooms to the well of a tower, then climbed circular steps to the top, where a soldier stood behind a sandbagged window, his cheek on the butt of a rifle that poked through the sandbags.

"*Shalom,*" Shulamit greeted him.

"*Chatzi-shalom,*"—half-peace, the soldier answered.

"Can we take a look?" Shulamit asked.

The soldier nodded. "But be careful. I think my Legionnaire friends down there have a rifle zeroed in on every crevice in this window. If they see movement they'll fire."

Evan closed one eye and looked through a pinpoint of space between two sandbags. The church tower had a spectacular view of the Old City. It looked down on the entire interior of the Old City in the vicinity of Zion Gate, which was only about fifty yards away.

"Look over to your right," Shulamit said, "at those destroyed buildings. See, where a few domes are left? That was the Jewish Quarter. The Arabs destroyed it house by house to get to the defenders." She also pointed out the Jewish cemetery on the Mount of Olives, held by the Arabs, and much farther in the distance, to the left, Mt. Scopus with its Hebrew University and Hadassah Hospital, now surrounded by the Arabs and useless.

[151]

"I feel like Moses on Mt. Nebo," Evan said. "I can see it all, but I'm not permitted to step foot on it."

"You'll be able to step foot on it," Shulamit said. "Everything you can see beyond this window belongs to us. One day it will be ours again."

The soldier, still peering through the sights of his rifle, chuckled. "This is beginning to sound like an Irgun travelogue."

Shulamit sent a dirty look in the soldier's direction, and Evan held back a smile that was beginning to form on his lips. He knew that he loved this Israeli girl, and he did not want to hurt her with humor that she could not appreciate. Certainly there was nothing funny about the ravished Jewish Quarter or the surrounded Mt. Scopus. But there was irony, too, in Jews discussing the capture of a Moslem city while standing in a church tower next to the site of the Last Supper. They walked back down the steps to the bottom of the tower and returned to the half peace of a Sabbath day in Jerusalem.

The room where they had eaten the Sabbath meal the night before was dark now, the last dim light from the departing Sabbath extinguished. They sat there in the dark waiting for Mr. Zephron to say *Havdalah,* the simple ceremony that marked the end of the Sabbath and the beginning of another week.

Shulamit had wanted to leave for the motion picture as soon as they had finished supper, but Evan had insisted on witnessing the *Havdalah* ceremony. It was a service he knew by heart, but he wanted the satisfaction of seeing his first Sabbath in the Holy City brought to its full completion. Shulamit, impatience showing on her face even in the darkened room, sat at the table while her father opened the drawer of the cabinet and felt for the multi-twined candle that, once lit, would bring light into the room and an end to the Sabbath.

During supper, Mr. Zephron had ignored his daughter, pretending, poorly, that she was not in the room at all. Only once did he drop the pose—this when Shulamit, speaking to Evan in Hebrew and making no attempt to lower her voice, suggested leaving for the movie before *Havdalah.* Mr. Zephron stared at her and through her before turning his eyes back to his plate, and his hand clenched around his knife handle so tightly that his knuckles became a row of small mountains.

[152]

As Mr. Zephron lit the candle and gave it to Carmi to hold, a tense darkness between father and daughter remained in the room. It played in the flickering shadows on both strong faces, and Evan was already regretting that he had opposed Shulamit's suggestion that they leave.

Mr. Zephron lifted the overfilled cup from the puddle of wine in the plate and began the *Havdalah* prayers. He shook the spice box and smelled it, passing it afterwards to Evan and his wife and son. He spread his hands toward the flaming candle held by Carmi and gave the thanksgiving for light. As he turned from the flame to lift the wine cup again, he stopped—they all stopped—as his eyes brushed across Shulamit. Her back was turned to the ceremony and she was sitting there catching the light of the *Havdalah* candle with the mirror of her compact as she applied lipstick to her lips.

Her father's hand trembled as he picked up the wine cup again. More wine spilled over the lip of the cup and dripped to the plate as he chanted the final prayer: "Blessed art Thou, O Lord our God, King of the universe, Who makest a distinction between holy and profane, between light and darkness, between Israel and other nations, between the seventh day and the six working days. Blessed art Thou, O Lord, Who makest a distinction between holy and profane."

He drank the wine, then took the candle from Carmi and extinguished the flame by grinding the wick into the puddle of wine and the plate beneath it. The room was plunged into darkness again for a minute until his wife switched on the light. Then Mr. Zephron let the *Havdalah* candle fall to the table and pointed a finger at Shulamit. "Get out!" he said. "You desecrate this home as much as you desecrate the Sabbath. Leave at once!"

"Gladly," Shulamit answered, snapping her compact shut and walking toward the door.

Mrs. Zephron put a restraining hand on her husband's arm. "Please. Please," she pleaded.

"No!" he said, shaking away her hand. "For the sake of the Sabbath I have held my peace. The Sabbath is over. This is not a place for her nakedness and painted face. Let her go to a *nofkie* house and live with the prostitutes and lewd men who can appreciate her."

"Shula!" Carmi ran to the door and put his arms around his sister's waist. He was sobbing. She bent down and kissed him on the cheek, then gently pulled herself away from him.

"*Shalom,*" she said and walked out the door.

Evan, as embarrassed and unsure of his ground as any wanderer into a family fight, went through the motions of saying a quick "goodbye" and "thank you" to people who hardly heard him, who would hardly be aware of his departure.

In the dark corridor that led to the street, he remembered that other arm, so many years before, pointing his way out into the dark. He was at a friend's house on Christmas Eve, waiting for his parents to glean the last Christmas Eve sales and come home. He watched his friend and his friend's mother trim the Christmas tree, the star at the top, the silver tinsel, the colored globes, the electric lights that blinked. The old man, the grandfather, came out of the room where he had been celebrating the birth. He was the same old man who had told them exciting tales of the hunt, of the faithfulness of dogs, of the Confederate Army, of the Ku Klux Klan. But now the breath of whisky preceded him like a dragon's vapor and he was unsteady on his feet. But the arm was steady and it pointed to the front door. The old man's daughter tried to hold him back, but the arm still pointed to the front door, and the voice behind it said simply, "Go home now. You don't belong here tonight." Out on the porch in the darkness of Christmas Eve, the door closed behind him, Evan wept, and in the light of Christmas Day, when the tears had stopped, he still felt the pain, the humiliation.

He walked up to Shulamit, who stood in the cobblestone alley waiting for him. She had done more to earn her expulsion than Evan had, yet he knew her hurt was deeper, though she was unlikely to admit it.

"You did that on purpose, didn't you?" he said. "But what did you accomplish? I don't think Carmi will remember this as a lesson in revolt."

"At least I made my father acknowledge my presence." Her bright red lips trembled in anger. "That's an accomplishment."

Evan reached down for her hand, to hold it while they walked out of Mea Shearim.

In his hotel room, she picked up her military bag and set it on the chair. "I'll go over to my uncle's tonight. I should have gone there in the first place." She looked at herself in the mirror on the dresser, and Evan walked over and stood behind her.

[154]

"Shulamit, there have been times when I thought I was lonely here, so far away from home. But you're much more lonely than I have ever been. Stay here with me." He put his arms around her and laid the flat of his hands on her stomach. She sighed and leaned back against him, pressing the roundness of her buttocks into his thighs and turning her head to the side and up so the high forehead nestled under his lips. Then she turned and faced him, her body very close to his. She reached up and stroked his smooth tan nose and cheek with her fingertips. "Such a *chocolatnik*," she said. "From the beginning, I thought I was seducing you. You've been seducing me." She stared intently into the two hazel eyes, then closed her eyes and parted her relaxed lips as the face came closer.

The khaki buttons were freed easily, quickly, and in a minute her khaki skirt was folded neatly on top of his khaki trousers, both resting on her military bag, while the two khaki shirts languished together on the back of the chair. She was on the bed next to him, wearing only a white brassiere and white panties. Her skin was an even golden brown, except between the brassiere and the panties, where it was a secret white. She lay on her side, facing him, letting him admire her and touch her.

Evan ran a finger over the whiteness, the roundness, the longness. " 'Return, return, O Shulamit; return, return, that we may look upon thee.' " He kissed the fragile nose and then the cleft in her chin. "Mordecai isn't here now to be embarrassed. Can I quote more?"

"Yes. Yes." She moved toward him, so near that she could feel the excitement in the hard, thin body.

He rested his hand on the elliptical face. " 'Thy body is like a palm tree, and thy breasts like clusters of grapes. I said: I will climb up into the palm tree, I will take hold of its branches, and let thy breasts be as clusters of the vine, and the smell of thy countenance like apples, and the roof of thy mouth like the best wine.' "

Their bodies were tight together, touching from their legs to their mouths, and in the unrestricted air behind her back his fingers searched for the lock to the band of white and found it. His hands slid down the dampness of her back and tugged gently, insistently at the elastic already well below her waist. And then they were free, suspended, it seemed, even above the sheets they warmed. They exchanged their warmth and multiplied it, embracing, entwining,

[155]

enfolding, enveloping, until they consumed the heat, consumed each other, in a tiny, muffled, throbbing explosion they shared as one.

Jerusalem was behind them early Sunday morning, and they were in Tel Aviv before lunch, much sooner than they had expected. They decided to see a movie before hitchhiking back to Haifa and then to camp. Shulamit chose *Gentlemen's Agreement,* a movie Evan had seen a year before in America, but only now playing at the Mograbi Cinema, the largest in Tel Aviv.

The Israeli theater annoyed Evan slightly. Competing with the regular motion picture image on the large center screen were two other tall narrow screens, one to the left and the other to the right of the picture. Hebrew subtitles were flashed on one screen and French subtitles on the other, each emanating from a separate projector that someone in the projection booth apparently cranked by hand. The person cranking the subtitles frequently fell behind, and the audience laughed at a humorous line in three different outbursts, seconds apart, each outburst coming from the segment of the audience that was listening to the English, reading the Hebrew, or reading the French.

Gentlemen's Agreement told the story of a magazine writer who pretended he was a Jew in order to do a series of articles on various forms of discrimination against Jews in the United States. Evan glanced around at the reaction of the audience to the motion picture. Almost none of them had ever seen America before or considered the interesting relationship of the American Jew to his Christian neighbors. They were emotionally captured by the movie. Whenever Gregory Peck became involved in an anti-semitic incident, some of the people near Evan would shake their heads despondently, as though re-reading a familiar story whose ending they already knew. Shulamit was engrossed. Several times Evan noticed her turn and look at him strangely, then turn back to the movie.

When it was over and they walked outside, squinting their eyes in the brightness of the sunlight, Shulamit said, "How can Jews stay there and be treated like that?"

"Treated like what?"

"Like animals, like subhumans, like the Jews in the cinema. I didn't know the Jews in America were so despised."

"They're not."

"The movie isn't true?"

"Yes, it's true in a way," he said. "But it's not just the Jews who are disliked. The different groups in our society have a natural prejudice against each other, that's all."

"Oh, I see. The U.S. is a country where there are many different groups, and each group hates the other," she said sarcastically.

"Hate's not the right word," Evan said. "This man went out looking for rebuffs. Things that might not happen to a Jew in a whole lifetime he made happen to him in a few weeks so he could gather material for a story."

"Then there is anti-semitism!"

"Yes, if you look for it. Sometimes if you don't look for it. But a Jew usually knows where he can live and where he can't live, where he can work and where he can't work. He doesn't look for trouble. My father can't belong to the country club in our city because he's a Jew. So he drives forty miles to play golf in another city. It's no great hardship. It's not like we're being made to wear yellow badges or being thrown into concentration camps."

"But it's a beginning," she said. "It begins with places you can't work in and can't live in and an insult in a restaurant. It ends with the crematoria."

Evan shook his head hopelessly. "Shulamit, it isn't that way at all. You've never lived in a place where the Jews are a small minority. You just don't understand."

"I understand," she said angrily. "I understand that a Jew can hold his head high only in Israel."

"It's no use trying to explain anymore," Evan said. "You can't comprehend. I envy you for that. You sabras are different from all the other Jews in the world. You're missing the 2,000-year experience of the exile. You've skipped a whole period of time from the Roman conquest to the present."

"The memories of the exile are part of us, too," Shulamit said, "but only the memories, not the realities. That makes us different from the rest of you. But all of you can be just like us. Now that Israel is here, you don't have to stay in other places and be inferior people. If you do stay in exile you'll always be inferior, and the only way you can stop being inferior is to stop being Jews."

"But you'll stop being Jews, too. In some ways, you've already stopped."

[157]

"We've stopped being Jews like my father, yes," she said. "But we'll be a nation of Jews. I know, that's a bad word in America. You American Jews don't want to be known as a nationality. But here we'll be a nationality. And you'll be a religion, nothing else. Maybe not even that."

"The brave new order of Jews," Evan said with heavy sarcasm. "You sabras already think you're better than the Arabs and Christians. Now you're going to be superior to all the other Jews in the world, too. *Eretz Yisrael über alles!*"

Shulamit glared at him. "You think we're Nazis?"

"No. Racists. You told me that first come the insults, then the crematoria. I say first comes the self-confident super-nationalism. Then comes the swaggering arrogance of superiority. God only knows what comes next."

There were tears of anger in her eyes. "No real Jew could see us with such horrible ugliness."

Evan stopped and grasped her shoulders. "Look at me and listen to me, Shulamit. I *am* a real Jew. But I will say what I think and I won't be bullied into silence by reprimands or tears. In the months that I have been here, I haven't noticed that anyone, including you, hesitated to tell me exactly what they thought about America and American Jews." He let his hands fall from her shoulders. "I'm sorry we saw the movie. It magnified a small ugliness in America. I suppose I've magnified a small ugliness I've seen here."

They walked together silently, each giving the anger a chance to subside. Then they caught a ride to Haifa in the cab of an army truck. Shulamit spent most of the time talking to the driver.

Chapter Eleven

AUGUST AND SEPTEMBER, LENGTHENED BY THE cloudless skies that appeared each morning and dissolved each night without variety, were months of half peace for Evan. His attachment to Shulamit became stronger, more intense.

They would meet at night and take long walks along the road toward Nahariya. Once they went into Haifa to visit Bernie and then saw a movie, a musical comedy. The argument outside the Tel Aviv movie had been put aside, but not completely forgotten. There were times when Evan felt that Israel, which had brought them together, was also a barrier between them. Shulamit seemed to demand of him the complete devotion to Israel's manifest destiny that she herself felt. Though he had grown fond of the land and the diverse people who were forging this new nation, he simply could not embrace Israel with the same passion and fervor as he embraced the Israeli girl.

And there were letters from his parents. They suggested that now that the Second Truce was dragging on interminably and it appeared unlikely that the United Nations would permit the fighting to resume, perhaps he should think about getting out of the army and coming home—if he hurried, he could probably arrive in time for the fall term at the university.

It was a half peace for the armored regiment, too. Men carried primed weapons on both sides of the truce line, and there were flare-ups at least once a week large enough to call for armored vehicle support. Then both the Israelis and Arabs would rush to file complaints with the United Nations observers, who dutifully wrote up reports and sent them off to the United Nations headquarters, which dutifully did nothing. The Israelis called it "The U.N. Comedy," and sometimes it was the U.N. tragedy, though they never called it that.

One night in September the entire regiment moved with darkened lights to Mt. Canaan by way of Haifa, Nazareth, and Tiberias, and made camp in the pine trees that overlooked Safad and the Sea of Galilee. The regiment crouched there, ready to assault the last Lebanese, Syrian, and Arab Liberation Army strongholds in the Northern Galilee. Before the regiment was able to spring on the enemy, however, members of the Stern Gang in Jerusalem assassinated Count Folke Bernadotte, the U.N. Mediator in Palestine. Orders came to cancel the plans for the attack.

The news of Bernadotte's death first stunned Evan, then made him apprehensive and melancholy. He warned Nahshon gloomily of the many repercussions Israel might face as a result of the Mediator's death: sanctions, loss of Jerusalem, blockade, maybe even loss of her independence.

"Oh shut up and stop looking like the world is coming to an end," Nahshon finally said impatiently. "We've lived through many things in the last few years. We will live through this, too." The Moroccan looked up and saw Shulamit returning from filling her canteen at the water tank. "Shulamit," he shouted, "the Yeled's angry about what your friends did to Bernadotte."

"Is he looking for an apology?" The tan eyes had a glint of amusement. "I'm glad they killed Bernadotte," she told Evan. "Does that shock you?"

"Yes."

"I thought it would."

"Do you think murdering a man of his importance has helped Israel?"

"Yes—but that shocks you, too, doesn't it? Did you know that Bernadotte was ready to ask the U.N. to give the Negev and Jerusalem to Transjordan? I heard rumors about it from friends in Jerusalem. Now his plan dies with him."

"So does the world's good opinion of us."

"Yes, but they'll have a new opinion of us two months from now and still another one two months after that. And a year from now no one will remember the name Bernadotte. But we will have the Negev and Jerusalem."

Evan and Nahshon watched her walk up the road through the pines toward the regimental headquarters tent.

"Shulamit is civilized," Evan said. "I think the boys who killed Bernadotte were civilized. What is it that drives a civilized person to think that the proper way to destroy an idea is to destroy a person?"

"A feeling, probably, that the only weapon they have to stop the idea is a gun. Do we have anyone in the U.N. whose voice is equal to Bernadotte's? Is there any country in the world that would rather take our advice than Bernadotte's? Maybe Shulamit is right. Maybe the Stern boys knew something we didn't. What would you do if you saw something that was precious to you being snatched away by a stranger, a stranger who had enough power to keep it or give it to someone else?"

"I would think of finding some way short of murder to stop him."

"That's an easy answer. Many of us in this country think in terms of violence because we have found in the past that someone else's fist was always stronger than our mouths. It is a costly lesson to learn—but then you never forget it. I learned it many years ago in Morocco. Moises, my father's cousin, had the fist. I had only the mouth. It started with a pair of sandals. Did I ever tell you, Yeled, that I was once a sandalmaker?"

"Yes."

"Well, not really a sandalmaker. An apprentice sandalmaker, Moises was the sandalmaker, and after my father left Sura and me with him in Demnate Moises taught me how to sharpen the tools and then use them to sculptor simple designs in the sandal straps."

He was a demanding master, Nahshon said. In the summer Nahshon and the other apprentices would have to work half the night. They would munch chickpeas and sunflower seeds, and sing Hebrew and Arabic songs to help them stay awake. They slept next to their benches and ate on top of their benches. Sura would bring them their meals—tea and bread in the morning, dried vegetables with oil and hot red pimientos for lunch, and spiced vegetable soup for supper.

Nahshon had learned the sandalmaker's trade quickly. Just before Sura's thirteenth birthday, he set aside a fine piece of leather and for several weeks took each moment of spare time he could steal to sew and tool and carve it into a pair of slippers for Sura. He etched into the leather tops the outline of the distant mountains and imagined that somewhere in the folds of the tooled design was the little village of Asabadin.

Nahshon gave the slippers to his sister on her birthday. She placed them on her small feet and cried with surprise and joy, and kissed and hugged her brother. She ran and showed them to the wife of Moises, who smiled when she saw them. But Moises did not smile. His eyes bulged with rage. He grabbed Nahshon by the back of his neck and shoved him into the shop. Moises flung him on the big bench and tied his hands behind his back. He then tied his ankles together with a leather thong and knotted one end of the thong firmly around a hook at the edge of the bench. He jerked Nahshon's sandals from his feet and reached for three long leather strips. As Nahshon lay on the bench, Moises whipped the bottoms of his feet with the long strips.

"Thief!" he shouted. "Are you now the owner of the shop? Would you take my lifeblood and the food from the mouths of my wife and children and give it away as a gift? So now pay for the leather and the time you have stolen with this, and this, and this."

Nahshon bit his lip to deaden the pain as again and again the leather strips whipped across the bottoms of his feet. Finally Moises stopped, threw the leather strips onto the bench, and walked out of the darkened shop. One of the other apprentices removed the thongs from his wrists and ankles. Because of the welts on the soles of his feet, Nahshon could not wear his sandals for two weeks. But Moises did not take the slippers away from Sura.

It was less than a month later that Moises announced that he had found a husband for Sura. Her husband was to be Shaul Ashkenaz, the green tea merchant. In the wretched *Mellah*, few men could afford to have more than one wife. Shaul Ashkenaz, not yet forty, already had two wives. Although the women of the *Mellah* speculated aloud about the affairs in a household where there was more than one wife, the men of the *Mellah* envied and respected Shaul's wealth. He and his father were given the positions of honor in their synagogue.

Sura's lips trembled when she heard the news. It was common for fourteen and fifteen-year-old girls to be married in the *Mellah*. It was rare for a thirteen-year-old to be given in marriage, especially one who had just turned thirteen.

"She is not yet old enough for marriage," Nahshon spoke up, trying to control his hatred and anger.

"Ah, we have here the *chachum*, the wise man," Moises said, reaching up to readjust the position of the skullcap on his shaved head. "We have the *chachum* who knows the Scriptures, the Talmud—and maybe even the Ten Commandments, except the one that has something to say about stealing. And what does the Torah say, tell me, *chachum*, about the proper age for a Jewish woman to marry a fine Jewish man?"

"Does a fine Jewish man have more than one wife?"

"How many wives did Abraham have? How many did Solomon have? Tell me, *chachum*." He winked at his wife. "Maybe even Moises Ibn-Eli would have more than one wife if he had a larger shop and honest apprentices."

"But there are other young men in the *Mellah*," Nahshon shouted

[162]

in anger. "There are those that would be content to love only one wife."

Now Moises was angry, too. He advanced toward Nahshon, grabbed him by the shoulders, and shook him. "Yes, *chachum*," he bellowed, "there are other young men in the *Mellah*. And are you going to give them a dowry, *chachum*? Are you going to pay for the wedding celebration, or would you rather have the wealthy Moises Ibn-Eli open his purse?"

Moises was still shaking the fourteen-year-old apprentice, whose head was bobbing back and forth on his shoulders.

"Moises, Moises," his wife called, putting her hand on his arm. Moises let his hands fall from the boy's shoulders.

"Shaul Ashkenaz has waived a dowry and agreed to pay for the wedding feast," Moises said. "Your sister will be a rich man's wife. She will have luxury that she has never known before. The matter is settled."

Later, Nahshon spoke to Sura and told her that Moises was going ahead with plans for the wedding.

"Let's run away. Let's run back to Asabadin," she said.

"They don't want us there," Nahshon said. "Besides, that's the first place they would look for us."

"I'm afraid to marry him." Her child's face was pathetic and imploring.

"But where can we go? Where can we go?" he asked helplessly. His sister began to cry. He lifted her hand and patted it. "Don't worry. I'll think of something."

On the night before the wedding, Moises bolted the door of the shop and placed his sleeping mat before it. Nahshon waited until Moises and the other two apprentices had fallen asleep. Then he got up from his mat and, holding his sandals in one hand, tiptoed to the back room where Sura and Moises' children slept. He awakened his sister.

"Where are we going?" she asked.

"I don't know. But we're leaving here."

They put the few clothes they had in a sack. They did not pack the purple velvet wedding dress and the white veil hanging on the wall.

Nahshon led her by the hand. "We can't go out the front door," he whispered. "Moises is sleeping beside the door."

[163]

They walked toward the back door. When they were several feet away from the door, they saw a body stir on the floor in front of it. It was Moises' wife.

"I'm awake," she said softly. "If you come one step closer, I'll shout for Moises."

Nahshon stared at her frantically. The only two windows in the narrow building had bars to protect the shop from thieves. "Let us leave," he pleaded. "You can say that you were asleep and we stepped over you."

"And Moises will beat me before I have time to explain. Besides, they would find you an hour after sunup. Where would two children hide in the *Mellah?* Where would two Jews hide outside the *Mellah?*"

Sura's fingernails cut into Nahshon's hand.

"Please," he begged.

"No," Moises' wife answered firmly. "Go back to your beds quietly and I won't tell that you tried to leave."

Nahshon went with Sura back to the bedroom. She collapsed on her mat and smothered her sobs in the crook of her arm. She wept for more than an hour while Nahshon rubbed her back and smoothed her hair. "I've failed you," he said over and over again, and his sister did not answer. It was almost the dawn of her wedding day when she finally fell asleep, her face still wet with tears. Nahshon tiptoed back to his mat in the shop. He lay there and tried to think of some other way he could escape with his sister. And then he broke out in a cold sweat as he realized there was no other way.

A large tub was brought to the shop of Moises, the sandalmaker, on the morning of the wedding. It was taken to the back room and filled full of water purchased dearly from the Arab waterseller. Late in the afternoon, in the deep tub of tepid water, Sura immersed herself ritually and then the wife of Moises and other women of the *Mellah* washed her soft black hair and helped the girl bride wash her body. They rubbed and dried her hair with towels and tied it into a multitude of small braids and one large braid. They dressed her in the purple gown adorned with gold embroidery and then arranged the large braid over the center of her face, so it hid her nose, her mouth, and her soft olive chin, and fell between the tiny mounds of her bosom. The women then covered her face with the white veil.

At dusk, the father of Shaul, the green tea merchant, arrived at the house of Moises to get the bride. The old man, clothed in his Sabbath finery, was riding a donkey and he was followed by many of the men, women, and children of the *Mellah*. Some of the people were carrying lighted candles. The old man turned the donkey around, and Sura, Nahshon, Moises, and his family followed behind the donkey to the large house of Shaul.

At the threshold of the house, one of Shaul's servants was holding a bowl filled with a mixture of honey and milk. Sura dipped her hand into the mixture and applied it to the wall of the house. The servant wiped her hand with a wet towel and then gave her a raw egg. She threw the egg up against the ceiling and the symbol of fertility smashed, spread, and dripped down to the floor.

Shaul, the bridegroom, came to the door to meet her. He was a heavy man with short-cropped black hair. He was wearing a white linen gown, a cylindrical white velvet skullcap, and golden velvet slippers. His temples were already beginning to turn gray. Shaul reached for Sura's hand and kissed it.

A rabbi stood before Shaul and Sura and hurriedly intoned the wedding contract. Shaul then broke a glass with his foot, according to tradition, and the marriage ceremony was complete. A trio of musicians began playing and singing Hebrew songs as soon as the ceremony was over, and the two families sat down at a long table in the large room for the wedding feast. There was tongue, stuffed chicken, boiled chicken, mutton, and other dishes piled on the table. They disappeared quickly into the seemingly starving mouths of the wedding guests, especially the children of Shaul and Moises. Nahshon noticed that Shaul's two wives quietly helped the servants replenish the fast-disappearing piles of food on the table.

After the prayers had been chanted at the conclusion of the meal, bowls of fruit and jugs of wine were set on the table.

The bride and groom rose from the table and walked to the far end of the room to the *mecreya*, a nuptial alcove built into the wall. The opening of the alcove did not begin until about two feet above the floor. The curtains were parted, revealing a mattress covered by white sheets and several pillows.

Sura had removed the white veil before the wedding feast began, although, like Nahshon, she had not touched a morsel of the rich meal. Now she stood before the *mecreya* as her husband told the wedding guests goodnight and encouraged them to stay late and enjoy the wine and fruit. The jet black braid still hung down over the middle of Sura's face and made a slight cleft in the full blouse of the velvet dress. Nahshon could see Sura's dark eyes. They were sad eyes and they were looking at him. Sura had not taken her eyes off the face of her brother once since the ceremony had ended.

Shaul, the green tea merchant, helped Sura climb up into the *mecreya*. She sat on the edge of the alcove and then swung her feet into the opening, also. The long velvet gown lifted above the thin olive ankles. Anguish coursed through Nahshon's chest. He saw she was wearing the birthday slippers with the delicate outline of the Atlas mountains tooled in the leather. Shaul crawled into the *mecreya*. There were lewd shouts from the male wedding guests as he pulled the heavy silk curtains together. Moises, who had already drunk too much of the wine, raised his cup and shouted a toast toward the alcove, "May it be God's will that the first one is a boy."

The noise in the room was as thick as the heavy wine in the jugs. The wedding guests toasted the bride and groom a dozen times, and Shaul's two wives appeared with ordered efficiency with jugs of fresh wine.

Nahshon stood against the wall, away from the table where the wedding guests were devouring the fruit and gulping the wine. Out of the corner of his eye he watched the curtains of the *mecreya*. Suddenly, he thought he heard a whimper, and the silk curtain twisted as though it had been kicked. In that moment he forgot the fear of Moises and Shaul and the *Mellah*. He ran over to the curtain. Reaching up with both hands, he pulled it with all his might and ripped it off the rod. There was the back of Shaul, covered with curly black hair. And there was Sura, the black braid no longer over her face. She was looking at her brother with surprise, and she was curling up her small naked body to hide it from the stunned, silent stares of the wedding guests. She was reaching frantically for the velvet purple gown to cover her child's body and her child's breasts.

Nahshon, who had made his move in a moment of violent action, now, in the flick of a second since the curtains had come down, stood frozen, looking dumbly at the nakedness of his sister and her husband.

In the next second, he held out his hand to her and shouted, "Sura, Sura! Come with me!" But Sura cringed away from him, pulling the gown in front of her body.

[166]

The wedding guests were now running toward him. "Bastard! Bastard!" "He has uncovered his sister's nakedness." "Shame!" "Stone him to death!" "Cover up the *mecreya!*" "Stone him to death!" "Dog! Dog!"

Hands were now reaching for Nahshon and flailing at him. Fingernails tore into the skin on his face. He felt his blouse pull and rip. He began to fight back, and using his fists as a wedge he plowed through the crowd of men and women to the front door. . . .

The agony on Nahshon's face as he spoke was as real now under the pines of Mt. Canaan as it had been in the *Mellah* of Demnate. And Evan, as he listened to the story, could feel the tragedy of the Moroccan brother and sister, even though he could not fully imagine the world in which they had lived.

"I got away and made my way to Palestine," Nahshon said. "There was a time when I would not have told this story to anyone—not even to the Yemenite family that sheltered me when I first came to this country. I thought I would be branded by shame if anyone found out. And then I found my story was mild compared to some experiences of my friends from Europe. Every story has its point, Yeled. Do you know what mine is? If I had to live it all over again, I would take the curved knife I used for cutting leather, and I would carve the heart out of Moises the night before the wedding. Perhaps the boys in the Stern Group were working from past experience."

All of the major Jewish holidays that year came in October. The season began on a particularly happy note when a letter arrived telling Mordecai and Aaron that their parents had been found alive and well in a D.P. camp near Naples. Mr. and Mrs. Kliger were being sent to a camp at Salerno, the letter said, and would be put aboard a refugee ship to Israel as soon as possible.

On the day before Rosh Hashanah, the Jewish New Year, tables were brought into the clearing outside the mess hall and the area decorated with colored lights. That night, following services in the little synagogue, the men of the armored regiment had a Rosh Hashanah banquet: vegetable salad, fried potatoes, fried filet of fish, and chopped mutton. Most delectable to Evan was the *chalah*, white bread, the first departure from the thrice-daily fare of rye bread since his arrival at the camp.

Almost everyone was restricted to camp during the holidays since it was feared the Arabs would take advantage of the season to attack. But only a tiny portion of the men in camp attended services on Rosh Hashanah eve and Rosh Hashanah day in the former British army day room now used as a synagogue. The religious Jews had completely whitewashed the walls and ceiling, built a pine ark on one wall, and painted the walls beautifully with scenes of the Tomb of Rachel and the skyline of the Old City of Jerusalem. It was a sight unseen by the majority. Netzer, a Palestinian on Evan's halftrack, had once said that his father had never missed attending synagogue on Sabbath and the holidays in Bulgaria, yet had never gone since arriving in Palestine before World War II. There was a feeling among many of the Israelis that their ancestors had kept the faith and preserved the Jews during the long exile, and now that they were back in the homeland again they could rest from their religious labors.

Evan wasn't in camp on Yom Kippur, the Day of Atonement. Several days before the fast day, his halftrack, two other halftracks, and three armored cars were sent to guard a new kibbutz scheduled to be established on the Lebanese border. The Arabs, it was feared, would be tempted to attack the isolated kibbutz before it could erect defenses. The armored vehicles and their men were to be a temporary show of force. The convoy left from Nahariya at nightfall with the armored cars and halftracks leading the column. Behind them were trucks loaded with prefabricated sections of buildings, tents, barbed wire, tools, and large square metal water tanks. About thirty boys and girls, the fledgling kibbutzniks, rode atop the cargoes on the trucks.

The convoy traveled east with darkened lights along the highway that paralleled the Lebanese border. The site of the kibbutz was a broad-domed hill adjacent to and commanding the paved highway. It was an unlikely spot for an agricultural settlement, but a prime place for a fortified hill. The kibbutz would be subsidized at first as a strategic outpost along the Lebanese border, and the youths could gradually begin to clear the surrounding slopes and valleys as farmland.

The armored cars remained on guard down at the road while the halftracks and trucks strained their way up a crude road to the hilltop site of the kibbutz. The men in the halftracks were then deployed to points halfway down the slope of the hill. By dawn barbed wire had been placed around the site and a basic system of defense trenches dug. During the morning the squads from the halftracks helped the young men and women—none of whom seemed to be over twenty, and some at least three or four years younger—nail together the prefabricated sections of their sleeping quarters, dining hall, and guard tower. They erected tents for supplies and lifted the empty water tanks onto wooden stilts.

The young kibbutzniks could have been a group of teenagers at summer camp, building cabins and a campsite that they would use until fall and then leave deserted when they returned home. The sunburned girls in their bloomer shorts or long khaki trousers worked next to the young men who were pushing the walls into place, and later they set out the bread and canned food for lunch on planks stretched across wooden crates. It should have been a summer idyl for these children, a few months in the mountains with other young boys and girls and chaperones. But it wasn't. They would live here through the fall and winter and marry each other and have babies. They would guard the highway and toughen their hands on a million rocks, working for the day when their kibbutz would be as comfortable and affluent as the older settlements in the Emek. Evan thought about those older settlements they had seen at dawn from the crippled halftrack and remembered how, from a distance, they had looked like part of a landscape from Lilliput. This then was Brobdingnag, where a closer scrutiny magnified the pores until one could see and smell the wads of dirt and fatty deposits in each one. It was a kibbutz populated with dark, dusty tents, unpainted shacks, and already close outhouses, all of it surrounded by trenches and careless turns of barbed wire. Evan could see the stains on the girls' blouses and smell the raw sweat as they passed.

The Emek and this hill were Israel. They were the tiny, handsome representative to the U.N. brandishing his miniature silver sword to hold off his ugly enemies and speaking in golden tones for his diminutive democracy, while at home his government argued among themselves about whether they should allow non-kosher meat to be imported into the country. They were the heroic little army venturing out into the hills at night to meet their foes, while at staff headquarters the generals debated whether they should courtmartial cooks who refused to cook a hot meal on the Sabbath for men preparing to go into battle. They were a nation that had proclaimed

[169]

the Law of the Return, and then reached out to bring the oppressed seed from far, while the citizen in Haifa was apprehensive that there would soon be more dark Jews in the country than light ones and that one of them might move next door.

How would historians a thousand years from now see this land, as Lilliput or Brobdingnag—or nothing? For it wasn't too difficult to believe that the feats of this little nation would be, in the eyes of the historians, eclipsed by the massive horror of the extended Dark Ages during which they were accomplished. The Twentieth Century was the miserable climax to a black millennium. It was a century when madmen stalked the earth like carnivores and slaughtered their fellow men for lust of blood. Among it all, the re-birth of the Jewish state would be as insignificant as the exodus of the Hebrews from Egypt had been to the historians of ancient Egypt.

And what would happen if the Arabs discovered what others had already begun to learn—that kindness would kill the Jew, would make him wither and die. Not pogroms, but brotherhood was the secret; brotherhood and peace until these Jews became Levantines, and their gods became mammon and nationalism. Was this then a new dawn, or an identical deceptive light, a twilight, a last chapter winding up an over-long, over-tragic story?

There was no trouble from the Arabs. The second night, after supper, some of the kibbutzniks built a campfire and Uzi produced his concertina. Except for the guards down in the trenches, everyone joined arms and began dancing the *hora* around the campfire. They had all been awake for more than twenty-four hours, but there was still a happy, untapped energy in the young sinews. They sang until they were hoarse. They scuffed their shoes and boots through the rocky dirt, shouting the words of the songs to the capacity of their lungs, as if daring the Arab soldiers in the Lebanese hills across from them to deny them their celebration.

The six vehicles from the armored regiment stayed at the new kibbutz until the morning following Yom Kippur. Then they returned to their camp, leaving a wisp of creation behind them on the hilltop in Galilee.

The holiday period ended in late October with an *isru chag*, an "additional celebration" on the evening that concluded *Simchat Torah*, itself one of the happiest holidays of the Jewish year. The religious Jews invited a Chasidic rabbi and three musicians to visit the camp and lead the festivities. Then they bought all the after-shave lotion in the post canteen and tore up newspapers into confetti.

That evening, as the celebration got underway, the synagogue was packed. Many men who had avoided the synagogue on Rosh Hashanah and Yom Kippur were crowded into the chapel, more out of curiosity than religious devotion. The rabbi, an older and smaller version of Mr. Zephron, led the congregation through the brief evening service. Then the festivities began. The band consisted of two elderly men with gray, stringy beards, playing clarinets, and one little boy, perhaps a year older than Carmi and looking very much like him, playing a snare drum. The band was unusual even for Chasidic Jews, since musical instruments were barred from the synagogue on Sabbath and most of the holidays.

As the music began to increase in pace, the men who were jammed around the walls of the synagogue clapped their hands with the beat of the drum. Two of the religious Jews danced in the center of the floor, holding the Torahs tightly in their arms. Then they passed the Torahs on to companions, who took up the step of the whirling dance. Other religious Jews sang the words of the song with them. They threw confetti up into the air over the dancers and poured the after-shave lotion into their cupped hands, then flung it into the air also. Sweat was pouring down the faces of the men now dancing with the Torahs. They were bending and whirling and shouting the verses of the song as though in a religious fit brought on by the screeching sounds of the two clarinets, the rasping sound of the snare drum, and the powerful rhythm of clapping hands. Evan stood against the wall and watched with the same fascinated interest he would have displayed if he were watching a Holy Roller prayer meeting. Nothing he had ever seen in Judaism resembled the emotional outburst of this religious orgy set to music.

The noise of the celebration had carried far beyond the walls of the synagogue, and other soldiers were shoving through the door to watch the proceedings. The men were now packed shoulder to shoulder in the chapel. The sharp sweet scent of after-shave lotion mingled with the smell of perspiring bodies.

Radhai stood transfixed in a corner of the synagogue, clapping his hands mechanically to the beat of the music. Hot beads of perspiration swelled out of the pores of his forehead and temple. As his hands kept time to the music, his thoughts pulled away from the whirling scene and drifted back through the lifeless seconds to the *mesgid,* where, as a boy for the last time and a man for the first, he had held the Book of the Law and danced to the song of the people of Debra Hakim and the music of the sacred instruments. And now these other men were dancing in the synagogue, singing in Hebrew instead of Amharic. The musicians were white and the floor was cement. A breath of air touched the perspiration on Radhai's face and chilled him. He squeezed through the clapping, laughing soldiers and made his way to the door.

As he opened it, a sergeant from one of the armored car companies ran in from the night, bumped him aside roughly, and shouted, "Air raid! Air raid! Out with all the lights! Quickly!" Someone pulled the light switches and the sergeant groped his way to the door, then hurried outside again. The music had stopped immediately, and now the men stood silently in the hot room, hearing only each other's breath, but straining for the sound of a motor. And then it was there, high and to the distance, a single engine, coming toward their camp from the north. Droning louder as it approached, it reached and maintained an even volume for what seemed like minutes over the darkened camp, then died away to the south.

The sound had hardly disappeared when it was replaced by the voice of Eliyahu, speaking from behind the bright beam of a flashlight at the doorway. "We have a report that someone was using a light at the Bahai shrine to signal the plane," he said. He swept the beam over a dozen faces. "You, you, you, you. Get your helmets, weapons, and twenty rounds of ammunition. Meet me at the hole in the back fence in three minutes."

Evan trotted grudgingly over to his barracks to get his helmet and Sten gun. He waited for the Falasha, who was walking toward him carrying his machine gun, and the two of them walked together to the fence.

The thin lieutenant, helmetless as usual, faced the soldiers. "You will follow me to the shrine as quietly as possible. Then surround the house. Do not fire unless I give the order."

He led them through the hole, across the hedge, and into the garden. Evan and Radhai knelt down fifty feet from the doorstep near which Evan had seen the big Persian digging in the flower bed those months ago. Eliyahu walked up to the door and pounded on it with his fist. A light went on in a back room; then the big Persian was opening the door. He was holding his bathrobe closed with his fist. Eliyahu spoke to him curtly in Arabic and the man went back into the interior of the house. He reappeared in a few minutes. Eliyahu snapped something else in Arabic and the big Persian pushed open the screen door and walked out into the yard, followed by an elderly couple. They were all dressed in nightclothes and slippers. The old woman's gray hair was tousled, and she tried to push the strands back into place with one hand while holding the top of her robe with the other.

Eliyahu asked them a question in Arabic in an uncivil tone of voice, and when they shook their heads the lieutenant began shouting at them. Evan had hurried away from the barracks without his jacket and now he shivered in the chilly night air. He could see that the Persians were cold, too, and frightened at the nature of the accusation. Embarrassed that he was playing any role in the torment of these people, he wanted to disappear, to vanish into the darkness before the large Persian saw his face and perhaps remembered it as that of a visitor to the shrine.

Eliyahu, however, his voice heavy with disbelief and sarcasm, would not relent. He kept them standing in the yard for ten minutes, receiving their denials and exchanging them for new charges. Then he let the three go back into the villa, and led his cold troops to the hole in the barbed wire fence.

The celebration in the chapel had resumed again. The lights were on and they could hear the whining music and the clapping of hands drifting through the darkness. While the others returned to their barracks, Radhai carried his machine gun and walked along the dirt path to the far edge of camp, where the music of the *isru chag* would be drowned out by the jackals. The dance in the synagogue, the plane, Eliyahu shouting at the Persians, they were all distorted pieces of memory. He sat down and tried to sort them out, to catch hold of them, in hopes that he could fling them back into the night.

There had been the dance on the Day of Forgiveness, and that night the people of the village had marked the end of the fast day with a community meal in the *mesgid,* Radhai sat with the other men of Debra Hakim on the dirt floor of the synagogue and listened to

[173]

a Falasha traveler who had tarried at the village to celebrate the Day of Forgiveness.

He had just come from the eastern slopes of the Semien mountains, the traveler said, where messages had been received that the white-skinned Romans had invaded the country, and, though they were Christians, had slaughtered thousands of Copts. They had taken the cities in the lowlands near the sea, and a few months before had captured Addis Ababa, setting the Christian emperor of Ethiopia to flight out of the land.

"Are these the same Romans who legends say invaded the Land of Israel and destroyed the new Temple?" Ya'qob asked.

The traveler nodded. "Only now, the people to the east say, the Romans have iron carts that move by themselves and shoot hundreds of bullets and big pieces of iron that burst into a thousand pieces. They also say that they have other carts that fly in the air like birds and drop the bursting iron from their stomachs."

The men of the village murmured and shook their heads in disbelief.

The next day, when Radhai and Ya'qob were down at the stream washing the togas they had used on the Day of Forgiveness, the youth asked his uncle if he thought the Romans had come to Ethiopia to kill the rest of the House of Israel.

Ya'qob smiled. "Whatever God wills will be. But if the Romans came to kill the House of Israel, why do they kill their fellow Christians? No, they came for the land, and the land has never been ours. We are strangers here."

"If God can send the Romans to Ethiopia," Radhai asked earnestly, "why can't He send the Messiah to take us back to our own land?"

"But He can, Radhai. He can. God could send the Messiah this very minute. But who are you or I to try to understand the Lord and His ways? It is very difficult for us even to understand ourselves. All we know is that our life is like this stream. It starts in the mountains from a drop of rain. The drop grows until it is a tiny brook, bubbling as it hits the small white rocks and widening here at our village, where it is smooth and mature and comforting to the people by its banks. Downstream there are rapids that fold the stream into powerful fists and then it is smooth again, until suddenly the falls send it out into space, terrifying the breath and dashing it into the rocks. But soon it is smooth again, and enters Lake Tana and is lost in the depth and the width. The stream is comforted and pacified, but it is never the stream again. And can we ask if its waters remain in Lake Tana forever, or are emptied bit by bit into the Blue Nile that flows for many thousands of miles to the land of Egypt and then into the sea? God has allowed us to know only so much. I believe I would be unhappy if I knew more."

There are times in a person's life when he instinctively knows that he has reached a summit of happiness, when it is quite likely that there will never be a happier time. The season that followed the Day of Forgiveness when Radhai was sixteen years old was the light-footed time of his life. The three-month rainy period that ended a few weeks before the Day of Forgiveness had been both generous and gentle, and wild raspberry vines flourished on the bare slopes that rose above the reeds on the banks of the stream. The grass even on the high slopes was thick and moist, and the earth was cool and springy under the hoofs of the cattle and the bare feet of the Falashas of Debra Hakim.

The season of life that had received such a wonderful initiation from the Day of Forgiveness coasted on, longer than usual. And in January the grass was still green, the wild flowers continued to grow. Then, abruptly, fiercely, the season of life ended.

Radhai heard the noise first. He and Ya'qob had left the village in early morning to check the cattle. They had wandered far upstream, and now they were driving the cattle back to the pastures near the village. The noise was that of a hornet. Radhai searched with his eyes over the tops of the deep grass, but saw nothing. The hornet sound was louder now and it was coming from the sky. Then he and Ya'qob saw them. They were large birds, with double wings like the dragonfly, only the wings did not move. Sticks joined the wings together, and two wheels hung down from the wings. There were three of the birds. They circled over Debra Hakim, then headed away. But as they headed away, one by one the large birds dropped away and turned back toward Debra Hakim. They were very low and as they passed over the village they dropped eggs from their wings. There were loud noises in the village and clouds of smoke rose up from behind the hedges and thatched roofs.

Ya'qob and Radhai began running toward the village, but there was the crack of rifles firing from up on the hill. The bullets hit in front of the two Falashas and they stopped running. Walking cautiously down toward them from the top of the hill were a dozen men. Eight seemed to be Amharas. Some of them had spears and the others held rifles aimed at Ya'qob and Radhai. The other four were dressed in light brown uniforms and wore boots. Three of the men had white skin, the first Radhai had ever seen. The fourth had black skin and might have been an Ethiopian. In the distance, Ya'qob and Radhai could see Amharas and white-skinned men in uniforms running toward the hedge that surrounded Debra Hakim, firing rifles. There were only a few answering shots from the village, and the men disappeared behind the hedge.

The three large birds were together again, flying away. It had happened so suddenly. For a fleeting second, Radhai believed that this might be only a bad dream, caused by the words of the traveler who had visited the village on the Day of Forgiveness.

The men from the hill came closer. One of the white-skinned men had a wide brown belt around his waist and a second that crossed over his shoulder. He stepped forward and said something in a strange language. The black soldier stepped up next to the man and translated into Amharic what he had said.

"Are you a Falasha priest?"

"Yes. Why did you do this thing?"

"Is this your son?"

"No. Why did you do this to my village?"

The man with the two belts, who was a full head shorter than Ya'qob, walked up to the priest and hit him on the cheek with the back of his hand, then spat out something else in the strange language.

"The captain says that it is he who will do the questioning!" the black soldier shouted.

The man began talking again and the interpreter continued: "We are occupation troops of the Italian Empire, conquerors of Ethiopia. Your Amhara neighbors in the village of Kumansa have told us that the Falashas will fight us. Therefore we have destroyed Debra Hakim. Go now to the Falasha villages to the west and tell them of the might of the Italian army. Tell them that it is useless to oppose us and that we come in peace. Tell them we have already conquered Debra Tabor, Gondar, and Debarech. Now go."

Radhai looked at Ya'qob to see what he would do. Ya'qob spoke to the interpreter. "Tell this hyena that I go back to my village now to bury the dead."

He took the arm of Radhai and began walking toward the village, brushing past the soldiers and Amharas. The grassland was now open between them and Debra Hakim. There was the sound of a gun firing behind their backs and Ya'qob fell to his knees. He held on to Radhai's arm for a second, then toppled over onto his side. Radhai threw himself down on the ground beside Ya'qob and cradled his head in his arms. The Italian captain was putting a black revolver back in the holster that hung from the wide brown belt. He spoke again to the interpreter.

"Go, now," the interpreter told Radhai. "Go, now, to the Falasha villages to the west and tell them what the captain has said."

Radhai put Ya'qob's head and shoulders back down on the ground. Ya'qob's eyes were open, but they did not blink. The priest was dead. Radhai stood and the anger in his heart absorbed the tears. He walked toward the stream, waded through the waist deep water until he came to the other side, then climbed the hills that led to the west. When he reached the first summit, he looked back. The body of Ya'qob was hidden in the tall grass. The Amharas from Kumansa were driving the cattle in the direction of their village, and the men in the uniforms were walking toward the silent Debra Hakim.

Radhai sat in a clump of bushes atop the bare hill all day, watching the soldiers and Amharas loot the village. In mid-afternoon the soldiers left, traveling north in the direction of Gondar. At dusk the Amharas left also, carrying bundles and baskets of loot on their shoulders and in their arms. One Amhara had a lighted torch. He set fire to each of the several dozen thatched roofs in Debra Hakim. The sun dropped below the hill behind Radhai, leaving the half-light in which the sky and the hills to the east were the same color. It had taken only a few minutes for the thatched roofs to burn. But now in the devil's light of dusk each stream of silver smoke marked a hut, and the largest stream of all came from the smoldering roof of the *mesgid*.

At nightfall, Radhai ran back down the hill to the body of Ya'qob. The priest still lay there on his back, the dark eyes staring toward the heavens, the white turban still in place on his head. Pieces of dirt clung to the soles of the feet that hours before had supported the tall body of the priest, but would never support it again. Radhai closed his uncle's eyelids, then lay down beside him to try to sleep away the evil dream.

The next morning he lifted his uncle on his shoulders and carried him into the village. Some of the men of the village lay dead near the hedge. Others, killed by shrapnel from the bombs, were grotesque studies in red and black. In the *mesgid* were the women and children of the village, huddled to one side of the house of prayer as if at a Sabbath service. Only now they were dead, the life having flowed out of them through the tiny perforations that leaked the red blood onto the earthen floor. Some of the mothers and children, side by side, still leaned toward each other for support in death as they had in life, and their bodies formed little pyramids. The others were sprawled on the floor, their bodies covered with burned particles of straw and reeds from the roof.

Radhai walked back outside the *mesgid* and searched for a tool to dig with. He found the head of an ax and carried it back into the *mesgid*. Beside the charred remains of the Holy of Holies, he dug a shallow grave, lined it with rocks, and dragged his uncle into it. He found flat rocks to make a vault over the top, and before he closed up the grave, he took the burned and disintegrating Scriptures and placed it on his uncle's chest.

Then he separated the dead villagers into little family groups on the floor of the *mesgid*, dragging in the bodies of the men and laying them beside their wives and children. Counting his uncle, seventy-three Falashas—everyone in Debra Hakim but himself—had been killed. Radhai piled stones in the two windows of the *mesgid*, then sealed the doorways with stones, also.

In the afternoon he went down to the stream and cut the tallest reeds he could find to make a covering for the *mesgid*. Now neither the wild animals nor the birds of prey could get to the bodies. Before dusk Radhai covered his head with dust, cut both arms with his knife, and chanted what he could remember of the prayers for the dead. He slept next to the stream that night, and the next morning repeated the prayers. There were no lambs left to be sacrificed on the altar outside the sealed-up *mesgid*, but Radhai prayed that the souls of the seventy-three could leave the Valley of Death and ascend to Heaven.

Radhai walked downstream and immersed himself in the cool

[178]

water of the stream. He washed the dust from his hair. He scrubbed his tunic and knee-length trousers against the rocks of the stream and hung them on the reeds to dry as he swam in the stream and washed his body. He put on his clothes, still damp, and walked downstream toward Lake Tana, not turning back again to view the Falasha village that had become a tomb.

Radhai followed the stream past the rapids and down past the steep waterfall. He turned to the west and stayed near the banks of the great Lake Tana, which would have looked like an endless inland sea except for the dark outlines of mountains to the south. Radhai examined each village he approached from a distance to see if it was a Falasha settlement. It took him only a short time at each village to find out. A woman—or a man without a turban—killing an animal, or a close up view of a villager with a longer, thinner face would indicate to Radhai that it was an Amhara village.

At first he had doubts that he would ever find a Falasha village. Then he had doubts that there was indeed a Falasha village to be found. And finally Radhai decided, hesitantly, then surely, that he was probably the last Falasha alive in the world. Why would the Italians destroy Debra Hakim unless they had already destroyed all the Falasha villages to the east? They had sent him ahead, he reasoned, so they could conquer the other Falasha villages without a fight and destroy them also. If it was the will of God that the Romans destroy all the Jews, then surely God had a reason for sparing him.

He had clung to that hope while serving Lij Hailu Balao, and he thought Wingate had fulfilled it. But in the seven years he had lived here in the Land of the Return he had new doubts, and now on top of the doubts there were flashing portents.

Chapter Twelve

THE THREE PLANES FLEW VERY SLOWLY AND IN A loose "V" formation. They were Italian trainers, bi-winged machines with two open cockpits. By military standards they were ancient and tortoise-like—they could barely make a hundred miles per hour. The three bombers of the Israeli air force were heading surely, if not swiftly, for a bombing run over Saf-saf, an Arab village in the Northern Galilee.

Once over the target, the men in the back cockpits would toss a few handmade bombs overboard to soften up Saf-saf for the assault by the armored regiment. Then the planes would turn back for Israeli territory. Such was the plan, and now, in the last hour of light on October 28, the Israeli pilots were executing it. The creeping planes broke their triangle formation and formed a single file, one behind the other.

All the vehicles in the armored regiment were in single file, also, on a road atop Mt. Canaan, waiting to move into the attack at dusk and clear the entire Northern Galilee of Arab troops. The regiment had been moved to Mt. Canaan two days after Simchat Torah, and now they were to make the assault that Bernadotte's death had kept them from making a month before. Soldiers were standing up in their halftracks and outside their armored cars watching the three Italian biplanes fly toward the Arab village that was hidden from the regiment's view by a fold in the hills.

A burst of smoke suddenly appeared in the sky, at least a mile from the planes. A few seconds later the men in the armored regiment heard the sound of a shell exploding in the air.

"Anti-aircraft fire," Uzi said. "God, their aim's awful."

A half-minute later there was another burst of deep brown smoke flowering out from a little bud in the sky, then dissipating into the air. This one was nearer the planes, but still a great distance away from them. Again there was the thumping report of an explosion in the air.

Then there were other explosions, but no bursts of smoke in the sky. The planes were flying over their target. Each plane tossed out two bombs and then turned slowly back in the direction of Mt. Canaan. They closed up into their triangle formation again. There were two more puffs of smoke, followed by explosions, far behind them. They were over Mt. Canaan, turning again slightly toward the direction of Haifa, and the men of the armored regiment shouted up at the planes and cheered and applauded.

Evan, tightly-wound and nervous, as he always was just before battle, still had to smile at the performance of the three planes. There would never be another war like this—one little nation fighting other little nations in the last little war in which the big powers did not intervene.

For three nights before the attack in the Northern Galilee, engineers had gone out behind Arab lines to remove roadblocks and fill in destroyed portions of road. Now, as the engineers went out into the darkness to remove the last roadblocks, the armored regiment left Mt. Canaan, followed the paved highway past Safad, then turned north toward the Lebanese border to strike into the heart of Arab-held Palestine.

This was the little war again. Thousands of bullets lunging past each other in the darkness, hundreds of bright tracers to count the thousands, and only one in a thousand finding its way into the soft flesh of man.

Saf-saf, the village the biplanes had bombed, was captured shortly before dawn. At dawn the regiment attacked Jish, a hill village that guarded a sharp bend in the road. Jish, built on the site of an ancient Jewish fortress that had held out bravely during the rebellion against the Romans, was ready for the attack. More than four hundred Syrian troops had been brought into the village by bus during the night.

The Israeli soldiers dismounted from the halftracks and ran in to attack the village under covering fire from the halftracks, armored cars, and mortars, which had been set up beside the road. To the left, running toward the village in a sweeping, flanking maneuver, were three squads of men. Through the slit in his window, Evan could recognize Uzi and the other men from his halftrack, and well ahead of them, running more upright than the others, Eliyahu, helmetless, his black hair bouncing with each stride. Little pockets of dirt erupted near the feet of Eliyahu, but still he ran, as though the winner of the race to the first building would receive a coveted prize. The dawn air was filled with the noise of battle, meshing small arms fire, the thump and then the blast of mortars, shouting men. There were several men lying very still on the slopes that led up to the village. An Arab ammunition truck exploded and came rolling crazily down the side of the hill, spewing fireworks in all directions. And then all the noises of battle were inside the village itself.

By early morning, Jish was captured. The armored regiment regrouped and refueled at Jish during the day, while the men in the infantry platoons took up positions on the hills and fought back a weak infantry counterattack. In the afternoon, when Evan was up at Nahshon's halftrack talking to Shulamit, the Arabs turned a 75 millimeter artillery piece on the regiment. The whistling, hurtling, invisible mass hit at first far off in a field away from the road. Then the exploding sprays of dirt came closer, in a broad arc, each one drawing nearer the vehicles. Evan and Shulamit crouched on the ground behind the halftrack. A projectile slammed into the hill forty yards above them, raining rocky dirt and then dust down on them. At the blast, both of them had fallen flat against the ground, their heads very close together, and Evan had bent his arm and made a shelter over her head. When they sat up again, Evan brushed the dirt from the top of her hair and then, in their hiding place behind the halftrack, kissed her deeply and felt her kiss back.

The arc moved past them and the next projectile crashed into the side of an empty halftrack. Then the screams of twisting metal clawing its way through the air stopped. The big gun, somewhere in the vicinity of Sasa to the west, had wasted several dozen rounds of ammunition in the empty fields, and now that it had found the range it mysteriously rested.

A jagged hole as big as a volleyball had been carved through the side of Zvi's halftrack, but the vehicle was still useable.

The regiment advanced again that night and attacked Sasa, which overlooked the junction of the last Arab-held roads from the interior of the Galilee. Most of the Arab troops had fled, however. Only a few snipers were in the village and it was easily taken. The Israelis also captured the French 75 millimeter cannon that had been used on them that afternoon, and immediately radioed back for an artillery crew so the gun could be used against the Arabs the next day.

They paused at Sasa during the morning, awaiting orders whether to press northeast along the border of Lebanon or push back along the border road to the west. Just before noon, a small pickup truck arrived from Safad with fresh food. The driver stepped down from the cab and went around back to examine his canvas canopy, rent by bullets in a dozen places.

"We have troops in Saf-saf, Jish, and here," the driver told the men near him, "but nobody in between. There were Arab snipers in the hills all the way up here. If I have to make another food run, I'm coming in an armored car." He reached into the back of the truck and pulled out cardboard boxes. Beef sandwiches, unwrapped, were piled up in each box. Some of the beef had spilled completely out of the slices of rye bread. There was a stampede toward the boxes.

"Slowly, slowly," the driver said. "There's enough here for everybody. You men must be getting sick of hazel nuts." He laughed as the men elbowed him aside to dig down for the sandwiches. "I've got mail, too. It came up to Mt. Canaan from camp the afternoon you left." He walked back around to the cab, pulled out a large bundle of envelopes, and ripped the string from around the bundle. While he called out the names of the men in the regiment who had letters, Evan chomped on the beef and groggily shuffled over to the water trailer to fill his canteen. When he returned, Uzi was waving an envelope in the air.

"A letter for you," he called to Evan.

It was from Evan's roommate at the University of Virginia. He sat down on the running board of the halftrack and opened the envelope.

October 12, 1948

Dear Evan,

I am now a confirmed Jew advocate. Last Saturday night Ted and I went to a dance at Mary Washington College and I got an Egyptian. They told me it was a girl. I'm still not convinced.

She told me she had five cousins fighting against you. I have already stuck a quarter in the Jewish Relief Fund and am going to insert more. If all the Egyptians are like that mealy-mouthed, fat, piggy little article, I'll come over and finish where you leave off. When I danced with her my right hand was squishing the fat back and forth about her waist. Long live Israel.

I have been corresponding with your mother, and I would say she is now over the real shock of knowing that you are in Israel. At least her letters to me seem a little calmer. I've already prepared for your admittance back into the University for the February term, if you can get back by then. Your mother asked me to do that, and I was glad to help in any way I could.

It looks almost certain that Dewey will be elected in November. I'm finally an American voter this year, you know. I'm going to cast an absentee ballot for Truman the next time I go home. I heard Norman Thomas, the Socialist candidate, speak on the radio yesterday and I'm going to hear fat-headed Wallace when he comes through Richmond next week.

[183]

When I was home last time I had a blind date with a girl who was so stacked I had to arch my back to kiss her. I'm getting to be a sex maniac. Don't forget, when you come back I want you to get me another date with Babs Wheater. I'm just mad about the way she bites my lower jaw when she kisses me. Feels like a close shave.

You're not converted to Mohamediasm yet, are you? Yeah, so I spelled it wrong. So what!

Try to kill off those five cousins, will you? Maybe she'll go back to Cairo then.

Yours in Protestantism, (I can spell that)
Allan

P. S. I'm thinking seriously of joining the Arab Legion, you old Jew you.

Evan read the letter over again, laughing at Allan's heavy-handed humor. He would write him back, he decided, and make up a big story about how a truck driver had risked his life delivering the letter to Evan, thinking that it might be important news from America. Evan remembered when Allan had returned to their room one day that past spring singing the latest ditty he had heard on campus: "Oh, you sons of Moses, with your long and crooked noses, fight, fight, fight for Palestine." And Evan had laughed and answered, "Today Palestine; tomorrow the world!"

Up ahead, he could hear happy shouting from one of the half-tracks. The men inside were leaning over the rim of the vehicle to pat Mordecai and Aaron on their heads. The twins had an arm over each other's shoulder and both were grinning ear to ear. Mordecai was flashing a letter in his free hand.

Uzi ran over to see what had happened, then came back. "A letter from Italy," he said, beaming. "Their parents were scheduled to get on a refugee ship that left Salerno three or four days ago."

"What was the name of the ship?"

Uzi called over to the twins and asked them for the name. Mordecai scanned the letter again, then shouted, "The *Pan York*."

The decision was made early in the afternoon to allow the armored regiment to press its advantage and advance northeast to the Lebanese border. The real fighting was over. El Kaukji's Liberation Army and the Syrian and Lebanese forces had been broken at Saf-saf, Jish, and several other points to the southwest. They were in rapid retreat from the Northern Galilee, and now that the junction at Sasa was taken they had lost their last paved road from the north-central portion of Galilee up to Lebanon. But they were retreating out of the pocket through mountain tracks that the Israelis did not yet control. And the villagers, getting word of the approaching storm, were leaving, too, though not as fast as the soldiers.

The road traveled due north until it hit the Lebanese border, then turned east to follow the border in a zigzag northeasterly direction. At sundown, the regiment captured Malkya, the last gateway to Lebanon still in Arab hands, and at dawn the next day, leaving almost half its vehicles and men to guard the junction, proceeded east toward Kadesh to link up with troops coming from the Israeli-held Lake Hula region.

The war in the north was virtually at an end. The Arab defeat in the Galilee was now complete, and Carmeli Brigade, stationed in northeastern Israel, was already occupying several Lebanese villages on the border. The armored regiment would roll a few more miles to Kadesh, touch hands with a brigade moving across from the east, and the formality would be over. The U.N. had already demanded a ceasefire and the Israelis were happy to comply. They had taken all their objectives and more.

As the armored column traveled along the curving, rolling asphalt road, the men in the halftracks rubbed the last bits of sleep out of their eyes and sat or leaned on the steel sides, watching the barren undulating hills of the Galilee slip by.

The armored cars slowed cautiously as they neared Kadesh, a place of less than a dozen crumbling mud buildings. Kadesh sat on a low hill off to the right of the road and barely higher than the level of the road itself. Strategically, it would have been a poor place to defend. The first armored car fired a long burst with its machine gun into the windows of the nearest mud buildings. There was silence. The Arab soldiers stationed there had probably left days ago for Lebanon, only a short march away.

The armored column turned off the highway into the narrow dirt road that ran into the settlement.

Then it happened.

The first burst hit Gingi, standing next to Nahshon in the halftrack ahead of Evan. The shoulders and blond head jerked backwards,

[185]

then disappeared below the edge of the halftrack. Two machine guns had opened fire from one of the buildings in the settlement and were spraying the entire line of jeeps, armored cars, and halftracks. The men in the jeeps rolled out of their seats and flattened themselves against the ground. The armored car observers and halftrack infantry troops dropped behind the protective armor plates of their vehicles like prairie dogs suddenly warned of danger.

It took less than a minute for the armored column to recover. The armored cars trained their machine guns on the windows of the building and fired long sustaining bursts at them. Radhai and Uzi quickly rolled their machine gun mounts along the steel track until the weapons rested on the side of the halftrack facing the building. Then they began firing, too. Hurried commands from sergeants and corporals crowded the sound of bullets in the morning air. The back doors of the halftracks opened and the infantry squads began jumping out to run in for an assault on the building, whose windows were still spitting out bursts of machine gun fire.

Under cover of the relentless hail of automatic fire from the armored cars and halftracks, the Israeli soldiers ran toward a low rock wall halfway between the armored column and the building. All but one man made it. At first Evan thought the man had fallen to the dirt deliberately for protection. But then he noticed that he lay there on his stomach, spread-eagled on the rocky soil, his right hand still gripping the stock of his rifle. The man wore short trousers and ankle socks. The helmet had rolled away from his head. He might have been a little boy who had stumbled in the dirt while playing tag, except the bullets in the air made angry noises and the boy did not move or cry.

The figure lay in the dirt only seconds before Mordecai leaped over the side of Nahshon's halftrack and ran in a crouch toward it. Mordecai was small, but he made a good target, advertised by the white circle with the red star of David on his helmet. One of the clattering machine guns from the mud building began firing at him. Mordecai dropped to the ground, but continued toward the fallen figure, crawling on his stomach. Tiny geysers of dirt hopped up around him. He crawled until he reached the soldier. Then the Arab machine gun turned away from him and tried to pick off the Israeli soldiers who were now dashing across the open ground to the flanks and rear of the building.

Mordecai, lying flat on his side next to the figure, pulled the strap of the first aid satchel off his shoulder and turned the body of the soldier over on its back so he could examine the wound.

Evan saw the man's face for the first time—Aaron! He grabbed his Sten gun, ran to the back door of the halftrack, jumped out, and began running toward the twins.

Not until he dropped to the ground next to them did he notice the sudden silence. The machine guns had stopped. A white cloth on the end of a crooked stick was being waved from the window of the mud building.

Aaron's eyes were closed; his face was ashen. There was a spreading circle of red just above the belt line at the bottom of his sweater. Mordecai ripped off his own fatigue jacket, balled it up and placed it under his brother's head. Then he unbuckled Aaron's belt and gently began rolling the bloodstained sweater up to his armpits. He unbuttoned the shirt and pulled up the wet red undershirt. Evan looked away. When he looked back, Mordecai was taping gauze over the wound.

Mordecai, his face now almost as pale as his brother's, glanced up at Nahshon, who had run over to them. "He's still alive," the medic said. "Into the stomach."

Radhai trotted up with the stretcher from Nahshon's halftrack and quickly loosened the straps to unfold it. Evan helped the Falasha slide Aaron onto the canvas. Radhai and Evan carried the stretcher over to the ambulance, then took another stretcher from the ambulance and carried it into Nahshon's halftrack. Gingi had been hit in the shoulder, and Shulamit was kneeling beside him, pressing a square of blood-stained gauze onto the wound. She walked beside them, holding the gauze in place, as they carried the captain to the ambulance, then crouched in the aisle of the ambulance between the two stretchers. Mordecai started to climb into the ambulance after her, but Gingi held up his hand.

"No, Mordecai," the captain said. "You might still be needed here. If this is the end of the fighting, Eliyahu will see that you join us in Rosh Pina."

Mordecai, his eyes pleading for an appeal to the order, turned to Nahshon. The Moroccan looked at him gloomily. "I'm going to escort the ambulance to Rosh Pina," Nahshon said. "It's only about twenty kilometers, so if the roads are clear Shulamit and I should be back in an hour or two. We'll let you know what the doctors say." He closed the back doors of the ambulance. The ambulance waited for Nahshon's halftrack to pull out of line, then followed it to the paved highway that would eventually bring them to Rosh Pina, a Jewish village above the Sea of Galilee to the southeast. The halftrack and ambulance sped eastward along the road, the first Jewish vehicles in many months to use that portion of the highway.

Evan, his Sten gun still slung over his shoulder, joined the cluster of men around the two prisoners who had surrendered in the building. One was a young, handsome man with light brown skin. His khaki uniform fitted him neatly. He wore no cap over his disheveled straight brown hair. But everyone was looking at his companion, whom Eliyahu was interrogating. The second man was a Negro. A giant of a man, he had thick lips, flaring nostrils, and large bulby cheekbones. He wore a U.S. army field jacket and olive-drab trousers. The sleeves of the jacket were at least four inches too short, and the bottoms of the wool trousers hit far above his black ankles. He was wearing low-quarter brown shoes and no socks. A French helmet, silver with a center ridge from front to back, looked absurdly small jammed down over the enormous head. The man was very frightened. There were tears in his eyes and his knees were quaking.

Eliyahu stood very close to the black soldier and shouted his questions with a snarl up into the man's face. Evan couldn't understand any of the Arabic, but he could tell that most of Eliyahu's questions were rhetorical. The Israeli lieutenant fired one after the other, interrupting the black man before he could complete an answer. Eliyahu's deep-set dark eyes flashed a cold, practiced anger. He now had the Negro so frightened that the man was virtually speechless.

"Search him," the lieutenant ordered one of the men standing nearby. The Israeli soldier felt the outside of the Negro's pockets and pulled a leather wallet out of one of them. Eliyahu opened it and pulled out a few bills. He tossed them on the ground. Then he pulled out another flap of the wallet and found another bill. He shouted something at the Negro and waved the bill in front of his nose. The Negro, trembling, tried to answer, but Eliyahu cut him off in the middle of a sentence with a crack across the Negro's cheek with the back of his hand. The Israeli lieutenant sneered another comment and turned away from the Negro.

Eliyahu saw Radhai standing at the edge of the circle of men, the butt of his machine gun resting on the ground and the barrel leaning against his leg. "You," he said, pointing to the Falasha, "and you," pointing to Evan, "guard these two men."

"Sorry," Evan said, "I'm a driver. I've got to see about my halftrack."

The lieutenant walked over to Evan and stood only inches away from him. "Listen to this, American," he said in English, speaking through clenched teeth. "I gave you an order. And I don't give a bloody damn if you're the driver for the brigadier. You'll obey it."

A few of the men near Evan laughed nervously. Eliyahu turned on them with a glare. They quickly walked away. He fixed his eyes for another moment on the flushed, humiliated face of Evan, then stalked off. Only Evan and Radhai were now left with the prisoners. Radhai moved away from them about ten feet and set his machine gun on the ground, pointing it in their direction. Evan slipped the Sten gun from his shoulder and cocked it, then walked over and sat down next to Radhai. The light-skinned Arab sat down on the ground and crossed his legs. The Negro squatted on his heels.

"What was that bastard Eliyahu shouting at the big one about?" Evan asked Radhai.

"I know very little Arabic. I think he was accusing him of being a Sudanese volunteer."

"Is he?"

"I don't know. Perhaps. Eliyahu found a Sudanese bank note in his money case. The man was saying he was an Egyptian and that he had stolen the bank note from a Sudanese. That's when Eliyahu hit him and accused him of lying."

Radhai stared intently at the tall Negro, whose skin was no blacker than his own. Radhai had seen Sudanese before. A company of Sudanese troops was attached to the 2nd Ethiopian Battalion when Wingate led them across the Sudanese border for the invasion of Ethiopia. Radhai was a Jew and this man was a Moslem, yet now, when they were both surrounded by white men, Radhai felt a certain closeness to the man—more of a kinship really than he could feel for someone like Eliyahu or even the young American sitting next to him.

The Sudanese was terribly frightened. His big bony fingers quivered as his arms rested on his knees, and he kept mumbling something in Arabic to his two guards. Radhai wanted to reach out and calm him. He could understand the man's fright. He had been frightened before, too. He was frightened now, but it was a fear of something he couldn't touch, a fear of something unknown hovering over his life.

It had started with the bombing of the Arab village by the three planes. No, it had started on the night after Simchat Torah, at the dance with the Torahs in the synagogue. It was a feeling that a dream was suddenly becoming real, or that reality was suddenly becoming a dream, but in either case with an awful distortion and an insistent repetition of the images.

The dance in the synagogue was the beginning, followed by the sound of the airplane and the raid on the Bahai shrine. Then the two-winged planes bombing a village he couldn't see, while he stood on a mountain and wore a uniform and watched. And now the Israeli lieutenant standing next to the tall black Sudanese and hitting him in the face. Yet they were images, twisted and endless. Radhai looked back down at his machine gun and checked the safety lever. If he could only rip the gun apart now and clean it, instead of guarding these prisoners, perhaps he could forget the fear and images that passed through each other in his head like weightless smoke.

"What's he saying?" Evan asked Radhai. Tears were running down the Sudanese's face and he was speaking imploringly in Arabic.

"He says please don't kill him." The words were English. They came from the light-skinned Arab.

"We're not going to kill him," Evan replied in English.

The Arab turned to the Sudanese and spoke to him in Arabic. The big Negro began rocking back and forth on his shoes, saying something else in Arabic to Evan.

"He says thank you very much, thank you very much, his life is yours," the Arab translated.

"Tell him to shut up," Evan said sternly. He felt such compassion for the Negro he could hardly bear to look at him.

The Arab turned and barked an order at the Negro. He closed his mouth and stopped rocking.

"Why were you two here alone?" Evan asked the Arab.

"There was a garrison of two hundred soldiers here yesterday. In the night we left and crossed into Lebanon. The Sudanese and I came back to see if we could find anything of value to sell."

"You were looters."

"All soldiers are looters. We did not expect you here so soon."

"You speak English very well."

[190]

The Arab looked at the young American evenly. "I worked for the British in their camps."

"Where are you from?"

"I was from Haifa. Now I am from nowhere."

"You could have stayed," Evan said.

"I could have stayed, yes," the Arab agreed, "and let the Jews be my masters."

"The Arabs will be treated the same as Jews in Israel."

The Arab curled his mouth cynically. "You are not a Palestinian Jew. Ask the officer who questioned us if he believes that."

"You're wrong. The Arabs could learn much from the Jews if they would forget their hatred."

"We have already learned much from the Jews. Someday you will see."

Eliyahu walked back over to them, unsnapped the leather cover over his wrist watch, and studied the dial. "We'll have to move forward within an hour. We can't take prisoners with us into battle, and I can't spare anyone to stay behind and guard them. Shoot them." He snapped the cover back down on his watch and turned to walk away.

Evan hoped he had misunderstood the Hebrew word. But shocked by what he thought he heard, he was almost afraid to ask for clarification for fear that he might have heard correctly. He glanced down at Radhai. The Falasha was making no attempt to prepare to fire his machine gun. "What did you say?" Evan called in Hebrew after the lieutenant.

Eliyahu turned and walked back toward Evan. "I told you," he said in English, slowly and deliberately, "to shoot them."

"When?"

"Now."

"No." Evan's voice trembled. He had been holding his Sten gun under his arm in a ready-to-fire position while guarding the two men. Now he let the weapon dangle, holding it only by the strap with his left hand.

"You Americans don't like to obey orders, do you?" Eliyahu said evenly, a honed edge to each word. He unloosened the canvas flap on his holster. "Now I give you a choice. You shoot both of them—the Arab and the *Cushi*—or I shoot you."

It happened so quickly that Evan was unable to sort his thoughts,

[191]

or remember later even a few of the courses his thoughts had been taking in those seconds. The Sten gun was pulled from his hand and the sound of three shots smashed against his eardrums. The big Negro fell back from his squatting position onto the seat of his pants. His eyes opened wide and he looked at Evan with a mixture of surprise and disappointment, the look of a man who couldn't believe that the most important promise of all had been broken. Stunned, the shots still ringing in his ears, Evan turned quickly and looked behind him. Mordecai was standing there with the Sten gun pointed at the Sudanese. He fired two more times. The Sudanese sat on the ground, taking the bullets into his big body. Then he closed his eyes and slowly toppled over onto his side, his knees tucked up almost to his chest, his chin almost touching his knees.

Radhai ran over to the Negro. The silver helmet was still clamped over the Sudanese's skull, and little streams of deep red blood were flowing out of both nostrils. The streams merged at his cheek, then dropped in a thin trickle into the dirt.

The light-skinned Arab had not moved from his sitting position. He stared in hypnotized fear at the muzzle of Eliyahu's Luger. "Now," Eliyahu ordered Mordecai, motioning toward the Arab, "the other one."

Radhai sprang from the side of the Sudanese like a charging panther and crashed into Eliyahu, sprawling him into the dirt. In the same motion he sat down hard on the lieutenant, knocking the breath out of him, and grabbed the gun hand and beat it against the ground until the Luger dropped free. Then he gripped his hands around Eliyahu's neck and began to squeeze with all the strength in his long black hands.

Some of the soldiers from the halftracks and armored cars were running over to them. They grabbed the Falasha and pulled and beat him loose from the dazed lieutenant. Radhai swung at them with his fists and kicked them to try to break free from their restraint. Then he stopped struggling. "I'm a *Cushi*, too," he sobbed. "Why don't you kill me?"

While Radhai was attacking Eliyahu, Evan had turned and jerked the Sten gun free from Mordecai's hands. He held the gun by its short barrel and flung it out into the field with all his might. "Great God!" he yelled at Mordecai. "Haven't you seen enough murder and death in your lifetime? Why? Why?"

[192]

Chapter Thirteen

EARLY THAT AFTERNOON, WHILE THE OTHER MEN were napping in the shade of the mud buildings, Evan dug a grave for the Sudanese. He did not dig very deep into the rocky soil, hardly deep enough to put more than a thin layer of rocks and rough dry dirt over the black man in the pathetically small silver helmet.

Almost minutes after Radhai's fight with Eliyahu, the regiment had received a radio message that the fighting was over, that the entire Northern Galilee was securely in Israeli hands. The regiment was to halt in Kadesh for the rest of the day and return to its base after nightfall. Eliyahu had sent Radhai and the Arab prisoner, both under guard, back to the base on the returning food truck. He had also sent Mordecai to Rosh Pina in a jeep so he could be with his brother.

As Evan dragged the Negro's body by its feet into the shallow grave, Nahshon walked up to him and stood there, his hands on his hips. Evan folded the Sudanese's stretched out arms into the grave, then began shoveling dirt on top of him.

"It was an awful thing to do," Evan complained.

"An eye for an eye," Nahshon said. "That's the stuff the world's made of, Yeled."

"But at least Aaron has a chance to live."

"He was still alive when we left Rosh Pina. But they don't live long, usually, with a stomach wound like that." The Moroccan looked back up toward the mud-brick buildings and the halftracks, jeeps, and armored cars clustered around them. "Kadesh. What is it taken from, the prayer for the dead?"

"I doubt it. The name is mentioned several times in the Bible. God commanded Moses to pick out six cities as places of refuge. Kadesh was one of them. If this is the same Kadesh, this miserable looking spot was once a Levite city. Anyone who had killed another man ac-

[193]

cidentally could come to this place and seek refuge, and while he was here the kinsmen of the dead man couldn't touch him. It wasn't much of a refuge for the Sudanese."

"Or for Aaron," Nahshon added.

Yes, Evan thought, it was ironic that a bloodthirsty little devil like Aaron had gotten his here, in the ancient sanctuary. "But Aaron," he told Nahshon, "was wounded during combat. Mordecai killed the Sudanese in cold blood."

"It's strange that you take out all of your anger on Mordecai. I am told that it was Eliyahu who ordered the men to be shot."

"Eliyahu is rotten. What he did was in character. But he didn't give the order to Mordecai, and Mordecai knows the difference between right and wrong."

"He knew the difference—before today. Now perhaps he has become one of us."

"There are still rules that civilized people follow, even in war," Evan said firmly.

"There are? When a man is told that it's legal to kill, do you think he worries about such small nothings as rules and right and wrong? He lies and loots and rapes, and his conscience is clear. He already has a license for bigger crimes."

Evan looked down at the low mound of dirt that covered the Sudanese. He would never be able to erase the image of the pleading Negro from his memory. He had promised him life, and Mordecai and Eliyahu had taken it away. Up toward the buildings of the village he could see Eliyahu striding officiously across the road. "The man without the helmet," Evan thought. He had out-bluffed all the bullets the lousy-aiming Arabs could throw. Evan hated the bastard for that, and he didn't know whether he hated him more for the bullets or for the Sudanese. For Eliyahu had tried to out-bluff Evan, too, and he had taken something precious away from Evan in the process. If Eliyahu had taken his gun out of his holster and cocked it, Evan might have killed the Sudanese, and possibly the Arab, too. Evan was not sure that he would have risked his life for the Sudanese, and that doubt would always diminish him.

The armored regiment left Kadesh at sundown with the lights of its vehicles blazing, a sign that the Galilee was now Jewish. There were no longer any Arab troops to be fooled or frightened in the dark. Eliyahu, who was now the acting company commander, stood next to Nahshon's seat in the first halftrack.

Nahshon drove the halftrack mechanically, not thinking about the speedometer, the shifting of gears, or even the twists and turns in the hilly road. What had just occurred at Kadesh saddened him more than had the death of Itzik. A few minutes in a stinking Arab village—what was it the Yeled had called it, a place of refuge?—had taken the lives and souls of these boys and kneaded them mercilessly. That was the problem with Israel. It was a nation of children, motherless children, who had been wrenched away from their homes and told to go out and start a nation. No matter that the world hates you and that you will be alone, go out and start a nation. They gave them children's weapons and they expected them to fight wars. They took away their parents and they expected them to be men. But they were still children, with a shouting enemy in front of them and a shouting enemy in back of them, and all they had was each other —and the hope that someday those they loved would join them. He knew. He had been a boy much younger than Aaron and Mordecai when he had run out into the dark street of the *Mellah*. The wedding guests were crowding out into the street to run after him. There were shouts, loud shouts. He could hear, "Stone him! Stone him!" repeated constantly. He looked back. It seemed as though everyone in the *Mellah* had joined in the chase. There were men, women, and small children running after him, shouting. Some people heard the shouts before Nahshon got to their doorways. He bowled several of them over as they stepped out of their thresholds.

Nahshon was approaching the narrow gate to the *Mellah*. He ran through it and out into the broad street of the Moslem section of Demnate. He looked over his shoulder. Almost everyone in the mob had stopped at the gate, shouting and raising their fists. A few teenagers chased him for another block in the Moslem quarter and then turned around fearfully and ran back to the *Mellah*. Nahshon ran and ran until he came to the outskirts of Demnate. He sat down against a building and panted for breath. He sat there all night, awake and alert.

At dawn, he begged a ride on a large horse-drawn cart full of skins. The cart was going to Beuguerir. He slept that night in a field outside of Beuguerir and the next day caught a ride to Settat, and then to Casablanca. There was a large Jewish community in Casablanca, but someday they would hear what he had done and they would stone him to death, too. He decided he would steal aboard a ship to France. He would become wealthy in France, and someday he would come back to rescue Sura.

Nahshon had discovered that the garbage cans behind cafes were a source of food if he was lucky enough to get to them before other scavengers in the district had made their rounds. He had eaten one meal a day while in Beuguerir and Settat, and now he found there were many more garbage cans—but more scavengers, too—in this huge city of Casablanca. On the first night in Casablanca he searched through five garbage cans, finding nothing but empty cans, entrails, and feathers. The sixth had a fresh supply of food. Nahshon filled a sack with half-eaten bread scraps, chicken bones, and a small, broken melon that had been thrown away because it was green.

Carrying the sack, the boy followed the alley to the port area. There were a number of freighters tied up to the dock. One seemed fully loaded. It had cargo lashed to the deck. Holding the top of the sack in his teeth, he grasped the shortest mooring rope he could find and climbed up it to the edge of the ship. He held onto the deck with his fingers and threw his right foot up onto the deck, rolling the rest of his body after it. The deck was deserted. Nahshon tiptoed around the deck, examining the cargo lashed to it. He found one good hiding place near the bow of the ship, but decided there would be too much chance of being seen from the bridge.

Halfway between the bridge and the stern, two large crates were lashed together, cushioned in the middle by a huge new tractor tire that stood upright between them. The top half of the tractor tire jutted above the crates, but the bottom half was hidden. The width of the inside of the tire, pressed between the two crates, was narrow, but large enough for a thin, fourteen-year-old boy to squeeze down into it. Nahshon dropped his bag of food down and lowered himself into the opening. He pushed the bag of food down into the tire. The boy's body was too large to fit into the tire, but he could rest on top of the two edges of rubber, with his knees pulled up slightly to allow for the curve of the inside of the tire.

He took out a crust of bread and ate it slowly. Then he sucked on a chicken bone. He would have to conserve his food. The trip to France might take three or four days, or maybe more. There was no telling how far France was from Morocco. He fell asleep, nestled in the semi-circle of the bottom of the tire.

Early in the morning Nahshon could hear the crew of the ship working on the deck, yelling orders, laughing at a joke. The thought suddenly occurred to him that perhaps the ship had just docked at Casablanca the day before. Maybe now they were preparing to unload the ship instead of getting it ready to set sail. He was afraid to peek out of the tire and see.

The sun was high over the ship when he heard the splash of the mooring lines falling away from the deck and felt the dull rumble of the screw as the freighter backed out into open water, out into the broad Atlantic that he had heard lapped the shores of Spain and France.

Nahshon used the stubby curved edge of his leather knife to cut a piece of the green melon. He sucked the moisture from it, spit out the seeds and then chewed the last drop of water out of the green pulp. That night, he ate another piece of bread and sucked a chicken bone.

The next day the ship turned toward the east. The sun was rising at the bow and setting at the stern. On the fourth day Nahshon sucked the last bit of juice from the melon and still the freighter had not arrived in France. On the fifth day, he was so thirsty that his tongue felt as though it were swollen to three times its normal size, and deep cracks split his chapped lips. A few pieces of bread and chicken bones were still left in the bag, but his mouth could not provide enough saliva to swallow the dry bread or suck the bones. On the morning of the sixth day the freighter ran into a small summer squall on the Mediterranean, but the top of the tire was a roof over Nahshon's head and he was afraid he would be seen if he stuck his head out. He pulled off his blouse and trousers and pushed them out onto the crate next to the tire. As they became drenched with water he pulled them in, sucked the water out of them, and then wrung the remaining water in them into the bottom of the tire. He put the clothing back on the crate and pulled it in again when it was drenched. The storm lasted only about fifteen minutes, but by the time the cloud had moved away Nahshon had a small reservoir of water in the bottom of the tire.

By the eighth day the last of the food was gone, but there was

[197]

a tiny pool of water still left in the bottom of the tire. The sun was rising now to the left of the ship and setting to the right, and Nahshon knew that the freighter was now headed on a due south course. It would never land in France. It had never intended to land in France. Perhaps it was turning back to Morocco.

That night he looked out from his tire and he could see the ship was moving steadily through a canal. It sailed through the canal all the next day and just after dusk it headed for open water again. Nahshon could see the lights of a very large city falling away to the right of the freighter, which was now close to shore, and he could see the lights of a smaller town coming up also to the right. To the left of the ship there were lights of a town, too, but they were far across the water. And in front of the ship, as far as he could see there was nothing.

Nahshon was very hungry. He had not eaten in two days. The ship was not going to France. He would have to get food and catch another ship that was going to France, where he could become a wealthy man and go back and get Sura.

The lights of the big city were receding rapidly now and the freighter was coming even with the lights of the smaller town. The shore was not far away, but he couldn't swim. The boy climbed out of the tire and onto the crate and then jumped down to the deck. It hurt to straighten his legs, which had been bent inside the tire so long. He took out his sharp leather knife and began to slice through the huge rope that bound the two crates together and sandwiched the tire in the middle. The rope was cut. He tried to pull the tire out, but it wouldn't budge. He tried to move one of the crates aside, but they were too big and heavy for him to move. He worked the tire back and forth. At first it moved a fraction of an inch, then a little more. The lights of the second town were beginning to move astern now. He pulled the tire free and rolled it to the rail of the freighter, just below the bridge. If only the men on the bridge wouldn't hear the splash when the tire hit the water. He was trying to wrestle the large tire up over the railing of the freighter when a man on the bridge glanced down.

"Hey! What the hell's going on down there?"

Nahshon couldn't understand what the man said, but he knew he was coming after him. He could hear the quick step of feet on the metal steps leading down from the bridge. He used his last ounce of strength to push the tire and butt it with his head over the side of the ship. It fell free and there was a loud plop as it hit the water.

"It's an Arab boy!" the man was shouting over his shoulder to another man on the bridge. "Come down here and help me catch him! Stop there, you little bastard!"

Nahshon looked down at the tire. He could see it in the moonlight. It was floating and beginning to drift away toward the stern of the moving ship. He ran toward the stern. He was still even with the floating tire. The man from the bridge was running toward the stern after him. Nahshon took a deep breath and jumped over the side. He held one arm straight out from his body, hoping it would hook the tire as he plunged into the water. After what seemed an eternity, his body hit the water and his arm slapped the side of the tire, but he was plunging down into the water too fast to hold on to the slippery rubber. The breath in his lungs brought him back to the surface. He flailed the water. His hand slapped the side of the tire again. He grabbed for it and clawed his fingernails into the hard rubber. Then he wrapped an arm around the tire and gasped for breath. He looked up at the ship. There was the foam from the propeller and the big tire was bobbing in the wake of the ship. Two seamen were standing at the stern rail trying to keep him in view in the moonlight.

"Should I reverse the propeller and put down a boat to get him?" one asked.

"Hell no," the other said. "That tire and the kid both will go under before we can get the boat loose from the ropes."

"We'll have to keep a twenty-four-hour guard on deck the next time we go through Suez."

"Yeah. The little thief must have sneaked aboard from the pilot boat."

The running lights of the freighter moved farther into the distance. Nahshon was connected to the boat now only by the white thread of churning water that it left in its wake, and soon this too would disappear.

Nahshon held on to the tire, pulled his knees in toward his stomach and pushed them out again, shoving at the water with the soles of the sandals still on his feet. The big tire was beginning to move slowly toward shore. The boy's strength was almost gone. He pumped for a few minutes, then rested, then pumped again. Gradually, the shore came nearer, but the tire sat lower and lower in the water as the sea slopped more water inside of it. Nahshon was in the water for what seemed a very long time. The skin on his fingers was wrinkled into cloth-like folds when the tire finally hit the shore. The boy stood in the waist-high water and tugged at the tire. It was heavy with water. He pulled one edge of it up onto dry land and then collapsed next to it into a deep sleep, one arm still wrapped around the tire.

Nahshon slept until about noon the next day. The sun was already very hot when he awoke and the tide had apparently gone out during the early morning hours, because the tire was now completely on dry land.

The boy was still weak from hunger. He grunted as he pulled the tire to an upright position and rolled it to the road which ran next to the water. Rolling the tire in front of him, half trotting at times to keep up with it, he followed the road in the direction of the last lights he had seen the night before. Several times he stopped and rested next to the road. He finally came to a small town. He heard the people speaking a strange dialect of Arabic and used simple Arabic words to ask the direction of a shoemaker's shop. He was understood and the people of the town pointed the way. It was a small shop and an old man was working on a tattered pair of shoes. There was no apprentice in the shop.

"Could you use a helper?"

The man looked up from his work. He saw before him a boy in beggar's rags, the dark hair growing short and stiff out of what had before been a shaved skull. The boy was very thin and there were dark circles under his eyes.

"I think *you* could use a helper," the old man snorted, turning back to his work.

"I was an apprentice to a sandalmaker."

"Does this town look so large that it can feed both a shoemaker *and* an apprentice?" The old man did not look up.

"I wouldn't want much."

"Anything is more than I have."

"Then how would you like to buy a tire?"

The old man put down his tools and walked to the doorway of his shop. He looked over the tire. "And what would I do with a tire?"

"You can probably sell it. It's new."

[200]

"Where'd you steal it?" The old man looked at Nahshon suspiciously.

"It's my tire."

"What do you want for it?"

"How many francs will you give me?"

"Did you come to this shop," the old man said angrily, "just to make a joke with an old shoemaker? This is Egypt. Who in this miserable village ever heard of a franc?"

Egypt! The land of the pharaohs. Nahshon could not reveal that he was a Jew, then. The Egyptians killed Jews. He did not know what kind of money the Egyptians used. If he bargained for money for the tire, he might receive only a few worthless coins.

"In Allah's name," he said carefully, "I do not want money. Give me some tools and food, and take the tire."

"What will you do, repair shoes on the street and take the business from an old shoemaker?"

"No. I won't use the tools here."

The old man walked back into his shop and fumbled in a drawer. He came back with a hammer without a handle, a loose pair of scissors, and three bent needles. He held them out to Nahshon.

"And some thread," the boy said.

The old man went back to his bench and picked up a half-empty spool of thick black thread. Then he went into the back room and reappeared with a half-loaf of round, flat bread and a wedge of yellow cheese.

"The tire is yours," Nahshon said, grabbing the bread and ripping out a huge hunk with his teeth. "Could I have water, too?" he asked through a full mouth of bread. The old man brought out a small earthen jug full of water.

"You're not an Egyptian," the shoemaker said. "How did you get here?"

"I hid on a ship."

"I see," the man nodded. "Then you stole the tire from the ship."

"Don't worry. The ship is a day's distance from here now. It won't be back."

The old man examined the tire, running his hand over the new tread.

"What is the name of this city?" Nahshon asked.

"This is Port Taufig, a dirt fishing village that isn't worth the stink of the half-rotten catch the fishermen bring back at nightfall. The big city back to the north is Suez, where they sell whores and cheap liquor to the infidel sailors who stop there, and murder to anyone who has half the price."

"Is this the Mediterranean Sea, then?"

The old man chuckled. "No, this is the Gulf of Suez, part of the Red Sea." He pointed to the southeast. "Over there somewhere is Mecca. So you'll know where to face when you're called to your prayers soon." Then he pointed to the east. "The other side of the Gulf is Egypt, too. That town across from us is El Shatt, another fishing village. And maybe two hundred miles behind it is the holy city of Jerusalem."

"Allah be praised," Nahshon said. "I never thought I would be so close to the holy cities of our faith."

"They aren't close," the old man said, rolling the tire inside his shop. "There are deserts and mountains and thirsts that make the holy cities very far from us."

Nahshon took another long gulp of water from the jug and tucked the bread and remaining piece of cheese under his arm. He picked up the tools and put them in his pockets, then walked away from the shop, taking a last look at the tire that had been his companion for almost two weeks.

The Moroccan boy walked down to the water's edge and found a shady spot next to a fishing boat that was lying on the beach awaiting repairs. He found a solid piece of driftwood and carved a handle for the hammer. Then he used the hammer to straighten out the needles and tighten the brad in the old pair of scissors. The boy searched for a flat, smooth rock, and when he found one he spent the rest of the day honing the blades of the scissors and leather knife and the points of the needles.

That night, when the beach was quiet and deserted, he dragged a small rowboat into the water and began paddling toward the lights of El Shatt across the water. He was strong now, and rested and determined. And he was a man. He would go to the Holy Land, to the land of the cool trees and the cool nights. He would grow up there and someday he would go back to Morocco and get Sura and Shimeon and his parents. So the Jewish boy paddled across the Red Sea. He was not chased by the troops of the Pharaoh. He was chased by the Jews of the *Mellah*, the Jews whose shouts of "Stone him to death!" he heard even now. And God did not part the waters of the Red Sea as He had parted them for Nahshon's ancestors. But He made the water calm, and He gave the boy strength and direction and the helping arm of night. And the boy crossed the Red Sea.

Nahshon hopped into the surf, pushed the boat back out into the water and waded ashore. He slept the rest of the night on the beach and the next morning walked into El Shatt to look for a way of getting to the Holy Land. He had to wait three days before he heard that a caravan was forming. On the outskirts of the village he found the camp. Bedouins in filthy headdresses were cursing the camels as they struggled to tie the big bundles on the one-humped beasts. They wrapped the stiff ropes under the stomachs of the big animals and then hooked the ropes around the camels' tails. The camels showed their yellow teeth and turned their heads to spit at the Bedouins, but the men shielded their faces and continued to work. A few of the docile donkeys in the caravan had already been loaded with staggering big bundles. Some cargo that had not yet been packed aboard the animals lay in the dirt.

Sharaf, a thin, black-bearded Bedouin, was owner of the caravan. Beads of sticky sweat covered his forehead as he shifted the load on one of the camels to give it a better balance. He turned to Nahshon.

"It is said you're going to Gaza in Palestine," Nahshon said.

Sharaf wiped his forehead with the tip of his headdress. His dark eyes stared at Nahshon. "A secret is hard to keep in this town of whores and pimps."

"I would like to go with you."

"You have money?"

"No."

"Then move along, you little beggar, before I quarter you and throw you to the fish. You waste my time."

"But I have something better than money," Nahshon said quickly.

Sharaf gave him a black, expectant look.

"I was an apprentice to a harnessmaker," Nahshon lied. "Look at the harness on this camel." He pointed to the camel whose load Sharaf had just adjusted. "It won't last the trip. See, I have all the tools. I can help drive the animals during the day, and I'll repair the harnesses at night."

Sharaf looked at the camel's harness and back at Nahshon. He walked over and felt the seam of the harness where the thread seemed to be coming unraveled. He did not turn around and might have been talking to the camel. "How much do you eat?"

"Next to nothing. A crust of bread a day."

"More important, how much do you drink?"

"Less than a lizard. A half a cup a day is enough."

"If you stagger or fall behind, we won't wait for you. The desert will be your grave."

The caravan left within an hour. Nahshon held the halter of one of the donkeys, and beat the little animal with a stick whenever it slowed or tried to wander off the road. The caravan moved up into the barren mountains of the Sinai Peninsula, up through Mitla Pass, where the dry, rocky peaks looked as if they might crumble at any minute and cave in on the caravan below. The Bedouins then followed a trail through the wastelands until they came to the oasis of Bir el Giddi. They also made stops at Bir el Hasana and Bir el Hadina. They entered Palestine at El Auja in the Negev Desert and then traveled up through Asluj on the way to Beersheba. When the caravan could, it would stop at one of these oasis towns, but sometimes Sharaf would call a stop just before nightfall next to the trail, and the animals would go without water for more than a day.

At night the Bedouins would bring Nahshon the harnesses that needed repairing. He would force the needles through the thick leather with the calloused fingers of his right hand. A year as an apprentice to Moises had given his fingers the sandalmaker's callous. Nahshon thought about the sandals he had made for Sura, and recalled with hot shame the last time he had seen them on her small feet. He whipped the heavy thread through the harness. It was all Moises' fault. One day he would go back to Demnate and punish Moises for the evil he had done.

They spent one of the last nights of the journey near Beersheba. Sharaf would not take the loaded caravan into the town because he wanted to avoid any contact with British police patrols. He had deliberately taken the most difficult way to Gaza instead of the easy route along the Mediterranean Sea because the British patrols were thick in that area. Sharaf did not want the British to inspect the cargo aboard his camels and donkeys. Inside the fat bundles were jewels for those who wanted to make themselves beautiful, guns for those who wanted to make others ugly, and hashish for those who wanted to forget for a few hours that there were such things as beauty and ugliness.

They stopped at noon a few miles from Beersheba and unloaded the camels and donkeys. Then, while a few of the Bedouins stood guard over the cargo, the others drove the animals into Beersheba for water and food. Beersheba was the most beautiful town Nahshon had ever seen, a peaceful desert crossroads, a caravan city as it had been for ages, with broad streets and low buildings of white stone sparkling in the sun.

While the camel drivers were watering their animals, Nahshon walked with Fuad, a ragged young Bedouin whose job it was in life to flail a donkey across the desert. They strolled along the main thoroughfare of the town and stopped in front of the mosque. Nahshon had seen larger ones in Demnate, Settat, and Casablanca. But this was a lovely little mosque, perfect in every simple detail of white stone, from the arch over the main door to the single minaret that shot up into the sky and overlooked the soft, smooth dome.

A young *muezzin* had appeared on the balcony near the top of the minaret and was calling the people of Beersheba to prayer. Some of the merchants threw down prayer mats outside their shops; others walked over to the courtyard of the mosque to kneel there. Fuad began walking toward the door of the mosque and Nahshon followed him. They took off their sandals at the arch and walked into the mosque barefooted. A few old men were inside, with their prayer mats spread in front of them. The large room was bare. There were no benches or furniture, and at the front of the room only a simple pulpit, where sermons could be made on Fridays, jutted out of the wall.

Nahshon knelt next to Fuad. He attempted to ape the other boy's motions, and watched Fuad's mouth out of the corner of his eye so he could say the same words of prayer a split-second after the Bedouin youth. Silently, the Moroccan boy asked God to forgive him for saying the prayers of the Moslems. They weren't really bad prayers, he discovered. Most of the words praised the power of God, and only a few mentioned that Mohammed was His prophet.

As they left the mosque and were putting on their sandals, Nahshon noticed another very large building, larger than the mosque, on the road that led to the north. He asked Fuad what it was.

[205]

"That's the fortress of the British police. They build them in the south to keep a caravan owner from selling his wares. They build them in the north to protect the Jews."

"Are there so many Jews in the land?"

"No, not so many now. But every month there are more." He ejected a thin stream of saliva through the gap in his stained front teeth. "Across the sea, the Christians throw them out of their lands, and the British bring them here. The Jews buy the land in the north and build villages. Then more Jews come and buy more land and build still more villages. Soon all the land will be theirs."

"Who sells them the land, the British?"

"No, the Arab landowners."

"Then why do they sell the land to the Jews?"

"Why does a dog of a farmer do anything?" An angry scowl crossed his face and he swept his hand around to the horizon. "They are like the British, who draw a line in the sand and say a Bedouin cannot bring his goods across the line. The Arab landowners mark off a few dunums of land, pile rocks around the borders, and call it a farm—their farm. As long as no one makes a claim on their few miserable dunums they don't care if the Jews buy up to the dust on their pile of rocks. This is what comes from the life of a farmer. A curse upon the breasts of their sisters, who are whores." He looked at Nahshon and grinned a dark-toothed grin. "But they are not all farmers and women in this land. There are some who worry about the Jews. After Sharaf has unloaded his camels in Gaza there will be fewer Jews."

The trip to Gaza was short. Nahshon helped unload the donkeys, then left the caravan. He walked along the road to the north, caught rides on donkey carts, then walked some more. One night, he slept beside the road near a Jewish farming village, but he was afraid to go into the village and speak to the people there. Their features, their skin, their clothes were different from those of the Moroccan Jews. They would never believe that he was anything but an Arab urchin.

Nahshon walked farther and caught more rides and finally came to the Arab city of Jaffa, just south of the Jewish city of Tel Aviv. At the edge of Jaffa, near the boundary of Tel Aviv, he found a Yemenite Jew, a shoemaker, who needed an apprentice. The Yemenite gave him a job in his shoeshop, bought him a blouse and a pair of short pants, let him sleep in the shop, let him eat at the family table, and gave him a few coins every Friday afternoon that he could spend on himself.

It was late summer of 1935, and in a month Nahshon had come halfway around the universe. He had crossed the Red Sea and the wilderness of the Sinai Desert. He had come to the Holy Land, and someday he would go back to Morocco and bring everyone he loved to the Holy Land, too.

Almost all of the Yemenite's customers were Arabs; the rest were Yemenite Jews who spoke Arabic. But the Yemenite shoemaker taught his apprentice to speak Hebrew, and on the Sabbath Nahshon would walk into Tel Aviv, where everyone was Jewish and where everyone spoke Hebrew. He would stroll down Allenby Road to the beach and sit there and watch the light-skinned Jews bathe in the surf. At night, before returning to Jaffa, he would buy an ear of corn from the vender with the boiling vat. The man would use a pair of tongs to pull the corn out of the vat, then wrap it in a corn husk and hand it to Nahshon. Nahshon would sprinkle it with salt and eat it as he walked back to Jaffa.

During the Arab riots against the Jews in 1936 and 1937 he was a listening post for Haganah, the Jewish defense group. Haganah chose him for the job because he looked like an Arab and spoke Arabic, and also was young enough not to arouse suspicion. He would walk through the streets of Jaffa at night, lounge outside the coffee houses, and listen while the Arabs inside discussed the latest rumors about the Jewish villages that were to be attacked and the number of Jews who would have to be killed before the British finally put a halt to Jewish immigration.

But the kindness of the Yemenite family and his own pride in his work for Haganah never quite comforted the loneliness in his heart. There was a longing for Sura, and for his parents and Shimeon in Asabadin. There were a few times when he decided he would write them and tell them he was safe in the Holy Land. But he didn't. He was afraid Moises would find out where he was and write the Yemenite that he had a runaway apprentice working for him—and even worse, Moises might tell why he had run away, why the wedding guests had chased him through the dark, narrow street of the *Mellah*.

Like Mordecai and Aaron and so many of the others, he had been

[207]

a child without parents in this country. He had been happy for the twins when they received the letter telling them that their hope was being answered. And now he was depressed that even the answer could not escape tragedy.

The convoy of vehicles drove along the Lebanese border to the Mediterranean and then down past Nahariya to their camp. The halftrack drivers parked their vehicles next to the barracks and the men stumbled out with their blankets and guns, but made no attempt to clean out the other debris of war that had accumulated in the halftracks for the past week—loose ammunition, spent shells, crumbs, mess gear, helmets, sweaters. It could all wait until tomorrow. The halftracks could wait, too. The drivers let them stand next to the barracks like unsaddled horses and went into their own barracks and fell onto their straw mattresses.

All but Nahshon. Nahshon went up to the headquarters building and made a phone call to Haifa. He was hanging up the phone when Eliyahu walked into the office.

"Eliyahu," Nahshon said, "I've just called Haifa about the parents of the twins. I've found that their parents are due in on a refugee ship tomorrow morning."

"So?"

"So I'd like to have a jeep to go to get them and take them to Rosh Pina."

"No."

"What?"

"No!"

"But the boy's dying."

"I'm sorry about that. But I can't spare you. What happens if the Arabs counterattack while you're gone? Are we supposed to walk up to Lebanon?"

"Counterattack?" Nahshon shouted, his eyeballs beginning to bulge out of his red face. "We have troops up there. And you know the Arabs aren't going to counterattack. They've had the whipping of their lives."

"Perhaps we should transfer you to the command staff," Eliyahu sneered. "You know exactly what the Arabs aren't going to do."

"I want that jeep!"

"For the last time, no," the lieutenant said angrily. "Now get out of here before I throw you out."

"You're going to throw Nahshon out?" the Moroccan asked incredulously. "Why you sniveling jackal, I'll rip you apart." Nahshon started around the desk toward Eliyahu. The lieutenant reached for his canvas holster and pulled out his German luger.

"Get out," Eliyahu said. "No more warnings."

Nahshon turned and stomped out onto the porch and slammed the office door with all his might, the sound of the crash preceding him into the night.

Chapter Fourteen

EVAN FELT SOMEONE SHAKE HIM. HE PULLED HIS shoulder away and buried down deeper into the blankets. Again he felt something pushing gently against his shoulder.

"Yeled," the voice whispered.

Evan pulled the blanket away from his head and opened one eye. It was still dark. Then Nahshon came into focus.

"Yeled," he whispered, "get dressed."

Evan yawned and sighed. He tossed the blankets aside and sat up on the side of the bed. Still partially in the grasp of unrequited sleep, he stepped into his dirty coveralls and pulled on his boots, tying them without bothering to put the laces through the top few holes.

He searched at the foot of his bed for his battle dress jacket, then stuck his arms into the sleeves and followed Nahshon mechanically to the jeep that was parked beside the barracks. It was a jeep usually used by one of the mortar crews, except now the ammunition trailer had been unhitched. A tall thin bar of steel had been welded to the center of the front bumper. Supported by two struts and poking up like a flag mast a little higher than the rider's heads, it was designed to keep the riders from being decapitated by a wire stretched across the road.

Evan settled himself groggily in the front seat of the jeep, and

Nahshon started the motor and drove down to the gate. The striped wooden pole across the entrance barred their way. The guard stepped out of his hut.

"Trip ticket," he said to Nahshon, reaching out his hand.

Nahshon searched in his shirt pockets. "I must have left it back in the barracks. I'll give it to you when I come back."

"Sorry, Nahshon. You know better than that. I have to have it now."

The guard expected the Moroccan to give him a loud argument. He was almost disappointed when Nahshon said with resignation, "All right. I'll go back and get it."

The corporal shifted the gear into reverse and began backing up the road. The guard turned and walked back toward his hut. Nahshon backed the jeep about fifty feet up the road and applied the brake. Then he threw the gear into first and jammed his foot down on the accelerator. Evan's head snapped back as the jeep shot forward toward the gate again.

The guard, who was just stepping one foot into his hut, turned and stared dumbly as the jeep hurtled past him. The upright steel bar on the front bumper splintered through the pole and bent back slightly under the force of the impact. Nahshon slammed on the brakes and skidded into a left turn to head down the highway. The skid almost flung Evan out of the jeep. He was wide awake now. He held onto the side of the jeep and twisted his body to look back at the entrance to the camp. Part of the pole was lying out in the highway and the guard was running out into the center of the road. Then darkness enveloped the scene and they were alone, racing down the highway.

Nahshon was pushing the jeep to its limit. The needle wavered at 55, then moved a fraction past it. Nahshon's hair was blowing in the wind. He was huddled over the steering wheel, watching the road intently.

"What in the hell is going on here?" Evan shouted.

"We're going to Haifa to get the twins' parents."

"Oh no we're not. Not me."

"You don't want to go?"

"No!"

"Then hop out." The sandy shoulder of the road was a white

[210]

streak fleeting by. Nahshon stared straight ahead, making no effort to slow the jeep.

"Look, Nahshon, I hope Aaron recovers. I feel sorry for the twins. I feel pity for them. I feel compassion for them. But I don't like them. I don't want to get involved in their lives, especially when it means we're going to end up in serious trouble."

"We start getting involved in other people's lives from the minute we're conceived."

"Yes, Mordecai got involved in the Sudanese's life, all right."

Nahshon took his foot off the accelerator and gradually applied the brake. The jeep came to a stop at the side of the road. "You've judged him, haven't you? You're the inspector general and you've come to Israel on an inspection tour, and everything and everyone has to meet your approval or you'll turn in a bad report. What do you understand about Mordecai or Aaron—or any of us? Who in the hell asked you to come here and judge us?" Nahshon sat there for seconds, giving his anger a chance to abate. Then he looked at Evan sadly. "You've been whining a lot lately about what civilized people do and what they don't do. I thought I could show you something today. Eliyahu gave you a choice yesterday between shooting the Arabs and getting shot yourself. Now I give you a much easier one. Come with me and learn something, or get the hell out."

Nahshon's assessment of him had been harsh—and true. Evan had made all the judgments, big and little, with tremendous ease. And now Nahshon had thrown them back in his face. Down deep, beneath the humiliation, he was grateful that the Moroccan had. Evan forced a smile. "It's a long walk back to camp, Nahshon. I'll go with you."

The *Pan York* was a toy boat, still far out in the bay, sliding slowly over the glass water toward the dock, hiding its uniqueness in the distance and in the haze. Evan did not have to see the details of the *Pan York*, though. He knew them by heart, and soon he would know them by smell, the putrid stench that would reach his nostrils before the sound of the ship heaving its rust-stained hull against the dock reached his ears.

If the Jews had tried to re-create a concentration camp and put it afloat, Evan thought, it would have to be something like this ship— if the *Pan York* could be called a ship. It was more of a ferry. The

Pan York had been built to ply the waters of the Carribean, hauling fruit and a maximum crew of thirteen. In her old age, she had been hastily converted to different waters and to a different purpose. Carpenters, not shipfitters, had increased the number of people she could carry to almost 3,000. The wooden latrines that lined both sides of her top deck were one example of the carpenters' handiwork; the ship's holds were another. Each hold had been divided into three deck levels, with ladder-like wooden steps plunging down to each deck at an almost perpendicular angle. At each level, three tiers of shelves a little less than six feet deep and three feet high had been built around the sides of the hold.

Each person on the *Pan York* could have a space on a shelf as wide as his body, as much fresh air to breathe as would filter down into the hold from the air periscopes on the deck, and as much light as came from the single electric bulb on the ceiling. He would have one glass of water a day, cheese and crackers for breakfast, broth and crackers for lunch, and sardines and crackers for supper. When he had enough energy, he could climb up to the crowded main deck to see the sunlight, to find a spot up-wind of the latrines where he could breathe deeply of the Mediterranean air, to wash his hands under the saltwater stream that dribbled into the discolored basin, and to brave the awful stink and filth in the gray, wooden latrines that cantilevered out over the sea.

When he returned to his space on the shelf, he could amuse himself by watching the little beads of perspiration roll into the faint wrinkles in his skin and make little gullies in the layer or two of dirt that coated his body, or listen to the occasional music of a scream followed by the rumble of a body playing a quick rhythm on the stairs as someone slipped on the black, greasy crust on the steps. And after four or five days he could wonder if the smells of the latrines, crushed crackers, sardines, exhausted air, used-up breath, and sweat had permeated one's skin for all time, as it had permeated the wood and metal of the *Pan York*.

The answer always came with the sight of land, when the fringe of the mountain appeared on the horizon, then began to reveal patches of light and shadow, height and depth, as the ship turned in toward shore. In Haifa Bay, the smells always disappeared, forgotten in the awesome presence of Mt. Carmel, pushing up and away from the water in a timeless mound.

It looked as though most of the people on the *Pan York* were now on the main deck, grasping with their eyes for the prize that lay ahead. They were standing on their tiptoes to look at the slowly approaching port. They would drop to their heels to rest their leg muscles a moment, then move back up to their tiptoes again.

There was a thrill to this sight which a thousand homecomings could never match. This *was* a thousand homecomings, for each person on the ship brought in his veins ten hundred wanderers back to the native soil. Some of the people shouted to each other and laughed. A few, the older ones mostly, wept silently. Most simply stared at the land that now surrounded them. Crowded close to each other as they were, they were completely unaware of each other for that last minute before the *Pan York* touched dock. There were almost 3,000 Jews aboard the *Pan York*. But this was not a mass return. It was the return of the individual, and each individual jealously tasted his own emotions.

The dock creaked as the ship brushed it. The drifting unreality came to an end. The *Pan York* was a mass of shouts, punctuated by the frightened wail of infants. Relatives on the dock were shouting names from behind a roped-off area. The passengers on the *Pan York* were shouting names back—first names, last names, nicknames. A few fathers held children high above their heads like legion standards that could be recognized amid the battle. There was chaos on the *Pan York*, a happy chaos that no one wanted to control or tried to control. Evan wondered if there were young men, unseen now on the other side of the ship, who were preparing to jump down to a rubber mat on a tugboat.

Dock workers lifted a rope-railed gangplank into place and then set up a small table and three chairs at the foot of it. An Israeli official and two U.N. observers sat down at the table, ready to check the papers of the new immigrants. One of the observers was a U.S. Marine major. The other, a Belgian officer, wore a pith helmet.

Nahshon went over to the Israeli official and told him whom they were waiting for and why. The man nodded, then searched for their names on a list he had before him and underlined them.

As the immigrants began to come down the narrow gangplank, single file, Nahshon and Evan stood to the side, a few feet in back of the table.

There were few children on the ship. Many of the passengers

[213]

were middle-aged men and women, copies of those who had made this trip with Evan in June, only dressed warmer now in the chill air of the first days of November. They held tightly to the ropes on the gangplank and walked heavily down the wooden steps, each carrying a sack or a piece of beaten luggage. Many took the last step from the gangplank to the Israeli dock slowly and deliberately, as if they wanted to record the sensation of their first contact with the land. Some took the step with trepidation, as though they feared —or hoped—they would suddenly be transformed into something bright and different.

And before them all was still the last table with the last non-Jews who would check the papers for the last time that certified them to be officially homeless.

"The last time I was on a ship was in 1945," Nahshon said. "I was in the Jewish Brigade and they were bringing a group of us back from Germany. I was lucky. The boat stopped for two days at Rabat, Morocco, to take on fuel and supplies."

He and two Palestinian friends, he related, rented a small pickup truck from an Arab, filled the back with gasoline tins, and drove along the rough road to Demnate. Nahshon parked the truck on the street that ran by the gate to the *Mellah* and told his friends to stay and watch the truck. It was very early in the morning, but in the *Mellah* the men and apprentices in the shops were already at work. The stench in the streets was worse than Nahshon had remembered it.

He went first to the house of Shaul, the green tea merchant. Nahshon's heart pounded as he saw a young woman open the door. He saw first the jet black hair, then the light olive skin, and then, in disappointment, the unfamiliar face.

"Is this still the home of Shaul Ashkenaz?"

She shook her head. "They have not lived here for two years." She closed the door.

He walked toward the shop of Moises, the sandalmaker. The buildings of the *Mellah* seemed to have expanded in toward the street, making the alley narrower than it had been ten years before. He stepped into the sandalmaker's shop. Two young boys were sitting at the benches. They had stopped work and were staring at the uniformed man.

"Is this still the shop of Moises Ibn-Eli?"

"Yes," one of the boys said. "We're his sons. Do you want us to fix your boots?"

"No, I'm looking for your father."

The boy motioned with his thumb. "He's in the back room on the right."

Nahshon walked back to the room that had always served as both the kitchen and bedroom of Moises and his wife. Moises' wife, who had never looked young to Nahshon, seemed to have changed very little. She was sprinkling water on the floor. Moises was lying on the bed, his chest bare and skull still shaved but without the skullcap he always used to wear. Nahshon could hardly recognize Moises as the same person. The chest and face were emaciated. His brown eyes were diluted with water and there was a few days' growth of stubble on his face. Nahshon was pleased that both Moises and his wife were obviously frightened by this soldier who had suddenly intruded into their bedroom.

"Do you know who I am, Moises?"

"No."

"I am Nahshon, the son of your cousin Yoseph."

Moises peered at him to make sure of the identification. His sick face reddened, and his brown eyes flashed the same fire Nahshon had seen the day he gave Sura the slippers.

"We had hoped you were dead," Moises rasped. "If I had the strength, I would kill you now with my bare hands."

Nahshon sneered and nodded. "Where is my sister?"

"So, you care about her now, eh?" Moises coughed and spat onto a piece of paper lying on the floor next to his bed. "You should have cared at the wedding feast."

Nahshon reached down, grabbed Moises' arm and pulled the man up to a sitting position on the bed. "I said, where is Sura?" His voice was threatening.

"Let go of me," Moises said. Nahshon released him and his head fell back to the mattress. "Sura is dead. She died a year after her marriage, in childbirth. The baby was a girl. It died, too."

Nahshon could feel a tightness in his throat, a strangling sensation of shock and hatred. "You killed her, Moises. You killed her when you made the marriage bargain for a child."

Moises looked away. He shook his head weakly. "No, you killed your sister when you put a mark of shame on her and her husband forever."

"Is she in the cemetery here?"

"Yes, but don't bother to look for the grave. Two years ago there was a pogrom in the *Mellah*. The Arabs in the Moslem quarter wanted to show their support for the Vichy government. They showed it by pushing over and breaking the markers in the cemetery, and looting the shops in the *Mellah*. Sixteen Jews were killed. Shaul—your brother-in-law Shaul—was one of them."

"Good," Nahshon said. "Too bad they didn't get all the scum. But breathe deep and cough deep, Moises. This is your hell. The *Mellah* is your hell." He left the bedroom and walked out to the street, then back to the truck where his friends were waiting.

The trip from Demnate to Asabadin that had taken his father four days took only a few hours in the pickup truck. The three soldiers left the truck at the edge of town and walked down the narrow street to the shop of Yoseph, the silversmith.

At least Asabadin had remained true to Nahshon's memory. Each house, each shop along the short street of the mountain village was just as he remembered it. The crack in a building here, a stone there. It was a timeless town, as timeless as the higher peaks of the Atlas mountains that loomed up gray in the distance. They were the benevolent walls that protected Asabadin, that held back the currents of change as though the village was a museum piece that needed to be preserved for all time. Nahshon wondered if perhaps the Berbers in the village unwittingly maintained the same rules of control for themselves as they held for the Ben-Mizrachis. Certainly, there seemed to be no new buildings constructed since he had left the village eleven years before. Were all the surplus youngsters sent off to the cities of the plains as Sura and Nahshon had been sent that morning so long ago?

There were children in the street, playing in the early afternoon heat. They ran to the doorways of their homes as the three soldiers approached. In the coffee houses there had been reports of a great war, far off to the east. But not since the French, many years before, had a soldier ever come to Asabadin.

The soldiers stopped at the shop of Yoseph. Nahshon stepped into the small shop first. He was followed by his two friends. Yoseph,

[216]

older now but still with the same gentle face that had told of the miracle of Passover, turned from his work to face the soldiers. The tiny hammer was still in his right hand. A young man, who could only be Shimeon, got up from his bench.

Nahshon, engulfed in emotion, had no desire to play a game. "Father," he said simply. "I'm Nahshon."

The old man disbelieved for only an instant. He shuffled over to his son and hugged him, and wept into the thick khaki of the rolled-up sleeve. Nahshon held his father tightly and fought back tears, while Shimeon smiled broadly and called for his mother. Nahshon's mother came into the room and cried first against the flap of the khaki pocket and then into her own hands, happy tears, not tears of sorrow. Then a young woman came into the shop from the back of the room and held back the small children who had followed her.

The little shop was crowded now with men and women and children. Nahshon's two friends stood in the background silently until he introduced them to his family.

Shimeon touched the shoulder straps of the khaki shirt his brother wore. "You are in the French army, then."

Nahshon shook his head proudly. "No, this is the Jewish army in Palestine. It's the uniform of the Jewish Brigade of the British army."

They walked into the back room and sat near the hearth. Nahshon told them about his life in Palestine, about his travels with the British army. His father told him that the grandmother had died many years before, and that Shimeon and his wife Rivka now slept in the grandmother's bed, and Shimeon's four children now slept on the mat on the floor where Shimeon, Nahshon, and Sura once slept.

"You know about Sura, then?" Nahshon asked, knowing that they did.

His father nodded. "I learned from Moises six years ago when I went to the *Mellah* to get Rivka for Shimeon."

"Do you despise me for what I did to her?" he asked.

Yoseph shook his head again, sadly. He held his hands out and looked at them. "The suffering, the blood of Sura is on these hands, not yours. I sacrificed the life of Sura to myself. God has punished me for it. I thought I had taken your life, too. I thank God that He was merciful."

They sat for a moment in silence. Then Nahshon said, "Take your tools, father, and your pieces of silver. Take mother and Shimeon and his family and come with us. We have a truck here and we can get you aboard our ship. You will come with us to the Holy Land."

Yoseph placed his hand on Nahshon's arm. "No, I must stay here."

Nahshon had not expected this answer. He spoke sternly, "In this village of Berbers? Do you think they love you here? What do the prayers that you say every day mean? You pray each day for the return to Zion, and when the chance to return is offered to you, you reject it."

"That is a prayer," Yoseph said gently. "I will still say the prayers. But this is my home. It was the home of my father and his father and his father before him. What is here I know. And the people who are here know me. They are not Jews, but they know me, and I know them. I would be a stranger in the Holy Land."

Nahshon looked at Shimeon. "Will you come with me, Shimeon?" It was a question that did not have to be asked. He did not have to hear the answer.

"We will stay here in Asabadin," Shimeon said.

Nahshon did not argue with them further. It was a child's dream that someday he would come back and get them, and that on a moment's notice they would pack up and go off with him to Palestine. He still could not fathom completely why his father wanted to stay here, in this place among Berbers. Perhaps it was because he had not seen Palestine as Nahshon had. But Nahshon had an uneasy feeling that even if his father could see Palestine, could travel from one country to the other, he would still want to return to Asabadin and live out his years here. Nahshon was fortunate. He had left this place as a child. The attachments were a child's attachments, and he could fling them off as easily as a blouse he had outgrown.

Nahshon looked at the children, sitting at the feet of Rivka, their young mother, and listening to the conversation of their uncle, the big soldier with the black mustache. The oldest child was a boy, five years old. The next two were girls, and the youngest, not yet able to walk, was a boy.

"Shimeon," Nahshon said, "when they are old enough to leave this village, don't send them to the *Mellah.*"

Shimeon nodded.

"Send them to me in Palestine," Nahshon said. "I'll make a home for them and find a life for them. Promise me that."

[218]

"You have my promise," Shimeon said.

Nahshon and the two soldiers ate supper with the Ben-Mizrachis. They sat around the table, which now seemed much smaller, while Nahshon's mother and Rivka put the food before them. Afterwards, they talked until late, and Nahshon translated some of the conversation into Hebrew so his two friends could understand it.

That night, the three soldiers slept on a mat in the courtyard behind the shop. They arose early the next morning, ate goat cheese on pieces of *pitta,* and washed it down with hot tea.

They prepared to leave. Nahshon kissed Shimeon, touched the heads of nieces and nephews with his fingers, then hugged and kissed his parents.

"I'll write you," Nahshon said. "I don't know if the letters will ever get to you up here. But I'll write."

The three soldiers had walked up the street a short way when Nahshon stopped and walked quickly back to the Ben-Mizrachis standing in front of the silversmith shop.

"Father," Nahshon said, "there's one thing I've always wanted to write you. I crossed the Red Sea."

His father smiled and nodded at him. But Nahshon couldn't tell whether his father believed him.

"I mean it. I really crossed the Red Sea." He turned and walked back up the street to join his friends.

Nahshon looked at Evan. "I don't know. He might have thought everything I told him was a lie. But I write them now and get letters from them, so at least he knows it's true that I'm in Israel."

"Do you believe Shimeon will send his children here?"

"Yes. I want him to and he knows it. That's what we're here for in Israel, to wait for the others."

"My father and mother are a world away from yours in every way possible. But if I asked them to come to Israel to live with me, I think their words would be almost exactly the same as your father's."

The Israeli official at the little table motioned to Nahshon. Standing in front of the table were a man and woman of almost the same height. They were both slender. The man wore a leather cap and a frayed, faded suit coat that didn't match his trousers. His collar was open, showing deep weather lines that ran along the sides and back of his neck and fanned out through the face and over the forehead. The woman wore a rough buttoned sweater over a loose-fitting print dress. A blue cotton scarf covered her hair and was tied under her chin. Her skin was very white, except at the swell of her prominent cheekbones, where it was orange, as if someone had dipped a chicken feather into beaten eggs and painted her cheeks and then baked them. The Kligers appeared to be in their late forties. Evan didn't know why, but for some reason he had expected them to look ancient.

The two soldiers walked over to the couple. Mrs. Kliger searched Evan's face expectantly, seeking some sign of resemblance to one of her twins.

"Tell them," Nahshon said to the official, "that we're friends of their sons and that we'll take them to the twins."

While the official explained to the couple in Yiddish, Evan and Nahshon picked up their suitcases, battered pieces of peeling luggage that were tied closed with pieces of rope.

Nahshon led them to the end of the dock and through several more tables of Israeli officials who filled out forms for them and gave them batches of papers with instructions written in both Yiddish and Hebrew. The two soldiers helped them into the back seat of the jeep and then fitted the suitcases into spaces between their legs and the sides of the jeep.

Nahshon drove back up to Acre and turned into the road that cut through the hills of Central Galilee and finally entered the mountain country, turning just before Saf-saf back up to Safad and then to Rosh Pina.

Nahshon did not speak during the entire trip. A number of times Evan glanced back at the couple, and it was always the view of a mother and father sitting very close to each other, hunching over in their seats and squinting their eyes as the wind whipped across their faces and fluttered the triangular tips of Mrs. Kliger's scarf. They had the stoical look of people who have learned and accepted that they are no longer masters of their own fate.

At intervals there were the rubble and shattered roadblocks of the recent war in the Galilee, but there were also the twisting, climbing roads up into the thin cool air of the mountains, and the higher they drove the more serene the land became. Below them were the soft round hills and rocky valleys of the Galilee, changed no more by a battle than by a raindrop, no more by a man than by an ant. This was the perfect spot to stand and admire Israel, Evan thought, to see it as through the wrong end of a telescope, because Israel was a world in miniature, and to see it up close, to give heroic scale to the problems which beset the world, was more than a person could bear.

Nahshon drove up to the clinic in Rosh Pina, hopped out of the jeep, and went inside while Evan helped the Kligers climb out of the back seat. The twins' parents were standing beside the jeep straightening their clothes when Nahshon came out of the clinic. The fatigue of the Galilee campaign had overcome him. The shuffling feet barely cleared the ground, his bloodshot eyes were tired and watery, and his shoulders drooped forward listlessly. He motioned for them to get back into the jeep.

Nahshon drove this time to a tree-shaded hill at the edge of town. The hilltop, cool and windy, looked down on the Jordan Valley and the flat blue Sea of Galilee. It looked up to the soaring, folding, softly swelling mountains.

There were already other people on the hill—a handful of soldiers and a black-bearded man wearing a broad-brimmed black hat and holding a tiny black book in his hand. The book was closed, but one finger was pressed in between the pages, marking a place. There was no grass on the hill, only the assorted round Galilean rocks. And there were tombstones and rock mounds scattered in clumps and indiscriminate patterns on the hill. The soldiers stood before three newly-dug graves. At the foot of each narrow pit was a new white sheet sewn into the shape of a long sack—and now filled.

Mordecai saw his parents as Nahshon and Evan were helping them climb out of the jeep. He ran over to them and embraced them both at once and then cried into the crevice where their shoulders touched. They patted his back and kissed him and wept the bittersweet tears of parents who had lost their young, not for the first time, yet still had a child to mourn with them and share their burden of sorrow.

But Mordecai's was a child's sorrow. The racking sobs sounded endless, but they would have an end, and the throbbing chest would become calm and the hurt would be forgotten.

Evan wanted to turn away from them and walk down the road and watch the burial from a distance, where he could not hear the sounds of grief or the noise when they began shoveling the rocky soil into the pits. Distance and silence could improve a burial, could make the principal actors the living instead of the dead.

He did not leave, however. His eyes were riveted on the weeping pyramid. He wondered whether the mother wept most for the dead son or the live one, and if she wept for both he wondered if the tears were the same. Looking at her, he thought of the mother of the Sudanese, living in some primitive place he could not imagine, unaware—he didn't know, perhaps uncaring—that her son now lay under a few inches of rocky dirt in a place called Kadesh.

And then he thought of his own mother. He couldn't calculate the time it would be back there; a little before dawn, probably. His mother's eyes were closed, but she was awake, and in the dark she reached out for the radio on the black piano stool next to her bed. And, trying not to awaken her husband, she turned the dial, moving in and out of the static and hillbilly music that sang from alien worlds, until she touched the distant signal that brought the news, broadcast ineptly by an announcer seeing the news copy for the first time as he spoke. There would be something about Palestine, a mention of ceasefires, and claims and counter-claims of dead and wounded and prisoners. A few words; no more. Then the inevitable music, but she would not hear, though she was still awake, and would be until the dawn.

The soldiers gripped the sewn edge of the sheet in which Aaron's body rested, carried it over to the grave, and, kneeling, let it down to the bottom. The rabbi opened the little book and chanted in a sobbing, breaking voice that he used only on these occasions.

"Oh merciful God who dwellest on high and art full of compassion, grant perfect rest beneath the shelter of Thy divine presence, among the holy and pure who shine as the brightness of the heavens, to our dear departed Aaron, son of Laban, who has gone to his eternal home. May his soul be wrapped in the bonds of eternal life. Grant that his memory will always inspire us to noble and consecrated living. Amen."

At the end, finally, when it was all over and the rabbi had closed his tiny book and left no finger inserted to mark a place, when the three soldiers wrapped in the white sheets had disappeared from the surface of the hill, three other soldiers, three living soldiers, took rifles that had been leaning against a pine tree and fired a single volley at the morning sun. The shots echoed against the fullness of the mountains and drifted away into the Jordan Valley.

Chapter Fifteen

THE JAIL WAS A SMALL CEMENT ROOM NEXT TO THE regimental police hut at the main gate. It had a locked and barred front door and a back door that opened onto a small dirt compound surrounded by barbed wire. Radhai, Nahshon, and Evan were the only occupants. The only other person Evan had ever known to be tossed into the jail was Shmuel, a large oaf-life sabra in Ephraim's halftrack who had been caught one night dropping a live hand grenade into the bottom of one of the latrines just to hear the noise.

Nahshon and Evan had joined Radhai in the jail late that afternoon. Nahshon had crashed the jeep through a new barrier pole at the gate when they returned and a livid Eliyahu had had them thrown immediately into the stockade.

Evan was sitting morosely in a corner of the compound, trying to force himself back into the sleep that Nahshon had snatched him from before dawn, when he heard an outburst of shouts coming from the front of the jail door. The Plugah Gimel cooks, all four of them, were standing there, their arms loaded with pots. They cursed the regimental policeman on guard at the gate and argued with him until he unlocked the jail door for them. Then they brought in the pots, grinning triumphantly and hailing the three prisoners like long-lost brothers. There was a banquet of chicken soup, roast beef, chicken, a mixed salad, and fried potatoes. The cooks stood there and beamed as the three prisoners gobbled the food. Then they left with the empty pots, again cursing the regimental policeman, who protested that he had nothing to do with the imprisonment.

At nightfall the other men from the company began drifting over to the jail. At first there were all the drivers, and then it seemed that every man in Plugah Gimel was there, more than a hundred soldiers, and they all had beer bottles cradled in their arms or hanging down from their hands.

"Refreshments for the jailbirds," one of them shouted.

"Where are the gallows?" another one called.

Uzi winked and passed opened bottles of beer through the barbed wire. "We've notified the Irgun to liberate you at midnight." Uzi snorted and raised his bottle in a toast. *"L'chayim!"*—to life!

The beer caps were popping off the bottles as the men sat down next to the barbed wire fence, shouting at each other and at the prisoners inside. Evan had never been fond of beer, and this beer wasn't even chilled. But it had a delicious bubbly-bitter taste and he took long swallows of it, then reached through the fence for a fresh bottle. Nahshon and Radhai were drinking with abandon, too, Radhai not showing the effects of the alcohol, but Nahshon becoming gayer with each mouthful. Nahshon ordered Uzi to go get his concertina, and when he returned with it the Moroccan led the laughing men of Company Gimel in the singing of "The Palmach Song," "God Save the King," and "Hatikva." Then he rolled into several bawdy Arabic songs that only a few of them knew.

The revelry at the stockade had become so noisy that men from other companies were drifting over to join the fun. Despite the merriment that surrounded him, Evan stood silently, groggily, behind Nahshon. For some reason, the beer was having a depressing effect on him, and the chopped-off thoughts going through his head had as bitter and bubbly a flavor as the brew in the bottle he now held.

He saw the horde of white faces on the other side of the barbed wire, and nearer to him, larger, wavering, the brown face of Nahshon and the black face of Radhai. White, brown, black. They were all Jews, and they were the history of the Jews, but not the meaning of the Jews. He could not grasp then the meaning of the Jews. Unless it was that God was never a vengeful God, never a great Jehovah who punished the guilty in His wrath and rewarded the innocent in His mercy.

No, God was a fun-loving God, a God who liked a joke. He was a big fat Uzi sitting up there trying to entertain Himself. He had picked out a tribe exactly like all the other tribes around them and given them a piece of stone. And because they had that piece of stone they thought they were different and fought everybody around

[224]

them. God laughed and laughed, and finally, tiring of the joke, He wiped the place clean and scattered the silly little people who thought they were different. And almost immediately, like chameleons, they began to look like the people into whose midst they were cast, but they kept pretending they were different, made themselves different, tried hard to maintain the difference, and they were so foolishly earnest about it that they suffered for their difference and died for their difference, when they weren't really different at all.

And God, the joke-loving, good-humored God, laughed at the funny little people. Then He made the biggest joke of all. He brought them back to the land that He had wiped clean. He brought them from all the places they had been, and now they were most certainly different. They were different from the people who lived around them and different from each other. Yet he and Radhai were alike. Radhai had spent half his life as a Jew among black men and the other half as a black man among Jews. Evan had been a Jew among Americans and now he was an American among Jews. But they were in the same boat, all of them. They were different, and yet not different. They were the same as each other, and yet the same as the Amharas and the Sudanese and the Arabs and the Americans. It was a mad joke, perpetrated by the Master Humorist.

Evan nudged Nahshon clumsily and pointed to his mouth that he wanted to speak.

The Moroccan held up a hand. *"Chaverim!* Quiet! The Yeled has something to say."

"What I want to say is this," Evan said drunkenly. "We're all Jews." There was a roar of laughter. He swept his hand in a wide arc. "And out there, they're all Jews, too. Everybody's a Jew." There was lusty hooting and applause. "The whole world is full of Jews."

Radhai put his arm around Evan's shoulder. "And Evan," he said thickly, "is the bravest Jew of all. Eliyahu couldn't make him kill the *Cushi.*"

Amid a new burst of applause and shouts, Evan was suddenly up in the air, sitting precariously on the two shoulders, holding onto Nahshon's neck with one hand and Radhai's with the other. He did not want to be up there, the object of the shouts and clapping. Maybe, just maybe, he would have killed the Sudanese if Eliyahu had cocked the pistol. But Mordecai had saved him. He had been saved by the bell rung by Mordecai.

Then Nahshon's knees buckled and all three of them went tumbling into the dirt. There was loud laughter as they lay there for a minute. When they looked up, Shulamit was standing on the other side of the barbed wire, grinning down at them.

"The three silliest geese in the Israeli army." She shook her head. "But I owe all three of you a hug."

"Uh-uh-uh." Nahshon had pushed himself up onto his elbow and was wobbling a finger crazily near his own face. "Careful. It's not us she loves. It's the barbed wire and prison smell. An Irgun girl can't control herself when she sees a prisoner inside a jail." He cackled and reached his hand through the fence to touch the tooled leather of her sandals. "Did I ever tell you," he said, not taking his eyes off the sandals, "that old Nahshon was once a sandalmaker?"

"Yes," she smiled, "I think you did."

A regimental policeman escorted them the next morning to the headquarters building. Evan's clothes were slightly wrinkled and his head felt as though he were wearing a steel helmet on the inside of his skull. Radhai, somehow, looked as sharp as if he were going to a parade. Next to him Nahshon looked especially disreputable. The Moroccan was unshaven and his eyes were a rich bloodshot red. Part of his black hair stuck straight up into the air and another part fell over his forehead.

Waiting for them in the company office was Gingi, standing behind the large desk. The captain's right arm was in a sling and the edge of a bandage was visible at the open neck of his shirt. Also in the office were Eliyahu, sitting on the edge of Gingi's desk with one foot on the floor, and Shulamit, seated at a small table with paper spread out before her.

Gingi walked around to the front of the desk and examined the three prisoners sternly—the handsome but inscrutable black face of the Falasha, the apprehensive, earnest hazel eyes of the American youth, set deep in the suntanned face, and the slack jaws and unbrushed mustache of the exhausted-looking Moroccan.

"Radhai," Gingi said, "do you deny that you assaulted Eliyahu?"

"No."

"Can you give me any reason why you did it?"

"He reminded me of a Roman," the Falasha said. Shulamit smiled. Eliyahu shot a black look in her direction.

"Any other reason?" Gingi asked.

"No."

The captain moved over to Nahshon, stared into the bloodshot eyes at length, then shook his head. "What charge shall I start with?"

"I'm guilty of them all," Nahshon said without remorse. "But I kidnaped the Yeled. He didn't know until it was too late."

Gingi turned to Evan. "Did you go willingly with Nahshon yesterday?"

Evan could avoid punishment completely now by saying no. It would have been partly true. But he found himself anxious to say yes. He and Radhai and Nahshon weren't gunbearers for anyone. They had defied authority to do what was right and good. If that made them guilty, he had a bursting desire to stand with his friends as a man and take the same punishment meted out to them.

"Yes," Evan said.

"Did you know before going that he didn't have permission to leave?"

"Yes."

Gingi flicked his eyes back at Nahshon. There was a trace of a grin under the Moroccan's mustache.

"All right," the captain said, leaning back against the desk and scowling at them. "Now I'll have my say. You," he pointed over to Radhai, "this isn't the African bush. This is the State of Israel, and our officers will be respected and obeyed, not brawled with as you would a village chieftain. And you," he nodded curtly at Evan, "you might learn that you are in an armored regiment, and an armored regiment dashing many kilometers ahead of its support troops cannot always take prisoners—or leave them behind. I have had the opportunity to see the bodies of some of the German soldiers captured by advancing units of your General Patton. And you," he turned to Nahshon and spoke in a scathing tone, "do you think this is some kind of tourist bureau that we send taxis out to meet arriving ships!"

He walked over to the window. "Shulamit, take this down. Radhai Hayehudi-Ha'acharon. Charge: Assault upon a superior officer. Plea: Guilty. Nahshon Ben-Mizrachi and Evan Copperman. Charge: Failure to obey a superior officer, theft of a government vehicle, absent from camp without leave, destruction of government property," he glanced toward the main gate, "two counts. Plea: Guilty."

The captain walked back to Shulamit's desk and stood behind her, watching her write. "Eliyahu," he said, "when were these men put in the stockade?"

"The Moroccan and the American were jailed yesterday afternoon as soon as they returned from Rosh Pina—about 4:30. The Falasha went in a day earlier."

"Good. All right, Shulamit, continue writing." Gingi ignored the three prisoners and fixed a narrow-eyed look on the lieutenant as he continued, "Sentence for all three men: sixteen hours in the regimental stockade on each count, all sentences to run concurrently, effective from time of imprisonment."

Chapter Sixteen

BEERSHEBA, CAPTURED ONLY A MONTH BEFORE, WAS a town of white, eerily-silent buildings when they delivered the British armored car there in December. Small and completely open to the desert and the desert sky, at night the abandoned Negev town had all the desolate qualities of a cavern. Voices and sounds were echoed and magnified by the smooth stone walls of the houses and shops, then were swept away into the infinite depth of the desert.

The armored car had been captured from the Syrians during the Galilee campaign, and Alex had worked on it for more than a month to make it serviceable, but then it was decided that the Negev forces had more need of it than the armored regiment. Gingi, probably at Nahshon's suggestion, had chosen Evan, Radhai, and Shulamit to make the delivery to the Palmach forces in Beersheba. They had left camp early that morning and hadn't arrived in Beersheba until almost nightfall. They talked little during the trip. The motor made a tremendous amount of noise and the racket seemed to become trapped in the small enclosure. Radhai stood with his head and shoulders out of the top turret, occasionally ducking back inside the compartment to point out a landmark to Evan and Shulamit.

Below Tel Aviv and the cities to the south, they passed orange groves and cultivated fields. Later there were only sparse patches of grass in the yellow dirt. And for the final two hours before they came to Beersheba there was a dry golden sea of rolling land, not a desert of sand but a desert of dirt that had lain fallow and thirsty for millennia. It had been plowed by the wind into the millions of straight, even, shallow furrows.

They turned left into a dirt road, away from the asphalt highway which continued on into Arab-held Gaza. Off to the right they could see the swells of sand that lay next to the sea, and the sun, beginning to drop toward the Mediterranean, backlighted the dunes and the city of Gaza into a silhouette before the glistening purple sea. Radhai tapped Evan's and Shulamit's shoulders with the toe of his boot and pointed to a spot in the Arab territory where a driver was leading a single file of three camels. They seemed to Evan almost as tiny and delicate as the silver camels in the window of the Jerusalem shop.

In Beersheba, they found the Palmach headquarters. A corporal on duty signed the papers accepting the vehicle, then showed them where they could eat the evening meal and spend the night.

The kitchen was set up in what had once been an Arab shop. Two girls, not yet twenty, in dusty wrinkled uniforms and Afrika Korps caps perched on the back of their heads, ladled the food into their plates. Radhai was holding his mess tins out for food when a boot rested for a second on the seat of his trousers, then catapulted him out of the line.

"Falashas eat last," a red-bearded youth smirked.

Radhai dropped his mess gear on the floor with a clatter, took two steps toward the youth in a crouch, then stopped, frozen. "Avinoam!" He jumped toward the grinning soldier, picked him up, and swung him around in a circle. "I had a hard time finding you in that beard."

Radhai introduced Avinoam to Evan and Shulamit as not only a fellow kibbutznik from Ein Dvorah, but also a member of the same pioneer group that would found a new kibbutz after the war. Avinoam came with them as they took their food outside, where it was nearly dark now, and sat down in the street next to the building to eat. Then the red-bearded soldier led them over to the mosque, a beautiful stone building that had windows shaped like keyholes, a small windowed dome, and a tall, slender minaret. They followed him through the dark interior of the building and up the winding stone staircase to the top of the minaret. A full moon shone softly on the stark buildings of Beersheba and cast a pale shadowy light over the surrounding desert. Atop the tall minaret they were suspended between the earth and sky, as close to one as to the other. Evan could not help noting the irony that this was the second tower he had climbed in this Jewish land—and the other had been on a church.

"When I see this," Shulamit said, "I find it hard to remember that the Galilee is in the same country."

"In many ways this is in truth a different country," Avinoam said. "It is a magnificent country, magnificently large and magnificently beautiful."

"And magnificently desolate," Evan added. "It's difficult to believe that even the Arabs could survive here."

"The Arabs survive, and the Jews, too," Radhai said. He pointed to the south. "There are already more than a dozen kibbutzim down there. There will be many more—cities, also."

Evan looked out over the barren vastness and wondered if such a prediction could come true. Radhai saw the doubt and added, "A group of us from Ein Dvorah already have a valley picked out. We call it Nabatean Dams."

"But why down here, where there's nothing?" Evan asked. "We've seen a hundred perfect places for kibbutzim in the Galilee. Why not there?"

"Because the Galilee has been conquered," Avinoam answered. "This is the land that needs to be won and tamed." He looked up at the magnificent sky. "A full moon. A good night for sightseeing. How would you like to see Nabatean Dams?"

"How far is it?" Shulamit asked.

"Only about half an hour by jeep. It's southwest of Bir Asluj."

"I thought the Arabs still had Bir Asluj," Evan said.

"They do. But don't worry about it," the red-bearded youth grinned. "We aren't going to drive through Bir Asluj. We can take a track off the main road. The Arabs never come out at night."

Shulamit and Evan were in the back seat and Avinoam and Radhai in the front of the jeep speeding in the night away from Beersheba. Avinoam had left them at the mosque and mysteriously reappeared with the jeep. He had screeched the wheels into a racing start on the street outside the mosque as though a dozen other goggled drivers were pushing him for the post position, and now he had the accelerator down to the floor, shoving the vehicle to its top speed. It was a type of recklessness typical of young Israeli army drivers; even behind the wheel they had to prove their disregard for danger and death. The number of Israelis they had killed and maimed rivaled the record of some of the Arab armies.

Avinoam turned off the highway a short distance outside Beersheba and onto a hard track that ran cross country. The desert changed from gently rolling land to an area of clearly-defined hills and valleys. Avinoam stopped the jeep. The four of them got out and stood at the edge of a hill. Below them, in the moonlight, was a valley much larger than the others. At its narrow end the valley was little more than a very wide wadi, a dry creek bed. But it widened rapidly and stretched out for more than a mile, guarded on both sides by a series of low hills until finally at its wide end the hills on either side stopped and the mouth merged into the desert.

Avinoam pointed to the wadis that ran down into the flatland, not only at the narrow end of the valley, but all along the sides, in the crevices of the small hills. The Nabateans, he said, had flourished in the Negev during Biblical and post-Biblical times by building dams across the wadis that caught the water from infrequent rains and channeled it via intricate canals to a central cultivated area. The Nabateans had thus grown crops by stealing the sparse rainfall from a large area and concentrating it on a relatively small area.

The remains of some of the dams were still in this particular valley, he said. The members of the Nabatean Dams kibbutz would attempt to rebuild the systems of dams and canals and plant crops in the fertile soil of the valley. Eventually, a portion of the Jordan River would be diverted down through the Negev in a large canal, and the towns and kibbutzim in the huge desert would have an additional source of water. But until the huge canal was built, which might be many years, the kibbutz at Nabatean Dams would try to prove that the Negev could flourish under desert conditions. If the Israelis held this territory and if the war were over by the next spring, he said, he and Radhai and the others in the pioneer group from Ein Dvorah would be here. They would spend the spring and summer rebuilding the dams and digging irrigation canals, and then they would await the thin winter rains to put their experiment to the test.

Radhai reached down and picked up a handful of the dry, sandy soil. When they had debated three years before where they should establish their new kibbutz, some had wanted to found it at a site near Ein Dvorah and others had wanted to come here. He had stood with those in favor of the Negev, and his side had won. For Radhai, there was more here than a new frontier for Israel. It would be Creation over again, an opportunity to start at the beginning, each man, each woman on equal terms. And in the first years, anyway, there would be too much of a challenge in this dry dirt, too much of a struggle against the desert itself, for a person to notice whether his fellow was white or black, Oriental or Western. This, at least, was Radhai's dream.

"A year ago," Avinoam was saying, "Radhai and I and eight others spent two weeks down here building a pilot dam and canals on the other side of the valley. I wonder if it worked during these first rains." He looked at the others. "Would you like to check it?"

"Go without me, Shulamit said. "I'm too tired."

"I'll stay here, too," Evan said.

"We'll be back in less than an hour," Radhai assured them. He and Avinoam began picking their way down the side of the hill, often sinking in the dry dirt to their knees. Shulamit and Evan sat on the crest of the hill and watched them shrink into small figures as they crossed the valley.

Shulamit placed her hand on Evan's knee. He moved closer to her and caressed the soft skin on her arm.

"Radhai is like a child with a new toy," she said. "I have never seen him in such a happy mood."

"Soon the troops down here will take the rest of the Negev and the war will be over. Radhai and Avinoam will be in this valley next spring."

"And you, where will you be next spring, Evan?"

It was a question that had to come. Evan wished he could put off an answer. "With you, I hope, Shulamit—and with my parents."

She looked at him, trying to understand the riddle.

"Shulamit, come back with me."

"You want to go back to America?" There was disappointment in her voice.

"Yes. For a time, anyway, until I have finished at the university."

"You have known this for some time, haven't you? And you didn't tell me. I thought we were so close."

"I was afraid of your reaction. I was afraid you would say no, you wouldn't come with me. I'm sorry now I didn't tell you sooner. It was cowardly."

She drew her hand away from his knee. "When did you make this great decision?" She put emphasis on the word "great."

"Do you want the hour, the day? I can't tell you. Maybe I've known it since the day I arrived in Israel."

"And from the day I first met you, I always thought you would stay in Israel. How could I have been so wrong?" She turned her head away from him and looked down into the valley.

He wanted her to understand, to feel the conflicting attractions that had been wrenching at his emotions. "You weren't there in Rosh Pina when they buried Aaron. Instead of the twins' parents, all I could see were my own, their loneliness for me and their hopes for me. I had a miserable feeling that I owed them better than they've received."

"Do you owe it to them to go back to a country where they hate Jews?"

"People are people everywhere. My mother wrote me that once and I've learned that it's true. You have your share of bigots, racists, bullies, fools, martinets. All Israelis aren't noble and pure."

"Did we ever tell you that we were?"

"No, you didn't. But that was what I expected, I think. And I believe I love Israel more now that I've found you aren't. Nahshon called me the inspector general, making my tour of Israel and judging everyone and everything. He described me perfectly. But what he didn't know was that he was describing the way I was in America, too. All my life I've been the inspector general, expecting everybody to conform to my standards, to respect my religion, to defer to my oppressed feelings. I don't think I ever tried to understand Americans any more than I tried to understand Israelis. I'd like to try living in America without being an inspector general."

"And if you try very hard," she said bitterly, "I'm sure you'll find there isn't an anti-Semite in the whole country."

"They're there. I know that. But are the Israelis so loved by the people around them?" There was an edge to his voice. "The Jew

[233]

is normal here, yes, but still hated. You have combined all the Jews into one Jew, and the one Jew that is Israel is still hated, feared, suspected by the other countries only because you are Jews. You've escaped nothing, simply consolidated it."

"Hated or loved, in Israel we are together with our own."

"Yes, that is what I love about this land. That and you are what draw me to Israel. But my own—my parents—are in America, and I love them, too. Your family is here. Nahshon and Radhai and all the others—they have no family or no homes to go back to. I am the only one who has a choice. That's the cross I have to bear."

"Oh, such a heavy cross," she said sarcastically. "And the easier life in America. Is that part of the cross, too?"

"Perhaps." He put his hand on her chin and turned her face so he could look directly into the tan eyes. "Come with me, Shulamit, and help me make the choice. In one year I'll be finished at the university. We'll give ourselves one year. And if you want to come back to Israel then, we'll come."

"No. If you go back, you go back alone. The luxury of America has seduced the Jews there. I would live in fear every day of my life that it would seduce me, also. I would rather my children carried loads on their backs and ate crumbs from a tin pail than know that I had borne them into a world that hates them, that will always hate them." She touched his arm. "But I won't let myself believe you'll go back, Evan. You're one of us. You'll change your mind and stay with us." She kissed him. It was a penetrating kiss, as though she hoped to change his resolve by invading him. He fell back onto the sand and pulled the face with the tan eyes and the liquid mouth down to his.

Later, when Avinoam and Radhai returned, they drove back to Beersheba as swiftly as they had come, leaving behind them the endless rolling dunes of the Negev and the secret valley of Nabatean Dams.

Chapter Seventeen

IT WAS ALMOST TIME TO LEAVE. THE NIGHT BEFORE, the drivers' platoon had thrown a party for Evan, and now he had spent most of the day turning in his equipment and saying individual goodbyes to his friends. His canvas suitcase, its blue sides bulging with the Israeli presents he had bought for his mother, aunts, and cousins, sat heavily on the bare wooden slats of his bed.

The War of Liberation was over. It had ended in the last week of December and the first week of January when the Israeli army routed the Egyptians in bitter fighting in the Negev and captured all of the southern desert except the thin Gaza strip. Armistice negotiations with the Egyptians were already underway on the island of Rhodes, but even before they began the army had announced that foreign volunteers would be released from the service, with college students receiving first preference for discharge so they could return to school in time for the spring semester.

There was still an hour before Evan, Radhai, and Nahshon would leave for Haifa in the jeep Gingi had given Nahshon permission to take. Evan left the barracks and walked along the damp path toward the headquarters building. Green blades of grass and here and there a short yellow flower had popped miraculously out of the sandy soil in the wake of the winter rains.

Evan stopped at Shulamit's room and knocked on the door.

"Yes."

Evan walked into the room. Shulamit was sitting on the edge of her bed, a pad of paper on her knees. Next to her were several envelopes. She was wearing the same skirt and peasant blouse she had worn the day they went swimming near the Bahai shrine. She had taken her hair loose from its bun, and it hung down now below her shoulders.

"We missed you at the party last night."

"Was there something to celebrate?" she asked coolly.

"Will you ride with us to the ship?"

"No."

"Why?"

"Because I read your orders yesterday when they came through the office. You're officially discharged the minute you leave Israeli soil."

"Is it so terrible to see someone leave the army?"

"It's terrible to see someone turn his back on Israel."

"I'll always love Israel."

"I'm sure you will," she said, touching her pen back down on the note pad, but not moving it from the first point it touched. "You can speak Hebrew to your rabbi now. And you can tell all your friends how you fought in the great Israeli-Arab war. The *chocolatniks* should be impressed."

"I'll come back."

"No. You won't."

"I love you, Shulamit. Can you stop loving me so easily?"

Her eyes held only contemptuous pity for him. "For the first time in my life," she said, "I am beginning to understand my father. If something we once held in affection turns awful before our eyes, it is best to make believe it never existed. When you leave Israeli soil you'll stop existing for me, just as you stop existing for the army."

"Both you and Israel will always exist for me."

"You fought next to us and you loved us," she said. "Now you reject us. And I reject you. Go back to America. Love us from a distance. And if your conscience ever bothers you, you can always soothe it by sending us money." She turned her head and shoulders away from him.

"I'll write you, Shulamit."

"Don't. I won't write back."

"I don't care. I'll write you anyway."

She did not answer him, nor did she turn around to look at him a last time as he stepped out of the room and walked down the path.

Evan, Radhai, and Nahshon ate supper at a restaurant in Haifa, then drove down to the dock.

The *Marine Carp*, owned by an American commercial line, was a converted troop transport, one of the smaller troop ships used during World War II. All its running lights were on and it looked very large and sleek beside the Haifa dock. The decks were clear, except for a bursar's officer in a crisp blue uniform who stood at the top of the gangplank, waiting to check the papers and tickets of boarding passengers.

Evan, dressed in the light summer trousers and corduroy sport coat he had brought with him to France, took the handle of the suitcase from Nahshon and shook hands firmly with Radhai. He started to shake hands with Nahshon, also, but the Moroccan pulled Evan to him awkwardly and embraced him. Evan stepped away from them and put his first foot onto the gangplank slowly, with almost the same sort of self-consciousness he had noted in the new immigrants alighting from the *Pan York*. With both feet on the gangplank step, he turned to face his friends again.

Nahshon smoothed out his mustache with his thumb and forefinger and smiled at Evan. "Let us know when you return, Yeled. We'll be here to meet you."

Evan stepped up to the top of the gangplank and showed his ticket and passport to the ship's officer. The man nodded him past. Evan walked to the rail and waved to Radhai and Nahshon. They waved back, then turned and left the dock. The young American watched them until they disappeared. He picked up his suitcase, went inside the ship, and began looking for his compartment. Ahead of him in the passageway was another man carrying a suitcase. He was wearing an overcoat with the collar turned up around his ears. As the man turned to enter the compartment, Evan recognized him.

"Deserter!" Evan called.

Bernie stopped and looked behind him. "Rebel," he grinned. His face was pale and thin. A wide, ugly red scar ran half the length of the right side of his throat, then curved around to the back of his neck.

"Looks like we're in the same compartment," Evan said. There were several dozen troop-type bunks in the large room. Evan dropped his suitcase next to one of the double-decker bunks. "Let's take this one. Which do you want, upper or lower?"

"Mocks friggin nix to me," Bernie said. "I ain't plannin' to spend no more time in it than I have to."

"It would be like old times if Gerry had the bunk next to us."

"That dumb nurse. We'll never see her again. She's got her hooks out for an Israeli doctor. She'll get him, too. Wouldn'cha know it. A doctor. Them Central Park West bitches never change."

Bernie pulled a bottle out of his suitcase and they went back up to the deck. They didn't speak as they leaned against the rail and watched the lights of Haifa—the fixed lights in the streets and houses that ran up the side of the black, invisible Carmel, and the moving lights of the cars and trucks winding up the slopes, luminous ants touching each other and moving quickly past.

Is that all they each had been to the other, ants touching antennae in a quick sign of recognition and then slipping swiftly past in opposite directions? There had to be more meaning than that to this year out of his life. This ancient land, this ancient kin had drawn him to them once. They would bring him back again.

And if not, he had at least put a fingernail on eternity. The thousands of Hebrews who went out from Egypt and the multitude of Jews who came back from Babylonian exile were faceless and nameless. And yet they had won an immortality for themselves by being part of the band that crossed over into the Promised Land and built and rebuilt a nation. There must have been those who went back later to Egypt and Babylon. But the Bible told only that they came.

Bernie struggled to get the bottle open. "When them Israelis put a cork in a friggin bottle, it stays corked," he said. Finally, the cork came out with a thud. He held the bottle up for a second toward Evan and said, *"L'chayim."* Then he took a long swallow of the Israeli cognac.